# THE DRACONEAN

JAKE & LUKE REAUME

ISBN: 1439268541
ISBN-13: 9781439268544

To our family and friends who always believed.
And Jess ... this one's for you.

ELËN
The Ashen Mountains
Northern Lake
Asgoth
Fishisha
The Fhisasgt Desert
Calle River
Hills of Asgoth
The Sea of Cathanlay
Lyiar
Jestiay
The Gaisiss Gullies
Pushwana
Norcrat
Dyrisza
Dohenneer
Zarinn River
Fwarra
The Umthar Forest
Soaier
Parisrw
The Alarian Hills
Iyillaz
Ethen-Jar
Serembal
Ethyen-Jar
Crystal Lake
Illyish
The Camodian Plains
Encorna Ilse
Tylii
Desert of Ethen-dith
Far'Camice
Arrash
Athprai Bay
Athprai Island
The Plains of Thorvana
Miishe
Wozar
Zyish
The Kyen Gullies
Watchers Bay
Farik
Heart Island
Asemican Cove
Siityth
Jujiss
Jitta
Sortaire
Oldo
Migste
Geeith
Sarr
The Mountains of Sortaire
Jara
Jimore
Koorast
Darsst
Alis
Parrie
The Devirius Marshes
Ojik
Gramal
Liaid Forest
Lamana
The Ridged Coves
Zyiad
The Fields of Tiuye
Dloire Mountains
The Plains of Horon
Horon
Zoron
Jinto
Stitar
Limore
Isen Cove
Gorgonathan
Limore Bay
Gorger
Sethen
Jusar
Mai
Sitiska
The Tombs
Minhera Mountains
Minhera Falls
Alsimo
The Plains of Duron
Seta
The Western Cove
Jymar
The Desert of Tiest
Oderon
Duron
The Silver Hills
Staro
Amarik
Marci
Zamar
The Gullies of Sanama
The Denn Flats
Duron Grove
Lare Forest
Fansy
Giam
The Fields of Fansy
Plains of Lia
The Mazarix Mountains
Moldost Tundra
Joserr
Moldost
N
S
W
E

THIÁ
Vearian Region
Zormian Region
The White Mountains
Lyix Lake
Mara
Mithall
Cira
UPPER NESMERESA
Emara
Tiae
Vera
Vearen
River of Queens
Zarise
The Sireth Fields
Lore
Gagji
NORTH SIRETH
Tork
Midozl
Pefthan (Northern Outpost)
The Jarah Desert
Aloric
Sea of Kyale
Deris
Sireth
The Islands of Andra
Barish Lake
Saida
Kiersyh
The Vihart Gullies
Garone
Nesmeresa
Thana
LOWER NESMERESA
Tarren
The Berrynf Plains
Gortha
Sham
Dasti
Bay of Pathpre
The Green Meadows
Len
SOUTH SIRETH
Fazial
Sahar
The Kurn
Koran
The Black Mountains
Clyss
The Sea of Belmese
Daghorn Marshes
Gulf of Thane
Parise
The Amainaf Wood
Gavin
The Gramanet Gullies
Sandar
Nefthan (Southern Outpost)
Leada
Norm
Bay of Belefliser
Sisc
Ziey
Drgael
The Tibean Marshes
Tarz
Yerna
Bearion
Gilyadae
Parvonai
Alyvia
Haysete Fields
The Plains of Arun
Desert of Ziin
The Ayinn Gullies
Draltis
Mayaze
Fyyrus
Chyeza
Famzeth
Morin
Sarae
The Garon Gullies
The Dariss Lake
Janst
Miess
Lyy
The Walltic Cove
Walltic
Castrious
The Black Plateau
The Ashwood Forest
The Forest of Amis
Odem
Barmin
The Plains of Zambris
Darhen
The Gulf of Sarlon
Gayll
The Arelli Tundra
Darnik
Raphi
Isirich
Mia
Huim
FAR ZARITH
NEAR ZARITH
Jagaz

Coldain Region
The Ashen Mountains
Northern Lake
The Gaisiss Gullies
Poshwana
Norcrat
Dyrisza
Dohenneer
Calle River
Asgoth
Fishisha
The Fhisasgt Desert
Hills of Asgoth
Sasier
The Sea of Cathanlay
Lyiar
Pargat
Jestiay
Zarinn River
Fwarra
The Urthar Forest
Parisrw
The Alarian Hills
Iyillaz
Ethen-Jar
Sarembal
Ethyen-Jar
Crystal Lake
The Camodian Plains
Encorna Ilse
Illyish
Tylii
Desert of Ethen-dith
Far'Camice
Arrash
Darvanis River
Athprai Bay
Wozar
The Plains of Thorvana
Miishe
Athprai Island
Crossing of Withgrop
Zyish
The Kye Gullies
Watchers Bay
rik
Heart Island
Asemicon Cove
Siityth
Jyyiss
Jitta
N
E
S
W

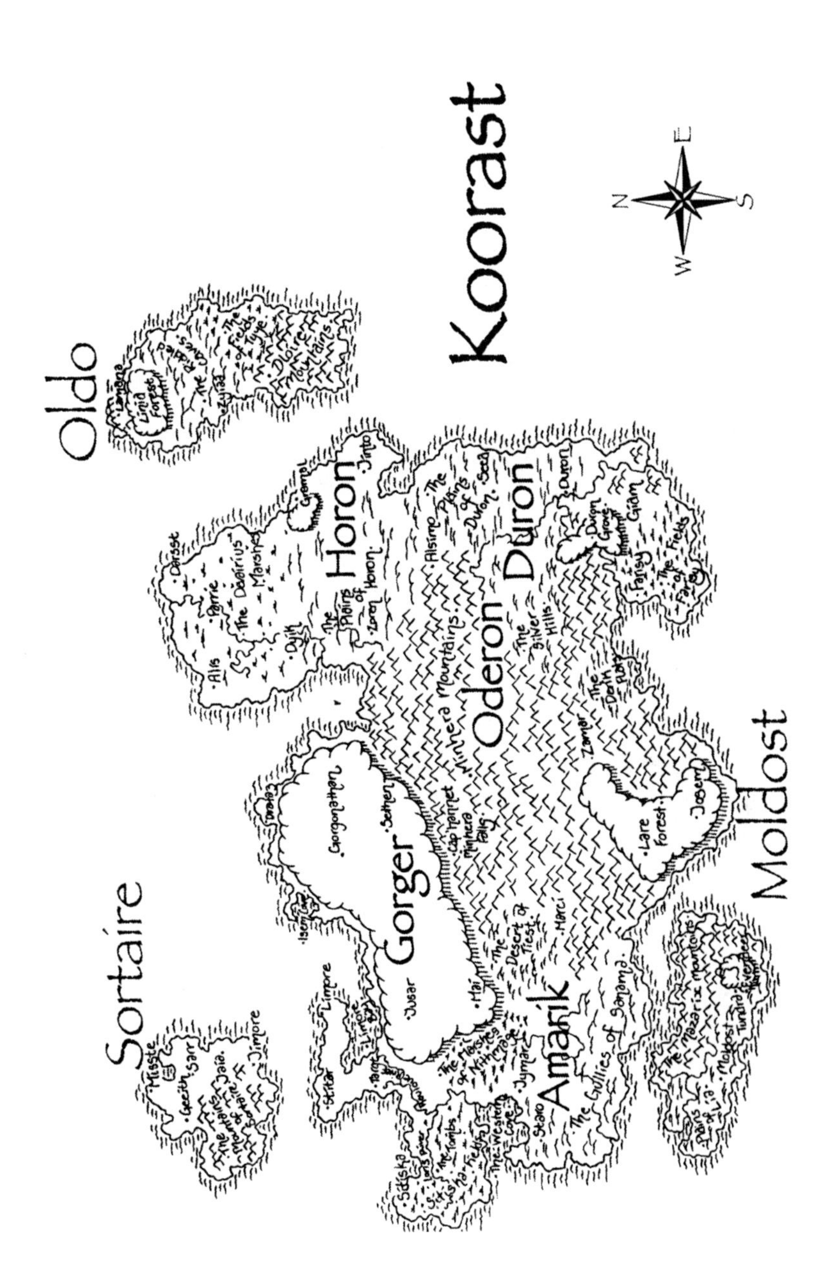

Oldo
Koorast
Sortaire
Moldost
Gorger
Horon
Oderon
Duron
Amarik
Linia Forest
Dloire Mountains
The Dalirius Marshes
The Plains of Horon
Minhera Mountains
The Plains of Duron
The Silver Hills
Lare Forest
Gorgonathen
The Desert of Tiest
The Gullies of Sanama
The Mazarix mountains
N
E
S
W

Vearian Region
N
W
E
S
The White Mountains
Lyix Lake
Mara
The Sireth Fields
Lore
Gagji
North Sireth
Tork
Midozl
Pefthan (Northern Outpost)
The Jarah Desert
Aloric
Sea of Kyale
Barish Lake
Deris
Sireth
The Vihart Gullies
The Islands of Andra
Saida
Kiersyh
Garone
Tarren
The Berrynf Plains
Sham
Gortha
Lan
Eposti
Bay of Pathere
The Green Meadows
Fazial
South Sireth
Sahar
The Kurn
Daghorn Marshes
Koran
The Sea of Belmese
The Black Mountains
The Amainaf Wood
Gavin
Nesthan (Southern Outpost)
Gulf of Thane
Sandar
Parise
The Gramanet Gullies
Clyss
Mithall
Cira
Upper Nesmeresa
Emara
River Tiae of Kings
Vera
Vearen
River of Queens
Zarise
Nesmeresa
Thana
Lower Nesmeresa

Zormian Region
N
W
E
S
Bearian
Haysete Fields
Gilyadae
Mayaze
Famzeth
Sarae
Dizael
Norm
Leada
Bay of Beleflise
Tarz
Yema
The Plains of Arun
Parvonai
Desert of Ziin
Chyeza
The Ayinn Gullies
Draitis
Sise
Ziey
The Tribean Marshes
Adyvia
Fyyrus
Morin
The Dariss Lake
The Garon Gullies
Jarist
Miess
The Ashwood Forest
Lyy
The Waltic Cove
Waltic
Castrious
The Black Plateau
Odem
The Forest of Amis
The Plains of Zamaris
Darhen
Barmin
The Gulf of Sarion
The Areili Tundra
Darnik
Raphi
Huim
Far Zarith
Near Zarith
Gayll
Isirich
Mia
Imfe
Tarra

# THE DRACONEAN

# PROLOGUE

*A cool breeze sighed gently, and the morning sun shone strong and true from a dazzling, cloudless blue sky, dissipating the first droplets of dew from the lush gold grasslands of Evendeer's meadows. Most were just waking, some turning to greet a sleepy companion.*

*While the rest of the city stretched and contemplated the day ahead, a young boy, awake since the predawn hours, walked through the crisp morning air enjoying the sensation of being the first to disturb the immaculate blanket of dew on the morning grass. Enticed far further into the forest than he intended, his eye was on the wooden figure fashioned only days earlier as a makeshift enemy and positioned for action this morning at the edge of a copse of trees. Circling it slowly, he lunged, spun, and thrust his sword, denting and slicing into the wood and cloth. His blood warmed, his young muscles began to loosen, and his movements became more fluid with each thrust and parry against his imaginary opponent.*

*He was a Draconean, already tall and strong but only thirteen years of age by the measure of men. An ancient race, Draconeans were immortal in times of peace, impervious to disease or the ravages of time. This Draconean's face was well shaped with a strong, squared jaw and thick, arched eyebrows. It was framed by hair black as a moonless sky, that fell flat across his forehead and low over his ears and collar. Distinctive, his eyes were a deep forest green with small, scattered spots of rich emerald, which made them seem to glisten in the morning light.*

*In those early morning hours, his young body loose and fluid, he felt awash with the vigour and optimism of youth. Not yet exposed to the fragility of time and the whim of fate, his energy was only just harnessed and focused, channelled into the discipline of his exercise. He flexed his grip on the leather-wrapped hilt of his new weapon, the intricately carved, vine-like patterns beginning to lose their rough edges as they absorbed his sweat and his scent. A recent gift from his father, it was heavier and considerably longer than he was used to. He could feel the pull and strain on his muscles as, brow furled with concentration, he swung the finely honed blade in a sequence of wide arcs.*

*Pausing for a moment to examine his blade and to catch his breath, he felt the loss of the sun's warmth as it crept behind a cloud. With the sudden and unexpected chill came a sense of unease. Noting the angle of the sun marking midmorning, he felt a jerk of panic.*

I've missed it!

*Weapons training with his father and brothers was not something to be missed. Ever. He put the whisper of unease he felt tickle his nape down to the anticipation of discipline he knew he'd receive from his father. He was already breaking into a long-legged lope as he sheathed his sword and headed for home.*

*What a day! Even old bones could enjoy a morning so beautiful. His Highness, Dray Sorzin, King of the Draconeans, stepped through the intricately carved arch of his doorway and beheld the glory of the morning. The tangy smell of the cedar from the nearby wood and the smell of rich grass laden with dew and a heady draught of fresh air filled his senses. Light breezes lifted his grey hair from his neck. Though not the heavily muscled warrior of old, his broad-shouldered, six-and-a-half-foot frame retained a stature that bespoke his position. The ancient city of Evendeer had been designed to complement and enhance the natural beauty of the surrounding landscape, and as his eyes methodically scanned it, he marvelled anew.*

*He strolled into the sunlight and toward a clearing in the trees where, under the shade of a wooden pergola, daily swordsmanship lessons were held. He could find six of his offspring but* where was that boy?

*At their father's approach, the six ceased their antics and quieted, taking their seats around the central arena. Sensing his unhappiness at their missing sibling, the eldest tentatively spoke up, "I think we should start without him, Father." There was a pause and a sigh, followed by a curt nod. With that, the daily training began.*

*The morning instruction complete, Dray stepped back to watch his sons thrust and parry, utilizing the practice strokes and techniques he had drilled them in that morning. He continued to feel unease at the absence of his youngest son. Allowing himself a fleeting memory and regret for other lost sons, Dray mused that a father wasn't supposed to have favourites. Though the boy was frequently the recipient of his ire, the lad held a special place in his father's heart. He had already shown a natural ease and grace, as well as a propensity for leadership that promised an extraordinary warrior.*

*Dray's only warning was a rush of unease that swept down his spine before the roof of the pergola above was ripped away and a meaty fist reached in to grab and clench him in fat, stubby fingers. As he was lifted through the air, Dray managed to reach around to the scabbard on his leather belt, secure his dagger, and tuck it within easy reach of his sleeve. Their world was filled with many strange creatures and while he would know the intent of this one before he acted, he wanted a weapon readily at hand if need be.*

*As the hand lifted him up and away from the ground, his worst fears were confirmed. It was a Tarnig, the largest and deadliest in the troll family. Far less intelligent than most of Elënthiá's creatures, this particular Tarnig stood over twenty feet high and, with its girth and short, fat legs, it was well anchored to hold the weight of a large animal, never mind a Draconean.*

*"I am Gaar, Captain of the Tarnig force," the creature bellowed. "We claim this city and these people for the great Lord Gorillian. We are to bring you and your seven sons also."*

*"We have ever been peaceful with the Tarnig race," Dray returned, indignant, his hope for a nonviolent resolution dwindling. "What quarrel have you with us?"*

*"You will come now! And your sons. Lord Gorillian has ordered it!" the creature repeated, more agitated.*

*Draconean soldiers had spilled out of buildings, arms at the ready. From that height, the king could see at least a dozen other Tarnig in or outside of the city and several battalions of fully armoured soldiers converging on the gates. It was an ambush. Peripherally noting that his sons and soldiers were frozen, awaiting his direction, Dray replied, already calculating, "I have six sons only. The other died just one year past. Take me, but leave my sons, for they are of no use to you. Do no harm to my people. I alone will go with you to Lord Gorillian."*

*"Foolish Draconean!" Gaar bellowed, bringing Dray closer to his face as his belligerence increased.*

*"You and your sons will come with us now. Or you will all die!"*

*Letting out a bloodthirsty battle cry, Dray pulled the dagger from his sleeve and rammed it into the Tarnig's eye, screaming to his sons, "Run! Run from this place and do not look back!" To his soldiers, he cried, "To arms!"*

*Taken off guard, the Tarnig dropped Dray as it screamed in pain and staggered back, holding grimy claws to its face to catch the gushing blood and fluid. Dray rolled easily to his feet and darted for his house and his battle sword. As he ran he could hear the first of the Draconean battle horns sound. Grabbing his sword and looping his battle horn around his neck, he ran back out into the streets, adding the blare of his own horn to the chorus now sounding. Hearing their King's call, the streets filled with Draconeans armed with battle-tried weapons, their courage, and their loyalty.*

*Sweat soaking his shirt between his shoulder blades, the boy made fast through the forest toward the well-worn and oft-trodden main path used by wagons, traders, warriors, and visitors as the main route to Evendeer. Finding it, he skidded to a halt and dropped to one knee to get closer to the unusual tracks he suddenly saw in the soft ground. The footprints were made by no man he knew, for they were as long as his arm and twice the width of his hip, toes sharpening to an ominous point. It could not be! A creature with a print so large must be at least fifteen feet tall.*

*He raised his emerald eyes and followed the path of the tracks until they disappeared in the distance. His heart lurched. They were headed for Evendeer. A shiver of dread rippled up his spine accompanied by an unmistakable premonition of evil. With that premonition came a rush of adrenalin as he surged to his feet ready to make haste to the City and to his family. Before he could fully rise, he heard them. The deep, sonorous moan of the Evendeer battle horns. "No..." he cried. "No!" and burst forward at a dead run.*

*The young Draconean broke free of the woods and once again skidded to a halt, blinking the sweat out of his eyes and shaking his head in disbelief at the sight in the distance. Smoke was rising over the trees, but he could only see the rubble of what was once Evendeer. The grass was singed and burnt away; as he stumbled forward, he began to see the first of the bodies. His friends. His neighbours. His life, all gone. Gone. Stumbling like a drunken soldier, he weaved and staggered through what remained of the streets unable to grasp either the carnage or the reason behind it.*

Father! *he thought suddenly.* Where is Father? *Hours passed as he searched, turning over bodies, gradually numbing to the horror of what remained of his home. No bodies of his father or brothers could be found. In exhaustion and despair, he stopped and stared around him. He was standing in the charred remains of an outbuilding near his house, the last place he could think to look for survivors, for remains. With nothing found, he turned to stumble away from the rubble and stench of death and the rotting Tarnig carcasses, thinking only to return to his beloved forest to grieve. He took a misstep, his foot catching on a charred and loosened board that flung ashes up into his face. With only a split second to react, the young Draconean turned his head. The quick action saved his left eye, but not his right.*

*He screamed in agony at the searing pain. It felt like his eye was on fire. Stumbling first forward and then back, he felt the boards beneath his feet crumble and the ground give way. Then he was falling, plunging into a dark void until his back hit the ground below with an unceremonious thud.*

*Winded, he looked around one-eyed, still grimacing at the searing agony in his eye. All he could sense in every direction was a thick blackness. As his good eye became accustomed to the gloom, and with the dusky light filtering down through the broken boards above him, he could begin to make out furniture and trappings of a room. Crawling on all fours, his eyes still both streaming with tears and pain, he found a table and pulled himself to his knees. He grasped a flint and the stump of a candle and lit it. There were shelves lining one of the walls from floor to ceiling, each laden and disorderly with scrolls and parchments.* What is this place?

*The boy fell to his knees, unable to take it all in. Dropping his head to his chest, his uninjured eye caught the reflection of something on the dirt floor. Reaching out he grasped it, recognizing as he did the distinctive silver dragon's claw wrapped around a round, royal blue stone and hung from a heavy silver chain. When last he saw it, it was hanging round his father's neck. With a cry of anguish, he clutched it to his chest and buckled at the waist. He curled into a ball on the hard dirt, hot, burning tears streaming down his cheeks and heaving sobs wracked his body as he bid his innocence farewell along with his heart and his youth. In the gloom and dirt he could only lament,* How did it come to this?

# CHAPTER 1

He crouched motionless, ignoring the frigid shards of cold that his inertia was allowing through the layers of his hunter's clothing. The tracks had led him close; now his stealth and the true aim of his arrow would make the difference between a kill and yet another day at the hunt. The sky above was slate blue. No wind today to carry his scent to his prey. Even though the winter sun was bright, it emitted little heat to warm the landscape. Breathing deeply and steadily through his nose, he could feel the bite and tingle of the air as it clouded and froze the tiny hairs in his nostrils with every inhalation. The light dusting of snow overnight had made tracking easy. Patience now...

Lathaniel Waythan was young. Though far from his mature height, he was already sturdy of form and figure, just shy six feet in measure. His carriage was strong and proud, and from his rugged and even-featured appearance he seemed far more a man than a boy. His long light brown hair curled restlessly over the collar of his tunic and fell unkempt across his forehead; his smoky gray eyes tended to shine in any hint of light. Beneath the soft hair peeked two slightly pointed ears. He was a Forsair: an ancient race with ancestry dating back to the early ages of Elënthiá. Half Human, half Elven—the strange combination brought him the grace of the Elves along with the size and hunter's instincts of Humans.

*Got you,* he thought, his young eyes drawn to a slight movement in the trees ahead. He was deep in the Linia forest, well south of Lamana, his home. This was the morning of his fourth day on the hunt. Winter had been bitter, and game had been scarce. They would all welcome the respite of spring this year.

Economizing his movements to avoid startling the deer or drawing attention, Lathaniel notched his arrow and raised his bow as he drew his elbow back in a slow, steady motion. Drawing his hunter's focus to a fine bead, he breathed deeply and with the beginning of a slow, controlled exhalation let loose his arrow. The deer, almost in premonition of the death upon it, swung its head to look straight at him. With no morning wind to waft or tempt it, the arrow flew true and buried deep in the white-crested chest of the young buck, dropping it where it stood.

Lathaniel loped to the fallen deer. The warm carcass steamed against the frozen snow, and with a quick prayer of thanks to the gods for the life given, Lathaniel relaxed. He would not go home empty-handed. There would be more meals and furs for his family to keep the winter at bay.

Efficiently wielding his knife, he minimally dressed the carcass, and with a grunt and a heave, he swung it across his shoulders and headed for home. Though he'd been hunting for four days, weaving and crossing the forest in his search, with the good fortune of an early morning kill he could still make it home by nightfall. Anticipating the warmth of a fire and the furs on his bed, Lathaniel shifted the weight across his strong shoulders and wound through the hills toward his valley and Lamana nestled within it. On warmer days he had whiled away hours sitting on these same hills, chewing on a stem of grass, lost in his imagination. And many times he would awaken early just to stand atop them to watch the sunrise in the distance. This was home.

To keep his mind from the weight across his shoulders and the burning in his thighs, Lathaniel lost himself in thought as he trudged onward. Life had become increasingly difficult for him. It would be two years before he would be of age, but he had been assuming more responsibility and leadership in the Waythan household; necessary, he felt, to deal with the increasing injustice directed toward them. Lamana was home, but so much of what was happening these days was unjust and wrong. Many felt that the injustice was increasing the closer Lathaniel came to his majority; for the Waythan family, all knew, were not mere Forsairs. They were heirs to the Forsairean throne - the true ancestral leaders of their people.

Lathaniel dropped the deer heavily on the ground beside him and sank to his knees, reaching for his water skin and a moment's rest. The fickle winds of fortune and time had seen the rule of the Forsairs handed to lesser men. And the Waythan family, driven to the brink of near extinction, had never regained the strength in numbers to retake its rightful place. Instead the Forsairs were lead by the Gramicy family.

The current head of the Gramicy family, Bracher, was as foul an excuse for a creature as any in Elënthiá. He used intimidation and an iron fist in his leadership of the Forsairean people. Understanding that he could not kill the remaining members of the Waythan family without incurring the wrath of the people, he nonetheless took every opportunity to impart unfair taxes and to delay or even ignore payment owed for lumber and other goods he took from them. The Lamanians saw these injustices and resented Gramicy and his hamfisted methods deeply. They considered armed confrontation a demonstration of weakness used only when all manner of negotiation and compromise has failed. As such, the elders continued to voice concerns on behalf of the people who, thus far, had made no effort to unite in protest. Without challenge to his power and having gathered sufficient muscle around him to support his bullying, Gramicy was now exercising these injustices upon more than the Waythans.

Resentment for him and his methods was escalating. More and more, Lathaniel felt a subtle pressure to act on behalf of his family and Lamana. More and more whispers were exchanged in the taverns and behind closed doors that change was coming, that soon a Waythan would once again rule the Forsairs. As much as he felt the pressure, Lathaniel did his best to ignore it, for this was his home. He wanted only peace. He did not want the burden of leadership. For now, he thought, *each day as each day comes.* Setting such troubling thoughts aside, he again slung the carcass across his shoulders and continued home.

It was dusk when he arrived. The smell of woodsmoke was heavy in the air, and the soft glow of lights could be seen behind shutters as all began to settle for the night. He headed straight for Chap Garous'. The Garous family had been butchers in Lamana for as long as anyone could recall. Getting the meat to Chap would give relief to his shoulders tonight and to appetites tomorrow.

"Now there be a sight for sore eyes," boomed a greeting from the shadows ahead. Out stepped Chap, his burly figure draped in furs and his face creased with smile lines and wreathed in a smoky cloud from his fragrant pipe.

"Have you brought me some work then, lad?"

"Aye," said Lathaniel, following him into his shop where he shrugged the heavy carcass onto a meat hook.

Noting the shadows of fatigue on his face and the weariness in his stance, Chap encouraged the young man, "Sit awhile, lad. There's much to tell." He led Lathaniel out of the cold storage and into the great room where the toasty warmth of the hearth beckoned. Sinking into a large wooden chair, he waved Lathaniel into another nearby.

Chap was a large man: fit, handsome, whiskered, and well over six feet, with a hard, lean wedge of a body, a jolly disposition, and a heart of gold. Just twenty-five years of age, he was in his prime.

"You're late, lad. We were getting worried. It be known that if there is meat to find, you're the hunter for it. But you were gone so long. Be there so little in the forest?"

Lathaniel shrugged, young enough to be uncomfortable with the compliment and unwilling to propagate the bad news of poor hunting.

"Just dress it for me, Chap, will you?" he sighed, rolling his shoulders, exhaustion settling in.

"A' course lad, it'll be done tomorrow. But…there be news."

Lathaniel could see him shift in his chair and a range of emotions play across his whiskered face. Whether the news to come was bad or good, it was obvious that his friend was fairly brimming with the need to tell it.

"I know you and your family have been having a rough go, but while you were in Linia hunting, your parents were evicted from your house. It's been boarded up…there was nothing we could've done, lad."

As he came to his feet, Lathaniel's face blanched. "Where are my parents?"

Chap gestured with his head to the stairs behind him just as Lathaniel's mother and father stepped down into the room, their faces creased with both worry and relief.

"I thought you wouldn't mind half a bit if I had 'em in my house 'til you returned."

Moving quickly across the room and gathering first his mother and then his father into a reassuring embrace, Lathaniel demanded, "Tell me."

Sayra Waythan was small in stature but a strong personality in his life. Lathaniel was struck for the first time by a sense of fragility about her he'd never sensed before. For a face lovingly painted with lines earned by life's joys and sorrows, hers always carried a welcoming smile. Lathart Waythan was a tall, quiet Forsair, no stranger to danger and adventure in his youth, but years and politics had worn him down. The burden of the loss of the Waythan heritage and the persecution he'd felt because of it had taken a heavy toll on him, and he looked older than his years. As Lathaniel grew, his father depended upon him more and looked to him for an opinion on family decisions. He was both father and soft-spoken friend to Lathaniel, and his devotion to his wife and son was unparalleled but circumstance and experience had made both his parents cautious people.

Lathart stepped forward and grasped both of Lathaniel's shoulders. "Son, there are matters we felt best not to speak with you about. Hear me now; let this lie. It is but a house. We will find other lodgings."

Lathaniel shrugged his hands away, agitated and tired of the secrets and the subterfuge. "Father, please! This is madness! That is our home—your home! Can I not know what has become of it?"

His parents exchanged a look then Sayra began, "There have been some issues with our taxes…"

Lathaniel made to protest, but she stayed him with a raised hand and continued. "Though he has never refused in the past, Gramicy now refuses to trade our goods for taxes owed. He came the day you left for Linia and told us he wanted coin for all our taxes, and gave us a day to come up with it."

His exhaustion forgotten, Lathaniel began pacing, furious at this latest news. Gramicy ruled Lamana with coercion and intimidation backed by his band of sycophants and hired mercenaries. He arbitrarily set taxes and penalties for items and actions where none had been before and enforced collection severely. He was beggaring the Forsairs, breaking their backs and their wills.

Lathart jumped in just then. "Lathaniel, please, for our sakes, make no more trouble. This will pass. You know that if we challenge him outright, it will only get worse. For your mother, for us both, let this go."

Lathaniel sensed that confrontation would not resolve a discussion that would be better addressed in the morning. "I'll sort it out with Bracher in the morning. For tonight though, I will take you back to our home. No," he said as he felt their protest rise, "I insist. As in the past, I will sort this out with Bracher. You must trust me. I'll get our home back. Go, please. Collect your things."

He turned to Chap. "My friend...my thanks for your help and your hospitality. "

The great clap he felt across his shoulders nearly felled him as Chap boomed, "Tis' no burden, lad. If you like, stay this night and be off home in morning."

Lathaniel shook his head. "No, Chap. The sooner we are back in our own home, the better."

Gathering bags and rope-wrapped bundles, the three trooped out into the night down the streets of Lamana to their home, where they found doors and windows boarded closed. Walking round to the back, Lathaniel found his axe leaning against a depleted woodpile; wielding it against the boards, he quickly opened access for his parents. A few armloads of wood and the touch of a flint to the hearth soon brought warmth to their home. With an exchange of smiles and a yawn, he gave into the exhaustion he had been fighting and collapsed into his bed.

# CHAPTER 2

Lathaniel woke early the next morning, the late-winter sun bathing him in a golden glow. Revelling in the comfort and familiarity of his own bed after nights on the cold ground, he drew a deep breath, savouring the faint smell in his bedclothes of the herbs and flowers his mother harvested and dried each year. Shrugging off the warmth, he shivered in the early morning air and dressed to face the day. A faint smile touched his lips as he looked around his room at the meaningful bits of this and that he had collected over his youth. Then his smile faded, and with a stern set to his jaw, he headed downstairs to stoke the fire and boil water for morning ablutions and tea. As the kettle began to bubble, he heard his mother call greetings down from the landing above him.

"You are awake early, son. I thought you'd still be abed, resting after your hunt," she said, making her way down the stairs to the hearth where she filled the pot for tea to steep and set cups, a loaf of bread, and preserves on the table.

Lathaniel didn't reply. He stared into the crackling flames considering, as he had so many times before, his heritage and his lineage. He was an only child, the last son of the last son descending from the ancient royal bloodlines of the Forsairean race. As the elders told it, millennia ago Lathaniel's ancestor

Jonas Waythan, a Human, secretly wed the Elven maiden Ethena. Intermarriage was forbidden and unheard of in their time, and they were ostracized from their respective peoples. Over time, other Humans loved and married Elves and found their way to the island of Oldo and to the enclave that Jonas and Ethena had established there in the secluded haven of Lamana. Thus, the Forsairean race was born and flourished, ruled benevolently across all but recent times by a member of the Waythan family.

The Gramicy clan had taken advantage of a strange sickness that had taken most of Lathaniel's extended family and had challenged Lathart's father for leadership of the Forsairs, promising clemency to the remaining Waythans in exchange for abdication. Rather than see his young son and wife killed, and out of concern for the welfare of his people, Lathaniel's grandfather had relented. The elder Gramicy was at least marginally honourable and had left the Waythan family isolated but in peace.

The same was not true of Bracher Gramicy, the most recent iteration of clan leadership. His treatment of his fellow Forsairs had deteriorated in recent years, and unrest was like a rising wave building across the small island nation. Gramicy misread the lack of overt defiance of his rule as weakness instead of wisdom and his harassment of the Waythan family had long since lost subtlety and had become blatant, especially in recent years as Lathaniel approached his majority.

Lathaniel looked at his mother and said without preamble, "They look to me to lead them, Mother. I want no part in this. My blood may be royal, but I am not. Nor am I a leader."

Sayra sank into the chair beside him and lay her hand across his arm. "I know you feel this way, Lathaniel, but the people will not have Gramicy for much longer. Whether you wish it to be or not; whether today or in the days ahead, there will be civil war. Lamanians only wait for a leader to take them through it."

Lathaniel met her eyes then. "Can you not understand, Mother? I am not that leader. I am not yet a Forsair fully grown. How can I lead a people to war and take responsibility for their life or death, for their well-being? I am a hunter, not a soldier."

"It is in your blood, Lathaniel." she said with calm resolve. "You would find the strength, and there would be many to help guide you. You've only to set your foot upon the path."

"No," he said flatly. "I will not fight. And I most certainly will not lead a war." He bent his head over his tea, holding the brew between his two hands and staring into his cup as if it held the answers.

Later that morning, Lathaniel opened his door to welcome three cloaked figures. As cloaks were shed, hands were warmly shaken and quick embraces exchanged with three of his most trusted friends. Jameth Panemon was a blacksmith. A goliath of a man, his head was closely shaven, but this morning his face was not as he regarded Lathaniel through serious eyes. The tall and thin weaver Mourir Dagin, and the shorter but solid Haug Fimmare, the baker, flanked him. Though older than Lathaniel, these men had looked out for him his entire life. He'd shadowed them as a young boy, trailing behind as they'd apprenticed in their trades asking endless questions. He'd borne their teasing, their taunts, and their practical jokes throughout the years. They were his friends.

"We heard you'd returned from Linia late last night. 'Tis good to see you're in your own house, lad," Jameth began without the traditional exchange of pleasantries, his usually easygoing demeanour noticeably absent. "Situations took a turn when you were away, and there's none of us happy about it."

Lathaniel gestured to three chairs by the hearth. Warily, turning his own chair backward, he straddled it and draped his forearms across the back, looking at the three.

Jameth continued, his agitation evident, "First the taxes and now this madness about coin! How is it that the Waythans are continually subjected to rules that the rest of the Forsairs are not? But then, if the past is a guide, Gramicy will first test if he can get away with imposing these on you…Then the rest of us will feel the bite of his demands next." Up he came from his chair, pacing in disgust and anger. "This cannot go on, lad. You have to know that this cannot go on."

At the sound of footsteps on the stairs, the four noticed Sayra and the others immediately moved to their feet. The three guests bent their heads and bowed their shoulders slightly in deference to her station. Gramicys may have believed themselves to be the Forsairean rulers, but centuries of tradition did not disappear so quickly.

"Milady," they murmured.

Still standing, Jameth turned to Lathaniel. "There is a small gathering at my house this night. I would be pleased if you could join us." As he spoke he looked pointedly at his friend, their gazes locking. Lathaniel gave a curt nod and saw the three out.

"Lathaniel…" his mother began. But Lathaniel knew she'd heard the conversation and raised his hand to stay the words he knew were coming. Without a word he slung his cloak across his shoulders and left.

The winter air was crisp under indigo skies. Beneath it, the woodpile beckoned. Mindless, repetitive labour was just what he needed to compose his thoughts and plan how best to address the latest development with Gramicy. He soon fell into the repetitive set, swing, split of the task as he worked his way through the woodpile, lost in thought. He sensed her before he actually saw her. In an instant, it was like the sun grew warmer and the air charged with energy, like just before a thunderstorm hit. He swung round, and there she stood leaning against the stone wall watching him, the wind gently lifting the ends of her long black hair, her green eyes soft and sparkling, her full lips curved in a warm smile.

Without taking his eyes from hers, Lathaniel set his axe aside and quickly crossed to her. He stopped, his toes very nearly but not quite touching hers, and simply stared down at her, his eyes searching her face, reacquainting himself with every fine line and plane, breathing her in through every pore. This was his Sabine. Lovely, devoted, his treasured companion and childhood confidante…and his only love. He reached down and gathered her close in his arms, lifting her to her toes and pressing her along his full length. Worries, plans, and plots all slid away in the slipstream of the afternoon's breeze.

"You found me before I could do the same," he said, smiling down into her eyes and dropping his head for a kiss.

Her eyes soft and blurred, she broke away at last and looked up at him. "No hello?" she teased. "You always did forget polite pleasantries, Lathaniel." Her smile slowly faded and her expression shifted to concern as her eyes, too, searched his face.

"I'm glad you're home safely, for my days have grown dark with worry in your absence. Bracher's latest madness is all that is spoken of. Have you found him yet?" Sabine knew better than most the increasingly difficult trials Gramicy visited upon the Waythans, trials more onerous than even Lathaniel's closest friends were aware.

"Hey, hey!" Lathaniel interjected. "What happened to taking a moment for pleasantries?" Gently tucking her soft hair behind her ears, he noticed the dark shadows under her eyes and the furrow in her brow. Determined to change the subject and bring a smile back to her pretty face, he gathered her close under his arm and pulled her toward the house. "I could use a warm drink and a moment or two with you. Come inside."

Working together, they prepared the tea, setting the cups and chairs in place, companionability and familiarity evident in their every movement.

"You were gone so long this time, Lathaniel. Is the game really so sparse in Linia?"

Rumours and gossip had filtered throughout Lamana that travelers passing by Oldo were venturing into the Linia forest, liberally hunting game. It was widely held that these were just that, rumours. Lathaniel told her about his trip and the lack of game. He also shared details of his conversations with his mother and with Jameth.

"You'll come with me tonight." It was more of a statement than a question for he knew that, as in the past, she would be by his side.

# CHAPTER 3

There were no strangers in the crowd gathered in the Panemon's great room. These evenings were becoming more commonplace as Forsairs gathered to discuss Lamana politics, taxes, Gramicy's latest idiocy, the strange whispers of a warlord beyond Oldo's shores named Gorillian, and the burgeoning resistance against him. Opinions were vociferously expressed and argued, and gossip was traded. But more and more discussions were serious and drew a bead on issues in Lamana; more and more their world was divided between those who were loyal to Gramicy and those who were not. More and more the outcry was for more than mere discussion - for action. More and more the subject of leadership and an uprising found its way to the forefront. And more and more Lathaniel Waythan's name and royal bloodlines were mentioned.

As Lathaniel and Sabine approached, expecting to hear the usual revelry from within, they noticed the gathering was strangely subdued. Lathaniel nodded greetings to neighbours he guessed were posted as sentries at the four corners of the house. He had heard that Gramicy was following their gatherings closely. Evidently, there was sufficient concern for Jameth to act. The door was thrown open to them before their second knock. Lathaniel handed off the keg of ale he'd brought along to Darryn Eariish, another of his childhood friends and reluctantly allowed himself and Sabine to be pulled into the gathering where there was much back slapping and laughter. No matter how many times, Lathaniel had reminded Jameth, and all of them, that he was simply one of them, he was still given quiet deference and a respectful welcome whenever he attended such functions. But tonight, in spite of the laughter and the raucous exchange of quips, there was an underlying tension in the air. It wasn't long before Jameth got the assembly down to business.

Lathaniel looked around the room nodding greetings to his parents - surprised that they were attending - and others he had not had a chance to greet on arrival. There were the usual faces along with many who had not joined such gatherings before. Ale was passed and pipes were lit. Once chairs were filled, folks found seats on staircases and rugs, settling in with a sense of anticipation that was new to such meetings. Jameth cleared his throat and addressed the gathered.

"Maria and I bid one and all welcome to our home this night. It is with a warm heart that I look 'round and see so many of my fellow Lamanians. As I cast my mind back to our earliest ancestors, I am reminded that when times called for it, loyal warriors gathered and renewed their oath as 'Brothers in Arms' sworn to follow and protect their leader."

As Jameth spoke, Lathaniel could feel a blush creeping up the back of his neck. He had known that this meeting would explore the topic of leadership—the gods only knew they discussed leadership at every meeting—but he sensed that tonight it was he who would be under the glare of a hot, harsh scrutiny before the night was done. His sense of unease grew.

Jameth continued, "While we can disagree on many things, we can all agree that the fate of Lamana and, indeed, of the Forsairean people has reached a critical crossroads. We have a tyrant in our midst. That we have let this go on so long is our own fault, and none but us can correct it. I can see now that by *my* own complacence I have supported the tyrant Gramicy as surely as anyone who has stood openly beside him. I have taken profit from sales to outfit him and his band of ruffians."

Around the room a deep silence fell as eyes dropped, none daring to look another in the eye.

Jameth looked around at them all. "It has been easier to go along than to fight, to believe that someday, somehow, it would get better. But we know this not to be true. The corruption grows more absolute by the day. Oppression, arbitrary taxation, punishment for actions that are crimes one day and not the next, crimes for one Forsair, but not for all...we are Forsairs, my friends! This is not our way. Across all the millennia of our race, this has never been our way. The Forsairs have always distinguished themselves by the justice they upheld, the values they embraced. Did we not choose the best of the Human and Elven worlds and make them our own? What has happened to us?" he cried out.

Still, not a sound was heard, and he continued, "I see now that we have been waiting, waiting for a leader, waiting for the right time to put Lamana to rights. I tell you, my friends, that time is now! I have watched with love, admiration, and fascination the boy Lathaniel become a man." All eyes shifted to Lathaniel. "Each time I look at him, I see the potential of our Lamana. I see hope. And I see our future. So it is with all this in mind that I pledge to you that from this moment I shall refuse all work for the tyrant Gramicy and his allies.

I urge you to do the same. I call for the ancient pledge of the Brothers in Arms and for every like-minded Forsair male to swear it!

"And," he continued, his voice softening and his eyes once again locking on Lathaniel's, "I beseech you, Lathaniel Waythan, step forward and claim the challenge of your heritage. Rule of the Forsairs runs in your blood. And your people have never needed you more!"

With that, the shouts of approval punctuated with the hammering of fists on tables became deafening. Jameth took his seat.

Lathaniel looked helplessly at Sabine, then across the table at his parents, all still seated and watching him carefully. The cheering quieted bit by bit until all eyes were on him, awaiting his reaction. Nearly a full minute passed before the sounds of Lathaniel's chair legs scraping the floor broke the silence. Lathaniel opened his mouth to speak then closed it again, composing himself, his mind desperately searching for appropriate words. His eyes swept the room, and in that moment he felt such a kinship with those gathered. They *were* his people. This was his land, his home. What should he do? The naïve boy in him wanted to agree to try and be their leader. But in his heart, he knew he was not ready to lead. And he still believed that there was a way forward that did not involve war.

Taking a deep breath, he addressed the gathered in a strong, calm voice.

"My friends, my neighbours, fellow Lamanians: there have been many words spoken this night by Jameth Panemon, and a great many of them are true. I, like you, despair over the current rule of our beloved nation."

He heard a general murmur of agreement roll through the room.

"Arbitrary taxation, oppression...Jameth is correct; such is not the way of the Forsair."

He paused and looked around the room at the expectant, upturned faces.

"But, I beseech you, think for a moment what armed conflict—in effect, a civil war—would do to our people. Neighbours, families even, would be forced to choose sides. And to bear arms. One cannot pick up a sword or a bow in anger if one is not prepared to accept the consequences of its use. Are you prepared to take the life of your neighbour—of a fellow Lamanian? I ask you this, my friends, because once we place our foot upon that dark road, we must be fully prepared to follow where it leads. Are we prepared for an armed resistance? Do we have an infrastructure in place to support such an effort? Warriors trained to face the likes of the mercenaries in Gramicy's employ? We have no idea what dark allies he has been consorting with and who would step up beside him if such a hand was played. Yes, we face trials today under his rule, but at least we can live in peace. You can live knowing that your women and children are not at risk. The action you suggest changes our lives on every level. Can you not see that?"

He paused. The silence was palpable. He knew he was asking questions that those gathered had been skirting around at every meeting. And he knew that in the asking, he was forcing the reality.

"You do my father, my mother, and me the great honour of recognizing our bloodline and encouraging the Waythan family to the fore of leadership again. Make no mistake, I am ever grateful for this honour. But with regret, I cannot."

Outcries of argument and disbelief echoed round the room. He put his hand up and waited for their silence, his voice dropping now, impassioned.

"Tomorrow I celebrate only my eighteenth year. Bloodlines aside, I know nothing of leadership, of warfare and strategy. I cannot take responsibility for the lives I see in this room nor those beyond these walls; friend or foe. I cannot. Beyond my lack of experience and maturity, I look to our past. Ours is a heritage of truth and honour, of peace and compromise. In dark times past, peace and truth have prevailed while war was a rarity. I am young, I know, and naïve. But I hold the belief that there is a way forward for Lamana and the Forsairs that will not see us war each with the other. In my heart, this I believe."

He paused again, looking at the sea of faces disheartened by his words.

Then he heard a voice from toward the rear of the room call out, "You are the only one the people of Lamana will accept. If you will not lead us, we are consigned to Gramicy and the despots like this Gorillian whom it is rumoured he consorts with..."

Lathaniel answered, "If by believing as I do, if by speaking boldly and from my heart to you here tonight, I have dishonoured my heritage or my country in your eyes, know that I am deeply sorry. Again, you honour me with your confidence and your belief in me. But I cannot do what you ask of me."

The silence was absolute. Not a word was uttered. He stepped back from the table and began weaving his way through the crowd toward the exit.

Just then the door was thrown wide, and a man Lathaniel recognized as one of the sentries yelled, "Fire! The Waythan home is afire!"

For a split second everyone remained frozen; then bedlam broke loose.

# CHAPTER 4

The snap and hiss of the remaining stubborn embers were a welcome relief from the earlier roar of flames that lit the night sky like a beacon and the hungry fire that, amid the screams and creaks of breaking timber, had swallowed the Waythan home. It was fortunate that Sayra and Lathart were at Jameth's, for it had not been their practice to attend such gatherings. Thinking what would have happened had they been at home made Lathaniel's insides roll. His face blackened with soot, his eyes red-rimmed, every muscle screaming from the effort to douse the blaze, and his heart heavy with the loss, he surveyed the scene, thanking the gods that no other homes had fallen.

Most of the crowd had dissipated, the biting cold driving them back to home and hearth. Sabine had taken his parents back to Jameth's. His friends remained. *brothers in arms*, he thought cynically before he could help himself. They huddled together; from the occasional curse and tone of their murmurs, they were obviously deep in a discussion.

As he drew near, he heard Chap say with disgust, "Lathart assures that the screen was across the hearth and the home fire nearly spent when they left for Jameth's. I tell you there is no good behind this, no good at all. And I'd not be guessing in putting a name behind it; it is the blackguard Gramicy, I tell you!"

Chap's statement echoed what Lathaniel had been considering only moments before.

Then, giving mortal form to the devil they were discussing, a voice called out from down the street, "What manner of ill deed has caused such a stir in my Lamana this night?"

Short and stout, fattened by too many meals consumed at the expense of others, Bracher Gramicy strode forward toward Lathaniel and the men. Draped in furs, the ancient Forsairean pendant of rule could be seen hung around his neck, its presence alone a taunt to the gathered.

"Ah, young Waythan," he began, his disdain and arrogance evident in his nasally tone, "I knew you to be hunting and wasn't aware you'd returned. I should have known to look for you where mischief is found."

Awash with anger, Lathaniel walked quickly toward Gramicy offering neither greeting nor the expected bow of respect. "There has been no mischief, Bracher, only a dastardly arson that has left my parents without their home."

Two of Gramicy's guards stepped forward thinking to thwart any threat from Lathaniel. He spun round to elude their attempts, kicking one guard in the knee knocking him down and landing a solid left on the jaw of the other. Sensing things were quickly getting out of hand, Jameth and Darryn surged forward and grabbed Lathaniel from behind.

"Easy lad," Darryn said quietly in his ear. "There will be a time and a place, but neither is this night."

The easy tone now lost, Gramicy stepped up to Lathaniel, his beady eyes glaring up at him as he spat, "Your *parents* have not lost a home this night, boy. *I* have lost a property taken in lieu of unpaid taxes. The loss is mine, not yours. And you will speak with respect to me or feel the sting of my displeasure!

A Waythan you may be, but like your cowardly father and his before him, you are a disgrace to your ancestors. How dare you speak to me as an equal and with anger in your voice? I am your leader!"

Gramicy stepped back now, his eyes sweeping the men gathered loosely around Lathaniel and addressing them with haughty scorn. "Are these your band of warriors, Waythan?" he sneered. "I suggest you tell them to return to their houses, for there is no telling how many laws they are breaking simply by gathering here. The gods only know, when my sheriff investigates, one of them just might be found as the arsonist that burned my house down this night."

Lathaniel felt a cold resolve settle over him. He gestured for Jameth, Darryn, Chap, and the others to step back. No matter the rhetoric of earlier in the evening, gaining the attention of this tyrant would bode ill for his friends, and he could not let that happen. At his nod they stepped back reluctantly but did not leave. Lathaniel stepped close to Gramicy looking pointedly at his guards then back at Gramicy whilst saying nothing. Not taking his eyes from Lathaniel's, Gramicy motioned to his guards to step back.

Lathaniel, his voice lowered and steady with both contempt and resolve, locked eyes with Gramicy.

"You can speak of respect? You speak of it as a currency, like another of your taxes or levies that can be demanded and paid. Respect is earned. And though you hold the seat of power in Lamana, you have not earned the respect of our people and you know it! That is why you surround yourself with guards. You know your control is tenuous and you foolishly believe that more force, more oppression and more fear are the answer. But know this, my lord," he said with contempt evident in his voice, "these last dark years have taken a toll on our people. For millennia, Forsairs have lived with honour and order, looking after their own with fairness and justice. The rule I see practiced across Lamana brings me shame when I think of our ancestors. If you do not change your ways and truly lead our people without the oppression you so liberally practice, you will lose your leadership, either to an uprising within Lamana or to a blackguard from beyond Oldo's shores. You think me a threat? I have no desire to lead Lamana. None. But be assured, I will stand for my parents and those I love. "

Gramicy's face had darkened, now blotchy red with anger. "You dare to challenge me, to threaten me, boy? I am the ruler of Lamana and you will respect me, by the gods! You think to speak to me as if I am your contemporary?...one of your lackey tradesmen companions? How will you stand for your parents, boy? You are naught but a child, a simple hunter with a blight of dishonour on his name who's attempting to ride the remains of a wave of achievements long dead. You dare to threaten me?" he bellowed.

His voice still tightly controlled, Lathaniel replied quietly, "Spewing words from behind your wall of guards is no large undertaking, Bracher. One day, you will stand alone and will account for your behaviour and your leadership. I pray there is still something left of Lamana when that day comes."

With that, Lathaniel turned on his heel, his young shoulders squared and his posture proud as he walked away flanked by Jameth, Darryn, Chap, and the others. He did not look back though he felt the piercing wrath of Gramicy's glare between his shoulder blades.

With his escort, he made his way back to Jameth's. The meeting, the fire, and his confrontation with Gramicy had left him exhausted both in body and spirit. He fell into bed where he slept hard, without dreams. So deep was his sleep that it took several hard shakes from Jameth before he awoke the next morning.

"Lathaniel! Wake up! You must wake!" Jameth was yelling.

Shaking his head to clear the haze of sleep and rapidly blinking his sleep-swollen eyes, Lathaniel muttered, "What?" Then coming to his senses, he answered loudly, "What! What has happened?"

Jameth's face was pale and drawn, his eyes wide with concern. "It's your parents, Lathaniel. They were taken in the night."

It was as if a blind had been raised, taking Lathaniel from drowsy and relaxed to instantly tense and alert. "Tell me," he said as he swung his legs over the side of his bed, pulling up his breeches as he stood and reaching for his boots, tunic, and sword.

"It's my fault," Jameth lamented. "I let the sentries go after the meeting ended and the fire was out. I didn't think we would need guards at my house. I heard nothing. I only know that their room is a shambles. They went quietly, but by the gods they did not go easily!"

"There's no blame to be placed with any save one. The blackguard, Gramicy has them. Of that, I am certain."

As he spoke Lathaniel descended the stairs strapping on his scabbard and throwing his fur-collared cloak across his shoulders.

"Wait!" Jameth pleaded. "Let me gather the men and we will stand with you."

Lathaniel ignored him; his full stride was already eating up the cobblestones, his focus on one thing only.

The Gramicy household was easy to find. It sat atop a hill overlooking Lamana village. Made of white granite mined from the cliffs along the northern Oldo shores, its facade boasted two supporting pillars between which hung heavy, double oak doors. Pink-toned tiles covered a roof marked by four solid brick chimneys, each of which was billowing smoke into the crisp, early morning air. It did not escape Lathaniel's notice that he was marching up the hill toward the bastion that had housed his ancestors for ages and, had the fates been different, could have been his own home.

The guards at the entrance to the stronghold were relaxing in the gatehouse not expecting visitors so early in the morning. Lathaniel was beyond them before they spilled out of the door and yelled at him to stop. Noting that he ignored their orders to halt, one grabbed a worn bellpull and sounded alarm to the house above. Lathaniel carried on. He marched directly to the double oak doors and pushed them both open, scanning the inner keep and great room.

"Ah..." he heard from within. "I wondered how long it would take you to get here this morning, boy."

Gramicy pushed himself back from the table where he had obviously been filling his face. Wiping the grease from his chin with a cloth, he threw it aside and rounded the table, strutting toward Lathaniel.

To his guards, he simply said, "Bring them."

Lathaniel had not moved from the threshold, but when he saw his parents shoved into the room in front of the guards, their clothing dishevelled and filthy, hands tied behind their backs, he surged forward. Before he could reach them, several other guards stepped between him and his parents, their swords drawn.

Lathaniel swung round to Gramicy. "What madness has taken you now?" he demanded.

Taking his time, Gramicy walked around Sayra and Lathart looking them up and down with smug distaste before turning his attention to Lathaniel.

"I have thought long about your impassioned speech in the streets last evening, Waythan. And I have decided that I agree with you. Lamana *is* fraught with unrest and unhappiness. But this has naught to do with me but rather to do...with you."

Lathaniel started, his face twisted in disbelief and bewilderment.

"You see," Gramicy continued, "I believe that my people are torn. They would like to embrace me as their leader, but they feel tied to the past. The Waythan name is synonymous with the past and, hence, their ludicrous attempts to hang on to it. They foolishly believe that their future lies in a Lamana led by a Waythan. I have come upon a solution." He paused, dramatically.

"Just tell me what you want, Gramicy," Lathaniel demanded, frustrated.

"It's simple," Gramicy said with a smirk on his face. "I want you to leave Lamana. Forever."

There was a gasp and outcry from Lathaniel's parents.

After a pause, Gramicy continued, "It really is quite simple, Waythan. You leave and your parents live. I will give them housing and leave them in peace. Provided your friends do not break my laws, they will be left in peace as well. You say you want order restored to Lamana. The unrest you say you detest is laid at your feet. Leave, and peace prevails. Stay, and you and yours will face the consequences. It is an offer on the table right now. One hour from now, it will be rescinded. So boy, what's it to be?"

Lathaniel remained silent and stood still, processing Bracher's words. In truth, he hadn't considered that he and the

Waythan name could be contributing to the problems faced by the Forsairs. That this could be the case was a blow to him. He would sacrifice anything for his family and friends, for his people. But could Gramicy be trusted?

"How do I know that if I leave you will not continue with your treachery?" he demanded.

The sneer was gone from Gramicy's face, replaced with a cold, hard look of calculation. "Quite frankly, boy, you do not. But I have given my word, and you will have to take that as it is given."

"No, Lathaniel!" his father pleaded.

Tears were streaming down his mother's face as she shook her head back and forth. "Do not believe him, Lathaniel. Do not consider this request, I beg you!"

Lathaniel was silent, considering. Then he turned to Gramicy. "I will need a moment with my parents and time to collect my belongings." His mother's sobs increased.

"So be it," said Gramicy, his delight barely concealed. He nodded to the guards, and they parted allowing Lathaniel to go to his parents. Unsheathing his knife, he cut the bindings round both their wrists freeing them. His mother threw her arms around his shoulders, through her tears still pleading with him to remain. As he held her, he met his father's tear-filled eyes.

"I must go," Lathaniel said. "If this guarantees your safety and a lessening of the trials within Lamana, then I must go.

"Do you not see?" pleaded his father. "His word means nothing! By removing the one rallying point for Lamana, his way is clear to torment and oppress with impunity. Your going will not change this, Lathaniel!"

"That may be so, Father, but it will save your lives. I can do naught but go. There is no choice. Know that I love you both and that in my heart I believe I will see you again."

He kissed his mother's forehead and released her, then pulled his father into a strong, quick embrace. Then, without another word or glance behind him, he walked out the double oak doors and down the hill past the gatehouse. As if somehow they knew something of great importance had happened, people came out of their homes and stood in their doorways, watching him make his way down the hill. Lathaniel saw no one. His face was impassive; his gaze was unblinking and steady as he walked. At some level he marvelled how he could feel both numb yet still like his heart was being rent from his chest.

Without pausing he walked into Jameth's cottage, began gathering his belongings, and stuffing them into his hunting pack. He paid no heed to either Darryn or Jameth's impassioned questions or pleas behind him.

In silence he turned and before he passed the threshold gathered first Jameth then his old friend Darryn into a quick embrace. "Look after my parents and Sabine, my friend," he said in Darryn's ear. "I am entrusting their safety to you. But now, I must go. I have no choice." He looked deeply into his friend's unbelieving eyes one last time then turned and walked out into the sunlight, not looking back.

He was nearly at the outskirts of the town when he heard his voice frantically being called from behind him. He turned to see Sabine running, pulling a loaded but reluctant ancient packhorse behind her. Her head was wrapped in scarves, and she had her winter woollens and furs on.

As she reached him, she panted, "I came as quick as I could. I have packed what I was able. I'm sure I have forgotten something important, but I brought what I thought we would need."

She was breathless and her words rushed out. Her face, beneath the flush from exertion, was dead white; and her voice held threads of hysteria. So caught up in his exodus, he had not given thorough thought to how his departure would impact her. How could he leave her behind? He placed both hands on her face, stared with anguish into her eyes, and then gathered her close in a bone-crushing hug. She cried out once. At some level she already knew he would not allow her to accompany him. But the reality of the good-bye was another matter. As he pulled back from her embrace, tears streamed down both their cheeks. He could not imagine a life without her, but he would not separate her from the family, friends, and life she loved.

"I must go," he whispered gently. He placed his hand gently across her lips to stay the protest she would have voiced. "To take you with me would be folly, Sabine. You know this to be true."

She was shaking her head, denying his words.

"You know that you have my heart," he continued, "that I have loved you since I was a boy and that I will love you always."

He gathered her to him again, breathing in the smell of lavender, sunshine, and woman; memorizing the feel of her. He stepped back again. Sabine straightened her spine and stepped back from him. Never taking her eyes from his, she gave him one barely perceptible nod and handed him the reins of the packhorse. She reached out and grabbed his other hand and forced a small piece of parchment into it. Tears still streaming down her face, she reached up on her toes and kissed him once gently on the cheek. Then she turned away and began walking slowly back to the city, never looking back.

Lathaniel could not bear to watch her walk away, so he turned and concentrated on placing one foot in front of the other as he left his life behind.

# CHAPTER 5

Under pensive, grey skies a cool west wind blew chilly breaths across the eastern shores of the island of Koorast. Gramal, a port city in the realm of Horon, was one of the largest bastions of sea trade in that part of Elënthiá. This day it was hunkered under overcast skies, its inhabitants pulling up collars against the damp and the chill.

Though his long leather tunic was damp from the weather, Jugarth Framir was anything but chilled. Adrenaline had his heart pumping and his senses acutely tuned to his surroundings. Hoping to elude notice, he entered the shop on the heels of two seamen from one of the vessels in port, come to replenish their supplies of tobacco and jerky. Once in the door he stepped quickly into an aisle stocked with rolls of sailcloth and made his way across two more, sliding into an aisle where gloves and other outerwear were displayed. He'd been in to reconnoitre once before and knew exactly what he was after.

He pretended to be looking at garment displays, but once the shopkeeper was engaged in a story with the seamen, quick as you will, he snatched pair of gloves and tucked them beneath his tunic, walking quickly toward the door of the store whilst doing so. He stole to eat—to survive. Otherwise, though it seemed contrary to what he'd just done, he did not steal. But then, these were gloves specially made for a swordsman, and that tipped the scale. He'd never be able to afford such a thing in a lifetime of saving. In his line of work, they'd be invaluable.

The door was thrown open just as he reached it, and a young, rambunctious boy of four or five ran in ahead of his father, filled with glee at the thought of the sugary treat he'd been promised. He collided with Jugarth, catching him off guard. The stolen gloves slipped from under his tunic and hit the wooden shop floor with a soft *thwap.*

The commotion was sufficient to draw the attention of the shopkeeper who yelled, "You! What have you there?"

The end of his question was drowned out by the slam of the door and the slap of Jugarth's feet as he fled. A block up from the shop, he slowed his steps to a fast walk, giving an occasional furtive glance over his shoulder and doing his best to meld into the traffic on the street. *Not good*, he thought. *Not good at all.*

He could hear the shopkeeper yelling behind him, "Stop that boy! That one! In the brown tunic. He's a thief!"

As he turned back, thinking it was time to forget blending in and just make tracks, he hit something hard enough to knock him on his backside. Looking up he saw only the leather jerkin-clad bulk of a city guard on street patrol, his arms crossed, staring forebodingly down at him. As he was dragged unceremoniously to his feet, he pretended to stumble and lose his balance, furtively tucking the stolen gloves down the front of his trousers and assuming his most innocent look.

An out-of-breath shopkeeper arrived on the scene and with a sound smack slapped Jugarth's face.

"You worthless little thief!" he panted out. "Where are those gloves?"

His cheek a blazing red, Jugarth stared unblinkingly at the man's angry face. "Why'd' you smack me? I stole nothing!" he argued.

"I saw the gloves fall from your tunic!" the man insisted turning to the guard. "Check his pockets. I'm sure you will find a very expensive pair of swordsman's gloves in them."

The guard patted the pockets of Jugarth's tunic and trousers. "I am not finding your gloves, merchant." Then to Jugarth, "If you did not steal the gloves, why were you running away?"

"For exactly this reason!" Jugarth tried to sound his most indignant, hoping to talk his way out of this. "It's always us that live on the streets that get blamed when things go missing. Why wouldn't I run?"

"I tell you," the shopkeeper bellowed, his face purpling in rage, "I saw him take the gloves!"

The guard intervened. "This is a case for the magistrate. If you have done nothing wrong, boy, you'll not mind waiting 'round 'til we can look into this, now will you?"

With a self-righteous nod, the shopkeeper backed out of the way while the guard, his hand firmly around Jugarth's upper arm, steered him toward the jail.

*Not good at all*, Juga thought again.

He sat on the damp dirt floor in the tiny cell staring at the uneven, grey stone walls, his knees drawn up and his forearms resting on them. If he read the light through the barred window high on the wall correctly, he'd long missed an important rendezvous with his Master. And missing meetings of that sort was definitely not good. He stood and began to pace. He was sixteen. Tall but slender, his musculature was just beginning to blossom and develop. He ran his hand back through his long, unkempt hair, making the ragged auburn locks stick up every which way. There wasn't sufficient fat on him to fry a bedbug, but his slender build belied the strength beneath the tattered garments.

"Guard!" he called out testily, blue eyes snapping with annoyance. "Let me out of here, and I'll tell my Master to spare your life when he comes to collect me."

He could hear the guard snort out a laugh in response then spit on the floor outside of his door. Jugarth figured he might as well rest while he could and sank back down against the wall onto the floor. As he shifted his backside trying to get comfortable, his eyes lit. He slid his hand down the front of his drawers and hauled out the gloves. Smiling to himself, he thought that at least the day was not a total waste.

# CHAPTER 6

Lathaniel had never been in this part of the Linia forest. Here the overstory was thick and dense, allowing very little sunlight to filter through to the forest floor below. As such it was difficult to use the sun—or the stars for that matter—to navigate. Game was so sparse as to be nonexistent. And there was a silence that was unsettling.

There was a reason the Forsairean people had chosen and settled in the remote enclave of Lamana. Oldo's island coasts were treacherous and inhospitable. Only the most seasoned of sailors could navigate to its shores, and only then during certain seasons of the year when the seas and the tides cooperated. Once ashore, even the most intrepid of explorers would find the outer rims of the Linia forest daunting. And, as Lathaniel trudged ever onward, he could truly understand why. He'd never been this far from Lamana, and though his hunter's directional instincts were finely tuned, he was admitting unease at his own navigational skills as he got further and further from his home.

His heart was sick, like a mysterious malaise had settled over the whole of him, sapping his energy and fogging his mind like the syrupy mists that clung to the forest floor. Over and over he rehashed his last days in Lamana. He could clearly see the anxious faces of his parents, the zealous Jameth, the abiding friendship in Darryn and Chap, the dastardly Gramicy. Had he done the right thing? Should he have stayed and accepted the challenge Jameth and the others had thrown at his feet? Would the gods ever allow him to return to his home and those he loved? These questions and a million more ran in a perpetual loop through his mind, kept company by the clop-clop of his packhorse's hooves as they moved steadily on.

The days bled each into the other as he continued toward what he hoped was the coast. His mind wandered back over many of the stories he'd heard from both his father and grandfather, stories that had been passed down from generation to generation, stories of journeys and battles and of ancient times when the Elves fought the evil Lord Morin, halting his destruction of Elënthiá. His recollections turned to the maps that his grandfather had sketched on parchment by firelight, giving life to those stories during long winter nights. These memories were sketchy and bittersweet, but through them he began to gain both perspective and purpose.

As he ate a solitary meal by his small fire a fortnight into his journey, he had a thought. If he was the first Forsair to leave Lamana, then he would keep maps of his travels. Who knew? Perhaps one day he would sketch his own maps by firelight for his own grandson.

That brought a wistful sigh as he thought of Sabine for the millionth time that day. But this time he gave a start, for he only just remembered the parchment she had tucked into his hand as they said good-bye. He had slid it deep into his pocket and had all but forgotten it was there. He stood and buried his hand in his pocket until he found it. He unwrapped it, recognizing what was inside even before he very nearly dropped it into the dirt. His eyes blurred as he recognized the fine silver ring that Sabine had worn every day he'd known her. The vine design on the band was unmistakable, as was the star sapphire that winked in its center.

He pulled a leather lace from his tunic and, running it through the ring, tied it securely around his neck before smoothing the folds out of the parchment and turning it toward the fire's light to read: *We will see each other again, either in this life or the next.*

Lathaniel had no hope of swallowing the lump locked in his throat. Carefully folding the parchment back into a neat square, he slid it into a small pocket in his pack and lay down beside the fire, silent tears drying on his cheeks as he slept.

Lathaniel was edgy as he walked the next day. He grew weary of the forest's gloom. The nights on its cold floor had done nothing to improve his disposition either. He instinctually sensed that he was coming to the edge of it; the overstory was thinning, but it was more the quality of the air. Forsairs were exceptional hunters, their senses finely tuned to the forest and to nature's ways. And Lathaniel's nose was twitching.

Perhaps he would reach the end of the interminable forest today, he thought, his pace picking up in anticipation. Over the next few hours, the foliage thinned and the ground became rockier, more rugged. More than once the weary packhorse stumbled. While Sabine had given her only horse to him, the beast hadn't seen spry for many a day. Lathaniel carried most of his essentials on his back; with the foodstuffs provided by Sabine long since depleted, the nag only carried extra bedrolls and utensils. The beast was clearly near exhaustion.

Finally, a full view of blue sky! Lathaniel took a moment to get his bearings, standing near the edge of a rocky outcropping, his hands on his hips. He had no clear view to the horizon. The Linia forest was behind him, and ahead were treacherous, jagged rock falls with barren, reddish-brown, low cliff faces.

He was certain he could hear the sound of rushing water but could not spot the source. As he considered the best way forward, he suddenly felt the ground beneath his horse and him give way as they both fell.

The horse's neck snapped on impact. And even if Lathaniel had been unconscious during the fall from the rocks above, the icy cold of the water he hit with a resounding slap would have snapped him back to reality. Turning onto his back, his feet facing into the icy current, he let himself be swept along as he hastily took in his surroundings. He had obviously fallen into an underground cavern of some sort. There was perhaps half a man's height between him and the roof of wherever he was; the walls around him were shiny with moisture. There was very little light, but the sound of the rushing water echoing off the walls was near deafening. He felt a lurch in his stomach as, carried by the force of the rushing water, he shot out feet first over first a small precipice and then out again into thin air as he fell to a pool of water below.

Weakly stroking to the shore, a relieved Lathaniel hauled himself up on solid ground. Wherever he was, the sun was strong. There was a strong smell of the sea in his lungs and the squawk and cackle of sea birds on the air. He'd made the coast. If his grandfather's stories were true and the gods were smiling, he might find a ship and catch a ride to the large island his grandfather had called Koorast.

# CHAPTER 7

The hooded figure sat quietly, his chair tilted back against the wall behind him. Painted in shadows, he could have been any weary traveler stopping for ale and a meal at the inn in Zoren. But he was not. The barkeep and his servers referred to him only as *sir.* Though his visits were infrequent—it might sometimes be months between them—he inevitably sat at the same table, his back to the wall, the hood of his cloak masking his face in shadows. Men would sometimes find their way to his table. Quiet discussion would ensue and the men would leave. Occasionally a voice was raised or the table pounded in frustration...but he gave little away. No niceties were exchanged; no details were offered. As always, information was the only currency that changed hands.

On this night, a drunk very nearly fell through the front door, righted himself, and weaved precariously through the scarred tables and the dim light toward the bar. Were those present able, they would have seen a grimace of distaste pass across the cloaked man's face, for he detested any behaviour which drew public attention. Hard-learned lessons in survival early in his life had taught him to skirt the fringes of society, drawing as little attention as possible. Those who knew the man beneath the hood called him Drake. That he was of the legendary Draconean race was a fact that few knew.

For tonight, though, a rendezvous at the inn as well as the ale and the slop in the wooden bowl in front of him were all a means to an end. He needed food, drink and an update on the Resistance. Beyond that, he was missing an apprentice. Three years of training he'd given the lad, and he was determined to protect his investment. Yes, it was information he needed this night.

A commotion at the front door drew his attention. A boy of about fourteen was standing just inside the door of the inn trying to gain entrance, his eyes scanning the crowds, barely giving attention to the barkeep's barking belligerence.

"I don't give a whit who you are here to see, I do not serve homeless children! Now out with you!"

Recognizing the short, sandy-haired lad, Drake stood hastily and quickly moved through the tables to the door. Stepping closely behind the barkeep, he leaned to his ear and quietly said, "He's with me."

The barkeep swung round saying. "I care not who he is with, he is not..."

His bellow faded mid-sentence when he realized who had spoken in his ear, noting as his gaze swept upward to meet the cold, hard eyes, that "sir" had never seemed quite so tall nor intimidating when he was seated. He opened his mouth as if to say more but at the steely gaze locking with his, stepped back, muttering to himself as he walked back to the bar.

The young boy was quickly whisked to the back table and seated. "Ziny, my lad, what news have you?" Drake questioned. "Come now...the walls have eyes and time is short."

Ziny's hazel eyes darted back and forth across the room as he sat, eyes that were wide with trepidation within his pale, oval face. He had heard stories of this mysterious man, but his personal dealings with him had mostly been at arm's length or with another informant present. Anxious to get to the point and get gone, Ziny quietly replied, his eyes never stopping their sweep, "I am told that Gorillian's armies have regrouped near the border of Ethen-jar to wait for both supplies and further orders."

Ziny was an informant working for the Resistance as they fought against the evil that was sweeping through Elënthiá. Working under the guise of a shop boy for a local merchant, he was one of a handful of spies positioned around Koorast, the main base for the Resistance. He moved in and out of the shadows within towns like Zoren, collecting bits and pieces of information from his own network of informants and from gossip on the streets.

Drake pondered Ziny's rely. Gorillian had been the bane of his existence and his sworn enemy since childhood. Drake had been tracking him century upon century, but each time the fiend was within his sights, he managed to elude Drake, returning to his stronghold in the poisoned realm of Ethen-jar.

"I need supplies, my young friend, and I need them fast."

Ziny's hazel eyes swung round then and locked with Drake's. "What have you need of?"

"Everything you normally get me."

Ziny nodded. "What else?"

Drake held his gaze but dropped his voice. "Would you happen to know where my apprentice is?"

"I do. But the news is not good. I was told only moments ago that he was caught stealing in Gramal. He is in jail awaiting sentencing." Ziny looked at Drake with concern. "If you go to Gramal to save him, you will alert Gorillian of your presence. He knows of your ties to the apprentice. The jails will be closely watched."

Drake sat in silence for a moment, deliberating his course of action. "I cannot leave him there. If not already, Gorillian will soon know of his arrest and will torture him, use him as bait to capture me. The lad does not deserve that fate for the simple crime of my acquaintance. 'Tis a chance I'll have to take."

If the decades had been marked by Drake's pursuit of Gorillian, the same could be said in reverse. The perpetual cat-and-mouse game they played had grown tedious, but the capture of the boy had upped the stakes. Every second now counted.

Drake turned his attention back to Ziny, who sat unmoving in his chair. Then, sensing their meeting was coming to a close, he made to stand. Drake reached across the table and grasped the boy's hand, holding him in his seat and slipping a leather pouch of coins into it as he did. By the gods, what had the world come to when children such as Ziny had to fight for freedom, he thought.

"Many thanks, my young friend. Have the supplies ready but in Gramal and at the usual place. I'll likely be coming through fast. Be ready. And stay safe.

With a nod, Ziny slid off the stool and into the shadows along the periphery of the inn's great room to the door, careful to draw no attention to himself. Drake paid for his food and drink, then stepped into the snowy street and easily disappeared into the crowds.

# CHAPTER 8

This was a fine mess, Lathaniel mused as he peered out from between the bars of the jail cell he had been thrust into. A day ago he was praising himself for finally have acquired his sea legs. A day ago he was sitting in the hold of a ship commiserating about the icy bite of the sea wind with his shipmates and sharing a mug of ale. He had been marvelling at the sleek build of the ship he rode upon, how it fairly skimmed across the tops of the choppy, white-capped sea. He had kept to himself for the most part, silently listening to the tales told once the ale was flowing about a warlord named Gorillian and those across Elënthiá who resisted him. Though he had heard the warlord's name even in Lamana, this talk of war and rebellion was all so strange and foreign to him. But that was all just a short day ago.

Now, because of this same Gorillian, he found himself behind bars in a town called Gramal. Their ship had been met as they docked by hooligans calling themselves the Black March. The entire crew was detained and accused of conspiring against Gorillian and of smuggling supplies for what they called the Resistance. Lathaniel had tried once to explain that he was only just catching a ride, but the bite of the knife wound he earned for his protest had kept him quiet.

The cell he'd been thrown into was small, and it took a moment for him to notice there was another pallet on the floor in the far corner. On it, a figure sat with his back to the wall and his arms wrapped around his drawn-up knees, studying him. The figure unfolded itself, and Lathaniel felt a moment of tension as a boy walked out of the shadows and stood before him.

"Welcome to my humble cell. It's not much," said a young voice with laughter in it, "but it's home. My name is Jugarth Framir, but most call me Juga."

Lathaniel hesitated for only a second before he clasped the outstretched hand now offered to him and shook it warmly.

"Lathaniel Waythan," he replied. The two young men fell into an easy conversation. Lathaniel, too used to keeping his own counsel and delighted to have someone nearer to his own age around, was quick to share the rudimentary details of his capture but careful to avoid either details of his full journey as well as his origins. Even in the dimness of the cell, Juga could see his pallor and that he swayed on his feet.

"Why don't you sit down on that pallet, my friend, before you fall upon it?" he suggested.

As Lathaniel bent to sit, Juga noticed the blood on his tunic. "You're injured." he noted. "Let me have a look at that."

With efficiency remarkable for a boy his age, Juga tore strips of cloth from a spare shirt he found in Lathaniel's pack and bound his wound. This was obviously not the first knife wound he'd tended.

"There is no water about to clean it properly, but it's not too serious," he commented. "An inch or two to the right, though," he smiled, his cocky attitude back, "and we would not be having this conversation."

The rest of the afternoon was spent with Lathaniel resting on the filthy floor pallet watching Juga shadow spar in the middle of the room. He hadn't spent much time in the company of Humans. Of course, Human blood was part of what ran in his veins, but he'd never really spent time with one before.

"Why are you in here?" he asked after a time.

Juga stopped his bouncing and footwork and turned to Lathaniel, just slightly out of breath. "I stole these," he said, raising his glove-covered palms in the air and wiggling his fingers, a slight smirk on his face.

"You're a thief then?" There was no accusation in the comment, merely a statement of fact.

Juga paused, looking straight at Lathaniel, the humour no longer in his eyes. "I steal to eat and to survive. I do not steal for sport, and I never, ever steal from those in need as much or more than I."

Then the smile was back. "But these, well, these gloves I just had to own."

The shadow boxing continued, and there was silence again for a time before Juga spoke again.

"You're a Forsair, are you not?"

His question completely took Lathaniel aback for, unless one knew to look for the special shape of the tops of his ears, now hidden beneath his hair, he appeared Human. He didn't answer, just held Juga's gaze.

The lad just harrumphed and went back to his boxing. "And here I thought I was in trouble. You'd best hope that no one else finds out. Humans still feel threatened by any of mixed blood. They'll kill you, you know."

Lathaniel did not reply and the lad said no more. But there was a wary tension in the cell now. Neither said a word as the late afternoon sun slipped deeper into the sky and evening approached. The silence was broken by the sounds of swords clashing. With a jaunty spring, Juga was off his pallet and standing on his toes, his hands on the bars looking with anticipation out the small window to the corridor beyond.

"I'll be saying good-bye to you now," he said, turning to grin at Lathaniel. "For, if I'm not mistaken, the sounds you hear are my Master come to fetch me."

Lathaniel hurried to his feet, grabbed his pack, and slung it over his head and shoulder, ready to greet whatever or whoever came through the door.

"Master!" he heard Juga shout. "In here."

With a clang and the rattling of chains, the wooden cell door was thrown open and its portal filled by a giant of a man, cloaked with his sword drawn. Juga grabbed his tunic and followed him out the door.

"Wait!" Lathaniel cried out. "Take me with you!"

The cloaked figure turned back seeming to notice Lathaniel for the first time.

Juga explained, "He's been jailed by the Black March for smuggling for the Resistance, Master. They're holding him for treason against Gorillian, but he says he's innocent." He paused and then lowered his voice to whisper. "He's a Forsair."

At that the tall man's head snapped around and the eyes beneath the hood of the cloak fixed Lathaniel with a hard stare. It was only seconds, but Lathaniel felt his burning regard.

"Keep up" was all he growled out before he turned and fled down the corridor, his cloak billowing out behind him, Juga and now Lathaniel close on his heels.

They leapt over two guards lying slumped on the floor by a table in the dirt corridor, grabbing their confiscated weapons as they ran by. A right turn down another corridor, then a left; a set of stairs down, and then another maze of corridors. The three ran on, Juga and Lathaniel grateful that their rescuer had some sense of the direction to their freedom. Especially since it was only a matter of moments before alarm would be raised and the jail would be swarming with guards.

Coming to a junction ahead, the tall man motioned with his hand for quiet and stealth and flattened himself against the wall, moving quietly forward. Ducking his head quickly out around the corner and then back again to ensure no one was about, he motioned them forward toward a door.

Opening the door slowly, they surprised two sentries who, before they could reach for their weapons found themselves laid out on the cobblestones, unconscious. Lathaniel's eyes were like saucers. Juga might be used to this cloaked man's fighting prowess, but he was not. He'd never seen anyone move so fast.

"Keep up," their rescuer ordered once again, and with that he took off down the street heading for the open marketplace where they might find some camouflage in the evening crowds. Behind them they could hear the peal of an alarm bell clang as the jailers discovered the wounded and the absence of two prisoners.

Drake slowed their pace, still walking rapidly but trying to blend in with the street crowds. At least his apprentice was unharmed, he thought. Still cheeky and arrogant, but unharmed. He would have many questions about how a Forsair could have been jailed as a smuggler for the Resistance, but he'd save them for later. For now, they had to put Gramal behind them, and as quickly as possible. The city was as much a stronghold for Gorillian's forces as it was for the Resistance. There would be spies aplenty on the streets willing to sell information to any who offered.

Seeing a familiar store, he detoured in the front door of it; as prearranged, the owner immediately closed the door behind them and locked it, flipping a "Closed" sign over and closing the shutters in the front window. He threw two bundles to Drake who, in turn threw one each to his followers.

"Find a change of clothes in these, and make haste. We've not a moment to lose." With that he shrugged off his own long cloak and rolled it tightly before attaching it to the bottom of his pack.

While Lathaniel pulled off his tunic and found clothing that fit him, he grabbed quick glances at the uncloaked stranger. He was tall, near to six-and-a-half feet, taller than Lathaniel had first imagined, with broad strong shoulders. He was built like a wedge, the breadth of his shoulders and torso narrowing to slim hips and long, booted, muscular legs. He wore his jet black hair long. His snug leather leggings were tucked into knee-high boots, also of well-worn leather, and the belt that hung low on his hips held both a dagger and a sword. He wore tooled leather gloves similar in design to those that Juga had stolen, with the last three fingers cut off at the knuckle.

The three finished switching clothes, all of them donning brimmed hats to alter their appearances and hide their features.

Four more bundles with straps were readied on the bench in the store's backroom. Giving one to each of the boys, the tall man donned the other two. A brief word and a coin or two were exchanged with the merchant, and then they were out the back door of the store looking nothing like the three who had, only moments before, crossed its threshold.

Twilight was giving way to darkness as they quickly moved through the streets to the gates of the village. Coming around a corner, they could see the gates ahead. The wound in Lathaniel's side had opened again, and he could feel blood trickling down his side. He knew if he didn't keep up, his new companions would not wait, would not risk capture for him.

The gatekeepers were moving to close the gates for the night, allowing the last of the stragglers to make their way through. Drake, Juga, and Lathaniel tried to blend in with these crowds. Just then they heard distant shouts from behind them.

"Close the gates! Prisoners have escaped the jail! Close the gates!"

The gatekeepers were at the end of a long day of guard duty and were slow to respond. The three took advantage of their hesitation to surge forward and through the open portal. The distant shouts of the guards grew louder. "It's them! It's the prisoners who escaped the jail. Stop them!"

The gate keepers sprang into action, but the three were making for the forest beyond at a dead run. The sentries on the wall loosed a volley of arrows that rained down around them. Frantic and breathless, Lathaniel could hear them streaking through the air and a soft *thwump* as one caught his rescuer in the calf. The man stumbled but kept moving. Lathaniel was near the end of his resources himself. His blood loss had sapped his strength, and he stumbled. He would have fallen flat on his face but for the strong arm that reached out and grasped his upper arm firmly.

"Steady" was all he heard.

And with that encouragement he kept on until they reached the cover of the forest and could stop and catch their breath. The night was fully upon them now. The darkness and the forest wrapped around them like a comforting blanket after the exposure of running through the open fields outside the town's walls. Chests were heaving as they all tried to catch their breath.

Lathaniel's legs had given out from under him; the other two were bent at the waist, their arms on their knees. Lathaniel reached into his pack and pulled out what was left of the shirt they had shredded to bind his wound earlier that day.

"I'm afraid I'll need your help for a moment, Juga," he panted. "I seem to be bleeding again."

Before Juga could move, his Master came down upon one knee beside Lathaniel. Pushing Lathaniel's hands aside, he peeled back his outer tunic and then the blood-soaked undershirt beneath it and surveyed the wound. Taking the cloths, he silently cleansed the wound with water. The he took some foul smelling salve from his pack and smoothed it over the wound, rebinding it with the cloths Lathaniel provided.

Then he shifted, settling himself on the ground beside Lathaniel where, with not so much as a sound, he yanked out the arrow that was embedded in his calf.

"Looks worse then it is," he muttered. "It caught more leather than flesh."

He pulled off his boot and swabbed the shallow wound with water and slathered on some salve. Moving to his feet, he stamped his foot back into the boot. Offering his hand to Lathaniel, he pulled him to his feet and said, "My name is Drake."

Lathaniel paused for only a second before grasping and shaking his hand. "Lathaniel," he replied.

"My thanks for your help. "

Drake didn't reply. His eyes moved to scan first the sky, then the darkened forest around them. Shouldering his pack he merely said, "Let's move."

The apprentice and the Forsair fell in behind him.

Dawn's light found the three companions well away from Gramal and waist deep in the grasses on Horon's plains. Lathaniel had passed tired hours before. His exhaustion was such that his mind was blank, all energy and concentration focused on placing on foot in front of the other. *Keep up. Keep up.* He tried to time his footsteps to that mantra, his gaze focused on Drake, who kept up a relentless pace with seemingly little effort. Even the ever-cocky Juga was silent, his gait uneven and his eyes glazed. The night behind them, they moved on through the day stopping only for water and to take food from the supply packs they carried. Lathaniel and Juga had stopped asking how far because the reply was always the same. Silence.

Drake seemed to have untapped energy reserves and a built-in compass that was steering him to some precise destination. While he gave Lathaniel and Juga breaks to rest, he backtracked, checking if they were being followed. Lathaniel doubted that anyone from Gramal could be close behind; such was the pace they had set. They were moving in and out of stands of leafless trees and across rolling hills that still held patches of winter snow and the dead remains of waist-high grasses from the previous autumn. The breeze moving across these and ruffling the tops gave the impression of a threadbare blanket wafting gently under the sun. Oft times there were rocky outcrops at the tops of the hills, and it seemed that it was to one such outcrop they were heading.

All of a sudden Drake fell back between the two and grabbed each by their upper arms, unexpectedly pulling them to the ground with him.

"What...?" they both began to demand only to be shushed by Drake as with a hand signal he bid them to stay low and follow behind him. Too tired to do anything but what he ordered, they obeyed, moving on their hands and knees for the most part but on their bellies as necessary so as to move unseen through the grass.

They reached the base of the rise of rocks where, following Drake's lead, they moved quietly from rock to rock, hard on his heels. They still had no idea what was driving his caution and stealth, but they did exactly as they were told. With a hand gesture, Drake bid them to stay put. He crept, soundless, farther up into the rocks.

Above them they heard a scuffle and a muffled cry, then Drake's familiar voice calling out, "It's safe."

Juga and Lathaniel scrambled up the remaining rocks to join him. Coming around the edge of a large boulder, they stopped dead in their tracks. At their feet was a bloody severed head. Lathaniel cried out and leapt back, his face pale and his stomach rolling at the sight. Juga stood expressionless.

When he had recovered enough to speak, Lathaniel yelled, "Are you mad? Who was that? You killed him!" all in the same breath.

Drake leaned over and wiped his sword off on the dead man's tunic, then sheathed his weapon.

"He was a spy sent to kill me," he replied flatly. "And he was trespassing on my property."

Lathaniel, still in shock, stared first at the body in the dirt and then at Drake, at a loss to understand what had just happened or why. He watched as Drake moved to a copse of bushes and bent into them, feeling around on the ground with his gloved hand. His hand found and then lifted a sturdy wooden handle from out of the dirt. He hauled upward on it and opened a portal the ground below, the outside of it still covered with underbrush and branches. No one could ever have found it were they not certain exactly what they were looking for and where to search.

Lathaniel watched, still incredulous. The three of them were in the middle of nowhere. What was below ground? Was it Drake's home? If it was, who or what would build a home like a burrow under the ground let alone locate it in middle of such a barren place? For his part, Juga's face remained unreadable, though when Drake grasped the corpse by the feet and began to drag it unceremoniously down the rocks to leave it in the long grass below, his apprentice moved to helped him. Drake walked back, and grabbing the spy's severed head by its bloodied hair, he hurled it down in the direction of the body.

"The scavengers will make short work of that," he muttered. With that he strode over to the mysterious trapdoor and bent over it. Juga squatted beside him, his face breaking into a smile.

Drake stood, stepping down onto the first stone step. As he did he grasped the inner handle of the secret door to close it behind them. Moving to the side he waited for his companions to follow. Juga was quick to descend the steps and disappeared into the ground below.

Lathaniel's feet were still rooted to the spot. It was like his mind was rapidly thumbing back through the pages of recent days trying to assimilate everything he'd been through. The images fell one over the other in his mind: the confrontation with Gramicy and the exodus from Oldo, his adventure on the sea and arrest for treason, a knife wound and a prison break followed by a gruelling trek to this place where he'd just witnessed his first murder. Murder? What in the gods' names should he do? If Drake could be so cavalier about killing that Human spy, what would happen when he went down those steps? Could he truly trust either him or Juga after an acquaintance of only two short days? Though he'd little knowledge of the local laws, he was certain that his life would have held little value had he remained in the Gramal prison. He could walk away from Drake and Juga right now But he had quickly learned that life beyond Oldo was fraught with more challenges than he had anticipated.

All of this raced through his mind in the seconds that he stood there staring blankly at Drake, who remained silent and expectant, still holding open the door. Lathaniel looked directly into Drake's emerald eyes. The eyes that held his in a hard, unblinking stare were ruthless, and they were cold. But Lathaniel saw no evil in them, and so, deciding to trust his instincts and remain with his new companions for a time, he moved toward the opening and stepped hesitantly down the first hewn stone steps into the darkness below.

# CHAPTER 9

The slam of the heavy door reverberated, the echoes resounding into the unknown and back until they were a mere whisper in the far reaches of the darkness that surrounded them. Drake, familiar with this dark world, could be heard rustling around until a flint was struck and the first torch lit.

Lathaniel stood motionless while his eyes adjusted, accepting a torch from Juga then stepping back, hugging the wall, and allowing first Drake then Juga to precede him as they began moving down the stairs. The torches cast long shadows but allowed a dimly lit arc in front of them. They were on a staircase that spiralled downwards into nothingness. The air was damp and, not surprisingly, held the strong smell of the earth; but, Lathaniel noted, the air was not stale, which meant there must be some manner of circulation.

With no sound but the rustle of their clothing, their footsteps, and the hiss of their torches, Lathaniel ventured, "What is this place?"

"My young companion, I believe this place has been called many things by many races throughout the ages, but for me it is home, though that might be too strong a word. Suffice to say that when I have had occasion to be in Horon, it has served as a haven for me." Drake replied.

He was silent for a moment and then continued, "It is a refuge. A place of peace in troubled times that, including the two of you, is known to fewer than my one hand could count. There are those who watch me closely who have surmised that there must be some secret place in this area, for spies shadow me constantly and are ever trying to thwart me when I near the entrance. Though, like our unfortunate friend providing dinner to the scavengers above, none have been successful in finding it.

"For my part," he continued, "I stumbled upon its existence by accident. I first thought it no more than a tomb dug to house the remains of the fallen. But over the centuries I have thoroughly explored these underground chambers and know it to be much, much more."

"Centuries?" Lathaniel blurted out, following along behind the two.

"Watch your step here," Drake cautioned as they continued.

"Save your questions until we have rested and eaten our fill, Lathaniel. These last days have seen your arrest, rescue from Gorillian, and a hasty flight across Horon that has been long and tiring. When we have rested, I shall answer."

With that, conversation ceased and they continued their single-file, downward spiral into the eerie darkness. Lathaniel reckoned they'd come down at least one hundred steps before they reached a landing where they began moving parallel with the surface above. They had entered a shaft wide enough that when he spread his arms the walls were still several inches beyond his fingertips on both sides. He was able to stand erect in the tunnel, but he noticed that Drake had to hunch slightly. The walls and the roof above were made of a wood that Lathaniel thought was oak. The floor was earthen though at some points firm, like well-packed clay, while at others his feet sank ankle-deep into a soft sand. Darkness remained a heavy curtain that rippled open then closed as they moved forward.

Though not uncomfortable with the darkness, Lathaniel was so filled with questions that he could not allow the silence to stretch further. "Juga, how did you come to be apprenticed to Drake?" he asked quietly.

Juga was silent for a moment; Lathaniel thought he might be waiting to see if Drake would object to his answering the question. After a time, he quietly answered as they walked on.

"I was just a boy of eight or nine and living on the streets of Duron City. A thief. Not a very good thief, mind you," he chuckled, "I was caught red-handed several times but always managed to lie my way out of it or get away. One day I met another thief, an old man who was sick. How I met him is a story for another time, but this old man and I came to an agreement: he would teach me how to be an excellent thief if I would give him half of what I stole in payment for living with him and helping pay for the house he lived in. I became a very good thief, and he paid off his house. It was a good arrangement."

Juga paused, and Lathaniel sensed there was much, much more to the story, but he said nothing. Juga continued, "One winter morning, I found him dead in his bed. The authorities quickly claimed his house for I was too young to assert ownership. I was a known thief. Though the local guards could never catch me, was closely watched. To tell you the truth, with the old man's death there seemed no purpose to either stealing or remaining in Duron City, so I moved north along the coast."

"Ahh, Lathaniel," he said with longing and wonderment in his voice, "there is no place in the whole of Elënthiá as beautiful as the north coast of Duron. I walked those cliffs for months watching the sea's dark blue waters crash and break against the rocks. I began to wonder what it would be like to be a sea creature, and if I sat in one place long enough, perhaps, I might see one. Or perhaps find a ship that was travelling to the realm beyond the sea. As a young boy I would take shelter under the porches of local inns or in the lofts of stables where I would sometimes hear stories of faraway lands told by travellers. Their descriptions made these places sound like they were the creation of the gods. It is said that Erénthoris, god of the sea, spent his life sculpting this realm and filling it with beauty from all over the world. I have never been borne upon a ship nor laid eyes upon any land save this. Drake has promised that one day we will travel across the Sea, and I live for that moment. Those days travelling up the coast of Duron were among the happiest of my childhood." Juga paused then and sighed, seeming to be lost in old memories.

"Duron?" Lathaniel prompted.

"We are presently in the realm of Horon, on the northeast coast of Koorast. The realm of Duron is directly south of us," Juga replied, annoyance in his voice at Lathaniel's ignorance. "Except for Gor'eans, the island of Koorast is home to Humans. Duron city is the seat of the Human King, Carnet. But he is old and weak and cares nothing for the troubles of his own people but only his own wealth," he said with disdain.

"Following the coast, I ended up in Horon and then in Gramal. I had learned my lesson in Duron with the old man. I knew that at my age and being homeless, if I continued to steal to eat I would soon find myself in trouble. So I found a menial job as a helper to an armourer in Gramal, and for nearly a year I learned to make weapons and armour. It paid just enough for me to eat, and it gave me a trade. The armourer I worked for liked his ale, though, and sometimes he drank away my pay. It was during one of those times when I fell back upon my old habits. Only this time, I was caught stealing. Not by the guards, but by Drake."

Lathaniel chuckled. "I would like to have seen that day."

Drake was now well ahead of them as Juga continued, "I thank Ruahr everyday for guiding me to Drake, for his acceptance of me."

"Ruahr? Do all in Elënthiá believe in Ruahr?"

"Yes, along with Erenthoris, god of the sea, Surias, goddess of the sky and Allimar the god of earth."

The question had sidetracked Juga from his story so Lathaniel prompted, "What happened when Drake caught you?"

"I knew in my gut that the only way to save my own life was to tell him the truth. And I did. He must have heard or seen something in the ragged thirteen-year-old he collared, because he took me in and fed me. He has been my Master these three years since."

"He calls you apprentice, and you call him Master. What are you being apprenticed in?"

"I am an apprentice in the art of war," Juga replied after a pause. "He schools me in the use of weapons and in battle tactics."

"Who and what is Drake?" Lathaniel rushed on. "What is he doing in…in Horon?"

His question was met with an instant tension and an end to their easy conversation. He wondered if Juga would reply, but when he did it was only to say, "You do not understand the privilege you were given when you were allowed along with us. When my Master has judged you worthy and when you are ready, it is his story to tell."

With that, Juga picked up his pace moving closer behind Drake as they continued along the dark tunnel. The young Forsair was left to wonder what Juga meant by *'when you're ready'*. Lathaniel picked up his pace and caught up with the other two noticing in the far distance ahead the faint glow of a light.

They entered a large chamber. Lathaniel and Juga stood still, and then slowly turned in a circle. The light within the chamber was dim but sufficient to make out its size and character. Light seemed to emanate from tiny crystals embedded in the rock itself. So tired and hungry were they that they were simply glad for some relief from the absolute blackness of the tunnels and gave it no further thought.

They moved to help Drake, and soon a blazing fire was raging in an oversized hearth. Drake lit torches held in metal sconces that protruded from the walls and before long the room was bathed in light and warmth.

The two could now see aged yet comfortable furnishings scattered about the floor near the hearth. On both sides of it and farther along the wall to the right were floor-to-ceiling shelves and cubbyholes, all unkempt and heaving with scrolls, parchments, books, and papers. The remaining walls were constructed alternately of the same wood that lined the tunnels, and of the rock in which the mysterious crystals were embedded. The ceiling was very high, and though the chamber was lit by the fire and the torches, the light did not reach it.

To the left of the fireplace there was a large desk laden with parchment and scrolls. Behind and to the left, they could see a large wooden door left ajar. Peering curiously inside, they could see its walls were similar to those in the great room, more shelves stuffed to the brim.

Moving back into the great room, they noticed that to the left of the small chamber was a very large stone arch with darkness beyond it. And further still to the left of the large arch were three smaller arches leading to what they assumed were other passages. Beyond the shelves to the right of the fireplace there was a scullery of sorts with a preparation table, cupboards, and some shelves. Beyond this were three more small arches. At the bottom of the chamber was the entrance to the tunnel through which they had arrived. Looking above this tunnel, they noticed four exquisite swords, polished to a shine and gleaming in the dim light.

The smell of the woodsmoke was soothing. Both Juga and Lathaniel shrugged off their packs and shed their outer tunics and hats as Drake unrolled one of his travelling packs on the preparation table in the scullery. From it he took a loaf of bread, a large block of aged cheese, and three plump red apples. Rummaging around in the cupboards, he produced crude plates and mugs and set these all on the table in front of the fire.

"Come," he ordered, "we will eat."

As Juga and Lathaniel took their seats in front of the fire and began to eat, Drake shed his outer tunic and the hat he'd been wearing since Gramal. Removing a leather thong that kept most of it bound, he shook out a shoulder-length mane of coal black hair that was intermittently shot with strands of silver. There, by the light of the fire, Lathaniel got his first real look at his rescuer.

The muscles of his shoulders and back rippled as he folded his tall body into a large chair nearest the hearth. His hair was parted to the side such that it fell across his eye on one side. He tucked the long hair on the other side behind his ear as he ate.

As if sensing his examination, Drake looked directly at Lathaniel, chewing and saying nothing. It seemed the two were each taking the other's measure. Lathaniel was most taken aback by Drake's eyes. From the one he could see, they were a distinctive deep green with a lighter emerald fleck in the irises that seemed to catch the light. They were old eyes, and Lathaniel had a fleeting glimpse of warmth, then sadness before they once again became veiled and watchful. The remainder of his face was a study in planes and angles with a square, stubborn set to the jaw line.

Juga began to talk while they ate, and Drake's attention turned to his young apprentice, allowing Lathaniel to continue to study his host while they were eating. Though his clothes were ragged and well-worn, there was a stature, a commanding presence to Drake that Lathaniel couldn't help but admire. He noticed a magnificent jewel hung around his host's neck that lay nestled against his chest. The gem was blue, a sapphire gripped by silver in the form of a dragon's claw and hung from a heavy silver chain. The pendant looked ancient, and Lathaniel wondered at the story of it.

Finishing the ale in his mug, Lathaniel sat back in his chair feeling relaxed for the first time in days. Juga had finished his report to his Master, and his eyes were heavy.

"Now, my young apprentice," Drake said gently, "it is time for you to take some rest. Find your quarters along the middle passageway and sleep in peace, for there are none that would disturb you here."

Juga stood, stretched, and left the great room. Drake took the plates away and returned with a jug, refilling their mugs with ale.

"It is time you told me of yourself, Lathaniel," he said as he sat and leaned back comfortably in his chair, fixing Lathaniel with his gaze. He sat in the silence that followed, staring at his guest expectantly.

Lathaniel felt a blush creep up his neck under this scrutiny. Gathering his courage he blurted out, "I refuse to tell you of myself until I know more of you…of who and what you are! Where are you from? What is this place? How long must we stay here? And why did you agree to bring me along with you?"

These questions all tripped out of his mouth without a single breath between them. He continued, "Juga tells me I am privileged to be here with you both, but there is so much I don't understand! I think that I must know some of this information before I say more."

With that, he closed his mouth and sat perfectly still, his face flushed, refusing to look away from Drake and waiting to feel his wrath at the impertinence.

Unexpectedly, Drake let out a snort of laughter, startling Lathaniel more than the shout he anticipated. "That must have taken all your courage!" he chortled. "I cannot recall when last someone has stood up to me and tried to stare me down. That was well done of you, lad! Well done."

He paused for a moment before leaning forward to rest his forearms on his knees. His smile fading, he continued, "In all seriousness, though, lad, I think that you must tell all and tell me now." He raised his hand to stay the protest Lathaniel was about to voice. "I will give you my word to do so in return, but there is much going on in this world of ours, and your story is important to my understanding of it."

He dropped his voice. "I sense there is betrayal in your past. I would have you know I will not betray you." His eyes held Lathaniel's as he spoke and again, as on the steps before they descended to this place, Lathaniel made a decision. With a sigh he sat back in his chair and began to talk.

"I am a Waythan, the only son of Lathart and the last of my line. I am eight and ten years of age and, as you now know, I am a Forsair. My home is Lamana on the island of Oldo, the only secret enclave of Forsairs remaining in Elënthiá. I know of no one who has ever left Lamana by decree or their own free will. Suffice to say that if any have, there is no record of their safe return. While my grandfather spoke of a time when there was movement between Lamana and the world beyond, those were mostly during times long past when both Elves and Humans vigorously hunted Forsairs for the crime of interracial breeding and we Forsairs had networks with the outside world to help those in need find their way to Lamana and safety. If there were maps to Lamana, they were kept secret.

"To my knowledge, there are no maps to Lamana left today. When I left, I travelled to the coastline where I happened upon a ship run aground on a shoal off the coast and waiting for the tides to turn before they could sail on. I know very little of the world beyond Oldo. With my grandfather's death, stories from the past were limited only to what my father could remember, and he did not share those with ease. From tales told I remembered the name of the island of Koorast. I convinced the ship's captain that I was harmless, and he gave me safe passage from Oldo and to Gramal where I had the misfortune to be arrested by the Black March and charged with treason against a warlord whose name I have heard only in whispers and about whom I know nothing. I survived a knife wound in the process, met Juga, and was broken out of jail by you. The remainder of the story you know."

Drake was silent for a moment, his gaze shifted from Lathaniel as he studied the flames in the hearth. Turning back to him after a time, he said, "You failed to say why you left Lamana."

"I did not omit it by accident," replied Lathaniel. "It is simply not something I wish to share with you."

Drake held his eyes for a moment before turning to stare back into the fire. Lathaniel's heart was thumping in his chest. He assumed their conversation was over. Then Drake said, "My full name is Drake Sorzin, son of Dray. I also hail from an island far from here. Though nothing remains of my city today, it was once called Evendeer. As to my age, it would be difficult for you to grasp it in your years, but suffice to say that I have lived longer than you can imagine. I am what was known long ago as a Draconean."

# CHAPTER 10

Lathaniel awoke with the word *Draconean* still on his mind. He lay on his cot thinking of his conversation with Drake the previous evening. There was so much to take in. Drake had made mention of his age in years being beyond his imagining. He'd also said he'd taken *centuries* exploring this underground haven. One thing Lathaniel was certain of, Drake was not a Human. He had no Elven markings either. Yet his size and stature were exceptional in every way.

Knowing that answers did not lie in bed, he swung his legs over the side of the cot. He had no sense of how long he had slept or whether it was day or night, so he dressed by the dim light cast by the wall crystals. Someone had left a pitcher of water and bowl on the table in his room along with a plate of bread and fruit. He completed his morning ablutions, finished the food and drink and went in search of his companions.

In the great room, the fire in the hearth had been well stoked. The torches from the night before were still lit, yet there was no sign of either Juga or Drake. Lathaniel crossed the great room to the passage that he had seen Juga go down the previous night. There he found a door. When he opened it he saw a similar cot with rumpled bedclothes, but no Juga.

The other archways led to storage rooms for food and wood and another, larger sleeping chamber that he assumed was Drake's. There was no sign of either of them. With the beginnings of concern, he called both their names out several times. Still, no answer.

He was beginning to panic when Juga came through the larger arch in the far corner of the room and cheerily said, "Good! You're awake."

"By the gods!" exclaimed Lathaniel. "I thought something had happened to you both. Where is Drake?"

"Come. I'll take you to him."

They headed through the large stone arch and into yet another wood-paneled passageway lined with torches. The ground sloped steadily downwards, giving the impression that wherever they were headed was farther yet beneath the ground. Juga moved at a brisk pace down a short staircase and another short torch-lit passage that opened onto a hall.

On arrival Lathaniel stopped short. The hall was lit by hundreds of torches, and the walls were covered from floor to ceiling on three sides with weapons, such a variety of which Lathaniel could never have imagined. On the fourth wall, he could see wooden replicas of many of the weapons which, he assumed, were used for training.

The cathedral ceiling was hewn out of rock as well and arched above them. The floor was firm but covered in fine sand. Drake stood at the far end of the room holding a long majestic sword. Lathaniel was struck anew by his size and stature. But for a piece that fell untidily across one of his eyes, his thick black hair was pulled into a queue again this morning and tied off with a thong of leather at the back of his neck. He wore his usual tall brown leather boots and leggings but had changed into a clean shirt that was open at the neck and rolled at the sleeves.

"Young Forsair!" his greeting rang out in the large room. "I hope you slept well, for you will have need of your strength today."

Lathaniel did not reply, uncertain of what this meant.

Drake smiled. "That is a mighty weapon you carry in your scabbard, young Forsair. Are you good with it?"

Caught off guard and unsure of where the conversation was leading, Lathaniel replied, "It's just a sword, and I can put a fair hand to it if needed. I also draw a steady bow. Why?" he asked pointedly as Drake strode toward him. On his way he veered over and pulled two of the wooden swords off the wall, tossing one to Lathaniel who grabbed it midair.

"Good," Drake commented. "Let us see how fair your hand truly is."

"Wait a minute!" Lathaniel objected warily even as he began to move keeping his eye on Drake, who was circling him. "You misunderstand. I did not come with you to learn to be a warrior nor to fight in your war."

Drake did not answer for a time; he merely kept circling Lathaniel. "I am not asking you to join an army, young Lathaniel. I merely want to see how skilled you are with a sword. It appears that the gods have placed us in each other's company for a time, and I would know the abilities of the man—or Forsair—" he smiled, "who stands beside me. Unless, of course, you are afraid to fight..."

Lathaniel was no fool. He knew Drake was taunting him, trying to prod his temper to get him to react. His eyes narrowed as he considered the Draconean. Calmly he tossed the wooden sword into his right hand, bending slightly at the knees as he considered his opponent.

"I do not believe in war. I am but a simple Forsairean hunter, nothing more. But I will humour you, Draconean." With that he stepped into an attack stance.

"Ahh, my young Forsair," replied Drake quietly. "You are anything but simple."

Drake opened their sparring match with a series of straightforward thrusts and parries, getting a sense of the young Forsair's balance and agility. Noting how easily Lathaniel responded, he stepped up the intensity of his attack, putting more muscle into his thrusts and forcing the young Forsair to increase his guard. Lathaniel held his own for more than a minute before misreading Drake's attack and finding himself on the floor from a hit to his back with the flat side of the Draconean's sword. He rolled to his side and, propped on his elbow, stared up at Drake.

"And what have you proven by this exercise? That you are a better swordsman than I? That is not in dispute. You have measured my abilities. Are you now satisfied?" he asked as he grasped his sword and moved quickly to his feet.

"Not by half," Drake replied and without warning went on the attack once again.

This time, Lathaniel was better able to hold his own, now having a sense of what to expect and of the strength and intensity of his opponent. The Draconean had nearly six inches on him in height and was half again his weight. It was obvious to Lathaniel that Drake was holding back and that, were he to exert the full force of his abilities as a swordsman, he would be formidable.

But for now, the thrust and parry went back and forth, the sounds of the weapons clattering within the chamber. Lathaniel felt sweat run between his shoulder blades and down into the waistband of his leggings. It dripped from his brow. Yet still he held his own until the wound in his side began to ache and his strength and concentration waned. Once again he felt the slap of Drake's sword across his shoulders and found himself on the ground panting with exertion.

Drake stood above him, neither winded nor sweating. He stared, consideringly, down at Lathaniel before calling out to Juga, who had been leaning against the wall observing the action.

"Juga my lad, I believe I have found you a new sparring partner."

With that he tossed his wooden sword to Juga and strode out of the arena down the tunnel toward the main great room without further comment.

The two stared after him, then at each other.

"This is ridiculous," Lathaniel exclaimed. "What is he playing at? "

"I neither know nor care," replied Juga. "But he's gone back to his scrolls and maps, and there's nothing else to do so...what do you say?" he asked as he smiled, tossing the sword back and forth between his hands and assuming an attack stance.

He was right, Lathaniel thought. There wasn't anything else to do, and if travelling with the two of them for an extended time was going to be anything like the last two days, brushing up on his sword skills wouldn't hurt. He smiled calculatingly back at Juga, and their sparring began.

So the days continued. Drake sat at his desk late one night, reviewing old documents and maps by torch and candlelight. He stopped to think about his young companions and marvelled that he seemed to have assumed the role his father had taken with his brothers and him a lifetime ago.

Mornings began with weapons training where he relentlessly put the two through their paces, introducing new weapons and strategies, personally sparring with each of them, then supervising their spars - pushing the two beyond what they thought they could endure.

Juga was ever the cocky prankster, quick to break tension with a jest or a self-deprecating comment. His skills were improving immeasurably by sparring with the young Forsair, who was nearer his age and a more realistic partner than the battle-seasoned Draconean. Drake delighted at the easy friendship between the two and at their shared passion for competition.

The serious young Forsair intrigued him. In the two thousand odd years he'd walked Elënthiá, there was little he had not heard about or experienced firsthand. While he had not revealed as much to Lathaniel, he knew the Waythan name and that his young charge was of royal lineage. He noted from what little information Lathaniel had shared that he was the only son of the last son. What fates, he wondered, had beset the Waythans that would see the one remaining heir leave his beloved land he did not yet know, for Lathaniel remained very closemouthed about the circumstances surrounding his flight from Lamana.

What touched Drake most about Lathaniel was the strength of his character and the depth of his maturity for one so young. Though naïve and innocent in so many ways, there was a solid, unshakeable core of honour and integrity in Lathaniel that Drake was growing to appreciate. What an unlikely threesome they made! For the first time in a very long while, Drake felt something stir deep within him, something that felt suspiciously like hope.

Days became weeks, and soon nearly three months had passed. These days in close contact saw the friendship between Juga and Lathaniel solidify and their respective relationships with the Draconean deepen. The three gained an understanding of each other's moods and personalities, strengths and weaknesses. Though it went unsaid, it was acknowledged that Lathaniel had also been accepted as Drake's apprentice, and that Lathaniel had put aside his objections to learning the art of war. As such, both were closely supervised and schooled in the use of all manner of weapons, stealth, hand-to-hand combat, and in the strategy of battle.

The tedium of weapons training was periodically broken by quick trips to the plains above where the three replenished their food supplies and enjoyed fresh air and sunshine. At other times, Drake would take them to the surface in the dead of night. There they would lie flat on their backs beneath the stars while Drake pointed out signposts in the night sky and their value in helping a traveler find his way. Day or night, these trips were never more than hours at a time and were always undertaken under very guarded conditions. But they were sufficient to keep Juga and Lathaniel from going stir crazy in the confines of the closed quarters below ground.

Late one day, when training had ended and Juga was busying himself looking at some old papers showing ancient sword designs, Drake summoned Lathaniel to join him at his desk. There, a large map was laid atop the documents and parchments. Drake stood with his arms braced on either side of the map and looked steadily at Lathaniel.

"It is time that you knew more of our world than what your limited experience and boyhood tales have taught you. This," he said with a sweeping gesture across the map in front of them, "is Elënthiá."

Lathaniel's eyes fell to the detailed map in front of them, drinking in what he saw, silent, waiting for Drake to continue.

"This is your island of Oldo," Drake said as he stabbed his finger to a place on the map. "You crossed the channel here to the port of Gramal in the realm of Horon on the island of Koorast."

Lathaniel nodded, his eyes eagerly following along. The island of Koorast was vast. Drake explained that it was largely inhabited by humans now and loosely divided into five realms; Horon, Duron, Amarik, and Gorger with the mountainous Oderon filling the center. The realm of Oderon housed the Minhera mountain range, once home to a race of giants called the Anulé. The rocky cliffs of Amarik's northern coast gave way to sparsely grassed flatlands to the far south, and marshes and forests to the west. It was home to Men.

Gorger was home of the Gor'ean race. Duron was the most populous region on the island and home to Carnet, the Human King. Duron City was a commercial hub where the fruits, vegetables, and livestock that thrived in the realm could be sold or traded. Horon was home to the most easily accessible ports on the east side of the island, its inland filled with rolling hills and grasslands peppered with the odd hamlet or village.

The island of Oldo was off the coast of the northeast corner of Horon. The realm of Duron was located in the southeast corner of the island. Amarik stretched along the west side of the island from north to south, and off its southern coast was the island of Moldost. The entire northern border of the island was home to the forested realm of Gorger; located between its coast and the coast of the Coldain region, was the island of Sortaire.

"And beyond is the Coldain Region." Drake pointed at the northwest corner of the map with disgust. "Ethen-jar is Gorillian's stronghold. It was once home to the Dwarves but they, like my race, faced extermination at his hands. Here," he stabbed the map again with his finger, "are the Elven lands. The Vearian and Zormian realms lie to the north and east.

We shall speak of these another time. But Koorast, lad, you must get your bearings here first."

Drake went on to describe the geography of the island and its peoples in the most general of terms, his emphasis principally on identifying routes through and between realms. Lathaniel listened, rapt, absorbing all he was told and asking questions when clarification was required. Drake straightened and rolled up the map. He set it to the side and reached for a pile of documents, handing them to Lathaniel.

"What are these?"

"It is time for you to know more of your world, young Forsair. What I have not told you, you can read. What I have not described, you can see on the parchment maps. When we leave this place, your mind and memory must be well schooled in the geography of Elënthiá as well as those races who would welcome us and those who would not."

Lathaniel was speechless for he knew the documents he held in his hands were ancient and of inestimable value to the Draconean. Humbled by his trust, Lathaniel moved to a table across the room to begin reading.

As he watched his two very different apprentices, Drake mused that the time was quickly coming when they must leave the safety of this haven and face the world above. Yes, it was coming quickly, he thought, and yet there was still so much to do.

# CHAPTER 11

Draconeans, like most Immortals, age by the measure of men for twenty years. Thereafter, they age one year for every one hundred Human years. The problem with being two thousand years old is that sleep does not come easily at times. And this was one such time. These last months had been a welcome respite from the solitary and nomadic existence Drake led. The energy and the inquisitive nature of his two charges rekindled feelings he'd thought long dead. But this night he lay awake deliberating over their departure from Horon and the journey ahead. He rolled to his back and scrubbed his hands over his face, pushing his long hair back over his pillow.

He would miss this place. It had taken him decades to shift all of the documents he had found that day so long ago to this place. In his youth he'd no idea of the treasures the parchments guarded, but he now knew that what he had accumulated in this sanctuary likely represented the only remaining record of the Draconean race.

He rolled to his side.

The young Forsair was never far from his mind. The lad was a quick study. His Elven heritage shone through when he sparred, for he was lightening fast in his reflexes and a natural athlete. Though Juga was strong and capable, a true student these past three years, Lathaniel had already surpassed him. Drake felt the gods' influence in bringing Lathaniel to him, but he was uncertain what to do with the lad. Should he insist Lathaniel travel with him and Juga or encourage him to seek his own destiny when they left Horon?

So many questions. Every journey began with a single step, and that time was fast approaching. Perhaps the answers would reveal themselves once the journey began. With that thought on his mind, he drifted off.

*"Drake," a soft, dreamy voice whispered. It seemed to float on the shadows through the silence.*

*"Drake," it whispered again. A sudden chill enveloped the room like a frigid cloak, extinguishing the last stub of candle that burned on the bedside table. Groggy, Drake forced heavy eyelids open and in the shadows above him thought he saw a woman's face.* I'm dreaming, *he thought. Certain he had heard the voice and seen something there above his bed, he rubbed his eyes and struggled up on one elbow.*

*A ripple of energy seemed to disturb the air, bringing with it a light so golden and warm that Drake could not only feel it on his skin but to his very core. The light began to increase in intensity until he narrowed his eyes and raised his hand to shield them from the brightness. Then, the light seemed to part like a transparent curtain, and through it stepped a women; the face he'd seen now was clearer.*

*As he opened his mind to embrace her arrival, she moved forward toward him along a corridor of light, the brilliance behind her making it difficult to see her features clearly. Drake sat up slowly and shifted himself back against the headboard.*

*"Who are you, Milady?" Drake asked, slowly swinging his feet over the side of his cot and moving to stand.*

*"We have met in dreams many times during these two millennia, Drake Sorzin, though you have chosen not to recall our meetings on waking, believing the memories to be too connected to the sorrows of your past."*

*Drake held her gaze, but his hand shifted neared to his dagger.*

*"You have no need of that, Drake Sorzin. Your weapons hold no sway over me. Please sit again, for we must speak and there is much to discuss."*

*"I would know your name and your purpose, Milady," Drake replied, sitting back on his cot, his dagger loosely held in his palm.*

*The apparition stood bathed in golden light, her hands loosely clasped in front of her.*

*"I am your past, present, and future, Drake Sorzin. I bring the light of both truth and knowledge. You asked as you fell asleep tonight what you should do about the young Forsair, Lathaniel Waythan.*

*"I have ever been close by you," she continued. "I offered you respite from misery and despair; I offered you hope when none could be found; I offered you life when nothing of your own remained. I offered these to you the day the Draconeans fell."*

*Drake, shaken, started to stand, but it was if an unseen hand held him in place. He did not know then if what he saw next were visions within his own mind or images cast by his golden visitor, but he was thrown back to that day in Evendeer. Arriving too late to prevent the destruction, walking through the wreckage, searching for his father and brothers, falling, and then…yes…as he lay upon the floor in the secret room, he let himself remember the appearance of a golden angel who called herself…*

*"Goddess! Suvillwa?..." he finished aloud.*

*She smiled, pleased with his recollection; then her face settled into a more serious countenance and she continued, "I must give you information no network of informants could possibly offer. There are circumstances in Elënthiá that you personally can no longer ignore,*

*Drake Sorzin. Your old enemy Gorillian's power grows. He and his armies are moving through Elënthiá like a black plague, taking advantage of the weak and complacent, imposing his rule and forcing allegiance.*

*"Full-out war is coming from which no race can escape. Even now, Gorillian's evil has footholds in the far north as well as the eastern lands. He focuses on the strongholds now...the Elven realms and Nesmeresa. Left with no other choice, the Elves defend their own borders and have not the resources to spare for the Resistance. Though if united the Men of the north would be strong, their tribes are divided, and many have joined with Gorillian to aid in his pillage of the southern realms of the Coldain Region.*

*"Siityth and Far'camice have been overrun, and it is rumoured that Gorillian will soon turn his sights to Illiyish," she continued. "But more urgently, here on Koorast, the realm of Gorger is in grave danger. The ancient city of Gorgonathan and its surrounding forests have long protected the Gor'eans, but the devil and his minions are truly at the gate.*

*"Gorillian's forces have an embargo in place allowing ships neither into nor out of Gorger's northern and eastern ports. With their backs to the Minhera Mountains and escape through the swamps of Amarik all but blocked, the Gor'eans are trapped, unable to open safe passage to the rest of Elënthiá and unable to bring aid in. Koorast is in grave danger. You know the weaknesses of the Human king and that Duron will not withstand a strategic attack from Gorillian. Here in Horon the Resistance is more organized, but faced with the full wrath of Gorillian's forces, how long they can hold is a matter even I cannot guess.*

*"You offer aid to the Resistance to thwart your old enemy when and as it pleases you, remembering that your leadership in past wars went unacknowledged once battlegrounds had cooled. But past wars were not as this one, Drake Sorzin. This time Gorillian has taken more of Elënthiá than ever before. There are those who fear it*

*may already be too late. You can no longer step away from this, my Draconean lord. You alone can provide the leadership that will turn the tides in this war. You alone."*

*A silence followed within the golden glow as Drake contemplated what Suvillwa had revealed. He knew well the burdens of leadership; in the face of past disappointments and betrayals, his idealism had long since faded.*

*His voice was filled with derision when he finally said, "If truly you can look behind and ahead, Suvillwa, then you will recall that my last interaction with the Gor'eans did not finish favourably. Were I to encounter even one who recognized me, the reunion would end in a deadly battle. Yet you ask that I intervene?"*

*Instead of answering his question, Suvillwa surprised him. "Your father gave you something in the moments shortly before his death. You possess it still."*

*Drake was taken aback. "How do you know of this?"*

*She ignored this question as well. "It currently sits in the bottom left drawer of your desk in the great room." She had his attention now.*

*"Yes, it is a map with no names, only descriptions of places that over the years I have deciphered."*

*"Have you deciphered where the map begins?"*

*"My father spoke cryptically of the wealth of the Draconean race being hidden in this place, though I thought it folklore, a bedtime tale told to young boys."*

*"Its existence is no folktale, Drake Sorzin. What you have in your possession is a map to wealth untold ... and to a forgotten city that plays host to the other half of your race."*

*Drake sat stunned as she continued.*

*"You have long believed that you are the last Draconean, but you are not. You have already surmised that the map leads to the Tombs. Trust your instincts in all things. You will find your kin… and a treasure that is the key to saving the Resistance."*

*Drake was silent as he digested what Suvillwa had told him. Then he asked, "What of the Forsair? I feel strongly that his sudden appearance in my life is no accident."*

*Suvillwa was silent for a moment. "Indeed, the young Forsair has much to do with your fate. He must go with you. Train and prepare him well, Draconean, for your life or death at the hands of Gorillian rests within his young hands. Without him there is no hope for you and none for the Resistance. But, as in all things, the choice is yours."*

*With that the golden glow surrounding Suvillwa began to fade as did her image, which seemed to grow smaller and dimmer as the light subsided. Before the light was extinguished, Drake heard her whisper, "Your road ends and begins in the Fields of Sitiska."*

Drake awoke with a jerk, bolting upright. Dazed, he looked around his bedchamber. The candles were nearly gutted but still alight. He fell back on his cot and lay there, staring at the ceiling.

It must have been a dream, he thought to himself as he lay there. Struggling unsteadily to his feet, he moved to the end of his bed and saw something lying on the floor. As he drew closer, he realized it was the parchment map given to him by his father - the map with no names. Reeling, he sat down hard on the end of his bed. It had been no dream.

# CHAPTER 12

The spring sun was strong as Juga lifted his face to a cloudless blue sky. Drake had set a brisk westward pace for them that morning, and they were nearing Zoren. They each carried packs - lightweight at present, but Drake had assured them that they would shortly be laden once they procured supplies in Zoren. In the three months they had been underground, winter had surrendered to spring, and it was if the world were reawakening around them. The three were quiet as they walked, each lost in his own thoughts.

Juga had always been a loner. His apprenticeship with Drake had changed that, as had his new friendship with the Forsair. As he walked he thought that while the two were his travelling companions, there was still much about them he did not know. He had long ago resigned himself to Drake's secrets, but Lathaniel seemed so naïve at times. Juga smiled to himself. Lathaniel was like a walking sponge, so filled with questions; though at times it was annoying, Juga did not really mind answering them. Lathaniel's apprenticeship and exceptional skills with weaponry had afforded Juga an opportunity to hone and perfect his own fighting abilities. These would stand him in good stead if he could ever make it to the mysterious camp at Cap'hannet and join the core of the Resistance. As they walked on, he daydreamed of fighting Gorillian's forces with the famed Gor'ean warriors.

Lathaniel dreamed of Lamana. The cerulean blue of the sky above him and the tart smell of spring in the air brought his home to mind and a pang of longing to his heart. He wondered how his family fared in his absence and once again hoped that he'd made the right decision in walking away. His gaze settled on Drake ahead of him. Their departure from the haven under the Horon plains had been hasty. He and Juga had awakened one morning to find Drake rifling through documents and scrolls in a frenzy, muttering to himself. He had been especially harsh in his sparring with them that morning and every morning since, pushing them harder, challenging them. Then he told them that they had to leave Horon immediately gave them scant information about where they were headed and the reason behind his urgency. And Lathaniel had caught Drake staring at him intently on several occasions.

Juga, Lathaniel thought with a smile, was more transparent. When the two were alone, he talked nonstop of his plans to join the Resistance at the first opportunity and fretted about Drake and how he would react when Juga asked to be released from his apprenticeship. Juga was a font of knowledge and gossip, and Lathaniel took every opportunity to question him, as he knew next to nothing about the Resistance.

"The Resistance," Juga had explained, "has been around for centuries, at times more active than others. But it began and exists today to thwart any evil that threatens the sovereignty of the many nations of Elënthiá."

He went on to recount that Gorillian in particular had been a force of evil in Elënthiá for many centuries, and that each time he rose in power the Resistance would rally in Elënthiá's defence.

"The Resistance includes many races but is principally led by the Gor'eans," Juga continued. When Lathaniel looked quizzically at him, he said in exasperation, "How can it be that you know none of this?!" but had continued in his explanation.

"The Gor'eans are Human...but in many ways they are not. In history we know that my people came to Elënthiá by ship. En route, they experienced a tremendous storm that saw their fleet halved. Half found their way to Koorast and the other to the Elven realms where they remained for nearly a century before reconnecting with their Human kin. During the years away, they embraced Elven ways and, on reuniting with their Human brethren found themselves ostracized and ridiculed for the new customs and habits that were now part of them. Feeling shunned by both the Elves and their own kind, they made their home in the deep forests now called Gorger and became known as the Gor'eans.

"They are as men," he continued, "but more fierce, more disciplined, and a fighting force to be reckoned with. Over the ages, when Elënthiá has been threatened, it has always been the Gor'ean Resistance that has stepped to the fore to defend it. It is said that they train at a secret camp in Cap'hannet in the Minhera Mountains, but no one is exactly sure where it is."

Lathaniel had quizzed him, then, on how Juga would find it on his own. Juga became despondent and told Lathaniel that when he summoned the courage to ask Drake for his release, he would also ask about Cap'hannet, as he was certain Drake knew of it. Thinking of all he had learned from Juga, from the maps and documents he had studied, and from the intense training he had undergone these past months, Lathaniel wondered what fate the gods had in store for him. For now he remained grateful that he had been arrested months ago and that the gods had steered him to Drake Sorzin.

They were approaching a small copse of trees. As they drew close, Drake called a halt and advised the two that they would wait there for the remainder of the afternoon and approach Zoren in early evening when the guards were lax, just before the gates closed for the night. Packs were dispensed, and the three sat leaning against trees taking water and some bread. Lathaniel later thought he would remember the conversation that followed for the whole of his life, for it was the first time that the Draconean had spoken of himself and his past.

"My father was a great man," he began quietly, staring off across the sun drenched plains, instantly gaining the attention of Juga and Lathaniel. "He was the King of Evendeer and leader of the Draconean race. Evendeer was attacked without provocation one morning when I was a young boy of ten and three years. I was not in the city when it happened. When I returned, the city was destroyed, and not a single Draconean had survived. Neither my father, nor my six brothers could be found among the bodies. I had no knowledge of what had happened that morning nor why until months later when a similar attack was launched on the Dwarven stronghold at Ethen-jar and it was determined that Gorillian was responsible for both.

"I was stunned to hear this, as his relationship with my father stretched back millennia to when Draconeans first came to Elënthiá. Gorillian was mortal then. He was gifted with immortality by the Elves and, on receipt of that gift he changed. He grew ruthless in his dealings with others in Elënthiá; obsessed with wealth and power. Their relationship had become strained in the years before my father's death but I was still shocked when I discovered he was responsible for the slaughter of my people. Fortunately, the Elves and the Gor'eans were able to bring a halt to his madness."

Lathaniel listened intently, feeling great empathy for the boy that Drake was describing and glad that he had questioned Juga so extensively and had at least some sense of the story unfolding.

"I took all of my father's parchments and scrolls from Evendeer and hid them until I could find a way to keep them safe. They now fill the walls of the haven we've just left. And it is from them that I have come to believe that there may be another city, a lost city filled with other Draconeans. This is important news to me, as I have long thought I am the last of my kind."

He looked gently at Lathaniel. "The last son of a last son..." Then his gaze became distant again and he went on.

"Certain...uh, circumstances in the last days of our time in the haven under Horon have confirmed my belief that my search for clues to my heritage should begin in Sitiska."

Lathaniel looked at Juga questioningly.

"Sitiska is located in the realm of Amarik," Juga said quietly, his attention not leaving Drake.

Lathaniel kept quiet, thinking to quiz Juga later.

Drake continued, "I have also come to know that there may be a treasure beyond imagining, the wealth of all the Draconeans, located there as well. Such a resource could do much were it to be made available to the Resistance."

Drake shifted his gaze to his apprentices, looking from one to the other. "It is to Amarik that we travel. We will collect supplies and information in Zoren. From there we will travel through the Minhera Mountains in Oderon into Amarik and then on to Sitiska. The traditional routes through the Minheras will be watched and will be dangerous. For this reason we will move underground, through the ancient land of the Anulé. It has been many years since I have attempted passage through there and what we will meet along the way, I cannot say. But you are both strong and competent warriors, and I know you can hold your own through this journey. Have no doubt," he cautioned leaning in toward them both, deadly serious, "we will be in harm's way from this point forward. I have no underground havens in either Oderon or Amarik. Our passage through Oderon will disturb the deadly Narcs who live there, and the likelihood of encountering Gorillian's forces is strong. You will need each and every skill I have taught you these months and your own wits about you to survive."

He paused for a moment looking from one to the other. "There would be no shame in walking away from this journey right now. No shame," he repeated.

Lathaniel held his gaze and shook his head firmly. He looked to Juga, who was doing the same. Neither would leave the Draconean. With a curt nod, Drake leaned back against the tree and closed his eyes, taking a last opportunity to rest before dusk.

The layout of Zoren was similar to Gramal and many Human towns on Koorast. It was walled with gates that were closed in the evenings, a safeguard still practiced from wars long past. The town was built surrounding a low hill with streets laid out in a grid-like pattern and lined by wooden, stone, and thatch dwellings on either side. The shops and businesses were situated in the outer ring of the town closest to the walls. Inward and uphill, the standard of the houses improved, growing larger and more indicative of the status of the residents.

In the time of the Anulé, Zoren had been a regional hub, an important stopping point for travelers entering Oderon through Minhera Mountains. But with the exodus of the

Anulé and the increasing age and disinterest of the Human kings, the town had fallen into obvious disrepair. Dubious local leadership liked to play both ends against the middle, welcoming both Gorillian and Resistance spies to the town and lining its pockets with money from each to look the other way.

The three travelers had entered the town's gates unnoticed at dusk and were making their way through the evening shadows to a merchant. It was all new to Lathaniel, who with his usual penchant for information gathering was peppering Juga with questions about the town's layout, history, who the leaders were, how the residents gained their livelihoods, and so on.

"And does Gorillian control this town?" he asked next.

Drake quietly answered this time. "No, but you'll find the streets of Zoren crawling with spies. These days no place is without danger. Do not let the absence of the Black March soldiers on the streets lull you into complacency. They were more obvious in Gramal because it is a port city and an entry point to Koorast. As such it is more important to both Gorillian and the Resistance. Zoren is just as dangerous, but of the two the Resistance is stronger here. Make no mistake, lads, there are eyes studying us closely. They have been since we entered the gates." With that he said no more.

Lathaniel looked at the faces on the streets with new regard, suspiciously wondering about this one or that, and which side they might be on. The three stopped on two occasions for Drake to participate in whispered exchanges. Juga and Lathaniel overheard the name Ziny and from prior conversations, assumed he was inquiring about the whereabouts of his young informant. It was obvious by the second conversation that Ziny was not about. Muttering a curse, Drake moved off along a different set of streets, modifying their destination.

He motioned the two to wait in a shadowed doorway and continued along a lane. Quickly looking first one way then the other, he entered a shop. Wanting to draw as little attention to themselves as possible, Lathaniel and Juga pulled the hoods of their cloaks farther down around their faces and remained still in the darkness. Minutes stretched. At a point when both apprentices began to fidget with concern, Drake appeared out of the shadows. Though his cloak was pulled low on his forehead disguising his expression, the two knew him well enough to realize that he was anything but pleased.

"Fool!" he muttered, moving off along the street.

Juga and Lathaniel did not question what had happened, merely kept close on his heels until Drake stopped several streets over.

After carefully checking to ensure they were alone, he said, "Gorillian has been alerted to the likelihood of our presence here. His informant's network is on full alert, and all are looking for us. That fool of a shopkeeper will take no chances in providing the supplies I want, fearing retribution from Gorillian when we leave. I think, young Juga, that Gorillian is most unhappy that you slipped through his fingers in Gramal and means to have us this time." His lips curled in a wry smile. "Unfortunately, we will have to disappoint him again."

"What about our supplies, Master?" queried Juga. "Where will we now go for these?"

"Same place," replied Drake. "But this time, we steal them."

The three huddled in the shadows while Drake outlined his plan.

In the early hours of the next morning when charcoal shadows were at their blackest and near silence settled over the streets, the three companions made their way stealthily back to the shop. As agreed, Drake approached it from a different direction to patrol the perimeter of the block, to watch for guards and to distract spies from both sides from the scent of their real mission. Juga and Lathaniel made their way to the shop's back door. There, Lathaniel took up his post as a lookout, focusing on the back alley and prepared to raise a quiet alarm to Juga if need be. As the seasoned thief, Juga was delighted with his role. He made quick work of the antiquated lock on the alley door of the shop, disappearing into the darkness inside. Drake had thoroughly briefed him on requirements for their journey. Having accompanied his Master to this particular shop before, Juga was familiar with where items were stored and immediately began to assemble their supplies.

Lathaniel was tucked into the deep shadows between the building that housed the shop and the one next to it. From the darkness he could easily see movement on the street. He and Juga had agreed that the call of a night owl would be their signal of danger. The sound would not raise suspicion, but on hearing it, Juga would exit the shop via the front door while Lathaniel sneaked away through the shadows at the back. The three would meet at an agreed rendezvous point where, after distributing the supplies between them, they would wait at the western gate to the town to exit at first light.

Lathaniel was tense. This whole business of stealing was new to him, and if he stopped to think about it all for too long, he found himself excessively uncomfortable at the thought of taking what was not his. He gave his head a small shake, refocusing on the task at hand. Call it hunter's instincts, but at that very moment he sensed movement off to his left even before he saw it. In the shadows farther along the street, he could make out the shadowy outlines of two figures moving his way.

Without hesitation he softly gave the agreed birdcall and shrank back deeper into the shadows. The direction the two were coming from effectively blocked his exit. He would simply have to rely on stealth and the darkness to conceal him. He froze, barely breathing, and flattened himself against the cold stone behind him.

Both figures were cloaked. One was tall and moved with fluid grace and ease, radiating both authority and confidence. The other was short and stocky and walked slightly behind with his head and shoulders hunched forward, giving the impression of both deference and a hierarchy to their relationship. As they approached, their murmurs became audible and Lathaniel could follow their hushed exchange.

"...continue with my plan as agreed," the taller one commanded.

"Begging your pardon, Master, but he has not come as predicted," was the tentative reply.

"You speak in riddles! Our spies report he is here in Zoren. What do you mean he did not come?"

There was impatience in his tone, and the shorter man was quick to reply, anxious to avoid his Master's ire. "He comes with two, my lord. He travels with two, not the single companion you warned of."

"Tell me more" was the clipped reply.

"One is as you said, a Human and heavily armed. The other is peculiar. I do not believe he is Human, yet neither I nor our spies can determine his race. He is tall and muscular, hooded like the other two, and also heavily armed."

Seconds of silence followed. The two were abreast of Lathaniel's hiding place, and he held his breath as they passed.

The Master spoke again. "Interesting. It is unlike him to carry a company. For centuries he has been a loner. The single apprentice was a surprise, but now there are two?"

They passed by Lathaniel, who was straining to hear their conversation.

"Let them pass," the taller man said then. "I must know more of these companions of his and of his purpose. I will make alternate plans. For now, allow their exit from the city, and then this is what I want you to do..."

Their voices faded as they continued down the darkened street.

Lathaniel let out a slow breath and relaxed cramped muscles, not realizing how tense he had been. Assuming Juga was clear with supplies in hand, he moved off through the night in the opposite direction, making for the agreed rendezvous and counting the gods' blessings for his near miss. He couldn't wait to share what he had heard with Drake.

# CHAPTER 13

The soles of his leather boots softly slapped the aged wood as he ascended the steps, their sound somehow reflecting his annoyance and disquiet as it reverberated through the empty western hall. His long brown cloak snapped and slapped the air as it billowed out behind him. The lightness of his step and his agility belied his age, but then, he had much on his mind as he reached the top of the hewn steps and entered a short, wide corridor.

Guards were posted at either side of a door that sat slightly ajar at the end of the corridor and from which a glow of light could be seen. The graceful arches carved into the wood on either side of the door peaked above its center and were inlayed with runes and symbols of the Gor'ean culture. The guards snapped to attention as he approached then swept aside to allow his entrance. He crossed the portal and stopped, sweeping his right hand across his torso to rest it on his heart then bowing his head in deference, awaiting his Fyyther's greeting.

For a room so large, there was a warmth and welcome to it that put visitors at ease. The walls on two sides ran at right angles to each other and were adorned with exquisite paintings depicting the rich history of the Gor'eans. The curved outer wall that joined the two was comprised entirely of ornately paneled doors that slid open in the daylight to entice occupants onto the terrace beyond. For tonight only two shutters were open to allow fingers of moonlight to caress the shadows and a slight breeze to jostle the candles that lit the room.

The figure at a large oak desk raised his head at the intrusion. He rolled his shoulders and rested against his high-backed chair.

"Lord Cindrick! Good evening to you. Enter and tell me what news you have of our armies."

"The grace of the gods and good evening greetings to you as well, Highness," Cindrick replied as he straightened and made his way to stand before the desk. The Fyyther waved him into a chair and bid him continue.

"Scouts report the Resistance maintains some pockets of strength in Jyyiss and Arrash, but otherwise the news from Far'camice and Siityth bodes ill. We have been forced to pull back, and in our stead, Gorillian's forces are now well entrenched. The Elves remain unable to assist. They resist Gorillian at their borders but have thus far resisted all attempts to draw them into the larger conflict, as they are preoccupied with their own civil war.

"Here in Gorger, matters are more grave. Gorillian's ships have a chokehold on our northern coastline that has all but stopped the flow of money and supplies into and out of Gorger. Drataz is still secure as, of course, is Limore. All our ships focus there and have successfully kept a corridor into and out of Gorger open, though our Captains run the gauntlet coming in and out of port. We have commandeered smaller ships from villages along the more remote stretches of coast and thus far have been sliding supplies and troops in and out of Gorger unnoticed in spite of the embargo. The Human King Carnet is little more than a puppet now. Gorillian has swung key members of Carnet's inner circle to his cause with promises of both power and riches under his leadership, and while we have a strong spy network in place there, Duron has, for all intents and purposes, fallen. Horon and Amarik remain strong, though for how long none can say. We continue to gather and then redeploy troops across Gorger and beyond through Cap'hannet. Thus far our interior borders hold strong, Highness," he concluded.

Acthelass Mar was the Fyyther of the Gor'eans, their King. In his day a ruthless soldier, he still held the carriage and authority of a commander though he had passed a half century in age. There was silence as he pored over the candlelit map of Elënthiá on the desk in front of him, considering all that he had heard. His relationship with Cindrick stretched back to the days before he was king and, at times, was uneasy. He knew jealousy factored into Cindrick's behaviour but the lord held a strong following in Gorger and, for the most part, Mar indulged him. He looked up at Cindrick, noting as he spoke his loyal lord's ill-concealed agitation. It was obvious to him that Cindrick had more on his mind than a troop update.

"That Drataz holds is good news," the Fyyther replied. "We are in desperate need of the supplies coming in from Nesmeresa. I have given orders that all shipments be sent directly to Cap'hannet. Decisions can be made there on deployment of resources as they know better where Resistance troops are in need. I have heard today that Jymar in Amarik was attacked by Are-Narcs. Though easily defeated, this boldness leads me to believe that we will shortly see a shift in emphasis in Gorillian's attacks, a shift that will bring him closer to our borders."

Seeing an opening to introduce the subject uppermost on his mind, Cindrick shifted his ramrod stance slightly before saying, "Then there are rumours, Majesty, rumours of the Draconean."

"I have heard these," replied the King. He tented his hands as he leaned back in his chair, eyes narrowing as he studied Cindrick closely. "It has been many years since news of the Draconean has reached this court."

"It is beyond news and rumours, Majesty," Cindrick rushed on. "The blackguard has been sighted in both Gramal and Zoren. Our spy network is abuzz with his appearance after these many years. He is accumulating supplies and collecting information. What intent the cur has in this is not yet known, but we know well he is no friend to the Gor'eans! After the debacle twelve years ago..." He trailed off and then pushed to his feet.

"He must be hunted down and brought to justice! You must deploy troops immediately to capture him such that we can perform his execution here in Gorgonathan before the Gor'ean people! Only then will justice have been served!" he ranted, leaning forward over the King's desk, fists clenched, losing himself in the ardour of his argument.

Leaning forward in his chair, his cold eyes narrowing and his curt tone a clear indication of his displeasure, King Acthelass snapped, "Hold your tongue, Lord Cindrick! You would be wise to remember to whom you speak and to guard manner accordingly. You are a Gor'ean and I am your Fyyther! Do not presume to tell me what I must and must not do unless you are prepared to accept the consequences. It is neither your right nor your place to command the armies of Gorger nor to dictate what happens within Gorgonathan. You overstep yourself!"

At Cindrick's raised voice, the royal guards moved immediately into the doorway of the chamber seeking reassurance that their Fyyther was in no danger. Realizing the gravity of his error and loss of temper, Cindrick quickly took two steps back and dropped to one knee.

"I beg your forgiveness, Majesty. The bitterness of my past interaction with the Draconean remains like a poison on my tongue. Forgive my outburst and my anger in your presence."

He remained on one knee his head bowed.

Acthelass left him there for a moment or two. In truth he had expected this reaction from Lord Cindrick, though the strength of his vehemence with so many years having passed surprised the King.

"Your bitterness clouds both your mind and your judgement, Cindrick," the King advised quietly. Cindrick raised his head and was gestured to his feet as the Fyyther continued, "Were history to be told impartially, it would show that the last Resistance would not have been successful were it not for the Draconean. As for the allegations you speak of, they were never proven."

He watched Cindrick's eyes darken though he held his tongue.

Then King continued, "Yours is not the only report I have received in this regard. The Draconean enters Oderon, though for what purpose we do not know. He will know that the travelled routes will be watched by Gorillian and will seek the ancient passages through the Minheras. Whatever your personal agenda in this regard, I wish to meet with the Draconean. I have dispatched my son to Cap'hannet with orders to send troops into Oderon to find and protect him by any means possible. The Draconean will remain unhurt and unharmed." Mar stressed the last three words. "And he will be brought here to me."

King Acthelass raised his hand to halt any further discussion on the matter and then lowered his head to continue perusing the documents on his desk, effectively dismissing Lord Cindrick. He could hear the snap and hiss of the angry

Lord's cloak as he whipped it around himself and left the room. The King once again sat back in his chair and listened to the staccato slap of Cindrick's boots on the stairs as he left the royal chambers. Turning in his chair so he could stare out through the open shutters into a velvet, starlit sky, he scrubbed his hands over his face and thought of the Draconean.

# CHAPTER 14

Gorillian was six-and-a-half feet of danger and hate, and he looked every inch of it, more so when attired, as he was now, in blood-spattered battle armour. His dirty blond hair was parted down the middle and hung well past the halfway point of his back. It was loosely tied in three places with leather thongs; once on either side of his face and the other at his nape. Between these the rest hung in knots and straggles, the darker hair beneath shot with grey. His beard was just as scraggly with moustaches braided on either side of his mouth. The coarse mass was gathered beneath his chin with another thong. The matted fur that fell from his jowls was also braided but left untied at the ends where it melded into the rest of the knotted snarl. His his fur-collared leather tunic shed, his massive frame was bent over a basin of water, washing the blood of battle from gnarled hands. Divested of his swords yet still clad in his chainmail vest and weapons harness, he looked up in the reflecting glass in front of him meeting his own tired gaze.

At times he could hardly recognize himself. The face that stared back at him had been Mortal once. How invigorating it had been to have such little time in this world; to feel the need to live each and every day as if it might be your last!

His memories were dusty and torn at the edges. He recalled only that there had been a time when every race in Elënthiá spoke his name in reverence, for he had once been a statesman and a scholar; a sought-after advisor to kings and queens, admired.

When he was gifted with Immortality, he had pictured spending the ages in the company of other scholars and among the elders of Elënthiá. That dream dulled and blurred, then disappeared forever. He learned that immortality draws its own hazards and extracts its own price. Allegiances were formed, debts acquired and blood oaths taken that fashioned a map for his future which had taken him so far from where he began that it was little wonder he could hardly recognize himself.

Where once his name was spoken in reverence, it was now spoken in fear. Where once he had kept company with the finest minds in Elënthiá, he was now surrounded by sycophants who cowered in terror in his presence, and by hybrid creatures spawned from beneath Oderon with the intelligence to fight and be killed – but little else. Gorillian started, then blinked. He had been lost in his thoughts. He stepped away from the glass and considered the latest intelligence he'd received.

How he longed for this centuries-old game of cat-and-mouse to be over. He hated Drake Sorzin with every fibre of his being. The hate and greed that had driven him to kill the Draconean King centuries ago and, indeed, to eradicate the Draconean race now seemed almost mild compared to the bitter loathing and malevolence roiling within him for the son, the last Draconean.

Over time, he had so many opportunities to kill him! And yet an ancient blood oath bound him to take the Draconean alive or lose his own life. Elusive though Sorzin had been in the past, by the gods he would trap him this time and be done with it! Once and for all he would rid himself of his obligation and of the despised Draconean. Sighing, he scrubbed a damp rag over his weathered face, eliminating most of the bloody remnants of the battlefield, then dried his hands and left his chambers.

Descending a narrow staircase, he entered a large, domed stone cavern. The Human awaiting him had been seated on a wooden bench against a wall but at his entrance leapt immediately to his feet, dropping to one knee and bowing his head in supplication.

"My lord Gorillian," he said, his voice a grating whine in the early evening silence.

The Human was reed thin and tall. His hair was sparse and a dirty brown, hanging in greasy straggles down either side of his face. His eyes were a dull brown and were perpetually watery, as if he had just inhaled the scent of the most potent of onions. He was a traitor to his race, banished for his treason, but as devoted to his new Master as one could expect a creature of such character to be.

"Arise, Pouris Gaul. What number of soldiers do you carry in your company?" Gorillian demanded, getting right to the point.

"A handful less than one hundred, my Lord," was the prompt reply. "Mostly Are-Narcs. We were due to connect with another battalion when we received your summons and diverted here." Gaul waited in silence as his Lord paced.

Finally Gorillian spoke. "I have word that the Draconean enters Oderon and will traverse through the Minheras, I presume heading into or through them into Amarik. Send scouts to watch the travelled routes and bridges," he directed. "Use the Are-Narcs. Instruct them to send word along to their kin in the caves to be vigilant in watching the entrances and exits to the ancient passages. Sorzin knows these well. Find the Draconean. And bring him to me..." He paused before adding with ill disguised contempt, "Alive."

He stepped close to Pouris Gaul then and used a single filthy, calloused finger to lift his chin and lock eyes with him.

"Do not disappoint me, Gaul. I want the Draconean this time. Fail me at your own peril."

Gaul was battle hardened, fearless, and possessing neither mercy nor a soul; but what threat he saw in his Master's eyes was real and he'd no doubt that failure was not an option. With a curt nod and a bow, he hastily backed out the door of the chamber where he turned, snapping out orders to his own minions to make ready for departure.

# CHAPTER 15

Looking at the three-forked options in front of them, they surveyed their choices.

"Which way?" Juga asked, turning to Drake.

"I am not certain," Drake replied, perplexed. "While I have travelled many of the ancient passages through the Minheras, I have only read of this canyon in my father's journals. They indicate that one of these forks leads to a door of some sort marked with anuléan symbols. However, while I am unfamiliar with this canyon, our Narc friends are not. We must move with haste but with care, for I feel certain we will encounter them before too long."

He paused, considering.

"I think it best that we divide. Juga, you take the passage straight ahead; Lathaniel, you take the one to the left, and I will go right. If what I have read is accurate, two will dead-end, revealing nothing. The third will also dead-end, but there should be a doorway of some sort. Those who find nothing should return here to this junction and await the others. If you encounter Narcs, do not try and manage on your own; retreat and draw them back to this junction immediately. Move with haste but with stealth and care. We may yet have to put your long hours of training to the test, but I would rather we found the entrance before nightfall."

Without another word, he moved off to his right. Lathaniel and Juga's eyes met. Excitement yet apprehension in both their eyes, they gave each other a nod and moved quickly into their respective passages.

Each of the three forks into the canyon was narrow, able in Lathaniel's estimation, to comfortably accommodate ten men riding abreast astride horses. Barren, smooth rock faces stretched straight up on either side like arms toward the heavens. Narrow as it was, the canyon floor would only see sunlight for the few moments during the day when the orb was directly overhead. Otherwise, it remained, as it was now: without vegetation and bathed in twilight and shadows.

As Lathaniel moved quickly forward, he felt his senses sharpen. Thinking preparation the better part of valour, he drew his sword out of its scabbard. His elven background lightened his footfalls, and he moved quickly over the uneven rocky ground in silence, frequently looking up to scan the high canyon walls for unfriendly eyes. He was thankful for the time underground in Horon; otherwise he might find the confining walls overwhelming.

Their departure out of Zoren and into Oderon had almost been too easy. He had recounted the whispered discourse between the two cloaked strangers in the alley to Drake, who had revealed little about who he thought the two might be. Lathaniel was only just realizing that by intertwining his fate with the Draconean's, he had joined the ranks of the notorious in Gorillian's eyes.

They had found entrance to this canyon in the high foothills of the Minheras. Moving under cover of darkness, the

Draconean had led them to a slim opening in a rock face, an opening that, even in the light of day, could have easily been mistaken for one of a hundred other crevices in the rock. Sliding sideways through it was a tight squeeze, especially for one Drake's size, but once through the three beheld this imposing, high-walled barren canyon.

Lathaniel continued apace. By his reckoning he had walked more than two hours before he stopped and took water and a piece of bread, still standing, not wanting to relax his guard. He continued at least two more hours before he sensed the end of the passage. He could see a wall in the shadows ahead of him but stopped several feet from it, sheathed his sword, and began to scan the canyon walls on either side looking for anything that might resemble anuléan markings. A fine thing, he thought derisively as he continued looking, given that he wouldn't know an anuléan carving if someone etched it into his hand with a knife. Lighting a torch, he looked carefully at the walls on both sides and even the floor of the passage for the last fifteen or twenty feet of it. Nothing.

Moving to the back wall itself, he was surprised to note that what had at first looked like the shadowy end of the canyon held, in fact, the entrance to a small cave. Entering this, he held his torch high. It was only the size of a small room and, as he rubbed his other hand over the rock surface, he felt slight indentations. Removing his glove, he ran a bare palm over the rocks' surface where he could detect a slight pattern of indentations in the stone.

*This must be it!* He moved quickly back out into the canyon and paused, listening carefully for any sounds and scanning the dim upper walls for intruders. With that, he extinguished the torch, again drew his sword, and moved quickly back the way he'd come.

He found Drake and Juga at the junction of passages, lounging on the ground, each with one foot stretched in front, the other knee bent with arms draped carelessly over them, patiently waiting for him.

"You have found the entrance, I hope. You've certainly been gone long enough," Drake drawled in a teasing tone.

He and Juga arose and shouldered their packs as Lathaniel updated them on what he had found. They quickly retraced his steps, aware of the lengthening shadows and the coming of night. Drake was loath to travel by torchlight as it marked their location to unwanted eyes. By the time they reached the cave, it was nearly dark. They lit their torches and slipped inside the small enclosure.

As Lathaniel had done previously, Drake removed his gloves and ran bare fingers over the hieroglyphics embedded in the stone, intoning a language with which Juga and Lathaniel were unfamiliar. Repeating certain passages again and again, he seemed finally to understand the ancient directions and instructed Lathaniel to stand on one side of him and Juga on the other. With his palm and fingers he cleared the dust and debris from three similar pictographs that, while not immediately obvious as being on the same linear plane, could be diagonally joined with a straight line. Following Drake's instruction, the three positioned their right palms over the pictographs and simultaneously pushed inward. The rock seemed to groan and protest but slowly shifted both backward and to the right, revealing nothing but an ebony gloom within.

Lathaniel's eyes were wide as he beheld the passage in front of them. Juga, too, was speechless. He had shared stories that he had been told or had overhead over the years with Lathaniel. They knew the Anulé to be a race of gentle giants but both were daunted by the prospect of entering their ancient underground world. Torches high, he and Lathaniel followed Drake forward, starting when they heard the solid granite panel slide closed behind them, enfolding them in unrelieved silence and blackness.

# CHAPTER 16

Once again, Lathaniel thanked the gods for the time he'd spent underground in Horon, else he would have panicked with the closeness of the air around them. Instead, he concentrated on Drake's lead and on the ground underfoot as they began to descend farther into the earth.

They had assumed their usual single file order with Juga following on Drake's heels and Lathaniel bringing up the rear. Though he moved them forward with haste, Drake exercised care, oft times stopping to check the terrain ahead for traps or crevasses, other times backtracking to take them down a different passage when a cave-in or the drastic narrowing of a tunnel made passage impossible.

To pass the time, both Juga and Lathaniel questioned Drake on the Anulé and their underground world, feeling the privilege of being allowed passage through this ancient kingdom and anxious for information. For the most part, Drake's answers were curt and uninformative, but when Juga quizzed him on what exactly the "deadly Narcs" were, he explained at length.

"The word *narc* is a shortened version of a nearly unpronounceable anuléan word for the creatures," he explained. "They originated from deep in the earth beneath these mountains and were used by the Anulé almost from the beginning of their settlement in the Minheras to mine these mountains. I guess you could call them slaves, though that implies that they were subjugated against their will. Perhaps "domesticated" is a better word to use. The Anulé fed and cared for the Narcs, and in exchange the beasts did their bidding. In many ways, their domestication over the millennia was to their detriment, as they all but lost the means to look after themselves. Throughout history they valiantly protected their anuléan masters against Gorillian but the Anulé were a secretive and shy race and the perpetual threat of evil drove them out of Oderon and beyond the borders of Elënthiá.

Lathaniel looked quizzically at the Draconean. "But why would they just leave, just walk away from a place that was their home for ages?"

Drake paused. "In the days before the advance of Gorillian's evil, Elënthiá was a place of peace. This suited the Anulé for they were not a warring nation. They were miners and artisans, able to create remarkable beauty from stone and metal. When evil began to spread across Elënthiá they could not bear to live under its threat nor to remain and watch the home they loved destroyed. So they left. Suddenly. Taking nothing with them but their tools. They called it the *mein naquivi* – the great depart." Drake sighed and paused for a time before he continued.

"In the absence of masters to feed and direct them, the surviving Narcs roamed wild through the Minheras, moving to the surface under cover of night to hunt and not particularly choosy about whether what they ate was animal, Human, or other."

The three continued to move on, Juga and Lathaniel rapt with fascination. "Gorillian found a few of the sealed entrances into this place and tried to take it as his own. The

Narcs weren't having any part of that and Gorillian grew tired of perpetually skirmishing with them, preferring Ethen-jar where he had eliminated all resistance. He left. But when he did, he took several thousand of the Narcs with him, likely with the idea of making them slaves. Over the centuries since, he has undertaken his own macabre breeding experiment, forcing Human female slaves to breed with his Narcs. As it turns out," he continued disparagingly, "it was a minor stroke of genius because they now make up the principle force of his army. He calls them his Are-Narcs."

"But, Master, how could two such different species breed?" Juga asked incredulously, sickened at the thought.

"Pretty much as you would imagine," Drake continued bitterly. "The rub of it is that the mix of the two has yielded creatures with the strength and physical attributes of a Narc but with a tolerance of light and sufficient intelligence for Gorillian to manipulate them to his own ends. Remember, they have always existed to serve. And believe me, his Are-Narcs serve him loyally without hesitation, without challenge, and without remorse."

"So are these mountains now filled with Gorillian's new Are-Narcs?" Lathaniel asked. "Is that what we are wary of running into?"

"Actually, no," Drake responded. "The Narcs that remained in the Minheras are loosely referred to as the Cave-Narcs, as they still live largely underground and usually only surface above under cover of night. But they have bonded into packs of anywhere between fifteen and fifty, depending on the strength of the dominant male. While they fight each other ruthlessly over territory or food, they band together against any outside intruder. That would be us. So, Lathaniel, to answer your question, it is the Cave-Narcs that we need be wary of."

Thinking it must now be well into the night, Drake called a halt. "We shall stop here for some rest and food," he directed. "I will take the first watch. Never, while in the Minheras, can all eyes rest at once," he finished ominously.

Lathaniel and Juga silently shed their packs, pulling out some dried meat and bread to take with some water, both thinking that perhaps they'd been better off not knowing about Narcs; their imaginations had them starting at every sound. But the night passed without incident, and the following day the three continued through the deserted underground kingdom.

They had ceased their descent. Here, so far below ground, the walls were again strewn with the same crystals as those in Horon, throwing sufficient light that torches could be extinguished. Each length of passage they traversed seemed to open onto a series of halls. Some were smaller, more utilitarian; some appeared to have been sleeping quarters with row on row of stone platforms with raised headrests; others seemed to have been meal halls filled with tables and chairs that were massive in proportion. The chair backs reached above Lathaniel's head and the tabletops stood at nearly five feet. All seemed as if the inhabitants had simply stopped what they were doing in mid-task, and walked away. It was haunting and eerie.

Some of the halls were empty, leaving the three to guess at their use. Others had obviously been used for specific tasks; there were an armoury, a massive scullery, and many workshops. Throughout the day Drake manoeuvred the three through a maze of corridors and passages while the apprentices absorbed every nuance of this monument to an absent race.

When they stopped to rest, Lathaniel broke the silence.

"Drake, you have told us of the Narcs but have given us no preparation in terms of their appearance or their fighting abilities. Can you tell us more?"

Sitting on the hard stone floor, Drake leaned back to rest against his pack and explained.

"Be prepared for a pick and an axe, for these they wield with both great strength and accuracy. They have had the anuléan armouries and abandoned tools at their disposal for many centuries and have learned to use these weapons with considerable skill. But as strong as they are, they are neither agile nor fleet of foot. We could outrun them in a footrace over a short distance but would be hard pressed to win against them were an extended flight required; though slow, they have the wind for endurance.

"You are right to question me about this, Lathaniel, for I forget that their first appearance may be disconcerting for both of you."

He was silent for a moment before continuing, as if trying to conjure a picture of one in his mind.

"You will find them repulsive and shocking at first. You may smell them before you see them, for they carry a peculiar odour. It is difficult to describe but once you have smelled it, the scent will be forever familiar to you. It is a bit like that of a decaying animal but with a sinus-clearing bite to it. If they are downwind from you, you may hear them before you see them for their breathing is like a hiss and in the larger chambers will tend to echo. I think they've learned to use that sound and the cloak of darkness to intimidate their prey during the moments it takes to ensure their advantage in a fight."

He paused again for a moment.

"In appearance, they stand almost as tall as you, Juga. Their backs are hunched and their spines are ridged, somewhat similar to a reptile. Their skin is a dirty grey and hairless. They wear no garments. Males and females alike are warriors. Females do not nurse their young, so the only way you will distinguish one from the other is by the genitalia. Do not imagine that the females are any less deadly, for you would do so at your peril.

"They have four limbs like us, but their arms are longer, allowing them to use these as support when they bend to move through narrower tunnels. They have four-fingered hands. One digit is shorter and acts as their thumb. Their feet are splayed with six toes all of which have elongated nails that are as deadly as any sword. Hard enough to chip away rock and always filthy, a wound from one will need special care. I've known strong soldiers to be felled within days from septic infection received from a mere scratch."

With that visual locked in his mind, Lathaniel could hardly suppress the shudder that rippled through him. Well, he *had* asked. Sometimes he wondered if not knowing was easier...

The following day passed much as the last with the three moving steadily ever westward. Random conversation periodically broke the silence, but as the trio moved forward they became quieter and increasingly more tense, to a one anxious to be out of the cavernous belly of the earth.

On the evening of the fourth day, Drake hummed quietly to himself as he took the first watch. His apprentices were fast asleep. He could see that their initial enthrallment with the anuléan kingdom had faded. Spending each waking moment in perpetual readiness for a battle that did not materialize was wearing; he knew this from long experience. By his reckoning, they were approaching the halfway mark through Oderon. They had crossed the same paths as Cave-Narcs on several occasions - more frequently now as they moved deeper into the Minheras. He had read the Narc spoor and knew that the three of them were tempting good fortune to have not met with Narcs already. He could only hope their luck held.

As he sat in the darkness, he thought of young Lathaniel for what seemed like the millionth time, recalling Suvillwa's prediction and pondering their intertwined fates. Lathaniel still had not divulged the circumstances surrounding his exodus from Lamana. But then again, there had been no opportunity for them to converse alone. On the heels of the melody he hummed, words from times long past followed and he softly sang them.

"That song and those words are familiar to me," Lathaniel murmured drowsily after a time.

"You should be asleep," Drake replied, uncomfortable at the attention.

"It should be nearing my watch." Lathaniel sat up and pulled his tunic around him, rolling his pack and preparing to exchange positions. "When I was a very young boy, my grandfather used to whistle that tune. Sometimes my grandmother would join him and sing the verses. How is it that you know a song that is familiar to me?"

Drake sat still, gazing out into the darkness. After a time, he replied, "It is a song about the beginning of your race, Lathaniel. About Jonas and Ethena."

Lathaniel was speechless. If Drake knew the tale of Jonas and Ethena, then he might know of Lathaniel's lineage. He tensed but said nothing as the Draconean continued.

"The two lived worlds apart. Jonas, as you well recall, was a Human Prince, the eldest but the only brother in his family not betrothed. As is sometimes the way between a father and his eldest son, Jonas and the King were ever at odds. The King sent Jonas away for most of his upbringing to apprentice with a Master of the Court, which in those times was a man schooled in the arts, both academic and of war. The tale is told that the two became very close, so much so that when his Master was killed by mistake in a random raid by the King's soldiers, Jonas took his revenge by killing his own father. The Human court was fraught with danger and intrigue in those times, and Jonas fled the kingdom abdicating all rights to the Human throne.

"He ended up in Nesmeresa where his former status as a Human prince allowed him reluctant sanctuary. Ethena was the youngest daughter of the Elven Queen. The two met by chance in the Nesmeresan forests and fell in love on sight. They met secretly for months agonizing over their love, the division of their two worlds, and the ramifications of a union between them.

"The Elven King and Queen were aware of their friendship but didn't know the depth of their commitment. When the two left Nesmeresa secretly, the Elven monarchy was stunned by this breach in protocol, for an interracial union was forbidden. When the Human monarchy heard of this, their reaction was the same. Emissaries from each met and determined that the two should be hunted and brought back to their respective kingdoms to be punished for such sacrilege. They were never found. Folklore passed down through the ages told of the beginning of a new race, the Forsairs. Over time, when other Elves and Humans met, joined, and disappeared, they were rumoured to have connected with Jonas and Ethena in some remote, mythical enclave. It became fodder for poetry and musicians: the romance of Jonas and Ethena...I have lived for more than two millennia, Lathaniel, and you are the very first Forsair I have had the privilege of meeting."

"And the song...?"

"It has many verses. The few you heard came to me here in the darkness. I am surprised you could recognize any of it, for I am neither poet nor singer."

"I never knew the entire story. I..."

Drake unexpectedly sat upright, instantly on alert. He held one hand to his lips to quiet Lathaniel and with the other gave a sharp jab to Juga, who awoke with a start.

"Make haste," he whispered. "Lathaniel, draw your bow for we will shortly have need of it."

# CHAPTER 17

With barely a sound, the three were on their feet. Lathaniel notched his arrow and began a slow draw back on the bow, prepared for a deadly release.

"Can you smell them?" Drake hissed. "Use your senses, lads. See the attack in your mind before you act; remember your training."

Nostrils quivering and ears straining, they could only just hear the sound of a soft hiss. It soon grew louder, as did a clicking sound that Lathaniel presumed were toenails tapping lightly on cold grey rock as the thing moved nearer. Leaving the safety of the circle of firelight, Lathaniel moved carefully through the shadows toward the noise. He sensed more than saw its shadowy outline and instantly let fly with an arrow. The *thwack* it made as it found its fleshy mark seemed to echo in the silence.

Lathaniel quickly notched another arrow and moved carefully toward it, senses scanning the area. Juga came up directly behind him, exclaiming as he held a gloved hand loosely over his nose, having had his first whiff of the stench of a Cave-Narc. Drake's large hand suddenly clamped on his sleeve and yanked him sideways. A small axe clanged off the wall behind where Juga had been standing.

"Do we stand and fight?" Lathaniel whispered.

Dropping all pretext of stealth, Drake grabbed his torch and took off into the darkness.

"No!" he yelled. "We'll need to make it to the stone gate that leads into the next hall before we are caught."

Juga didn't know which was worse, the sibilant hiss that echoed and re-echoed off every stone wall and surface again and again until it was almost deafening, or the orchestra of clicking toenails that tapped like a million tiny castanets against the mountain floor. The three fled through the darkness.

"Ahead! Faster! Can you see it?" Drake called back to them.

The doorway was cut as an enormous triangle inset within a triangle inset within yet another, colossal triangle. There were no hinges, no handles. Running across its portal, Lathaniel skidded to a halt and turned, looking frantically from left to right at the gaping threshold.

"How do we close it?" he yelled.

Drake had stopped and was standing in the center of the portal just inside the opening. He intoned the Anuléan words, *"seeis harvat toomal dyquiray"*

From the bottom right-hand corner of the triangle, a panel began to slide across to join another solid rock panel that slowly moved inward from the entire left hand side of the triangle.

"Faster! They're almost upon us!" roared Juga as the cacophony of clicking and hissing rolled toward them like an ocean wave.

"To the side!" yelled Drake. "Move to the side!"

A volley of small axes and rudimentary daggers came pelting through the ever decreasing portal opening, clattering on the stone floor just inside the door. The sonorous slam of granite hitting granite was nearly deafening as the portal shut. The instant quiet that followed was almost as unsettling as the previous roar of noise.

"Well," said Juga matter-of-factly, breaking the silence. "Nothing like a brisk midnight run for your life through pitch blackness to get the blood pumping." He uncorked his water skin. Lathaniel swung away from the portal and caught his eye, taking the water offered. Juga's face broke into a huge, white-toothed grin. "Better than sparring in Horon," he stated, taking another swig.

Drake was already scouting the hall they'd entered. "We've not seen the last of them. There are many avenues through these mountains. We need to move or we'll find ourselves trapped."

The trio moved quietly forward into a gargantuan chamber. Even in the minimal light, the two apprentices found themselves in rapt awe at the grandeur and majesty of the massive, columned granite hall they had entered.

"What *is* this place?" Lathaniel whispered in awe.

"I've travelled through several of the ancient underground passages. But I have not been in these before. I believe we are in the royal quarters." Drake quietly replied, his eyes sweeping the incredible chamber.

The hall they'd entered was long and rectangular, the ceiling held up, they presumed, by columns that stood like parallel rows of sentinels along its length. The columns themselves were marble and inlaid with colourful floral designs and encrusted with semi-precious stones. Drake could recognize lapis lazuli, red agate and amethyst, abalone shell twinkling, even in the dull light. Ornate vines crafted out of coloured inset marble wound around the columns disappearing into the darkness above.

To their left, another similar chamber intersected with the room at its midpoint. The three moved to investigate it. In the dim light they could see that its design was identical to the main hall, but rather than plain white marble flooring, inset mosaics made of tiny tiles paved the hall. Impressive, massive statuary filled the spaces between ten pillars that supported the grand architecture of the room.

"This is the Hall of Kings," said Drake quietly. "It is the throne room." He knew that they should make haste through this hall but his own awe and curiosity overcame practicality and he allowed his company to linger.

As the three walked up the long room, they could see that each statue was a huge monument in the likeness of Anuléan Kings that had ruled across the ages. Each statue was at least three times the height of Drake, the statues closest to the entrance appeared to be the oldest and most weathered. Each King was sculpted holding what could have been either a tool or a weapon. On a lower console carved into the base of the statue at a height that would have been waist-high to the Anulé, lay the original implement.

Drake and Lathaniel moved on ahead, but Juga lingered at each statue marvelling at the gentle features mirrored in the stone effigies and fingering the blades and the hammer headed tools in wonder and appreciation. He moved from figure to figure until he reached the top of the room. There the last King's statue sat behind and atop a massive marble throne.

Juga studied the chiselled features of the last Anuléan king. His eyes settled on the king's weapon, a long-handled hammer that lay across the seat of the throne. He moved up the three steps before the throne and reverently picked up the ancient massive mallet. Surprisingly it was far lighter than he'd imagined, lighter than his sword, though its appearance belied that fact. It fit comfortably in his closed fist as he wielded it back and forth experimentally. Intrigued by how the design of it differed from the other hammers held by previous kings, Juga moved down the room to investigate and compare.

Drake and Lathaniel had moved off to the left of the throne investigate another doorway. It led into a smaller antechamber. As with the throne room and the rest of the royal chambers, the stonework within this room was exquisite, decorated with the precious jewels and rare coloured marble that could only be found in the Minheras. Although every item in the room was hewn of rock, there was an intimacy to the space that reminded Lathaniel of the Drake's great room under Horon.

There was an ornately carved stone desk. It was in disarray, littered with dusty tomes and parchments, yet still as sturdy and strong as if newly carved. It was flanked by two large cabinets brimming with scrolls; the walls on either side of these were lined with shelves and cubbyholes filled with more of the same. Shallow trays on the desk were filled with a dried, black substance that Lathaniel assumed had been ink. Feather quills were laid carelessly aside as if the owner had meant to return. Lathaniel folded himself into the huge stone seat and set his legs beneath the enormous desk.

"Are you aware that you are seated at the last Anuléan King's own desk?" Drake asked quietly from behind him, his back turned away as he perused the contents of the shelves behind the desk.

Lathaniel popped instantly to his feet and stepped away from the massive desk.

"He's long dead, Lathaniel," Drake said drily. "I tell you only so that you will know more of this chamber. You show no disrespect by your actions." With that he continued his review.

Lathaniel sat back at the desk, imagining its owner. The light in the room was only that offered by the wall crystals, so it was difficult to read anything on the scrolls - impossible given that even if he could see, he didn't read Anuléan script. He thumbed through some of the dusty maps left open on the desk noting that while the script was different, the drawings were similar to those he had pored over with Drake whilst in Horon. They showed all of Elënthiá but were of a larger scale, including places beyond their world about which he'd not heard.

Sifting through more of the ancient documents, he came across a detailed ink sketch of a Human standing beside a regal looking but stern-faced Anulé. The human's head reached only slightly higher than the Anulé's waist. In the dim light he could make out Human script below the portrait that said only "King Morbit and Genisar." The Anulé carried a powerful hammer with a solid stone face and an intricately carved handle; the weapon was nearly as long as he was tall. The Human held an oval shield strapped to his left arm and a long, elegantly curved sword in his right. Lathaniel sensed that the two were friends. He recalled Drake saying that many allied against Gorillian during the Great Wars; such a friendship between an Anuléan King and a Human would not have been unheard of.

"Lathaniel!" he could hear Juga softly call. "Lathaniel!"

"It's time we moved on anyway," Drake said as their eyes met.

Lathaniel pulled an arrow from his quiver as, bow in hand, he and Drake moved quickly back into the throne room. Juga was midway down the room. In his right hand he held what looked like a heavy ancient Dwarven hammer. He was standing in front of a statue holding a similar weapon.

"You have to see the workmanship of this, Lathaniel! It is incredible."

The two bent nearer to the statue to examine the weapon, and as they did Drake saw an ominous shadow move across the entrance to the throne room beyond them and cursed himself for indulging his curiousity.

"Lads," he whispered urgently. "We've got more company."

# CHAPTER 18

The three froze in the half-light. Drake slowly lifted his right leg and slid a dagger from his boot. As if sensing their presence, the Narc slowly turned just as Drake let fly with the dagger. The screech from the beast peeled through the caverns and was abruptly silenced as the dagger embedded itself in the soft flesh of its throat.

The three were already in motion. Lathaniel pulled an arrow from his quiver readying his bow. Juga had his sword in one hand and the ancient hammer still in the other. Drake paused for a heartbeat to extract his bloodied dagger from the fallen Narc, and then the three were sprinting up the marbled main hall toward the next huge triangular gate at the far end.

However, under the apex of it, a battalion of Are-Narcs stepped forward in formation, their armour glinting in the half-light, their weapons drawn. The three skidded to a halt a hundred feet away from the gate. Though they did not look back, they could sense that their pursuers had halted a similar distance behind them. They were trapped.

The three gave each other their backs, forming a tight triangle of their own and shifting in a circle, eyes evaluating their enemy and their options. Slowly Drake leaned down and replaced his dagger in his boot. He reached across his torso and drew his sword in its stead. It was magnificent, in itself daunting. Nearly four feet in length, the engravings of three vines entwined round the two-handed hilt and extended up the blade. Embedded within the hilt was a large silver star, and to its right a smaller black one. Above these, a single perfect emerald winked, gathering all available light and reflecting it outward like a blinding beacon.

Following his lead, Lathaniel shouldered his bow and returned his arrow to its quiver. He unsheathed his sword and gripped it in readiness. Juga held his sword in one hand and the ancient anuléan hammer in the other. The three formidable warriors confidently faced off against impossible odds.

These were no Cave-Narcs but Gorillian's trained mercenaries. The two forces of Are-Narcs shifted to each side, forming a circle three deep around the companions. With a roar from their commander, the first line of Are-Narcs attacked, pulling the three from their tight circle into the larger fray.

Are-Narc warriors were skilled swordsmen and tough adversaries. But in a battle with a two-thousand-year-old, six-and-a-half-foot, rock solid, angry Draconean, more than skill was required. Drake wielded his enormous sword like a scythe, sweeping it back then forth and severing heads and limbs. He moved like a dancer, easily evading attacks with an agile side step then swinging around yet again with his deadly sword. The smooth marble became treacherous, its surface slick with blood and the bits of flesh scattered across it.

The hours, days, weeks, and months of sparring and anticipating what-if close combat scenarios paid off. Lathaniel fluidly stepped to the side, avoiding one advance, and in to intercept another. The block brought him face-to-face with a foul-breathed Are-Narc, and as he got his first close look at one, it blinked. And so did Lathaniel. The Are-Narc's eyelids flickered closed over flat black irises but the eyelids closed from the sides - not from the top! The split second it took to register his shock and surprise cost him a bloodied nose and a hard hit to the gut. Annoyed now, he drew his sword back and swung it, beheading the Are-Narc in front of him before another of its odd blinks could pass.

On the backswing of that attack, he swung his elbow up to clip the chin of one behind him, snapping its head back and giving him time to swing his sword around and remove its arm at the elbow. Ignoring the scream of agony and the arc of blood that hit him in the shoulder, Lathaniel continued to face the onslaught. He saw more than felt a blade slash across his chest. In annoyance he gripped the hilt of his sword with both hands and swung it around into his attacker's abdomen, nearly cleaving him in two. In his peripheral vision he saw that Juga was surrounded, his tunic and leggings slashed and seeping blood in a half-dozen places. He began to make his way through the fray toward him.

Juga was using both weapons in two-handed attacks. He became quickly adept at using the long-handled hammer head to butt his opponents in the face, gut, or knees; anything to disable them while he wielded his sword with effect. While this strategy worked well with his back against a wall, it did not allow him to easily protect his flank whilst in the open. An Are-Narc swung a club, catching him across the back of the neck. He fell to his knees before Lathaniel could reach him.

"Drake!" Lathaniel yelled.

The Draconean had been holding off five Are-Narcs and swung his head around just in time to see his Human apprentice fold. With his attention fractured, his attackers were on him. He gave a great cry that seemed to tear from deep within him and surged upwards, flinging them away, leaping over corpses and fallen bodies, and sliding on the slick marble as he made for Juga.

With Juga down, the Are-Narcs had Lathaniel fully engaged; he was outnumbered. As he fought to get to Juga, Drake marvelled at the Forsair's calm resolve and maturity as he lost the advantage in defending himself. He reached Lathaniel as the remaining Are-Narc's pressed in around them both. With no space to swing a sword, the two began to use the hilt of their weapons along with their fists and legs to battle the onslaught. Lathaniel cried out as he saw the swing of a club arc toward Drake's head. It was the last thing he remembered before the world went black.

# CHAPTER 19

The Are-Narcs parted and stood at attention as Pouris Gaul stomped down the corridor and into the cell.

He paused on the threshold. "Are they alive?"

"Yes, sir. Unconscious only. We had to use clubs on all three to restrain them. Minor wounds and headaches. No more."

Gaul walked over to the largest of the slumped figures and gave it a kick. Nothing. Thankfully, he would not have to disappoint Lord Gorillian. He reached down and hauled up the head of a second body.

"The Human…yes." He let go of Juga's hair, pushing the limp head away from him as he moved to the last motionless body.

Grabbing a handful of Lathaniel's hair, he lifted. "And what have we here? Hmmm…not an Elf yet not a Human either. Lord Gorillian must know of this."

He let go, and Lathaniel's head fell heavily back on his chest. Gaul dusted his hands on the thighs of his leggings, delighted.

"Excellent! Dispatch a runner to Lord Gorillian immediately."

Consciousness came slowly to Lathaniel. His first coherent thought registered at the same time as the pain. Unmoving, he did a slow inventory of his surroundings. He was on his knees, his arms pulled behind him and tied at the wrist to a stake anchored in the ground. The pain in his head was blinding; from the feel of it, he'd been struck more than once and a heavy hand had been used.

His shoulders screamed with pain at the position; his hands and arms were numb, as were his legs and feet. He concentrated on opening his eyes. At first he thought they were swollen shut, but with effort he opened them. Not swollen, he thought with relief, just caked with dirt and the remnants of the battle.

He let his eyes shift to his left and right. He did not want to reveal his consciousness just yet nor did he want to aggravate the already blistering pain in his head. Juga was to his left, slumped forward, still unconscious. To his right there was another empty stake. Unless Drake was bound behind him, he was not with them in the torchlit cell. Lathaniel suppressed the panic he felt at the thought that Drake had perished.

Juga moaned. He was regaining consciousness. Lathaniel heard a voice at the door call out, "They're awake!" and girded himself for what was to follow.

The two were doused with buckets of icy water. That brought Juga to immediate consciousness with a jolt and a yell as he, too, felt the repercussions of his injuries. Juga and Lathaniel made no further sounds, fearlessly locking eyes with their Are-Narc guards, who stood silently near the entrance to the cell, their watery, black, side-blinking eyes watching them.

The two beheld the Are-Narc soldiers before them. They were more human-like than their Cave-Narc cousins, standing almost upright with only a slight stoop forward. Thick-necked and thoroughly muscled, their clothing and armour made it difficult to tell if their spines were of the same reptilian shape as their unclothed relatives. Their skin was the same dirty grey, but their limbs were proportionate. Hands and feet were uncovered and similar to the Cave-Narcs. The breastplates of their armour were roughly made from two separate plates of pounded iron. Spiked pauldrons were bolted on to each to protect their broad necks. They wore rounded helmets with large eyeholes. The faceplate left their nostrils and mouth free but tapered down on either side of their heads to two fang-like spikes. Beneath the breastplates they wore a sheet of rough chainmail. Both their greaves and vambraces were designed with spiked thorns that, like their long, filthy fingernails, could inflict a deadly wound.

Shifting his gaze to Juga, Lathaniel quietly asked, "Drake?"

"I saw him here when I awoke before. He's alive."

"Where are we?"

"Not the royal chambers," Juga replied derisively, "... but still in the Minheras, I think."

"How badly are you hurt?"

"Hard to tell. Apart from a blinding headache, everything is numb but nothing broken. Just a few slices here and there."

The two were silent for a time, then Lathaniel whispered, still staring at their captors, "Assuming we get out of here, I now get why you would want to join the Resistance."

"Well, first I need to get myself another weapon. But then I'd still need to find a way to get to Cap'hannet to join the Gor'eans."

"Is Cap'hannet a city?"

"I'm not exactly sure, but I know it's the base of Resistance operations. It's said that it is run mostly by Gor'eans but that spies of other races come and go with war reports from across Elënthiá. I know that Drake has been there. Though he's never said, I've always wondered if he would take us there en route to Sitiska. Unless he turns up soon, we may never know."

An hour, maybe two passed in silence, both Juga and Lathaniel conserving energy for whatever lay ahead. A disturbance outside the cell could be heard before two Are-Narcs appeared in the doorway dragging a semiconscious and thoroughly beaten Drake between them. He was unceremoniously thrown to the floor by the third tether then wrestled into the same position as the two other captives and securely tied. The two Narcs departed leaving the original four still at their post by the entrance. The four remaining guards seemed lax and disinterested and paid little heed to the three; instead, lounging on the floor against the far wall of the chamber and talking amongst themselves in strange hisses and grunts.

"Master!" Juga whispered loudly. "Master! Can you hear me? Awaken! Can you hear me?"

Drake stirred lifting his head slightly. "Help..." he croaked. Then again, "Help...is coming..."

With that his chin dropped again to his chest. Lathaniel and Juga locked eyes, uncertain if they'd heard correctly. Regardless, the information gave them new resolve, and both began to subtly shift and move their limbs trying to coax feeling and circulation back into them. Hours of waiting rolled by. Drake was still, unmoving. By turns the two tried to rouse him but without success.

The Are-Narc guards were joined at evening by a new cohort who held bowls of fetid water before them, forcing them to lap at it like dogs. A chunk of stale bread was stuffed into both of their mouths nearly choking them, but slowly they chewed and swallowed it down, anxious to keep up their strength for the promised rescue.

The two were grateful when a fire was lit to take the chill from the room. The fire drew their attention to the roof of the cell which seemed to contain several shafts three or four feet in width. When the guards nodded off, their bellies full in the now warm chamber, the two whispered suggestions back and forth regarding how these could be used for escape—all fruitless given the strength of their bonds and the fact that even if they were free and had the means to climb up and out them, they'd never leave Drake behind.

He worried them. It had been hours since he'd been brought back to the cell, and yet he still had not moved. Both watched him closely and quietly commented that his wounds seemed to be less extensive than they had been when he first arrived, almost healing before their eyes. Yet still he did not move.

A strong hand came across Lathaniel's mouth, suppressing any sound he might have made and jolting him awake. For a split second he thought the Are-Narcs had come to take them away but quickly realized the hand belonged to no Narc.

They were being rescued! In the darkness he felt a blade slice through the bonds around his wrists and ankles. He nearly cried out, so painful were his shoulders from having been bound for so long. The hands massaged his shoulders and upper arms until feeling returned, then cupped his elbow when he stood until he could steady on his feet. He could sense several people in the darkness, all moving in utter silence. He could feel the moisture at his wrists and knew they were weeping blood from the tight bindings.

As his eyes accustomed themselves to the semidarkness, he could make out the shapes of both Drake and Juga. Drake, miraculously, seemed hale and hearty. Juga, like Lathaniel, was stiff and sore and seemed only slightly the worse for the wear. The Are-Narc sentries remained fast asleep, still leaning against the wall near the cell entrance.

Whoever had arrived to save them numbered twenty-five or more from what Lathaniel could tell. Though not a sound was uttered, all followed the hand signals of a single tall man. At his direction, several positioned themselves in front of the sleeping Narcs with arrows notched. At his signal arrows were loosed, killing the sleeping Narcs with deadly and silent accuracy. Only then did Juga and Lathaniel hear the mysterious stranger speak.

"I believe these are yours," he said quietly to Drake handing him his long-handled sword, Juga's sword, and the elongated leather-wrapped bundle that Drake always carried across his shoulders. "We also found this." He gestured to two of his men who, between them, struggled beneath the obvious weight of what was carried forward. They set a blanket on the ground before Drake and unwrapped it.

"I don't know how you were able to carry this. It has taken the best efforts of two of my men to bring it from the Are-Narcs. I assumed it was of some value or significance to you."

The blanket was pulled back revealing the long-handled anuléan hammer. Juga exclaimed from across the room and quickly moved to the weapon, easily grasping it by its handle and lifting it. "I thought this would be lost forever," he said, his attention riveted to the weapon, missing the looks exchanged between the stranger and Drake.

"I do not know what weapons you carried," the man spoke quietly to Lathaniel, "but we found only this bow and arrows."

These were returned to Lathaniel, who nodded gratefully.

"Wait," Drake quietly ordered. He reached into the bundle he had shrugged across his shoulders and extracted a single sword. It was a long, hand-and-a-half sword. Beyond the crescent-shaped hilt guard, it waisted slightly before stretching out into a thin, finely balanced, deadly blade which bore three intertwined vines. The hilt itself was braid-wrapped with royal blue leather. Where the leather met the hilt guard, an exquisite blue sapphire was inset.

He presented this to a dumbstruck Lathaniel. "You will have need of this."

"We can stay no longer in this place," the stranger interrupted before Lathaniel could reply. "We must leave immediately before we are discovered."

Led by the tall stranger, Drake then Lathaniel, Juga, and the remainder of their rescuers moved out of the cell and into the dark corridors beyond. The company moved soundlessly through the darkness stepping over more Are-Narc corpses en route. Juga and Lathaniel could sense an incline in the floor below them. The rise led them through a close series of short tunnels that opened onto a cavern of massive proportions. It seemed almost like a great granite chimney to Lathaniel. A wide stair spiralled both above and below them into the darkness. Noiseless, they began a rapid climb to the surface.

The broad spiral stair abruptly funnelled into a narrower step that hugged the cold mountain wall. At a gesture from the man in the lead, the soldiers quietly unsheathed their weapons and made ready for engagement. Drake and the lads did the same. As they approached the top of the steps, they could smell woodsmoke ... and Narcs. And they could hear the murmurs of those who warmed themselves by the fire, unaware of the danger about to descend upon them. The stair spilled out onto a wide platform, three sides of which overlooked the abyss beneath.

Hugging the wall, the company kept to the shadowed perimeter until all were on the platform. By Lathaniel's count two dozen men or more warmed themselves by the fire while as many others lingered around and outside of what appeared to be an exit to the open air beyond.

The Narcs didn't stand a chance. Drake, Lathaniel, and Juga fully supported the soldiers accompanying them, and before their weapons could even be drawn, to a one the Are-Narcs were slaughtered where they stood. Soldiers fanned out around the perimeter of the platform and then cautiously to the exit into the open air beyond, killing the remainder.

In the firelight, Juga and Lathaniel had their first real glimpse of the man who led their rescue. Lean and muscular, he was shorter than Drake yet only slightly taller than Lathaniel. His leggings were soft brown leather and his boots, knee-high. His over-shirt was a close-fitting dark green covered by a tunic of such a deep green as to almost be black. He was fair, the long hair at the front of his face gathered back from his forehead and held in a thong in back of his head. Light blue eyes were inset in a tanned, closely shaven face. His demeanour left no doubt that he was a warrior, but there was stillness and a steadiness that drew and held attention. He bore seven lamed pauldrons that looked as if they had been made to fit him perfectly. A magnificent quiver, designed with an engraved falcon, lay across his back as was his strung bow.

Drake and their mysterious rescuer conferred quietly for a moment before joining Lathaniel and Juga.

"It's time you met the esteemed Captain of our rescue team. Lads, I make known to you Hanna Janheoanus Caapri, a lauded Captain in the Elënthián Resistance. Captain Caapri, may I introduce Jugarth Framir and Lathaniel Waythan."

The Captain met the eyes of each and gave a slight nod of acknowledgement.

"I am pleased to make the acquaintance of any who accompany the Draconean though regret the circumstances of our meeting. I must excuse myself to see to my soldiers and prepare for our journey away from this place. By your leave," he said quietly as, after another slight incline of his head he quickly moved about his men who were foraging for additional weapons and supplies.

"I know his name is Captain Caapri," said Juga. "But who is that man?"

"That lads," replied Drake, "... is a Gor'ean."

# CHAPTER 20

The company emerged from the depths of the Anuléan kingdom to behold the blurry mists and the soft light that heralds dawn. Lathaniel raised his face to feel the caress of fresh air and to deeply inhale the rich smells of the earth, the forest, and life itself, only now realizing the depth of deprivation his soul felt after more than a week underground. As the mists lifted and the sun awoke, he could see that they were moving along the valley floor through a deep cleft between the mountains. Ramrod pines, still silver-dipped from the previous night's late spring frost, lined the steep slopes shoulder to shoulder, a silent audience to their passage.

The pace was brisk, and the troupe trekked along trails that quickly moved them farther up the bowl of the valley into thinner air and the more densely wooded higher country. The other Gor'ean warriors were dressed and armoured similar to Captain Caapri, their economy of movement and swift passage up the mountain path testament to their familiarity with the landscape. Juga and Lathaniel had no trouble remaining apace of the Gor'eans, though their single-file passage limited any opportunity to converse. Lathaniel assumed that they were remaining with the Gor'eans only until the threat of the Are-Narcs was behind them, after which they would continue on to Sitiska. But as Drake had taken the lead next to Captain Caapri, there had been no opportunity to speak to him.

Only a single short break was taken at midday to replenish water skins and allow for scouts to move both ahead and behind to ascertain if they were being followed and to cover their tracks. Then the company resumed the gruelling pace until heavy dusk made it impossible to continue. Camp was struck at the edge of a small clearing, but no fire was lit. While polite, the Gor'eans seemed to keep their distance; it was unsettling but at least allowed Lathaniel and Juga an opportunity to speak to Drake, who offered no additional insight into their hosts or destination. The Gor'ean Captain was being markedly vague, Drake reported, insisting only that the three remain with his company.

Three days of travel followed characterized by the same polite silence. The fourth day saw the troupe round the shoulder of a mountain following a path just below the skirt of the tree line and then begin a steady descent into the lush green, thickly forested valley below. The demeanour of the Gor'ean soldiers seemed to relax somewhat as they moved steadily toward lower altitudes.

Their narrow and overgrown path spilled out onto the mountain floor and into a thin ribbon of meadowed clearing. To their immediate left, the cliff faces of the Minheras rose starkly, a sheer vertical wall that kept the clearing in shadow until the sun passed their peaks at midday. About five hundred feet to their right stood the edge of the Gorger Forest, a dark, daunting, impenetrable bastion. Drake explained that the strip of land between the two was known as the Clarin Vargor, which loosely translated meant "peace among the trees," so named after the Clairadonean Treaty struck between the Anulé and Gor'eans an age or more earlier and allowing each unfettered access. The few entrances to it were known only to the Anulé - now long gone - and to a handful of only the most trusted Gor'eans.

An early halt was called in late afternoon, and hunters were sent into the forest to gather fresh meat for the evening meal. A warming fire was soon crackling, a welcome respite after the cold nights during their exodus. Uncertain how best to be of assistance, Juga and Lathaniel thought it better to find a spot and stay out of the way. Drake soon joined them.

It wasn't long before Captain Caapri came to sit with the three travellers. "You have surprised me." He directed this comment at Juga and Lathaniel. "We are unused to any other than a Gor'ean able to keep pace with us, yet you seem to do so without effort. Have you a hidden skill or are you of a special race?"

Juga replied first, smiling. "I am an ordinary Human apprenticed to an extraordinary Draconean."

The Gor'ean's lips lifted in a slight smile and his eyes shifted expectantly to Lathaniel who, though he met his gaze openly and without rancour, offered no explanation. Caapri's eyebrow lifted slightly at his silence, then went on to address the three.

"I take you to Cap'hannet. It is a four-day journey from this place." He paused as if considering whether or not to continue. "We were sent into Oderon with explicit instructions from our Fyyther himself to find and bring you there. I must ask your pardon of my soldiers, for we were given no reason for your summons. There are few of significant importance to receive such a summons. You either carry information of great import, or you have committed a severe transgression against our people. I ask for your understanding for, until we understand the reason, my soldiers remain cautious."

"We are no enemies of the Gor'eans," Drake quickly replied, his mien serious. "We were merely passing through Oderon on our way to Amarik. Whatever reason behind your Fyyther summons, it is not treason."

"Be that as it may, you will accompany us to Cap'hannet. The Fyyther's own son has been dispatched to meet you there."

Drake looked taken aback. "It has been many years since I was a guest in Gorgonathan, but I was unaware the King was blessed with a son."

Caapri did not reply but instead turned away, bringing the conversation to a close and leaving Drake alone with his two apprentices.

"We will go to Gorgonathan instead of Sitiska?" asked Lathaniel quietly when they were alone.

"We will go to Cap'hannet and meet this Prince," Drake replied. "Then we shall see."

Juga didn't bother to contain his excitement. "Cap'hannet!" he exclaimed. "Lathaniel, that is the seat of the Resistance. It is at Cap'hannet where the elite of the Resistance troops are trained and then dispatched. The best of the Gor'ean's best warriors train there." His voice trailed off. He was clearly caught up in his musings and had missed Drake's close scrutiny as he spoke.

The three were quiet then, each lost in his own thoughts. Staring into the flames that evening was the first opportunity for Lathaniel to process the momentous changes the past few weeks had brought to his life.

Slowly he began to accept that by uniting with the Human and the Draconean, the gods had fashioned his fate as a warrior, at least for now. He sighed as he recalled that not so very long ago his life had been so different, his days spent as a simple hunter. His heartache for the loss of his Lamana was a near tangible thing. He fell asleep dreaming of his home and refusing to consider whether his departure had guaranteed his family's safety or their demise.

The next three days fell into the simple routine of travelers. The company rose with the first light of dawn and kept a steady pace until the sun fell, stopping only to take water and a bite to eat at midday. Their pace was such that there was little opportunity to converse. In the evenings the Gor'ean warriors, though exceedingly polite, continued to keep both their distance and their silence. On the morning of the fourth day, the forest, which had so steadily kept its distance on their right, began to veer sharply inward until it crowded them into the mountain walls and then completely blocked their passage.

The company fell into a single file as Captain Caapri led them along a barely discernible path that threaded through the tangle of trees and undergrowth. Of a sudden, the trees gave way to a solid wall of rock that reached from their feet into the sky, how high Lathaniel could not have guessed. There was a surreal hush in the air; no forest sounds, not so much as a whisper of wind moved the leaves. Hugging the wall, they followed it until they stood at a precise spot beneath massive wooden gates. There was no blare of horns nor fanfare to herald their arrival nor special code to announce their purpose. Only a deep voice that seemed to reach through the thick wood to quietly demand, "Speak!" The Gor'ean Captain leaned close to the wood and quietly replied, "Captain Caapri returning from Oderon"

"... and the password?" was the deep-voiced reply.

"Reairyss" Caapri quietly replied.

With a great creak and a moan, a smaller door inset within the massive wooden gates swept inward. Captain

Caapri turned to the three and said with a sweeping gesture, "Welcome to Cap'hannet."

Juga did not know what he had expected these many months when his imagination painted Cap'hannet, but it was nothing like what lay before him. With the opening of the gates came a flood of sights, sounds, and smells: shops in full commerce, horses pulling wagons laden with barrels and crates, and the inhabitants, soldiers and civilians alike, briskly and purposefully moving about their business.

The backdrop to the scene was a mighty waterfall that even from their distance seemed to find its origins at the very peaks of the Minheras before it fell in a sheer drop to crash into a massive pool at its base, creating a cooling mist. Cap'hannet had been built into a natural grotto inset into the mountainside. With the waterfall and the pool forming the back of it, sheer rock faces stretched out on either side where they stopped just short of embracing, the solid wooden gates completing what was now a massive, almost circular enclosure. Juga could see Lathaniel was doing much the same as he, his head swivelling left and right, eyes drinking in all that they beheld.

As they moved beyond the cluster of shops near the gates, flat arenas filled with soldiers engaged in various military drills could be seen, some in swordplay, others in hand-to-hand combat, and yet others marching in formation. The perimeter of the training fields was lined on three sides with low, rectangular, utilitarian structures that could only be barracks. There was a crisp, military orderliness about the entire scene that underscored the deadly discipline of a well-trained fighting force.

The company drew to a halt parallel with these training grounds, and Caapri issued a sharp order, dismissing his men who, with nods to the three, excused themselves and moved to join their comrades.

"I am to take you directly to the residence of the High Prince," said Caapri as he again moved along. Drake met both Lathaniel and Juga's eyes and the two refocused, once again wondering why they had been summoned to meet the mysterious Prince.

The Prince's residence sat atop a slight rise well to the right of the waterfall and appeared to have been partially hewn out of the actual mountain face. Nearly the full front of it was comprised of a large half-circle of steps, four high. Atop the steps was a platform open on three sides. Lathaniel thought it a perfect stage from which to address troops and wondered if that was its purpose. They climbed the steps and crossed the platform to massive oak doors with guards on either side.

Caapri drew himself to attention and saluted, crisply announcing their arrival. "Captain Caapri with three guests to see His Highness, the Prince."

Saying nothing the guards crisply stepped back with their right feet, pivoted, and grasped the brass handles on the doors to push them inward, moving in perfect unison. The company entered a small courtyard. To their left was a fountain and seating area. Enormous pots held leafy trees. Numerous, slightly smaller pots brimmed with bushes and flowering shrubs, effectively mirroring the Gorger Forest outside the camp's walls. They passed through the lush courtyard and another set of double doors where they entered a gallery lined with dark wood panels. Torches in elaborate sconces lit the room, allowing Lathaniel and Juga to view massive paintings of battles and landscapes that hung on either side. Lathaniel could hardly contain himself; he wanted nothing but to stop and examine each of them and find a willing tutor to answer the million or more questions that had his mind so full it was nearly seeping out of his ears.

Doors to their right were thrown open, and the four swung immediately toward them. Captain Caapri saluted smartly then dropped to one knee and, with his right hand on his heart, bowed his head.

Their host was slightly over six feet in height and well muscled. His fair hair hung past his shoulders, and eyes the blue of a summer's day shone from a lightly tanned, unmarked face. His under garments, tunic, and leggings were the same shades of green, beige, and brown of his soldiers, and his demeanour and carriage bespoke a leader. He addressed Caapri first.

"Rise, Hanna Janheoanus. I convey your Fyyther's gratitude for bringing our guests safely to me. Please, join your men and take your rest. Your duties here are finished."

Captain Caapri rose and with another slight nod of deference turned smartly on his heel and excused himself. Their host gestured for them to enter the room. For their part, though their greeting had thus far been amicable, the three companions remained wary.

"It has been a long, long time since my eyes beheld your face, Drake Sorzin," their royal host began as he stepped forward.

Bewildered, Drake still said nothing.

"Do you not recognize me, my old friend?" asked the Prince. "It is I, Athron. Athron Mar."

# CHAPTER 21

Pouris Gaul was on his knees. The sweat that beaded on his forehead and ran between his shoulders was not indicative of exertion but rather the icy chill of fear he felt as he faced the wrath of his Master. For his part Gorillian appeared calm, relaxed almost. He had interrogated Gaul extensively until he had heard every detail of the capture and subsequent escape of the Draconean and his apprentices in Oderon. Gaul's thin, stringy hair fell limply across his face and eyes as he sensed the questioning was coming to an end. Uncomfortable with the silence in the room as Gorillian paced the floor behind him, he chanced a plea for mercy.

"We did all that we could, my Lord," he whined. "But the Draconean still has many allies in Elënthiá. And what of the strange being that travels with him? Who knows what alliances he has made with the Gor'eans? I exist only to serve you, my Lord. I have ever been faithful and loyal. I will redeem myself if you would show me the face of your mercy."

His last plea tapered off to a mere whisper. Gorillian paced a moment more than walked behind Gaul and snatched a handful of his oily hair, yanking his head up and backwards.

"Is this the face of mercy?" he demanded, his obsidian eyes boring relentlessly into Pouris Gaul's. "No ... this is the face of vengeance, the face of retribution and of power, the face that brings fear to all that look upon it. But it is not the face of failure. And it is not the face of mercy..."

The dagger barely whispered as it left its leather scabbard and sliced both the air and Gaul's throat. Deftly stepping away to avoid the gush of blood that shot forward as the artery was severed and a dark stain crept across the stone floor, Gorillian thrust the body away with disgust.

Gorillian was an Immortal of few remaining emotions, save cunning and hate. But a bubble of acid anger rose within him as he contemplated what Gaul had just told him. *Drake Sorzin!* How he despised that name! He had once called his father, Dray, friend. He had been Dray's guest in Evendeer; feted and celebrated. With his Immortality, their relationship changed. It was the Draconean king who betrayed him by announcing his secret alliances to all of Elënthiá. Were these to have remained secret, Gorillian would not have become an outcast and lost all. Ah yes! ... he had his retribution. He had wiped out Dray's entire race – save one. Surely it couldn't be *this* difficult to eliminate one last Draconean. Over the years he had lost thousands of troops directly and indirectly to the cur. And now, yet again, Sorzin had moved beyond his grasp.

His ability to evade had obviously rubbed off on the Human who travelled with him. But most interesting was Gaul's description of his third companion. If he was neither Elf nor Human but carried the characteristics of both, then the rumours of a race called the Forsairs were true. This, more than anything, was unsettling.

Gorillian's spy network within Elënthiá was extensive. On two or three occasions across thousands of years had he received intelligence regarding a race of peoples calling themselves Forsairs, but he'd never placed much credence in it. If indeed it was true, what did that mean? Had the Forsairs established allegiance with the Resistance? Was there a secret army training to move against him? If this was the case, the three rescued companions were now united with the Gor'eans and in the hands of the Resistance.

*Resistance*! He nearly spat at the thought of the label for the rabble that fought against him. It was *his* fate to lead the whole of Elënthiá! It was only a matter of time. His armies now held more of Elënthiá than in any previous age, and he was unstoppable. The Draconean and his companions were only annoyances that he would deal with in time, he told himself.

He flung himself across his throne, his arms loosely draped over the cold granite armrests and his legs askance. He recalled the exact day when he'd made the deal with the Tarnigs to join the attack of his Black March and destroy Evendeer. Dray Sorzin and his six sons were taken captive and brought to his fortress in Ethen-jar. From his many visits to Evendeer, Gorillian knew the Draconeans had amassed a treasure beyond belief. He had obliterated the Draconeans but that wasn't enough; he also wanted their treasure. But even under torture, the Draconean king would not disclose its whereabouts.

He had staked the king to a tree and made him watch as, one by one, his sons were tortured and killed. The Draconean had later pretended to be mad with grief at the loss of his sons, and Gorillian had foolishly lowered his guard. Dray Sorzin escaped and took the swords of his six sons with him. Then it was as if he fell off the face of Elënthiá.

Gorillian scoured Elënthiá for him for months until, unexpectedly, the old king was spotted roaming the wilderness on the island of Koorast. He followed Sorzin's trail from Koorast back to the island of Moldost, and it was only then he discovered that the seventh son still lived.

He caught up with the Draconean king in time to see him pass something to his son - a bundle of some sort. The son escaped. The deposed king had been clothed in filthy rags when he found him; no vestige of the mighty race he led remained. Yet he stood tall and proud, quietly mouthing a Draconean prayer as Gorillian approached him. As he watched Gorillian draw his sword, he looked him in the eyes and smiled. The memory of that smile ... of the Draconean standing placidly as Gorillian's sword pierced his heart, still haunted him.

Even as a young boy, the last Draconean had eluded him. Pursuit of the fully grown son across century after century had driven him to a point near insanity. It was as if he were a pawn of Ruahr himself in some perverse game of chase and release. He had tried to believe that the fabled treasure had been lost forever but his dreams told him otherwise...and with the reappearance of the last Draconean at a critical juncture in the battle for Elënthiá, he could not longer assume anything. If the treasure did exist and the Draconean had discovered the means to get to it, Gorillian did not want to contemplate what could happen ... what an infusion of such resources would do to turn the tide of this war.

He pondered all angles of the thing, and then began to wonder if Ruahr had perhaps placed the last Draconean in his path at this point not to foil him but to assist him. To foil the last Draconean and take the treasure at this point, when the war was so firmly in his favour, would seal Elënthiá's fate!

As the near-black blood from the cooling corpse in front of him crept slowly across the cold flagstone and congealed into puddles at his feet, Gorillian's madness lent a strange glow to his black eyes and brought an evil half-smile to his lips. He stared off into space contemplating how next he could trap the Draconean and his companions, and how he could use this new player, this Forsair, to his advantage.

# CHAPTER 22

"Can it be you?" Drake grasped Athron by the shoulders as he searched his face. The two embraced briefly, each giving the other hard claps on the back. "How can this be? Look at you!" he said, his eyes scanning the face before him. "I can hardly find the boy I once knew."

Lathaniel was wondering how Drake could be excused from treating a High Prince with such ribald familiarity but was relieved at their reception. Drake seemed to remember he was not alone and stepped back to draw Juga and Lathaniel forward.

"May I make you known to my apprentices: the Human, Jugarth Framir..." he said with a grin as Juga executed a respectful bow. "...and Lathaniel Waythan," he paused as Lathaniel also bowed and then added, "...a Forsair. Lads, I give you His Highness Athron Mar, the High Prince of the Gor'ean people and our host at Cap'hannet."

Ignoring protocol, Athron reached out and firmly shook first Juga's hand and then Lathaniel's, whose he held for a time, looking at him closely. "A Forsair, did you say? This is quite an honour for me, lad, for I'd always thought Forsairs to be a folktale. I was unaware that any existed."

"But for the assistance of your soldiers Your Highness, this Forsair may not have," Lathaniel replied warmly. "It's a pleasure to meet you."

"Come!" Athron welcomed, drawing them further into the room. "There are twelve years' worth of tales to be told, and I would hear them all." He gestured to two soldiers standing off to either side of the entrance. "Take my two young friends to quarters where they can bathe and change clothes; then return them here so that we may take our meal together."

Lathaniel and Juga looked immediately to Drake, their hesitation obvious.

"Go, lads," he said. "You need have no fear in this place, for you are among friends."

With a respectful bow to the High Prince and a nod to Drake, the two departed.

Drake turned back to Athron and the two shared warm smiles and another hard, hearty embrace. As they pulled apart, Drake responded to the seriousness he saw in his friend's face.

"What is it?"

"There is much to tell you, old friend, but first the most urgent. Have you any idea why you have been summoned to Gorgonathan?"

Drake frowned. "I agreed to accompany Captain Caapri to Cap'hannet, my friend. I never agreed to go as far as Gorgonathan. I am here mostly out of curiosity for I was told I would be met by the son of the Gor'ean King. What last I knew of the Gor'ean court, King Forginn ruled and he had no son. At some point you must tell me how Acthelass came to be King, but for now know this; I do *not* respond to summons, and I have no intention of continuing to Gorgonathan."

The ease and warmth so recently shared between the two abruptly cooled as each stepped a pace back.

"Drake, the past will not simply disappear. There are Gor'eans on the Supreme Council who still call for a formal hearing into the incident. Twelve years has not dimmed their memories."

"I have explained what happened on the battlefield that day," Drake countered. "It was a tragedy. But the business of war is filled with tragedies."

"Then go to the Council. State your case. Clear the record once and for all."

"I am a Draconean! An Immortal!" Drake raised his voice now, clearly annoyed. "I do not respond to summons from the Supreme Council, nor do I answer to its members. I have neither a case to state nor a record to clear! How conveniently does the Council erase, then resurrect! Do the Immortals among them not recall sending emissaries to track me down and plead for me to intermediate with the Elves during the Great Wars? Do they remember that the tide of the war turned in the favour of the Resistance thereafter? Theirs are memories of convenience! I explained what happened. Once. I will not stand before them with my cap in my hands, responding to questions long-answered to ask forgiveness for an outcome that was neither my fault nor by my design!" The Draconean turned on his heel and stalked to the fireplace in the corner. There was silence for a time.

Athron was torn. Drake Sorzin was closer to a father than any he had known, though his own was hale and hearty and not three days' ride away. The Draconean and he had found an affinity from the earliest days of their acquaintance. He had saved Athron's life when he was little more than a toddler, gifted him his first real sword when he was deemed old enough to wield it, and scrupulously schooled him in the arts of a war as a young boy. The Draconean was the patient but firm parent Athron had always wished his father could be.

Athron detested having been put in the position of bringing Drake back to Gorgonathan, but his father, his King, had ordered it. In fact, Athron felt his father was testing his allegiance by insisting that it be he who brought the Draconean before the Council.

"It grows late in the day, and you have travelled far," he said quietly. "Though I am charged with bringing you back to Gorgonathan with me, those orders do not stipulate that you must do so as a prisoner. Quarters have been readied for you, the same as you occupied in years passed. I bid you go there now. We will speak again."

The Draconean did not reply. He turned to his former protégée and looked him steadily in the eye. With a marked nod of deference to his new station as High Prince, he left the room.

The three returned to the High Prince's chambers for the evening meal. The food was simple but plentiful, as was the wine, and the stilted formality the two young warriors had initially felt in the presence of Gor'ean royalty disappeared as the evening progressed. Juga and Lathaniel were soon animated in recounting their adventures in the Minheras to their host, who chuckled at their descriptions and recollections.

Both Juga and Lathaniel noted that Drake was decidedly more reserved with Athron than he had been on arrival. As conversation shifted to the politics of the Resistance and the most recent edicts of the Supreme Council, the atmosphere became more serious.

"Forgive me for my ignorance, Highness," Lathaniel said. "Drake and Juga have told me much of Elënthiá, but I know little of the Supreme Council. Of whom is it comprised?"

"If you are aware of the different realms throughout Elënthiá, then you are already well on the way to understanding its composition, Lathaniel. The leaders of all realms and races across Elënthiá are automatically eligible to sit on the Council. Some choose to abstain and continue to live in isolation. Others are uncomfortable with the politics of the Council and elect to attend only if there are matters directly related to the sovereignty of their realms. For the most part, however, its members come together to discuss matters of common importance to us all: matters of economy and commerce, matters of law and order, and unfortunately, these days, matters of war."

"How often does the Council meet and where?" Lathaniel pressed.

"In times of peace, it typically meets once in each season and always at Gorgonathan. The meetings used to be hosted by a different Council member each season, but this became difficult. Gorgonathan is large, and it is secure. Especially in times of war, safety is a concern for all its members. My father and the Gor'ean Kings before him have embraced the role of host, for we are a warrior nation, committed to preserving our own sovereignty as well as peace in Elënthiá. Gorgonathan was a natural choice."

"Speaking of Gor'ean Kings, this is a perfect opportunity to share with us how your father came to be King," Drake interjected quietly.

Athron's face seemed to sadden, but his tone was flat. "I rose through the ranks such that I was assigned the post of King Forginn's personal guard. We were ambushed returning from Nesmeresa, and the King was killed." Though he tried to school his features, it was obvious the loss still pained him. "My father was personal advisor to King Forginn and himself a distinguished army General. On the King's demise and in the absence of a blood heir to his throne, it was decreed that my father, Acthelass Mar, be King Forginn's successor."

Given the power Mar held within the army, his role as Chief Advisor to the King, and in the absence of any other suitable contenders, Drake wasn't surprised. The conversation shifted back to the war and the Supreme Council.

"What remains of the Council is strong," Athron reported, "but former leaders of the realms now under Gorillian's control are either dead or in hiding. Those who still hold their thrones have devoted all their attention to saving their own peoples and all their available troops to safeguarding their own kingdoms. This has placed the whole of Elënthiá in peril. The Elves support the Resistance by defending their own borders but are otherwise mired in a bloody civil war that shows no signs of abatement. As you well know, our own lands present natural barriers to invasion and have always withstood Gorillian's advances. But ours is a culture of warriors, men whose profession as warriors is their livelihood. With supply lines all but eliminated and Gorger's own financial resources severely depleted, the future of the Resistance is grim indeed. Apart from the Nesmeresa, Gorger remains one of the last strongholds. After all that I have shared, you can imagine the state of the rest of Elënthiá."

There was silence for a time after his bleak update.

Drake raised his glass of wine and drained it before setting it firmly on the table in front of him. "Athron, my old friend, I have not crossed half of Koorast to visit with you, nor is it my intention to divert my journey for a useless trip to Gorgonathan."

Athron sat forward and began to mouth a protest, but Drake stayed him by raising his hand. "I would ask for your assistance. We must travel and travel with haste to the far western side of this island. Your knowledge of the terrain and your exceptional abilities as a warrior will go far in aiding our cause."

Athron interrupted then, incredulous. "After all I told you earlier this evening and knowing that aiding you would directly contravene an order from my father, the Fyyther of Gorger, you can *still* ask this of me?"

Drake looked round the room to ensure they were indeed alone; then he lowered his voice and leaned toward Athron. "I have a map, an ancient map that leads to the accumulated treasures of my entire race."

Now he had the attention of Athron, whose eyes widened. "Where did you acquire such a map?"

"It was given to me by my father."

"Your father? Your father died nearly two thousand years ago. How is it that you came to have it only now?"

"A map was pressed into my hands by my father only moments before Gorillian took his life. It was encoded with riddled directions that have taken me nearly two millennia to decipher. But the riddle is a riddle no more. I know where the treasure is held, or at least I have irrefutable clues to its location. I have no doubt that Gorillian is tracking me and it will only be a matter of time before he ascertains that there is purpose to my travels. Were he to become aware of the treasure, he would know that such resources in the hands of the Resistance could turn the tide of a war that finally shows clear signs of victory for him."

Drake leaned forward, eyes locking with Athron. "Help me. Help me, and I will provide you with sufficient resources to fund not only the Gor'ean Resistance efforts but those of the entire Supreme Council. But know this: if you help me, if you leave with me on this quest, it must be done immediately and in absolute secrecy, for time is of the essence and I trust no one."

Athron stood suddenly, his chair thrust backwards and sliding across the stone floor behind him as he began to pace in agitation. "Do you know what you ask of me, Draconean?

To do as you ask means I must disobey a direct order from my King. I must place my lot in league with an Immortal already in ill favour with my people. And you!" Athron turned now, returning to the table which he leaned across confrontationally. "What want have *you* with treasure? You have eschewed wealth for all the years I have known you and beyond. Is it treasure that you seek now?"

"I have never required wealth, nor is it wealth I now seek," Drake replied quietly. "I have received information from an impeccable source advising that there are documents to be found with the treasure, documents including another map...a map that will lead to a lost Draconean city. It seems, my young friend, that I am not the last Draconean after all."

He was silent then, watching a range of emotions play across the young Prince's face, for Athron knew well the history of Drake's people and of their fate. He also knew that an Elënthiá that could once again rely on the remarkable skills and support of Draconean Immortal soldiers could forever be at peace. And with a treasure also at its disposal...Athron swung away, again pacing in silence.

Drake pushed himself back and stood. Lathaniel and Juga, who had been witness to the exchange and listening in wide-eyed silence, did the same.

"I have left you with much to consider, your Highness," Drake said quietly. "I can spare one week only. I will give you this time to consider your options. Thereafter I will depart Cap'hannet with or without you."

He turned and left the room, Juga and Lathaniel at his flank.

# CHAPTER 23

Acthelass Mar, Fyyther of the Gor'ean people, paused at the threshold of the entrance to the Elënthián Supreme Council chambers. An immaculate cloak of white fox fur fell loosely across his shoulders. Simple but opulent royal blue robes beneath the cloak fell to the floor and were laced with gold threading around the cuffs and collars. He bore an ornate sword at his waist. There was a small Gor'ic symbol just above the hilt, and its distinctive pommel featured the four colors of the different sects of the Gor'ean Army: black, bronze, silver, and gold. Another smaller dagger was strapped above his right hip, concealed by his cloak.

Time had not been kind to Mar, and his body was failing. Most of his fifty-six years had been spent serving his nation as a warrior. His face was deeply scarred, his eyes were the cold blue of winter ice, and his thin lips were perpetually drawn into a grim line. He had timed his arrival such that he would be the last to take his seat on the Council. He had relished each and every moment of his role these last nine years as Fyyther of the Gor'eans, especially his role within the Council. While fundamentally his belief in the Council was absolute, it was the power and the politics he relished most. He felt no small pleasure in knowing that the rulers of Elënthiá awaited his arrival beyond the doors in front of him. He nodded slightly to the Herald, who thrust open the Council chamber doors.

"The Gor'ean King and Fyyther, His Royal Highness Acthelass Mar." The Herald's voice rang through the elaborate chambers, drawing the attention of the elite that had gathered.

The circular Elënthián Supreme Council chambers were built around a small center platform upon which stood the Adjudicator, of no rank or title but appointed and empowered by the Council for administrative oversight and to ensure order in the Council's meetings.

The Chambers were built at the apex of five of the tallest and most ancient treetops in Gorgonathan. Their ceiling was open to the sky providing natural light for meetings, the elements kept at bay by a spell of Elven magic. The amphitheatre was richly appointed with balconies for each of its members and galleries along its uppermost reaches for spectators when allowed.

Acthelass's gaze swept the chamber, noting more were absent than usual, no doubt as a result of Gorillian's expanding evil across their land. The Elven Queen attended, coolly distant and lavishly attired as always. She was flanked by an entourage of Elven Lords, their blond hair catching and reflecting the light. Her husband was absent, concerns over the Elven civil wars and security for their monarchy the likely reason.

Fae and Gnoman delegates were present, but their royalty was noticeably absent, doubtless fearing travel in such uncertain times. No Centaurs attended. Representation from the Sixteen Realms of Men was strong with twelve Kings and their entourages in attendance. Gor'ean Lords were present to a one and stood in deference, heads bowed and right fists over their hearts at their Fyyther's arrival.

The Adjudicator called the meeting to order. "Your Highnesses, Excellencies, Lords and Ladies of our great Elënthiá, I call this meeting of the Elënthián Supreme Council to order."

A great, sonorous gong was struck, echoing through the Chambers and marking the beginning of the meeting.

"We have but two items on our agenda this day, both of dire importance. Scouts newly arrived this morning bring news of the Are-Narc attack and slaughter of three Elven supply caravans passing through the outer reaches of the Nesmeresan realm."

There were gasps of dismay heard across the room. The Adjudicator raised his hand for silence.

"Strategy of how best to deal with increasing power of the evil Lord Gorillian will be discussed in due time. But first a matter has come to the attention of the Council, and several Gor'ean members have demanded discussion."

The delegates settled in to hear more.

"Reports from Cap'hannet reveal of the arrival of three individuals accompanied by a Gor'ean scouting party. One is a Human. The other…" he paused for effect, "a Forsairean." Again more gasps and murmurs across the Chambers. He waited until he had silence once again.

"And the last is a Draconean."

The room erupted into outcries and catcalls of disbelief as many members called across the Chambers and turned to discuss the information with their entourages.

Acthelass Mar stood.

The Adjudicator, loudly intoned, "His Highness the Gor'ean Fyyther wishes to speak."

The room gradually quieted.

"With respect, may I ask for details on the Gor'eans who comprised the escort party?"

The Adjudicator consulted his parchments and then replied, "Our scouts advise it was led by Captain Hanna Janheoanus Caapri."

The Gor'ean Fyyther announced, "It was I who ordered the three to be found and taken to Cap'hannet." The hall fell silent at the King's words.

A Gnoman representative ignored protocol and rose to his feet. "We must have more information! How is this possible? Were not all Draconeans destroyed by Lord Gorillian centuries ago?"

Before the Adjudicator could return the gathering to order, the King of the Realm of Asgoth stood and called out, "If one Draconean lives, perhaps there is truth to the ancient tale of that more exist." The room once again erupted with discussion and shouts.

The Adjudicator banged his gavel, repeatedly calling for both order and silence. Acthelass Mar remained standing; by protocol he was the last to be given the floor and held it still. As silence fell and attention returned to him, he spoke once again.

"To my knowledge there is but one Draconean alive today. And it is long past the time that discussion of him be brought before this Council." That statement riveted all attention on him. "For my part, my first memory of the Draconean dates back nearly thirty years. He arrived at one of our Resistance camps holding my son in his arms; the boy had been lost in the Gorger forests. I was Chief Advisor to King Forginn at the time. We had dispatched soldiers to search for my son, but all had returned empty-handed. There was great joy in Athron's safe return, and the Fyyther requested the stranger be brought before him. It was during his audience with the Fyyther that he revealed himself as a Draconean. Both the Fyyther and our Gor'ean scholars questioned him at length and determined that he was indeed who he claimed to be: an Immortal, the only surviving son of the Dray Sorzin, the last Draconean King."

The room erupted once again in incredulous discussion. When there was silence, Mar continued.

"In researching his heritage, our scholars reported countless instances in the previous two millennia where a man – they surmised it was the Draconean - surfaced to be of assistance to the Gor'eans. At times he was summoned when situations were at their most dire. At other times he simply arrived at a critical juncture. On every occasion, his presence had the effect of turning the tide of the conflict in favour of the Gor'eans. And on every occasion, the opponent was Gorillian. The Gor'ean tomes speculated that he was even an Elven General at one point in time."

At that an Elven Lord took offense "And speculation it shall remain! A Draconean has never stood at the head of our armies!" As he sat, he turned in question to his monarch. Queen Allivaris kept an expressionless look on her face and said nothing. The room was filled with politicians used to the nuances of life within the Council. Not a single one missed the significance of her silence. The room quieted once again, anxious to hear more of this incredible tale.

"Knowledge of his true heritage remained known to only a few – most in Gorger simply thought him a Human from one of the Realms of Men. He trained and fought alongside Gor'eans and lived among us. There was no reason to bring him to the attention of the Council. King Forginn embraced the Draconean and gave him control of a full legion of Gor'eans. I can tell you that his skills as a warrior far exceed that of even the strongest and most seasoned Gor'ean. In my own years as a soldier I have travelled far and fought alongside the best that Elënthiá has produced. His abilities are formidable, beyond those of the Elves, perhaps even Gorillian."

The silence and tension in the room was almost palpable as Mar continued, "He is quite simply the perfect soldier." Mar paused allowing his words to settle with the Council before he continued.

"The Draconean is a ruthless warrior. Much of the manner in which Gor'ean warriors are now trained can be traced back to his influence. He fought at our side for eight years until Gorillian was all but paralyzed within Elënthiá once again. Twelve years ago, hearing that a legion of Gor'ean soldiers was embattled in a skirmish led by the Gorillian himself, the Draconean marched his own soldiers out into a blinding snowstorm. Days later we had word of a Gor'ean legion having been ambushed by Are-Narcs. Our Scouts came upon a gruesome battleground. The original legion was found dead, but their bodies riddled with Gor'ean arrows – from the legion lead by the Draconean." There were gasps across the chambers.

"The Draconean's legion was also found dead, slaughtered to a one by Are-Narcs. The only survivor was Drake Sorzin. The circumstances were suspicious, as it appeared that the Draconean had led an attack on our own forces. Soldiers were sent to detain him and return him here to Gorgonathan for an investigation and trial if need be. They did not find him, but he returned of his own accord.

"The Draconean explained to Lord Cindrick, who was the General in charge of Cap'hannet at that time, that Gorillian had held the Gor'ean legion at the center of his troops on purpose so that any concerted attack by arrows would be fatal to our own troops. Unaware of this, the Draconean's legion attacked Gorillian without mercy and unknowingly, according to the Draconean, killed our own Gor'ean soldiers. The Draconean claimed he only survived the attack on his own legion only by virtue of the fact that he is an Immortal. The General arrested him so that he could be returned to Gorgonathan to face a tribunal on the incident. How, we do not know, but the Draconean escaped Cap'hannet and has not been seen nor heard of until these last days when word spread of his travel through the Minheras."

As Mar continued, the Adjudicator whispered something to an assistant who scurried from the room.

"When I heard the Draconean had resurfaced and was passing through Oderon, I ordered him intercepted and escorted here to Gorgonathan. I have dispatched my own son, the High Prince Athron Mar, to Cap'hannet to see to this task. He will not fail me."

---

Gorillian briskly walked through the corridors of his fortress at Ethen-jar. The Draconean was being held at Cap'hannet. Gorillian knew that the Gor'ean King would not pass up an opportunity to question the Immortal on the incident twelve years passed. If they got him to Gorgonathan, the Draconean would be lost to him. He had not yet penetrated the bastion of Gorger let alone the fortress of Gorgonathan. He had to act before the Draconean slipped through his grasp yet again.

Sorzin's movements showed purpose. Gorillian's second sense about this had been confirmed in yet another dream the previous night. The Draconean was indeed moving to claim the fabled treasure. If he accessed it and, worse, utilized it to support the Resistance, the war would be all but lost. Further, there were now whispers that where he found the treasure, he would also find information about a lost city; a city with other Draconeans. If such was the case, the consequences were beyond imagining.

He swung to his right entering an antechamber. The lone occupant immediately dropped to one knee, bending his head in supplication before drawing to his feet once again. This was Karget Gash, one of the few in his entourage in his trust. He was his chief advisor, a General in his army and his greatest warrior. The man was a solid mass of muscled fighting machine nearly seven feet in height weighing near to three hundred pounds. His skin was polished black, and he was entirely hairless; the absence of lashes, brows and moustaches lending further intimidation to his features. His scalp, face, and bulging arms were a landscape of scars. There was not a single spark of humanity to be found in his flat brown eyes, which at this moment were trained on his King and Master.

Report!" Gorillian barked impatiently.

"Highness, your forces in the Vearian Region are holding. We've lost yet another scouting party in the Ashen Mountains. The unpredictable weather there prohibits a full investigation, but avalanches are presumed the cause. When we can get in, scouts will investigate. We've shifted six thousand troops to the borders at Nesmeresa. We have word that battles amongst the Elves are especially bloody of late and their attention is drawn within. With your leave, we will strike now when they are most vulnerable. Meanwhile, the naval embargo around on Koorast is proceeding as planned. We await your direction on the next phase of the battle plan there." Gash knew to keep his reports succinct and to keep his tongue while his Master assimilated the information.

" It will be a day of celebration when I bring Allivaris and Naris to heel. Send riders to Nesmeresa with orders for all six legions to attack. Continue the campaign on Koorast but focus all efforts on the Gorger borders. Find me a way into Cap'hannet! If we can learn the location of a passage into that camp, we can destroy it and completely disrupt Resistance efforts and leadership. The Gor'ean realm must fall!"

Gorillian paused for a moment before continuing. "Overt military action against Gorger will draw out the Draconean. I know him. As in all previous campaigns, he won't be able to resist coming to the rescue of the Gor'eans. That will give me the opening I need."

With a gesture he dismissed Gash who turned to leave the room. "Send my scribe in as you depart. I must contact my Generals."

# CHAPTER 24

Juga felt that if there were a heaven for warriors, he was in it. He detested giving in to exhaustion at night and could hardly wait for each new day to begin. Cap'hannet! How long had he dreamed of being in this place, of training with these warriors!

His easy manner and open-faced smile had won over the reluctance of the Gor'ean warriors to include him in their training. He was an apt pupil, already so skilled and eager beyond measure that soon he was the target of lighthearted jests and pranks and readily included in each day's rigorous training exercises.

Juga had developed a taste for gambling and spent the hours after each evening meal cavorting with the soldiers. His years as a thief had left him with a sleight of hand that allowed him to occasionally cheat when the game wasn't going his way. The stakes were always small, so no great loss was incurred, but the Gor'eans sensed they were being fleeced by the cocky Human teen though they could never quite catch him in the act. The tension had almost erupted in fights on several occasions but always ended without proof and with the Gor'eans believing Juga the lucky recipient of a winning streak.

Lathaniel remained on the fringes, more a willing observer than a participant. His keen, inquisitive mind looked beyond what was happening around him and more for the how and why of life at Cap'hannet. Like Juga, the fact that he had free rein to wander coupled with his youth and genuine interest in all that he saw, soon won over the Gor'eans and all gladly took time to answer his questions as best they were able.

The week of waiting gave him much needed time to regroup, to process all that he had experienced and heard during the past incredible months. More so than Juga, he understood clearly now that his fate was finely interwoven with that of the Draconean. The Immortal's past was revealed in bits and pieces through conversations with people like Athron - frustrating, but intriguing. Lathaniel catalogued all that he saw and heard, slowly adding pieces to the puzzle. His thoughts frequently turned to Lamana and his people. He perpetually swung between the belief that he had done the only thing possible by leaving Lamana and the sickening feeling that he had abandoned them.

For his part, Drake used the respite to revisit secret exits out of Cap'hannet that he knew from his periodic stays there over the centuries. He also pored over the map he carried and strategized on how best to travel to Sitiska and where to begin their quest for the entrance to the Tombs on arrival.

Thoughts of his youngest apprentice caused his mouth to curve into a smile. Juga had dropped sufficient hints that he wanted to join the Gor'ean Resistance. He was fascinated by the weapon the lad had carried out of Oderon. While it took the best efforts of two of the strongest Gor'ean soldiers to heft it, Juga easily carried and wielded the ancient Anulean hammer as if it were weightless. He had confronted the boy with the fact that he had taken the ancient weapon out of the Minheras, effectively robbing the last Anulean King. The lad was only partly contrite, arguing that the action was not done with forethought, only as an accident of fate during their flight from the Are-Narcs.

Examination of the great handle of the hammer had shown it inscribed with the Anulean word "*Ehamsen*" for "iron shaft." Anulean legend had that a tool chose its master and, once affiliated, it could be wielded by no other. Some Anulé magic evidently saw Juga worthy of the ancient weapon.

The young Forsair continued to intrigue Drake. He kept to himself, often spending hours alone by the waterfall or in the wooded areas within the camp. When not alone, he was forever questioning the Gor'ean warriors, their Captains, the shopkeepers, and the scouts arriving daily from across Elënthiá. His curiosity knew no limit, and both his mind and memory were keen. He seemed to drink in details of maps and tales of other parts of Elënthiá. He did not often engage in training skirmishes with the Gor'ean warriors, but on the few occasions that he had, Drake received reports that he crushed his opponents with embarrassing ease. This and his innate reserve enhanced the aura of mystery surrounding him. That he was a Forsair was now widely known. While he would have been vilified by both Humans and Elves, the fact that Gor'ean history had given them exposure to the best and worst of both cultures prompted their easy acceptance of him - and their fascination. After all, before meeting Lathaniel it was widely believed that a race of Forsairs was the subject of myth and folklore. His heritage and race aside, the Draconean was still at a loss to understand what made the Forsair so unique and guessed that time and the fates would reveal all.

Drake met with his apprentices each evening to take a meal and to quiz them on their day. Juga was always filled with anecdotes and tales of skirmishes with the Gor'eans. Lathaniel said little. And the week slipped away. On the eve of the seventh day, Drake awaited Lathaniel and Juga, who were in the baths and would join him shortly. In his mind he reviewed his father's riddle:

*It is to the West you must go,*
*To the land of the flattened mountains*
*Only the greatest Prince would know*
*The secret of the lock in the Fountain*
*Into the Hill*
*And you will find your fill*
*Strength, courage and cunning – more than mere knowledge*
*O'er the brother's breasts find the matching edge*
*Only the worthy may decipher the pledge*

Suvillwa's final clue had been all he required. After all these years, he was so close.

The Gor'ean Lord Garnec Cindrick paced in his chambers in Gorgonathan awaiting the return of his administrative apprentice, who would bring the most recent updates from Cap'hannet. These would determine Cindrick's course of action. The young Gor'ean arrived, breathless, his robes flapping behind him.

"My Lord, the Draconean remains at Cap'hannet still. Reports advise that he and his apprentices have settled in for what appears to be an extended stay."

Cindrick's face lit up; he was clearly delighted with the news. It had taken all his political acumen to lobby the Adjudicator to accept his recommendation to dispatch an additional escort to Cap'hannet, and to sell it to others on the Supreme Council without having it appear to challenge the Gor'ean Fyyther's own actions regarding the Draconean. He took care to plant just enough seeds of concern over the High Prince's close friendship with the Draconean to suggest that an additional escort might be prudent. He understood the risks he was taking with his relationship with the King, but he could not help himself. He had never recovered from the humiliation of Sorzin's escape from Cap'hannet twelve years earlier. Nor had he recovered from the fact that King Forginn and Acthelass Mar had not included him in the small circle of confidants that knew that Sorzin was a Draconean. Cindrick's captains had held him responsible for the escape and the shame of it haunted him still.

The Elven Queen along with six Kings from the Realms of Men had voiced support, sufficient, the Adjudicator felt, to justify the additional troops and to placate the Gor'ean King if the action was challenged. The Council's willingness to accept the Adjudicator's recommendation stemmed from curiosity. If the Draconean was all the Gor'ean King described then they wanted a chance to see him for themselves. Cindrick had learned from his outburst with his King that his own emotions need be kept closely veiled when it came to the Draconean. Inside, the bubbling pot of his rage was soothed by the knowledge that after twelve years he would take a personal role in bringing the Draconean outlaw to justice for the Gor'ean lives that were lost and be vindicated as the General in charge of Cap'hannet who let him escape those many years ago.

"A half legion of soldiers should suffice. Assemble them," he ordered.

"My Lord, with respect, there is but a legion in total guarding Gorgonathan at present. All others are dispatched to fight across Elënthiá. To do as you ask would reduce by half the guardians of this great city."

"Two hundred and fifty then" was the disgruntled reply. "Have you not heard? The Draconean is described as the near perfect soldier. He must not escape us again!"

His apprentice nodded, bowed, then scurried out to do his Lord's bidding.

# CHAPTER 25

The Draconean, the Human, and the Forsair made their way through the half light of deep dusk to the gates of the High Prince's residence, where guards quickly gave them entrance. They waited only a moment or two in the gallery entrance before Athron appeared, his face grim and unsmiling. Drake opened his mouth to speak ...

"Before you begin Draconean, yes, I know what day it is and I know why you have come."

His gazed travelled over the three, noting they wore both their weapons and travel packs.

"There is time for neither discussion nor excuses, my young Prince," Drake said. "What is your decision?"

The Gor'ean High Prince locked eyes with the Draconean in a hard stare that lasted the better part of a moment, neither breaking the gaze nor uttering a sound. Then: "I will accompany you."

Drake grasped him by both his upper arms, continuing to hold his gaze. "Any dishonour from this will fall on those who would doubt your loyalty to Gorger and its people. You have made the right decision both for the Gor'eans and for Elënthiá," he said quietly.

Athron gripped his upper arms in return and yanked him closer, looking up into the Draconean's face. "Do you swear to deliver what you have promised? If you do not, may death find you quickly; for you shall find me close behind until it does!"

The Draconean nodded his assent but said nothing. The two released each other.

"I am ready," Athron said quietly. "I have but to complete some final preparations. I require the assistance of one of your apprentices."

Drake nodded to Juga, who immediately stepped forward to follow the Gor'ean Prince across the gallery and into an antechamber, honoured by the opportunity to assist him. If Drake was a father figure to Juga, then Athron had quickly been cast in the role of the elder brother he never had. Juga held him in high esteem; in equal parts hero worship and awe at the calibre of soldier, and indeed the man, he had dreamed of becoming.

The young Human helped the Prince strap on his armour and weapons and prepare the last of his supplies in a travel pack. The pair worked in silence, Juga ever at Athron's elbow. Then the two rejoined Drake and Lathaniel in the gallery, and the Prince led them all out a side door and across a shadowed, empty courtyard into a small outbuilding that appeared to be a small chapel.

Inside altars were positioned against each of the four walls, before them bits of candle stubs and dried greenery lay, left in worship. The walls above the altars were adorned with elaborate paintings depicting both Elënthián and Gor'ean gods. Statues of individual gods stood on either side of each altar. Inside the building, standing in the shadows, travel packs astride their shoulders and fully armed, were four Gor'ean warriors. They snapped to attention at their Prince's arrival but remained silent.

Drake turned a stern and questioning eye to the Prince.

"Do not challenge me on this matter, Drake," the Prince asserted. "These men are my most loyal Lieutenants. They accompany us of their own free will. While they have been made aware of what you have shared with me, each would die before revealing such knowledge. If the journey ahead is as you say, then the extra hands will be necessary."

Drake looked from soldier to soldier, taking his own measure of each; then he nodded.

"There will be time for introductions later," Athron said quietly to Lathaniel and Juga. "For now we must be away."

He walked across the room to a statue depicting a half-man and half-bird. Gor'eans were a tree people, influence of a century spent with the Elves remaining strong down through the centuries. Their homes were built in the trees. Their entire capital city was built high among the trees. And they felt most at home when they were closest to trees, the more proliferate, the better. This affinity had seen them develop the ability to leap high enough that they could mount a large tree limb well above the ground in a single leap. Alternately, they were able to jump down from heights, landing with grace and only the slightest of sounds. Their communion with Gorger's trees and all creatures that lived within them were the reason birds were revered in their culture and worshipped with the same devotion as was given Surias, the goddess of the sky.

Athron grasped the statue's stone bow and yanked firmly downward. The statue shifted under his efforts until it moved back into the wall revealing a staircase. The descent was not long, and their way was lit by the torchlight that flickered at the base of the steps. The steps opened into an armoury, deserted at this hour. He and his men were suitably armed, but Athron gestured to the three to take what arms they required from the plentiful racks and shelves. Juga immediately spied and claimed two identical knives that fit a harness, which strapped across his shoulders and around his waist. The scabbards for each weapon extended down his back to almost his hips. When sheathed, the hilts of each knife would be within easy grasp should he reach behind his lower back at either side. During the week in Cap'hannet, he had worked with a tanner to fashion a leather harness for the ancient hammer. With the two knives, the hammer, the sword Drake had gifted him two years back, and the daggers in each of his boots, he felt ready.

Lathaniel was hesitant. He already carried the magnificent sword gifted to him by the Draconean and felt awkward accepting weapons, especially since their departure was under less than auspicious circumstances. But at Drake's urging he selected a beautifully crafted dagger for each boot and traded his well-worn bow for a new longbow nearly as tall as he and stained the blue-grey color of the sky on a cloudy day. Its range would far exceed his own. A soft leather quiver filled with more than forty arrows completed the set. He kept his own worn quiver, already brimming with arrows as well, for one never knew when a surfeit of arrows would be required, and the promise of more battles during their newest adventure left him anxious to be well prepared. Lathaniel caught the High Prince's eye and bowed his thanks for the weapons.

Athron then rolled a small map he had retrieved from his pack out on the table. The remainder of the company silently gathered round.

"Here is Cap'hannet," Drake began, indicating a point on the map. "The route for our exit from Gorger I leave to Your Excellency, but I respectfully suggest we exit here to avoid the Desert of Tiest, or alternatively here, so that we spend as little time as possible in the open dunes. "If we enter the Marshes of Nithmage here," his finger stabbed at a section of the map where the Marshes touched the western borders of Gorger, "I anticipate we can pass through them in two days if we follow this route. Passage will be unpleasant, so we will want to move through them with all haste. From there we cross the Sitiskan Fields to begin our search for the entrance to The Tombs. What challenges await there I cannot begin to guess, but excluding our exit from Gorger, I put our travel time between two and three weeks."

Athron's nod was curt as he rolled up the map parchment and stowed it, offering no insight into how the company would exit Gorger. It was obvious his decision to support the Draconean was still weighing heavily on his mind. Drake asked no questions.

From the armoury they exited through yet another concealed passage that emptied out directly into dark forests beyond Cap'hannet's walls and the cool of the night under a moonless sky. Lathaniel drew the night air deeply into his lungs as the company set off at a brisk jog through the darkness. The respite at the camp was welcome after Oderon, but he was just as happy to farewell the Gor'ean stronghold and its undercurrents of politics and animosity. He felt a shiver of excitement at the mission they had undertaken for, if they found success, the world of Elënthiá would be changed forever.

At that moment, a tall and handsome figure was stumbling slightly as he took his leave of a tavern. He had eaten and drunk his fill for the evening - silly to celebrate that exactly thirteen years before he had left his home on a mission he had yet to complete, but he was lonely for his homeland and his people and took solace in the mugs of ale that he'd consumed.

He was in the port city of Limore on the northernmost tip of the Amarik realm on Koorast Island. It was one of the few port cities held exclusively by the Resistance. His name was Layne Rev'eara. His unusual height and solid build marked him as a stranger among Limore's inhabitants. His size and height had stood him in good stead as, in his own land, as soon as he was of age he had joined the army. Through his own efforts he had been promoted through the ranks to Captain. There was but one General in the army he served, and he had long since retired. In its wisdom the High Council that governed his people had decreed the highest rank in the army would remain as captain. With no imminent threat to his people they'd felt adding the additional rank to be redundant. He did not agree.

Word of his abilities as a soldier – and of his ambitions – were widely known but he was still surprised when he received a summons from the High Council. He was offered this mission and promised that if he completed it successfully, the rank of General would be his. He could not refuse. Little did he know that accepting it would take him from his homeland these many years. And little did he know that completing the mission would be so difficult.

It was supposed to be simple; information had reached the Council that they wished verified. There was word of a solitary Draconean living in southern Elënthiá. He was tasked with finding out if this was true and, if so, with bringing the Draconean before his Council.

So he had travelled south many years ago. His discreet inquiries had led him to the Gor'eans of the Gorger realm where he was told of an Immortal that was being sought for war crimes. There were rumours that this Immortal was a Draconean. But the trail went cold from there. For the past twelve years he had followed leads all over southern Elënthiá, but to no avail.

Layne Rev'eara dressed as a peasant and carried only weapons that could be concealed beneath his robes. He had become an expert at blending in, at moving like a shadow through southern Elënthiá. His resolve remained strong even after thirteen years. And, thus far, the reason behind his inquiries needed to remain a secret. For if any knew who and what he was, his cause was lost.

# CHAPTER 26

Late summer was comfortably ensconced in the Gorger forest, bringing a chaos of greens, blooms, and blossoms, the gallery of leaves overhead a welcome shelter from the sun. On the forest floor, the palette of color from flowering bushes and shrubs was stunning against such an emerald backdrop. For most of the first and second day, the company moved through and between the trees of the thick forest following no discernible path. Using the position of the sun to track their direction, Lathaniel understood that they were weaving hither and to, seemingly directionless, to throw off or at least deter any who would follow, both losing and gaining them valuable time.

Their path was now threading steadily west. The company moved at a perpetual jog, the ground-eating pace allowing them to cover considerable distances without overtaxing their strength. The rigor of the past months had seasoned the two youngest members of the company, and they kept apace with ease.

Conversation between Drake and Athron remained strained during those first days. Drake gave Athron the space and time to fully come to terms with his choices. Athron's soldiers took their cue from their Prince and spoke only when spoken to. For his part, Juga gravitated to the Gor'ean Prince. While little was said between the two, Juga automatically appeared at Athron's side to assist him with his armour at day's beginning and end, to clean and polish his weapons, to lay his kit out each evening and collect it each morning. Unobtrusively and without becoming an annoyance, he assisted the Prince.

While Lathaniel and Juga's experiences these many months had cemented the friendship between them, the differences in their race were such that they had not developed the affinity that Juga seemed to feel for the Gor'eans. Lathaniel did not begrudge Juga this; in fact, he felt a kind of envy that the young Human seemed to have found a niche for himself in the confusing world about them.

For his part, Lathaniel found himself gravitating more and more to the Draconean. He positioned himself directly behind Drake on the trail and to his right when they were at rest. Conversation between the two was easy, with Drake often pointing out edible plants and medicinal herbs or drawing Lathaniel's attention to wildlife or some notable natural geography or geology. Lathaniel was ever the apt and rapt student.

His feelings for the Draconean were complicated. He felt almost a visceral pull toward the Immortal, feeling their lives were becoming like the vines that wound around the trees in the Gorger. The Draconean was becoming mentor, brother, and friend to him. In itself that was as disturbing as it was comforting.

During the third night in Gorger, he'd joined the Draconean for his watch. As he dropped down beside him in the dark, Lathaniel told him all: of the fall of the Waythans, of Gramicy and the deterioration of his Lamana, of his people's cry for his leadership in war, of Sabine and his dear friends, of the threat to theirs and his family's lives, and of the ultimatum that led to his departure. Drake sat beside him, saying nothing. After a time, he stood and placed one large hand on Lathaniel's shoulder for a second or two before giving it a comforting squeeze. Then he left on his patrol of their camp. Though the Draconean had not uttered a single word, the young Forsair had felt the weight of guilt and self-doubt ease, and the relief was immeasurable.

That had been two nights ago. Lathaniel was taking his turn at watch and completing a quiet patrol of the camp perimeter. The night was crisp and clear. The new moon offered little light to the sky, but the blanket of stars more than made up for it. It was a perfect time to hunt the creatures that were about in the moonlight and to try out his new longbow. Perhaps fresh meat would entice the Prince to agree to a fire and a warm breakfast.

Lathaniel broadened the circumference of his patrol. As he headed further north and west, his nose twitched. He was downwind of a smell that was frighteningly familiar. Keen ears detected sounds that froze him in his tracks; he quickly squatted in the overgrowth on the forest floor.

Are-Narcs! Slowly inching back to his full height, concealed in the forest darkness he surveyed their camp, executing a quick count and an assessment. Backing soundlessly away until he felt he could move undetected, he turned and darted back toward his company.

*The company had moved to the edge of steep cliffs so high that the ground at their base was steeped in darkness. As if the gods themselves had shaken out a great dark blanket, a heavy cloud descended upon them from the skies, enveloping them and lifting them from the earth high above Elënthiá. He fell to his knees before Nesmeresa, the goddess of Nature, and the Great Ruahr himself, god of all the gods, begging for the lives of his companions. But the gods charged him with black deeds, recounting each and every one...deeds he had no memory of doing. When Ruahr dropped his mighty hand, he began to fall. Down through the thick, dirty clouds, the four lands of Elënthiá rushing up to greet him. Just as his body was about to be impaled on stone and rock...*

Athron awoke with a jerk, disconcerted, sweating, and disoriented. Only a dream, he thought, but what a dream it was. The camp was silent. He'd made no outcry in his sleep, thankfully.

Looking at the sky he thought it near to dawn. A quick review of bedrolls showed Lathaniel's to be empty; he must be on patrol. It was a warm night, and like the others Athron had removed his shirt to sleep. Quietly he began to dress.

A twig snapped behind him, and honed reflexes had his dagger in his hand in a blink as he wheeled to challenge the intruder. It was Juga. Sensing the Gor'ean had risen, he had also stood. The young man raised both hands until certain the Gor'ean knew he was no intruder, and then watched silently as Athron turned away to roll his bedding and pack his belongings.

"Highness, forgive my boldness, but how did you come to have that?" Juga gestured to the colourful symbols on Athron's bare back. The background was an elaborate golden crest; atop it was the outline of a great tree, and in the foreground two majestic birds battled.

Athron looked over his shoulder and smiled. "It was applied as an initiation to the Royal Guard, a demonstration of commitment and loyalty to the Guard at the price of great pain."

"Is it paint, then?"

"No. It would be no hardship if it were only paint. Artisans mix different coloured pigments with a special ink. Using fine bone needles, the pigment is applied just beneath the skin one dot at a time until the chosen picture is complete. It is done for hours each day. Depending upon the design, it can take weeks to complete. A necessary though not particularly pleasant process," he said drily. "But it is a symbol to all that I am or have been a member of the Royal Guard. The additions that have been made to the original design here and here," he wrapped his arms around himself and tapped the spots, which he knew by memory, "now mark me as a member of the Gor'ean royalty. Such body markings are a tradition among our people."

The two were silent then, for the remainder of the company had awoken and begun preparations for departure.

Lathaniel sprinted back towards their camp, easily leaping over fallen debris on the forest floor but careful that his rapid bolt through the woods was as soundless as possible. Approaching their clearing, he ducked his head to avoid a low-hanging branch and, as he skidded to a stop, found himself face-to-face with the image of two crimson birds with emerald, sapphire, and golden wingtips poised to strike at each other. Disconcerted, he was speechless for a moment. *Athron?* he thought as the man turned.

He shook off his surprise and his questions, eyes darting around the camp until they locked on Drake's. "Are-Narcs" he said quietly. "A half legion or more, camped not more than a league to the northwest."

Athron whirled to look to Drake. "We are at the edge of Gorger's borders. They cannot be trailing us, or they would be coming in from the southeast. They likely came ashore at Limore or in the northwest. We are well patrolled there. If they have entered Gorger, then it will have been at the expense of a Gor'ean patrol."

The Gor'ean soldiers were standing at full alert, an invasion within their borders unthinkable. Athron's eyes had not left the Draconean's face as he spoke, but his mind was racing. "I cannot walk away from this knowledge, Drake. I will not compromise our enterprise, but neither will I abandon my people when I have the information and means to warn them of an imminent attack."

The Draconean nodded in agreement. Athron swung briskly around to his aides.

"You will all pack now and make haste to Cap'hannet with this news. Take the most direct routes but travel with care, for if Are-Narcs have penetrated one of our borders, there is a strong possibility it is part of a larger, more strategic initiative."

His soldiers slapped their right fists against their hearts, bowed, then turned to ready their weapons and packs.

"Jacon." Athron touched the shoulder of one of his Lieutenants and drew him aside. "There are two messages you will carry. One you will give to the General in charge at Cap'hannet; the other, to my father. Deliver it personally if you can. If you cannot, send one whom you trust. May the gods speed and guard your journey."

He gripped Jacon's shoulder and gave him a slap on the back. With a last bow to their Prince, the four loped out of the camp. Shortly thereafter the four remaining companions left in haste heading for the border of Gorger.

Garnec Cindrick entered the Supreme Council Chambers and took his seat high in the Gor'ean balcony next to the Fyyther. It was midday, and the Council had been called into an emergency session. Every available General in the Gor'ean

Army had been called back to Gorgonathan. Every Gor'ean Lord was present. The summons had been flagged as urgent. For what reason, no one knew.

The Adjudicator came to his podium in the center of the room far below and began. "You have all been gathered here this day to hear urgent news of the war." A wave of anticipation rippled through the room. The Adjudicator was briefly distracted by the delivery of another missive by an aide.

While they awaited his attention, Lillandra, queen of the Fairies and newly returned to Council, stood and quietly asked, "What of this Draconean and his companions? We have heard no news on this. Was not Lord Cindrick charged with their safe return to Gorgonathan?" The fairy queen had only just returned to Gorgonathan and the Council from the Amainaf Wood on the southern tip of the Vearian region. She did not fill a chair as did others on the Council. Her diminutive stature was such that it was more comfortable for her to hover above the chair. Her elegant and near translucent wings fluttered slowly, allowing her petite two foot body to remain in place. Hair of the deepest crimson cascaded down her back over shoulders garbed in a richly embroidered tunic. Her pale green eyes were tired. Like many others within the Council, all was not well in her homeland. Her gaze held Garnec Cindrick's expectantly.

Cindrick could feel a hot blush creep up his neck as his Fyyther turned to stare at him. He rose to his feet to reply. "On this matter I can reassure you, Excellencies. At the Council's request, I sent a contingent of two hundred and fifty of Gorger's finest soldiers to Cap'hannet to escort the Draconean to Gorgonathan. They are expected any day now." He stressed the word *Council* in a meagre attempt to placate the Fyyther, from whom a decidedly cool tension was emanating.

One of the Kings from the Realms of Men stood in his balcony across from the Gor'eans and shouted, "For your sake, my Lord, let us hope you prevail." There was a light ripple of laughter from several of the balconies; none had missed the King's reaction. Cindrick squirmed in his seat.

The Adjudicator banged his gavel for silence. His visage was clearly pale and his tone serious as he announced, "We've just this moment received a messenger from Cap'hannet. The contingent of two hundred and fifty Gor'ean soldiers you dispatched are all dead, Lord Cindrick, slaughtered in an Are-Narc ambush near the southern border en route to Cap'hannet."

There was a collective gasp from the Council. Cindrick fell back in his seat, his chest heaving as he absorbed the news.

The Adjudicator continued, "Cap'hannet stonewalled a direct attack by Gorillian's troops on the Camp. Nearly five hundred Are-Narcs were slaughtered, including those that tried to escape back into the Minheras. It is hoped that none eluded our troops to report back on their route into Cap'hannet, but we cannot be certain at this time. A count shows Resistance injuries are limited; only a handful are life-threatening."

The Adjudicator paused then, and the Council knew that more bad news would follow. He continued quietly, "All are accounted for except eight, among them His Excellency the High Prince Athron Mar."

There was absolute silence in the Chamber as all eyes shifted to the Gor'ean Fyyther, whose face had paled into a cold, expressionless mask.

"The Draconean and his two apprentices are also missing. The other four are seasoned warriors and known personal favourites of the High Prince. Lieutenants Horgon, Tmark, Syctris. . .and Cindrick."

Garnec Cindrick leapt to his feet, his face nearly purple in shock that his son was among the missing and renewed rage at the Draconean's escape. "If this company has survived and my son is a part of it, then he only participates at the direct order of His Excellency, for he is a loyal servant of Gorger and Elënthiá." His temper broke then. "The High Prince is a known ally of the Draconean in spite of the cur's role in the death of nearly a full legion of his own people!"

So close to treason was his outburst that nary a gasp could be heard in the Chambers. The silence was deafening.

The Adjudicator interrupted, "Please, Lord Cindrick. Take your seat, for there is more." He waited until Cindrick was seated and the room quiet again before continuing. "As scouts reconnoitred after the attack on Cap'hannet, they found the four Lieutenants. It appears they stumbled upon the Are-Narcs in the Minhera pass whilst trying to return Cap'hannet. All are dead."

A cry of anguish erupted from a distraught Cindrick. At a nod from the King, several Gor'ean Lords assisted him from the Chambers.

The Council was alarmed, for Gorillian's armies had never discovered the access to Cap'hannet. That was what had always made it such a valuable stronghold to the Resistance. That Cap'hannet had been attacked and that two hundred and fifty Gor'ean warriors had also perished along the southern borders of Gorger meant that Gorillian was stepping up his campaign, and the kingdom faced a dire threat. The Council relied on the Gor'eans to hold firm in spite of what was happening across Elënthiá. As in all ages past, it was upon the Gor'eans that hopes for the Resistance rested, especially given that the Elves could not enter the fray.

The Adjudicator brought the Chamber to order once again.

"Two messages were found on the body of Jacon Cindrick, both from His Excellency the Gor'ean High Prince. The first was addressed to the General in change of Cap'hannet. The message reads:

*"'Gorillian Are-Narcs inside northwestern borders of Gorger ten leagues from the Marshes of Nithmage. Half legion or more. Watch all borders. Warn all patrols. May the gods guard our land.'*

"There was a second note addressed to his father, the Gor'ean Fyyther. The seal on it is intact. I will deliver this to you personally, Highness."

The Adjudicator called for the Generals and key military from across the Supreme Council to join a special session to discuss troop deployment in the face of this most recent news and the Council was adjourned.

# CHAPTER 27

The Sitiskan Fields were rather like the plains of Horon but with more rolling hills and sporadic gatherings of light forests and orchards. The evening prior had marked the equinox, and the skies were that particular shade of blue seen only in autumn. The goddess Nesmeresa was preparing her world for the long sleep of winter and used each and every hue in her pallet to ensure that autumn's exit was spectacular. Grass, wildflower, shrub, and tree alike were afire as they reluctantly surrendered to seed. There was a bite to the morning air, a portent of the icy winds that would whip across the lands in a few short months.

The four companions had exited Gorger where the tip of the Marshes met it, eliminating travel in the open dunes of the Tiest Desert. The Marshes of Nithmage had not become any less unpleasant with the passage of time, Drake thought as they moved along. The pungent smells emanating from the murky sludge bordered on the intolerable. They had camped one night but continued on through the next, picking their way along little-known trails, willing to travel any distance to speed their departure from the swampy lands. With firmer land beneath their feet and the stench of the Marshes now downwind, the four moved across the Sitiskan Fields at a brisk pace in the early morning air.

At every break during the day, over each meal, and in the hours in between and before they took their rest each evening, the principle topic of conversation was the ancient riddle. They'd about worn out the map Athron carried debating the best routes and what inferences could be made from the riddle. That the entrance was near water was a given, but which water and at what juncture?

The Rauloue and Loris Rivers cut through the Fields. The entrance to the Tombs could be anywhere along either. All keenly felt the pressure of time and, though the gods had been kind to them thus far, felt the harsh regard of many in Elënthiá and knew that several factions were now hunting them.

That first evening in the Fields, after staring at the map until the light of dusk made it almost impossible to continue, Drake blurted out, "It's the Loris. Not the Rauloue. I could not tell you how I know this, but I feel that it is to this river we must head."

It was the first time he'd been that definitive about their starting off point. He was an Immortal, after all. If he felt strongly that the Loris would reveal all, then they were inclined to follow his lead.

But where on the Loris? That subject launched Athron and Drake into their next round of heated discussions about regional geography as it might relate to the riddle. Both had travelled extensively in the region. For their parts, each day brought Juga and Lathaniel to new vistas; they had little to contribute.

"I can agree that it is unlikely it is the Rauloue for it only runs high when the early spring runoff overfills its banks.

Otherwise it tapers to a mere stream in places. With its origins in the Minheras and its flow strong, the Loris is more robust during its entire course, right through to where it empties into the basin of the Western Cove. I think it best we begin at the Cove and work our way back along the river searching for possible connections to the clues." Athron was adamant.

"Think of the geography, Athron!" Drake replied in frustration. "We've had this discussion before. If even a portion of the legends are true, then the Draconean treasure vaults are full beyond imagining. The practicalities of bringing treasures in volume, undetected, from that end of the Loris are impractical. Remember the salt marshes all along its estuary? No, I think we should commence our search here." He stabbed the map further inland.

Thus began the volley back and forth as each argued his point, conceded on some minute issue but then found another to dispute. The younger companions rolled away and let sleep take them as the Gor'ean and the Draconean continued their debate.

Layne hopped on one foot then the other, stumbling across his small rented room above the smithy as he pulled his breeches on and up. He stamped his feet into boots and with his shirt tails flapping pulled on his tunic and cloak and ran out of his room, nearly falling down the flight of steps that took him to street level. The quantity of ale he'd imbibed the night prior had left him with an inordinate sensitivity to bright sunlight, and as he stepped out into the street he felt himself near to blinded until his bleary eyes adjusted.

A pounding on his door earlier had pulled him from his stupor, but the message delivered had jolted him into immediate alert. A barman had sent word to him: "a matter of great importance," he was told. It could only be one thing; there was finally news!

Kanea the barkeep was polishing mugs at the rear of the room when he entered the tavern.

"Layne, m'lad. It's a pleasure to see you this fine morning, though you look like you'd be happier if the skies were cloudy and the sun not so bright this day." He smiled. "I see my man found you."

"Good morning to you, too, Kanea. I came as soon as I received your message. Please, tell me your news.

"There were Resistors in here last evening. Drinking ale back there in the corner table and talking all quiet-like, they were. Shooed the barmaid away and would only let me take their drinks back. Kept looking round my place as if they expected trouble at any turn. Twice when I took them ales, I heard mention of a Draconean. My ears perked up just then remembering that you said you'd pay for any news of such a creature, so I listened well."

Layne could hardly contain himself but kept silent as the barkeep continued.

"They got to talking of those Gor'ean tree dweller folk what live in Gorger. That they are chasing down a company. Four in total, I heard them say: a Gor'ean Prince, a Human thief, something what they called a Forsair, and a Draconean. Said they were heading west."

"West? Where were they spotted and how long ago? Did they say where the four were headed?" The questions tripped over themselves on their way out of Layne's mouth.

"There weren't no more said that I could hear after that," said Kanea. "What exactly is it you want with this Draconean? You never did say."

Layne had set a small pouch of coins on the counter in front of the barkeep and was already turning away. "Believe me when I tell you that it is far too long a tale. My thanks, Kanea."

He left the bar with a brisk step, leaving the barkeep to polish his glasses and consider how best to spend the gold he had just received.

# CHAPTER 28

"Concentrate, Lathaniel!" Drake bellowed as the young Forsair lay on the ground, having been easily thrown there during an extended training skirmish with the Draconian. Coming slowly to his feet, Lathaniel once again assumed an attack stance. Drake immediately lunged, whipping his sword arm around such that his hilt clipped Lathaniel's wrist, and his sword fell from his hands. The Forsair sank to his knees, his face dripping sweat and his arms trembling as he rubbed a bruised wrist.

The Draconean looked off into the horizon, annoyed, then dropped down on his haunches and spoke quietly to the Forsair.

"How many days has it been, Lathaniel? How many days with little or no sleep?" He knew it had been at least three, so he continued without waiting for an answer, now angry. "I should have left you in Cap'hannet or turned you loose months ago! I can ill afford to child-mind now, when we are so close and when Gorillian and half of Elënthiá is hard on our heels." Lathaniel remained quiet, his expression closed.

Juga stepped up and quietly intervened. "Master. Go easy. He just needs sleep."

"What he needs to do is to *choose* to sleep, to *choose* not to rehash again and again that over which he has no control and to *choose* to concentrate on what tasks the gods set in front of him today! Today!"

Juga stepped back, speechless. It was out of character for the Draconean to show either of them a temper.

Drake focused on a point over Lathaniel's shoulder and took a deep breath. It had been so very long since he had cared enough about anyone to get angry at them. He wasn't entirely certain he liked the emotions that he was feeling, and seeing the Forsair this distracted made him feel helpless, an emotion he never embraced easily. He lowered his voice and softened his tone. "Whatever it is, you have to let it go for now, lad. Not forever, but for now."

He stood and, bending at the waist, extended his hand to Lathaniel. After a second or two, he reached up and took the hand offered pulling himself to his feet.

"That's it for today. Clean yourself and take food. Perhaps the exercise will help you sleep." He clasped Lathaniel's shoulder for a second or two, regretting his words and show of temper, then walked away into the dusk. In Gorger, the lad had finally shared details of his exodus from Lamana. But these last days the Forsair had grown more quiet and withdrawn. Drake's efforts to draw him out had been met with vague replies and were dismissed. Frustration with his young friend had brought on the temper. Drake could only think that the lad's family and the situation in Lamana was what weighed heavily on his mind. Unfortunately that path could only be walked by the young Forsair; he had to find his own way.

Five days later, the four were running along the banks of the Loris River. They had picked up the Loris at the point where its estuary ended and were working their way quickly inland. Fresh fish coupled with the harvest of autumn fruits and nuts found in the woods near the shoreline filled their bellies each evening. Coupled with the fresh air and the vigorous pace, they were thriving.

Late that afternoon they came to a junction in the river where a smaller tributary veered east. Drake left them to make camp while he scouted the tributary and further upstream on the main channel to the west. He wasn't back by nightfall, but then he often scouted well into the night. As an Immortal he required very little sleep.

Lathaniel came awake with a start, his dagger in one hand and the other reaching for his sword, certain that Are-Narcs had come upon them in the night until he heard Drake's quiet whisper, "It is I."

Willing his heart out of his throat and back into his chest, Lathaniel fell back on one elbow. "Trouble?"

"No. But I believe I have found the entrance to The Tombs! Wake the others. It's nearly dawn, and there is no time to waste."

The Draconean led them away from the riverbed, up steep banks, and along the ridge of an escarpment. Intermittently they could still see the river to their left. Off to their right, the Fields of Sitiska warmed beneath a rolling golden of blanket of grasses in the early morning breezes.

The spine of the escarpment gently curved higher as they moved along it. Before long they could hear the distant hiss of water, which grew ever stronger the farther along it they moved.They entered a clearing at the bluff's edge to behold a horseshoe-shaped fall of water that plummeted into a clear pool below, the impact fountaining the falling water and creating a silver mist that refracted in the morning sun into a million tiny rainbows.

While the sight was spectacular, the three looked expectantly at Drake; for if there were caves or entrance to behold, they were missing it.

"Remember the riddle. '... *The secret of the lock in the fountain...*' Study the pool, the bottom of the pool. Can you see it? *'The secret of the lock in the fountain'* doesn't have to mean a lock and a key. A 'lock' can mean a bridge between two bodies of water as well."

"Yes!" yelled Juga, pointing. "I see it. Look! There, at the pool's bottom. Do you see the shades of grey in the shadows? They're only noticeable from this height and only if you're looking for them. From the shore it would look like any normal pool." Juga's excitement suddenly waned, and he abruptly fell quiet. His companions were busy exclaiming over the find.

"Following back along the escarpment and making our way back up the river bed will take too long," Drake explained. "I have tested these." He gestured to the thick vines that grew over the cliff and clothed its faces in greenery. "We should be able to climb directly down."

Preparations began, and soon the four were descending down the cliff-face to the pool below.

"Now we take some food and water and rest a short while. Thereafter, we swim."

They looked at Drake in confusion.

"I thought you meant that the shadows directed us to a place behind the waterfall. Where are we swimming to?" Lathaniel asked.

"To the bottom of the pool," Drake replied impatiently. "The entrance to the Tombs is at the bottom of the pool!"

Juga blanched, for this was what he had feared as soon as he knew they were descending the cliff face. He was quiet for a moment before saying, "I mayn't have mentioned this before, but I cannot swim."

Drake chuckled. "You mean we have finally discovered a task that the Human finds daunting?"

Athron intervened, "Have no fear, lad, for you will travel to the bottom of the pool holding my shoulders. We will leave no one behind at this point, for we know not what we may find below."

That comment sobered the four, and they quickly went about the business of eating and preparing their belongings for a chilly swim.

Drake dove into the pool. He was the strongest swimmer and wanted to ensure he knew what they faced at the bottom of the pool before the four of them swam down to it. He was gone more than four minutes. Lathaniel began to pace, his eyes never leaving the water's surface; Juga sat stone still on the shore, white-faced. Only Athron looked unconcerned. There were two very deep sighs of relief when Drake resurfaced.

He pulled himself out of the pool and shook his body like a great wet wolf. With his long black hair slicked back off his face, Lathaniel saw his sightless left eye clearly for the first time. It was strangely clear and, like its mate, the flecks of emerald green within the pupils caught and reflected the midday light.

"It's there at the bottom of the pool, just as we thought," Drake reported.

Bending down, he picked up a stick and drew a quick sketch in the sand. "The water falls down into the pool here. The sides of the pool come down on either side like a bowl, except the two sides don't meet at the bottom. Instead, here, on this side, the pool bottom is higher. It overlaps, like so."

He dropped the stick and stood.

"Once you reach the bottom of the pool, it is a short swim through the tunnel—ten or fifteen feet, no more. You will come up on the inside into a small pool." He looked pointedly at Juga. "You can do this."

Securing their weapons and packs, Lathaniel and Drake dove into the pool and began to swim toward the waterfall. Juga and Athron walked into the water; then, towing Juga behind him, Athron swam out to join them.

Drake gave final instructions. "Three deep breaths in and out. On the fourth, we dive. Keep your eyes open and follow me." He breathed with them, and on the fourth, they descended into the clear, cold depths of the pool. The transition through the short tunnel was made with ease, though Juga surfaced in the small pool coughing and muttering, "never again," much to the amusement of his companions.

*Yet again*, thought Lathaniel with an inward sigh, *we are back underground.* But this was a far cry from the warmth of the haven under Horon or the cold opulence of the Anulé chambers within the Minheras. Here the tunnels were dank and moist with walls that dripped condensation. Their soaked clothing and the squish of their wet boots against the rough stone floors did nothing to alleviate the cool dampness in the air or their shivers as they made their way along the main tunnel.

As they moved away from the pool and the waterfall, the tunnel began a slight incline before it levelled again, and the rock and air around them became drier, dust and cobwebs replacing the mould and damp. The tunnel emptied into a small room roughly hewn out of rock. In the torchlight they could see the walls were covered with strange, colourful symbols. Three dark holes signified other tunnel branches.

"What language is this?" Lathaniel asked as he traced his fingers over the runes on the walls.

"Darrish. The ancient language of the Draconeans," Drake replied quietly, distracted.

Lathaniel watched his fingertips dance over the runes along the wall first here, then there, and imagined what it must be like for him to finally find this place after centuries of searching; to be the last of his kind among the remains of his kind.

"It's this way." Drake abruptly moved off into one of the tunnels.

As they followed behind him, Juga asked, "How do you know which one to take? Is the answer in the runes?"

"The runes only reveal more riddles. They are there to confuse any who would stumble upon this place. Even understanding Darrish, the way forward would be difficult to determine. My father's papers told of the Tombs, of the route we must follow...and I have had nearly two thousand years to memorize it. It was the starting point that always eluded me."

They followed Drake through the tunnels turning this way, then that, weaving through a maze that sometimes doubled back across paths they'd taken already and through other smaller chambers, the walls of which were covered with more of the ancient runes. Drake's concentration was absolute, and the three were silent as they followed his lead.

The passage of time was difficult to gauge in the dark, but as his three companions began to grow weary, the company came upon another larger chamber. Without exploring it, Drake swung his pack from his back.

"We will rest here and take some food."

The three discharged packs and opened water skins, collapsing on the hard ground, grateful for the reprieve.

The chamber was large, larger than any they had come through. Drake moved about, lighting torches to illuminate it more fully. Once it was fully lit they beheld a massive stone door on one of the walls. It was elaborately etched in geometric designs and more Darrish runes. At its center, about waist height to the Draconean, an exquisite stone was inset. It winked in the firelight as Drake lit torches on either side of the great door.

He moved away to sit near his pack, facing the door and staring at it in wonder.

"The final quest begins."

# CHAPTER 29

"Take out your swords," Drake instructed hours later. They had eaten then slept; deep in the Tombs, it was difficult to measure time, but all were refreshed, still spralled along the cave floor but anxious to continue. Athron, Lathaniel, and Juga withdrew their swords and laid them across their laps.

"Juga, I gifted you with a sword one year after you became my apprentice. Lathaniel, your sword was given to you after our escape from the Minheras. And you, Athron—yours was given when you were much younger and apprenticed to train with me. The three swords you hold in your hands, together with the three I carry across my back, are the keys to the lost treasure of the Draconeans."

The company was silent, their eyes glued to Drake as he continued.

"Gorillian executed every member of my race, save my six older brothers and my father, the King. My father was tortured mercilessly to gain knowledge of the location of this place, and when he refused to reveal it, my brothers were tortured and murdered before his eyes."

Drake paused for a moment then sighed, the memories still difficult for him.

"My father knew that Gorillian would have tortured and killed all of them anyway. The bodies of my brothers were burned and the ashes scattered, but Gorillian kept their swords as trophies. My father kept the secret of these Tombs through it all but feigned the loss of his sanity. Believing him completely mad, Gorillian relaxed his guard, and my father escaped taking my brother's six swords with him. I carry three of these swords with me. You each hold one of the other three."

Three sets of eyes dropped to their own laps realizing the import of what they had been told and the inestimable value of the weapons that lay there.

"This was not the first tragedy in my father's life, but as an Immortal, such things happen. When he was much younger he and his sons—his first six sons—were caught unawares by a freak storm high in the Minheras. My father survived. Not being full-blooded Immortals, his sons did not. He returned in the thaw to claim their bodies and their swords. His first six sons are buried here, in these Tombs, each in a separate chamber. Each chamber is protected by the power of their swords. We need to retrieve their six swords, and together with the ones we hold, we can open the great vault and claim the Draconean treasure."

"Protected?" Athron asked. "Protected by what, or by whom?"

"While my father's journals detail many things about this place, description of the protection on each Tomb is absent. I know he enlisted the assistance of other ancients to activate these protections and may not himself have fully understood exactly what each entailed. I know only this: a sword must be retrieved from each of the funerary chambers and only my brothers or one who wields a sword that once belonged to them may face the protections found in each of the chambers. All others are forbidden to enter."

"The sapphire in the hilt of my sword matches the one embedded in that door." Lathaniel gestured to the ancient portal across the room. "Is it the same with all chambers?"

"Excellent observation, Lathaniel. Yes, the jewels in the portals should match those set into the hilts of each of your swords and those that I carry. Since each of you has accepted ownership of a Draconean sword, I believe that you must be the ones to enter the chambers and face their tests. We will decide who best to wield the three remaining swords once you've broken the protections on the first three."

Drake paused again, his eyes moving from one to the other. "I cannot adequately express my gratitude for your presence here nor your assistance this day. Beyond reclaiming my heritage, what we find in the vault should forever rid Elënthiá of the evil cloud that hovers above it."

There was silence as his three companions absorbed the magnitude of his words.

Drake stood abruptly and dusted his hands on his leggings. "Let us be about it."

Lathaniel stood before the great door. He unsheathed his sword and slid the blade slowly into the slot below the jewel. He felt a click as he buried it to the hilt. Following Drake's instructions, he then twisted it three full turns to the right. After a series of loud clicks and a great groan, the door shifted back, releasing his sword. It parted in the middle, opening to reveal the chamber beyond. What faced the four left them speechless.

It was as if someone had cut a body of water in half and they were looking into a dimly lit, murky cross-section of it. Lathaniel slowly thrust his hand forward to the elbow. His arm easily moved into the wall of water, and when he withdrew it, his arm was soaked. As the ripples caused by his arm stilled, they could see the blurry outline of a tall, squared passage beyond which was a large,domed room. A crypt was situated at the far end of it. Suspended vertically and rotating above it was a sword.

Lathaniel shed his tunic, pack, bow, and quiver but kept his sword and daggers. With a quick look at Drake he took a few deep breaths and stepped across the threshold into the water.

After only just a few strong strokes into it, it was as though the heel of an unseen hand hit him hard in the center of his chest. Startled, he instinctively opened his mouth in a gasp. In doing so his lungs drew in a great gulp of air. *Air? By the gods, what has happened to me?* Tentatively he opened his lips the slightest bit expecting his mouth to fill with water. Instead, more fresh air poured in. Fascinated with the sensation he opened his mouth wider to take in more air and let his chest rise and fall in normal rhythm. He guessed that this mystic reversal of the elements must somehow be connected to the protections Drake told them about. Still suspended in the water, he clawed at the water and swung back around. Drake and the others were peering worriedly through the ripples no doubt wondering why he wasn't making haste toward the main chamber. He gave them a curt nod of reassurance then with long, pulling strokes and strong kicks propelled himself up the passage and across the chamber. As he reached the crypt he hesitated, looking both up and down for signs of any traps. Tentatively he reached forward and grasped the hilt.

As soon as his hand touched it, he heard a strange garbled grating. Quickly looking up then down he could see that drains had opened in the stone floor. The water level began to drop rapidly. Believing the protections had ceased with his retrieval of the sword, he relaxed and pulled for the surface above him. As he broke the surface he opened his mouth to take in a breath of air only to feel the hard punch in his chest once again. He opened his mouth, gasping now. He could take no air into his lungs! Panicked he slid below the water's surface to find that he could breathe normally there as before.

The water level was continuing to fall. Understanding his peril now, he swung toward the tunnel and the entrance beyond it, arrowed down toward the floor and swam for all he was worth. He had just reached the entrance to the tunnel when he swam full tilt into a wall of rock that was moving upward from the floor. The jarring impact stunned him, throwing him backward. With the rapidly decreasing water level, his first instinct was to stand – and to breathe. The now familiar punch to the chest reminded him again of his peril. As he looked down the passage toward the entrance he could see two other thin stone walls pushing up from the chamber floor toward the ceiling. The water level was at his waist now. Bending forward, he thrust his head beneath the surface to quickly gulp in fresh air and stood once more flipping his hair back off his face. The unexpected wall had risen just above waist height and rising. He easily hefted himself sideways and vaulted over it as it continued its push upwards.

Another wall, now higher still, was ascending in front of him. Still holding his breath he hoisted himself up and threw a leg over its top, sliding down the other side. His air was almost gone but the last wall between him and the entrance was already above his head. The water was ankle deep now. Dropping to his stomach he thrust his face into the little water that remained and gulped in a short breath. He had to get over the last wall before it sealed him in!

He leapt to get a grip on its top. His heart was pounding, the small gulp of air he had taken not nearly sufficient. His lungs started to burn. He could feel his strong arms quiver as he hauled his body upward, again swinging his leg up to gain purchase on the top of the wall. Using first one leg, then the other to help propel him upwards, he squeezed through the diminishing space near the ceiling rolling off the wall and dropping like a stone to the floor on the other side.

But for the odd puddle remaining, the water had completely drained. Starbursts were exploding behind Lathaniel's eyes and his lungs were on fire. It was a dozen feet or so to the chamber's entrance and the great stone door was steadily closing. Barely conscious, he could see the others waving and screaming his name but could hear nothing. He forced himself to stagger forward a few steps then gathering his last remaining strength he threw himself forward barely registering the great hand that reached out to him. Locking wrists with Drake, he was unceremoniously yanked the final few feet and through the gap in the door to fall flat on the floor of the main antechamber soaked, barely conscious. The mysterious reversal of the elements ceased at the door to the chamber. His chest heaving like a bellows, he gulped in fresh air. There was a second or two of complete silence.

Standing off to one side, an ashen Juga quietly remarked to no one in particular, "I hope they're not all filled with water."

A short passage took them to another antechamber. The door was of the same design, but the jewel embedded in it was a diamond; a match to the jewel in Juga's sword. The procedure to open the portal was repeated, and when the great stone doors shifted back and parted the four were surprised to see a simple chamber, the same size as the one before but showing nothing significant save the crypt at the far of the room and the sword hovering above it.

They traded uncertain glances. Then, it was as if the room suddenly elongated, pulling back and away from them, the crypt and the sword suddenly pulled away into the distance. From the floor and the ceiling a great moan was heard before thick green vines and trees began to fill from top and bottom, weaving hither and to. The thundering of air and the rush and moan of creeping trees and a jungle of greenery stopped abruptly...directly in front of Juga.

Like Lathaniel, Juga shed his tunic and pack. He removed the great Anulé hammer from across his back and shrugged out of the harness for it. Beads of perspiration dotted his brow as it furled in concentration. He unsheathed his sword and also pulled one of his sharp Gor'ean knives from behind his back Thusly armed, he stepped forward, swinging his sword in front of him like a scythe hacking a path through the dense growth and alternately swiping the shorter knife into the vine creepers that hung from above. Soon he was beyond the view of his companions who awaited his return in anxious silence.

Dripping with sweat and panting from the exertion, Juga continued forward until he found himself in a clearing about eight or ten feet from the crypt. Though exhausting, it had seemed a fairly simple endeavour thus far. He stood for a moment in front of the crypt. Similar to the tomb in the first chamber, the lid of it had been carved in effigy of the lost son. In spite of the circumstances of his death, the young man's face was portrayed in peaceful repose.

With a quick prayer to the gods to guard the souls of the lost, Juga reached above the tomb and wrapped his fist around the hilt of the hovering sword. He had expected the worst, but nothing happened. The sword fit loosely into his own empty scabbard. Still, nothing happened. Nothing until he placed a foot back into the undergrowth. Then a great thundering seemed to roll around him. The trees and plants seemed to come alive, swiping and slapping at him.

Instinct had him surging forward. But roots shot up from the ground and out from the dense growth around him and quickly clasped his ankles tightly, yanking him from his feet. His collision with the hard earth left him breathless and momentarily stunned. He was dragged along the ground on his back by his feet! He frantically grabbed at the undergrowth as he sped by it but his hands slid down and off the slippery vines. Holding one of his forearms in front of his face to protect it, he raised his head. The roots were rapidly pulling him toward the gnarled and knotted base of a massive tree.

As he neared it his fist curled around some sort of thick vine. His body jerked to a stop and stretched painfully as the tree roots continued their attempt to pull him in. The vine held! The huge tree's roots relaxed for a split second as if gathering strength for a renewed effort. It was just the opening Juga needed! He sat up and heavily thrust his short Gor'ean sword into the thickest of the tree roots that bound his feet. The air was filled with a deep, sudden, almost pain-filled moan as the huge tree shuddered and its roots released Juga. He kicked his feet and hands free from the remaining vines and roots and leapt to his feet, running back up the path he'd been dragged along. *There it was!* The path of vines and brush that had been crushed beneath his dragged body dead-ended ahead where it intersected with another path he recognized as his. He took a sharp right heading for, what he hoped was, the chamber's entrance. The volume of noise around him was increasing. A quick glance over his shoulder revealed the undergrowth was rapidly filling in behind him, erasing all trace of his path. The groan he had heard when he thrust his sword into the tree limb had intensified. It was as if every vine and plant had been given voice and all were shrieking in outrage.

Branches whipped across his face and shoulders breaking the skin; a thicker limb snapped back and caught him across the bridge of his nose. Eyes streaming and blood gushing from his nose, he plunged on. He could hear the frantic cries of Drake and the others in the distance, so he knew he must be nearing the exit.

Swiping the back of his hand across his face cleared his vision enough to see that the great door was shutting. It was only with a final leaping dive and a corkscrew turn in midair that he was able to slide sideways through the narrow opening and roll to the antechamber beyond. An ear-splitting crash of granite hitting granite echoed as the door to the crypt slammed shut.

The ruby in the crypt door winked in the torchlight. Its sister, embedded near the hilt of Athron's weapon, winked back. It was his turn. He slid his sword in place and awaited the slide and parting of the great doors to the next funerary chamber. What they saw inside of it left the four, again, in awe.

Instead of a chamber like the previous two, a long, thin stone walkway extended nearly one hundred yards directly in from the entrance. At the end of the walkway was a narrow stone platform upon which the crypt of the next brother sat. Above it, a sword hovered. There seemed to be no ceiling to the chamber, rather a sky filled with rolling, ominous clouds. A wind whipped through it. As to the floor, on either side of the walkway it seemed to fall away into a black abyss the depth of which one could only guess.

Divested of all but his sword, the Gor'ean High Prince stepped across the threshold and onto the walkway. At his first footstep, a great growling peal of thunder boomed across the chamber, gale force winds whipped through the chamber and sheets of driving rain pelted down but, mysteriously, immediately above Athron only. Undaunted he bent into the tempest and continued. With each step he took, the thunder grew in volume and the wind and rain increased in strength. Evidently the protections for this chamber called upon the elements to do their worst. With a now clearer sense of what might lie ahead, Athron kept his focus on the task at hand and pressed forward.

As he neared the midway point of the gangway, the rain and thunder abruptly stopped and the temperature within the the chamber plummeted well below freezing. The winds that had whistled and roared their accompaniment to the rain, now carried first a heavy hail and then driving snow upon them. Unprepared for the freezing termperatures, Athron wrapped his arms around his own torso and bent into the winds as he continued his surge forward.

As he stepped onto the platform that held the crypt, the wind and driving snow suddenly ceased leaving a strange echo of quiet in their wake. The rain in his hair had frozen into icy ropes and frost dusted his eyelashes and moustache. He paused there, rubbing his arms vigorously and stamping the snow from his boots whilst carefully scanning the crypt and the sword circling above it.

With his first step toward the tomb a burning circle of light arrowed down upon him from the betwitched sky above, the swelter from it was immediate and intense. So acute was its strength and ferocity that it seemed to evaporate the moisture from his clothes and body almost instantly. Squinting into the glare, Athron quickly moved the final steps and grasped the hovering sword.

The second his fingertips touched the hilt of the hovering sword the brilliant light was extinguished and, out of the absolute darkness a bolt of lightening shattered a portion of the platform upon which the crypt sat. His eyes still unfocussed from the quick switch from blinding light to blackness, Athron relied purely on instinct has he turned and took off at a dead run back toward the chamber's entrance. It took every bit of his natural athletic skills to maintain his footing as lightening bolts zapped down from the phantom sky, hitting the narrow pathway at his heels and disintegrating it behind him.

As he crossed the threshold at a full run and skidded to a halt, the deadly spears of lightning abruptly stopped. In the eerie silence that followed, the four watched as the great doors to the chamber slid slowly shut.

The next antechamber was a surprise, for the great door to the crypt held three jewels at its middle instead of one: a black opal, an amethyst, and a deep green jade. Drake stood in front of the door, pondering what this meant. He removed the remaining three swords from the leather scabbard he wore across his shoulders and unwrapped them. Though he took the harness off each evening when he slept, none of them had ever seen what the wrappings held. In it they saw the remaining three swords each bearing a jewel to match those inset in the portal. They looked to Drake for explanation.

"I can only think that this is perhaps because the three youngest brothers were gifts from the gods, all born the same day and at the same time. Their mother was of mixed blood and perished from the struggle of birthing them. Even though my father's love for my own mother was strong and true, he carried the loss of his first wife close to his heart for all of his days. The three boys were in their thirteenth year when they perished in the Minheras. It appears that they have been buried here together, joined in death as they were at birth."

He handed one of the three remaining swords to each of his three companions.

"As you all now carry the weapons of my brothers, I feel it is only right that you act as brothers to wield these final three swords," he said.

Each grasped one of the remaining swords and proceeded to the chamber door.

The chamber it revealed was plain and unadorned. The three final crypts lay at the far end of it, and three smaller swords rotated in ghostly harmony above them. The three stepped into the chamber simultaneously and cautiously, anticipating the worst with every step. Nothing happened. They stepped up to the three crypts and positioned themselves to take the weapons. Still, nothing.

At a nod from Athron they each grasped a sword at the same time. The room began to instantly fill with a thick mist. Before they could step away from the crypts and head toward the door, it enveloped them. They found their voices locked in their throats, and none could cry out.

*Out of the mist Athron could see himself upon his knees before his Father with the entire Elënthián Supreme Council looking on. His wrists were weeping blood from the bite of the rough ropes that bound his arms behind him. His clothes were in tatters, his flesh torn and oozing in the aftermath of a severe beating. He was stunned and confused, overcome with intense shame and humiliation. Allowing his gaze to sweep the ramparts of the Supreme Council chambers he could see only the angry and disapproving glares of the Council who, without exception, leaned over the railings to witness his disgrace.*

*"Traitor!" Acthelass Mar yelled. "You are a traitor to your people and to Elënthiá, and you must die!"*

*"But, Fyyther, please listen!" Athron begged. He could not fathom the depth of his father's anger and struggled to articulate his defense "The treasure—" He didn't get to finish.*

*"Treasure!" the Fyyther spat. "It is but a myth, a fiction. You have brought shame to this throne, to your family and to your people. You are naught but the lackey of a Draconean outlaw. There is no treasure; there never was."*

*"Shame? ... That was never my intent father. You know me to be loyal and true... I am your son ..." His voice trailed off.*

*The Fyyther continued as if he had not spoken, his pronouncement echoing in the cavernous chamber. "I condemn you to death for your treason and your treachery. You are no son of Gorger. And you are no blood of mine."*

"Noooo!" Athron found his voice finally. He shook his head to clear it of the poisoning mists. At his outcry he heard Drake's voice, "Athron! Athron, can you hear me? This way! Come this way."

Following Drake's voice he stumbled through the mist and out of the antechamber, gasping and falling to his knees.

"It's the mists, Drake! They creep into your mind and rob you of all reason, showing you the worst of what you fear"

Drake looked worriedly back into the swirling grey, concerned for his two apprentices.

*Juga looked down and found himself in ripped, filthy clothes, smelling of sweat and vomit. He was battering the gates to a Resistance stronghold, begging to be allowed inside.*

*A disembodied voice jeered, "Go away, Human. We know of your performance in battle. You could not hold your own against Gorillian's forces so you fled—a coward! And because of you hundreds died. Because of you!"*

*"No! That cannot be true," Juga croaked out, great tears filling his eyes, blurring his vision. "I am a strong and loyal soldier of the Resistance, a true warrior. I would never abandon my post. I would never give up, never give in."*

*"Warrior," the guard said disdainfully. "You are no warrior. You never were... You cowered in fear when faced with the shadow of Gorillian just as your parents did. You are no soldier! Only a weak, spineless coward."*

*Juga punched his fist against the grey-black planks of the gate, splitting the flesh of his knuckles. "Do not speak of my parents! Face me and repeat those words and I will skewer you upon my sword like foul carrion!"*

*His threat was met with a scornful laugh. "Empty threats from a pathetic coward."*

*Enraged, Juga pounded both fists against the solid gate before stepping back and savagely kicking at the wood again and again until it splintered and broke from its hinges. He surged through the opening only to find himself in darkness. Spinning around and then around again he screamed, spittle flying from his mouth, "Face me! You label me coward but it is you who hide. Face me!"*

*Suddenly the tattered door was gone and a stifling blackness pressed in on him. A disembodied voice seemed to whisper to him from all sides. "The mere mention of your name will bring a curse from the lips of all who hear it until it remains forever unspoken." Juga dropped to his knees in despair, his hands over his ears and tears streaming down his face as the voice continued, softly jeering and relentless. "You are weak. You have failed. You are naught but a coward ... a disgrace."*

"Liar!" It was as though the word had been exorcised from his very soul. Juga screamed it, his anguish pouring out in that single drawn out word. "You lie..." he whispered again.

"Juga! Juga, lad, can you hear me?"

Drake's voice seemed to come to him from a great distance, but once he focused on it, he realized he wasn't more than twenty odd feet away. Juga stumbled toward the sound.

*Lathaniel stood on the hills above his beloved Lamana. The skies were the blue he loved so dearly; the Linia forest with its emerald trees beckoned to his left. On the ground before him, he saw the graves of his mother and father. He felt a clutch in his stomach that bent him double before the weight of his guilt and grief pulled him to his knees. He was locked in place. His face was twisted in agony but he couldn't seem to cry out or to move, so deeply felt was his anguish. He had failed them.*

*As he lifted his eyes, he saw the markers for grave after grave begin to emerge from the ground: Chap, Jameth, Mourir and Haug, Darryn, and his own Sabine…all gone. He slid sideways until his hip hit the ground and he was leaning heavily against one arm. He could read the names of more and more of his neighbours and friends as the markers multiplied before his eyes. He was overcome with a sorrow so keen, so overwhelming, he felt it at his very core. And with this sorrow a paralyzing blackness began to creep over him.*

*Mocking laughter caught his attention, and he swung his head round to see Bracher Gramicy and his benchman standing off to the right. "Did you really believe I would spare them? They were all dead before nightfall the day you left. You are a fool, Lathaniel Waythan. A fool! Lamana is well rid of you and the poison of your kin. I have allies now, strong and immutable. By the time I have finished there will not be a single Lamanian brave enough to utter the name Waythan! Lamana is mine now! Mine!"*

*His maniacal laugh seemed to go on and on. Lathaniel covered his ears and sank to the ground weaving back and forth in his anguish, oblivious to all around him.*

*After a time he could hear a voice; a deep, calming voice that seemed to penetrate the fog of his great grief.*

"It's an illusion, lad. Only an illusion. You must walk away from it now and come back to us, for none of it is real..."

Lathaniel tried to focus on the voice. It took him several tries before he could find his voice.

"Drake?" he called out.

"Here, lad. I'm over here. Stand now and walk away from this madness."

Lathaniel pulled himself to his feet and stumbled out of the mist.

Gorillian stood on the top of the escarpment with his arms crossed on his broad chest. They were close; he knew it. He had pulled information from every link in his network and used his best Are-Narc trackers. Tracks had led them to the Sitiskan Fields, and then here to a waterfall on the Loris River. But from here it was like they had vanished into thin air. He had patrols on both sides of the river, systematically working their way inland looking for any tracks or trails. If the Draconean had disappeared, that meant he'd gone to ground; and that meant that he'd likely found the lost Draconean treasure or was searching for it. The greed that had driven Gorillian to slaughter an entire race drove him still. He wanted that treasure!

The spy networks were humming. He was no longer the only one in pursuit. The Gor'eans were reeling at news that their High Prince had thrown in with the Draconean and, like Gorillian, had troops scouring Amarik for any sign of the company. His Are-Narcs had already clashed with Gor'ean patrols on several occasions with considerable losses to both sides. His only advantage, to his mind, was that the Gor'eans believed they were tracking a criminal and a deserter, not a mythical lost treasure. If the Resistance knew what the Draconean searched for, Gorger—indeed, the whole of Elënthiá—would be emptied of soldiers trying to assist him.

As it was, he had deployed troops to keep the Gor'eans busy. Incursions on their northern and southern borders had them scrambling to protect their own. A debacle at Cap'hannet had meant the loss of a half legion of his Are-Narcs, who'd stumbled inadvertently across the entrance to the Camp. Not a single soldier survived to share directions to the entrance! Gorillian gave himself a mental shake and set that aside. Sufficiently concerned with the capture of the Draconean and his treasure, Gorillian had left Ethen-jar to supervise the hunt personally.

# CHAPTER 30

The four companions pressed onward. They allowed for a brief break to regroup after the challenges of the funerary chambers, principally because the ordeal had so shaken Lathaniel. While the others had found their way out of the deadly mists within a quarter hour, Lathaniel had been subjected to them for nearly an hour before he could shake off their influence and find his way out. He was drawn and pale; he'd said little more than a handful of words in the hours since the incident.

They now carried the six ancient swords retrieved from the Tombs but did not have to travel far. Not fifty yards up the passage from the final antechamber, it opened into a wide, high-ceilinged corridor. Ancient paintings graced the walls, recording the history of the Draconean people. Drake promised himself that he would return in more peaceful times and reacquaint himself with his ancestors, but for now they wasted little time in moving forward and through the large arch at the end of it. Once through, they lit torches to illuminate a large chamber ... perfectly round.

There was a large circle suspended at the center of it, perhaps thirty feet in diameter and accessible via four thin gangways that joined to the outer, much broader circle where they now stood. The means of its suspension and what was in the blackness below the gangways was unknown. There were pillars around the edges of the broader circle that supported an upper gallery.

Drake set his pack aside and began to explore first the perimeter of the outer circle. Finding nothing of interest, he crossed one of the gangways to the inner circle, dropping down on his haunches to inspect the raised markings on the floor of it.

"Here," he said. "It is here."

Athron, Juga, and Lathaniel gathered the six swords and crossed to join him.

"See these slots in the floor? It is a variation on the doors to the funerary chambers. Find the jewels that match the swords we retrieved, and slide the swords into the corresponding slots."

The three followed his instructions, dusting dirt and debris away from each of the openings. There they could find the jewels and slots for two blades, one for the swords taken from each of the chambers and another for those belonging to Drake's own brothers. One by one they worked to slide the twelve swords into the stone sheaths in the floor of the circle. Athron's two were the last to be inserted.

The four looked at each other expectantly. Nothing happened.

Drake looked about in confusion wondering what he had overlooked. Lathaniel quietly touched his shoulder and pointed to the center. "There is a space for yours, Drake. As the thirteenth son, and the last living Draconean, yours is required to open the vault and claim the legacy of your race."

Silently, Drake went to the center of the circle. There beneath the dust and beside a gleaming emerald was a final, single slot. He looked from one to the other of his companions, not certain what would happen next, and then slowly slid the final Draconean sword into its ancient stone sheath.

As the hilt of Drake's sword locked into place time itself froze. Drake lifted his head in surprise and stood as he looked around him. A strange golden glow had filled the chamber bringing each and every detail of it into a fine focus. Lathaniel, Athron and Juga were frozen in their squats by the other swords still staring expectantly at him, unblinking. The air felt charged with a strange energy and the hair on the back of Drake's neck lifted as he felt a presence, a warmer light behind him.

Slowly turning into it, he blinked several times trying to reassure himself of the vision before him. There amidst the dust mites that hung suspended in the golden, supercharged air, stood his father. Not the rag-clad fugitive he saw die before him, but the father his memories embraced. The father that stood strong and solid in buckskin leggings and tall boots, his grey hair groomed and rippling back from his face. The father of his childhood at whose knee he had thrived and whom he had loved unreservedly.

"Is this some dream? ... some magician's illusion?" he whispered.

He saw a gentle smile spread across his father's face. "No dream, my son. It is I." Still smiling, he moved toward Drake, his figure shrouded in an otherworldly bluish glow. He came to a halt a few feet from Drake who remain stunned, speechless.

"You found the Tombs and have claimed what is rightfully yours at last. My pride in you knows no bounds. But Drake, my son, you must release the sorrow and guilt that your heart has held so tightly to. The gods intervened that day. You were not meant to be in Evendeer. You were meant to survive – you were always meant to survive."

The tears that had blurred Drake's vision slipped free and rolled unheeded down his cheeks.

His father's face became serious as he turned and glanced over his own shoulder. "I have so little time ... you must listen closely for what I tell you now, you are long overdue in knowing. The goddess has already revealed that you are not the lone survivor of our race. I have come to tell you why," he sighed then, his expression softening as he looked with thirsty eyes at his son. "Feeling we were outgrowing Evendeer and the island of Moldost, an age or more ago our race set out to build an enclave in the northernmost mountains of Elënthiá. It was a time of peace between races then. We had little contact with any but our own but we enlisted the help of the Dwarves and the Giants for our undertaking in the north was of a scale that it could not be accomplished on our own. In the last years just prior to its completion there was a schism among our people. There were those who felt that our allegiance should shift from Suvillwa our beloved godess of light, to her mate Dyvariiare who, as you know is the god of darkness and who we worshipped as only a minor deity. We couldn't reconcile our differences.

"As Dray Sorzin my allegiance to Suvillwa was strong ... but as King of the Draconeans I made a decision to separate the two factions for a time – a calming period, if you like. Nearly three thousand Draconeans left the island of Moldost on ships sailing north. The coasts were not watched in those days and their movement north was, as we planned, secret. In the years that followed, we came to a compromise and planning was underway to vacate the south and to unite the northern and southern Draconeans. But not long after you were born Gorillian began a campaign for control of Elënthiá. As you now know, it was not his first such campaign but Elënthiá was not organized to unite against evil then, and communication channels were tenuous. From the time we first heard of this here in the south, we forbade any mention or discussion of our northern brethren for we feared for their safety and wanted to ensure our own when we moved north.

"You know what became of Evendeer," his voice dropped and his eyes clouded, "and you know of my fate and that of your brothers. When I finally found you that day so long ago, there was no time to tell you, and you were not of an age that I could give you precise directions to the north. Instead, I gave you the swords and the means to find your way here so that you could find the map and re-join our people."

If the presence of his father had, in itself, not been enough, Drake was stunned by his father's revelations. As if some unseen voice was prompting him, Dray Sorzin continued hurriedly, "My time with you is coming to an end but know this my son," he leaned in closer to Drake, his eyes serious and penetrating, "your duty is not done. Find the map, for you are urgently needed in the north. While you live, it remains your sole duty to avenge your family and our people but you must also know that the threat to Elënthiá will not end with Gorillian's demise. Only when *two* perish will this darkness lift." With that he took a step back. That motion seemed to snap Drake into action.

"No!" he blurted, stepping forward. "Please! After so long, you cannot think to leave me yet – to leave me again?"

"Hold your companions close to you, Drake. Though you have sacrificed much, still more will be asked of you."

"There is so much I don't understand ..." Drake's hand reached out to his father but felt nothing but the warm glow of the air around him.

"You will in time, my son. I have long watched over you and will watch over you still ..." The edges of light surrounding his father began to blur and his figure began to recede into the golden flush still permeating the room.

*I love you ...* Words that, for two millennia, a boy had yearned to say to his beloved father remained unsaid.

"And I, you my son" was the whispered response.

Blue light was embraced by gold ... and then the gold light faded slowly away.

"Drake? ... Drake?" Lathaniel called his name once again. Disoriented, Drake jerked his head around to lock eyes with Lathaniel who was studying him curiously. Athron and Juga were also on their feet looking at him expectantly.

Just then, they braced their feet as the floor beneath them jerked and began to shift clockwise; the walls of the circular chamber shifted counterclockwise. Drake gave his head a shake and tried to bring his concentration back in focus. As the room rotated, an entrance to another chamber was revealed. When the walls and floor stopped moving, they gathered torches and moved into the newly revealed adjacent chamber.

It was also circular but with no central, separate circle. When they had set the locks in motion in the original chamber, it must have triggered a concurrent lock in the adjacent room; for when it stopped moving, a large open archway on the opposite side of it was revealed, likely an exit.

However, the four were not concentrating on the exit just then but on the incredible sight before them. Statuary, both small and gigantic, depicting Draconean gods and inset with precious and semiprecious stones, was everywhere. Between, among, and around them were chests opened and overflowing with gold coins and jewels, exquisite jewellery and all manner of opulent adornments. Finely crafted vases and vessels of all sizes and description spilled over with gems and gold, colourfully shimmering in the torch light. The four were held breathless in the face of a treasure gathered across an eternity by a people now all but extinct.

Drake reclaimed their attention. "We must be mindful of selecting only that which is most valuable and easily accepted as currency across Elënthiá," he cautioned.

"It must be the gems, then," Athron replied. "They can be carried easily and in quantity and won't belabour our efforts in battle nor arouse suspicion whilst we travel."

Drake agreed and went about sourcing four sturdy leather receptacles in which to carry the gems, and then selecting the contents for each. This finished, he said, "I now need your assistance, for this chamber is large and what I must find will not be obvious. I am looking for a map, scrolls, a pouch of documents…something that might have been left here for my attention. Spread out across the chamber and help me search."

They fanned out into four quadrants, trying hard to concentrate on the task at hand and to ignore the incredible vista of wealth that surrounded them.

Lathaniel began his search at the perimeter, thinking to work his way inward. As he methodically swept back and forth across the area, he noticed a golden structure about ten feet in height and rectangular. It was like a cabinet, but the lower face of it was enclosed and covered with gold inlay. The upper portion was open and framed by an elaborate arch. Within the opening was a single shelf upon which sat an elaborately jewelled chest. Intrigued, he opened it. The size and beauty of the sapphire he found inside it took his breath away. He lifted it reverently from its nest of rich fabric and examined it turning it this way and that, admiring the warmth it emitted when it captured the light. He was still holding the stone when Juga called out.

"Here, Drake! I may have something."

Lathaniel tucked the stone in his pouch to show the Draconean and headed across the room to where Athron, Drake and Juga were now congregated.

"Good work, lad. I think this is it."

Juga had discovered a cabinet against the wall in his quadrant. In it were several leather-wrapped parchments. On quick but careful examination, Drake found what he was looking for. His face was solemn as he unrolled the ancient scroll. What he saw turned the bones of his legs to liquid, and he sank to his knees.

"It's true," he whispered. He looked up at Lathaniel through eyes that were at last unguarded. "It's as he said it would be. There *is* another city of Draconeans, hidden these many years here…" He gestured to the map, and the three of them leaned in to see what he was pointing at. "Here in the Coldain Region.."

Looking from one to the other of them, his usually sombre and serious face broke into a huge, white-toothed smile, the first true smile that any could recall having seen. He ran his fingers lightly over the parchment muttering almost to himself, "The Darrish clues are cryptic but not insurmountable... protections ... hmmmm." Then it was as though he gave himself a mental shake. He stood and said, "We have what we came for; we must now make haste to finish our mission." He rolled back on his heels and came to his feet, rolling up the leather–wrapped scroll as he did. He slid it into his satchel then began barking out orders to the three of them. "Go back to the central chamber and gather all the swords; we must secure this place before we exit."

They hastened to follow his instructions. That done, they took a moment for dried meat and some bread, eating while all torches but for those they each carried were extinguished; packs and weapons were collected and shouldered. The four then made their way into the dark corridor on the far side of the treasure chamber.

Just beyond the exit, they found a large stone panel higher than a table with the face of it sloped toward them. Within half of it were empty slots for thirteen swords, each, again, clearly marked with corresponding precious stones. There were several verses of runes on the other half. Drake ran his fingers across these and translated while his companions held their torches over the panel.

"This instructs that the swordbearers must leave with the weapons they carried to this place. All others must remain." he deciphered. "According to this, by virtue of your efforts here, only you, as the original bearers of the Draconean swords used to master the protections can return to this place via the exit ahead." He turned to look at them.

"The runes bid you guard the Draconean sword you now own, and your life, well. For the secret to the Draconean treasure now rests with not one but four races in Elënthiá."

Drake then instructed them in the opening of the vault should they come back to this place alone. The nine remaining swords were then slid into their respective slots. As soon as the first sword slid into its sheath, they heard a now-familiar series of clicks as the locks and tumblers shifted. By the time the last of the nine swords was sheathed, the granite doors of the circular treasure vault and the chamber beyond it had closed.

Just up the tunnel from the vault exit, the four companions hit a dead-end, their further progress blocked by another stone door. In the manner of the Tombs, sliding any of their four swords into the single slot would release its locking mechanism.

Before he did so, Drake turned to his companions. "We cannot be so fortunate as to have escaped undetected during our exodus from Gorger. There will be scouts from all sides hunting for us. The moment we step from beyond this door, we will once again be in harm's way. By my estimation, it will be dusk, and the shadows will be long."

He shrugged off his pack, then the satchel he wore across his chest, leaving them with Juga and Lathaniel. He unsheathed his great sword.

"I will open the portal and exit first. With this call of a night owl…" he demonstrated… "I will signal the way clear. Exit one by one but not until you hear my call. Precautious, I know, but rather that then the opposite."

There were nods of ascent all around, and all torches were extinguished.

Drake inserted his sword into the slot in the door and they heard a click, albeit a very quiet one. The locking mechanism released the door and allowed them to slide it very quietly to the side, sufficient for Drake to squeeze through. The fresh evening air rushed in through the thin opening along with the sounds of the forest in early evening and the last dusky rays of daylight. Beyond the door way was a thick veil of vines and greenery. Drake slipped out and away into the half light. At his call, Juga followed carrying his pack, then Athron followed by Lathaniel who looped Drake's satchel over his shoulder and with one last look slid the door to The Tombs shut.

There were twenty-five of them in total. An Are-Narc patrol charged with scouting the riverbed of the Loris for any sign of the Draconean and his company by direct order of the great Lord Gorillian, who was himself supervising the search from downriver. They were five staggered rows of soldiers, each five abreast with five shoulder lengths between them. They worked in coordination with another patrol doing the same immediately inland from them and with two other patrols doing the same on the other side of the river. Every bush, clump of brush, and copse of trees was prodded, poked, climbed on and under; no area was overlooked as they methodically scoured the shores of the riverbed.

Lathaniel and the Are-Narc scout saw each other at the same time. Lathaniel let fly with a dagger at the same time as the Narc loosed an arrow. Lathaniel saw the dagger embed itself in the Narc's throat just before he felt the arrow pierce his left shoulder, the impact of it lifting him from his feet and hurling him backwards against the rocks ... and blackness.

"Give it to me," Gorillian growled in a deadly quiet voice. His General handed him a worn leather satchel. Gorillian snatched it from him and walked over to stand near the campfire. He flipped it open and rifled through the contents, throwing bits onto the ground in his impatience. The last item he extracted was a roll of leather tied off with a thong. Pulling at the knot, he yanked the thong away and rolled open the leather.

His face stilled, the anger falling away. His hurried movements ceased, and he finished unravelling the leather with great care. He sat on a low stool, leaning in closer to the fire and tilting the document within the leather toward the firelight so as to see it better.

His eyes raised and he stared off into the distance, his mind first numb as he absorbed what he was seeing, and then racing with the implications of it.

A lost Draconean city! So it was true… He'd heard the occasional myth across the ages but had disregarded it as the hopeful musings of his detractors across Elënthiá. There had never been a single shred of evidence to support the tales, and he had given them no credence. His eyes dropped again to the map.

The city was somewhere in the Coldain Region. The exact location was not clear, the likely directions buried in the Darrish runes that footnoted the scroll. His brow furrowed. It had been centuries since he had seen Darrish, and the runes would take time to decipher—time that he did not have to waste.

"Break camp immediately. We must hasten back to Ethen-jar."

# CHAPTER 31

*The grey, swirling mists of oblivion were punctuated with short, sharp stabs of the most intense pain he could imagine. It became unbearable ... so he reached once again for blackness. No luck. The pain had a tight grip on him and was dragging him up, and up again. He could hear voices, as though in a dream or from a far distance. He tried to marshal his thoughts to decipher what they were saying, as at some level they felt familiar. His eyelids fluttered.*

"There must be something else you can do…something else you can give him."

*Drake's voice?*

"I was certain he wouldn't make it through another night, but the lad is strong."

*That voice was unfamiliar. A calloused but familiar palm pushed his hair off his forehead. Then the pain sharpened once more.*

"Must you do that! Can you not hear him moan?"

"This is near to the last of it. I have tried to do this in stages, mostly when he is unconscious, for I am aware of the agony of it. But there are still places on his torso where pieces of his shirt are burned into his skin. We must remove these, else risk an infection that he is too weak to fight off."

"And his shoulder wound…?"

"I removed the shaft and cleansed the wound thoroughly. In truth, it is the least of his worries now. I will finish with the burns then wrap them. Beyond that, I can do more as a healer. His survival is with the gods."

That last sentence seemed to fade as Lathaniel surrendered once again to the blackness.

Juga leaned against the column outside of the building, staring off into the night. He felt a hand on his shoulder and turned to Athron.

"He will live," the Gor'ean Prince reassured him. "He is young and strong, a warrior. He will live."

Juga smiled weakly and turned again to stare into the night, but the door opened behind him. Both he and Athron turned to see Drake exit looking haggard and drawn. Their eyes searched his face expectantly, hoping for good news.

"He lives. But only just. If he survives this night, then the gods are with us."

Drake moved to stand beside Juga, leaning on the opposite side of the column, sadness and exhaustion filling every fibre of his being. A low, keening cry of agony seeped beneath the doors to reach their ears, twisting their hearts in the process, for it was not the first they'd heard. Juga turned to look at Drake, who stared sightless into the night. A single tear slipped down his cheek and disappeared into the folds of his collar below.

Lathaniel's eyelids felt as though sap had sealed them shut. It was a matter of a moment's struggle to focus his efforts and attention on opening them. He could hear raised voices nearby. One was Drake's. The other he didn't recognize. From the bits of their conversation he could hear, he presumed the other man was a healer. He tried to raise one hand to wipe his eyes but only managed to lift it a few inches before it fell heavily back on the coverlet. The movement caught Drake's attention, and he was instantly at Lathaniel's side.

"Lathaniel? Lathaniel, can you hear me?"

Lathaniel nodded slightly and tried to lick his lips, realizing how parched his throat was. The Draconean was a blur above him but a welcome sight.

"How do you feel, lad?"

It took effort but Lathaniel rasped, "Pass me a sword and I am yours to command." He smiled weakly then closed his eyes again.

The Draconean's shoulders seemed to sag as he let go of the tension he'd carried since the Forsair fell on the Sitiskan Fields. He rinsed a clean cloth in a basin of water near the bed and dribbled water onto Lathaniel's grateful lips. He continued until Lathaniel signalled he'd had enough.

With a somewhat clearer voice, Lathaniel asked, "What happened?"

Drake pulled a chair close to the head of the bed. "We were surprised by a scout party of Are-Narcs shortly after we left the Tombs. You took out the scout with your dagger but not before you took an arrow in your left shoulder. You were knocked unconscious. Gorillian had troops on either side of the Loris from its estuary almost as far north as the Marshes. We carried you away and into a copse of trees until you could regain consciousness but a scouting party tracked us and there was a skirmish. They lit the trees on fire to flush us out. It was a time before the three of us could get to you, lad, and you were burned...your side, some of your upper chest and a bit of your back."

He held Lathaniel's gaze as he recounted what had happened, the emotion in his eyes raw and obvious.

"In the heat of it, a stranger arrived astride a horse and threw his lot in with us. Another soldier. His name is Layne Rev'eara. He has made himself scarce these last days but I am certain you will shortly make his acquaintance. With his assistance, we killed the Narcs but knew others were on their heels. Layne was charged with getting you to help. Juga, Athron, and I laid down tracks in the opposite direction and gave Gorillian and his Are-Narcs a chase. We lost them in the Marshes and came directly here to Limore to find you. Limore, Lathaniel. That's where we are now. I don't know if you remember your maps, but—"

"I remember," Lathaniel softly interrupted. "How badly am I hurt?" He paused again before asking, "Will I live?"

"Yes, lad. You will live. By the gods there have been days in the past fortnight where it did not seem that you would, but you are a warrior. Yes, you will live," Drake repeated, the last three words said with a catch in his voice that he cleared with a cough. The two were quiet for a time while Lathaniel absorbed what he'd been told and marshalled his remaining strength.

"Juga and Athron. They are well? The treasure…?"

"As well as two such scoundrels can expect to be," he smiled. "Juga's eyes were blackened from his adventure in the Tombs, and his nose was broken. That baby face of his has a bit of character now."

More seriously, he continued, "Some knife wounds. Athron took an arrow to the flesh under his arm, but it was really nothing. They left for Gorgonathan two days back, once they knew that you would survive. It is time that Athron cleared his name, for the Gor'eans scour Koorast to find him. More importantly, the Resistance is in dire need of the resources they carry."

"And the map?" Lathaniel asked. "It was in your satchel and I was carrying it. Did you get the map?"

"Aye, I got the map. But in during the fight with the Are-Narcs, I lost it. It will now have found its way into Gorillian's possession, I'm sure."

Lathaniel started, the movement bringing a grimace of pain to his face.

"Shhh, lad. Be still. I had enough of a look at it to know that the lost city is called Dohenheer and is located in the Ashen Mountains far in the north of the Coldain Region. To find its exact location I would have needed to study the runes. But we have no worry of that now that we've made the acquaintance of Layne."

"Can we trust him, Drake? Are you certain he is no enemy?"

"He is no enemy, Lathaniel, of that I can assure you. He is a Draconean."

# CHAPTER 32

A few tenacious leaves clung to the trees, their mates long since fallen to the ground and were crackling into bits under their footfalls. There had been a light rain the previous evening, but Juga and Athron had awoken to clear dawn skies. They certainly weren't travelling at a speed that allowed one to enjoy the view Juga thought as he kept apace of Athron, who was hastening back to Gorger at a ground-eating rate.

Athron was preoccupied. What they carried upon their backs was crucial to the Resistance, and both he and Juga felt the weight as if it were boulders they carried instead of gems. This, coupled with the questions surrounding the reception they would receive, hung above them like a thick cloud.

With only Athron's back to stare at, Juga's mind wandered. At some level he wondered if he were racing back to Gorger to face execution for his allegiance to the Gor'ean High Prince. *So be it!* he thought. Rather to die alongside a great warrior then alone as he was in that horrid dream in the Tombs!

On the other hand, Juga considered it could not have turned out better. If Athron could satisfy his father and the Supreme Council of his loyalty, then his allegiance to the Prince could work to his favour. Juga was an optimist. But as much as he held Athron in high regard, the circumstances of his life had also taught him to be an opportunist.

"Athron..." he panted as he trailed behind. "Must one be Gor'ean bred to join your army?"

"Yes," was the curt answer. And then after a half minute or more, "Unless extraordinary bravery in service to Gorger has been demonstrated. In that case, an exception can be made, but only by royal decree."

"And the Royal Guard...can that same decree allow a non-Gor'ean to guard the royal family?"

There was silence for another moment. "Yes, it can."

The two ran on for another mile or two before Juga again broke the silence. "Do the Gor'ean artists you told me of do other kinds of special body markings, or only those for the Royal Guard and the royal family?"

"As I told you, body painting is an integral part of our culture so, yes, others beyond the Guard have markings, but none exactly the same as mine for it is forbidden to carry such a marking falsely. Any who have the markings usually depict birds of some sort, for these are sacred in our culture."

The Human lad smiled to himself knowing that the next time he saw Drake and Lathaniel, he would be the proud bearer of some colour.

Juga was restless that night, he was thinking about Lathaniel and Drake and was facing some difficult truths, truths that forced him to let the last of his adolescence go and step forward as a man.

If he was honest with himself, the close relationship between the two bothered him. He had been Drake's sole apprentice for three years, and though their relationship had grown and flourished, he knew that he and Drake would never share the ties that he witnessed between the Draconean and the Forsair in the short time they'd been together. He knew that the rare emotion Drake showed in Limore would never be so for him.

Jealousy? Perhaps. But then there was Athron. He felt as strong a pull toward the Gor'ean Prince as he imagined Lathaniel felt toward Drake. As he considered how the gods had fashioned his fate, he realized that all was as it should be; in fact, beyond his imagining! He had the good fortune of being trained in war by inarguably the most accomplished warrior of their time. Though still years from his actual majority, he had already distinguished himself as fearless and competent in the few battles he had engaged in. He was companion to the Gor'ean High Prince, and if the gods were with them and Athron was embraced in Gorger, he was well positioned to petition for consideration by the Gor'ean Army. His lifelong dream of joining the Resistance was closer to a reality than ever.

He rolled again to his other side as these thoughts settled his mind. Yes, the sooner they returned to Gorger, the better.

They crossed the border into Gorger the following morning. The Prince seemed to relax marginally now that they were on Gor'ean land, but he remained cautious, saying little. Their passage into Gorger did nothing to ease their pace; if anything, it increased. Juga could still feel Athron's anxiety and desire to face his Fyyther.

Athron played out alternate scenarios repeatedly in his mind as they ran on. A central core of duty and honour was bred into every Gor'ean. It was in their genes and an integral part of their makeup. Contravening an order from his father and deliberately casting himself in a role of a deserter was as foreign to him as was imaginable. His father had considerable influence with the Supreme Council, but these were extraordinary times. Even if Acthelass Mar believed him and welcomed him with open arms, there was still the Council to worry about. Thank the gods for the contents of their packs, for it might only be this that would turn the tides in his favour.

He worried about his Human companion and hoped that, whatever the fates brought to him, Juga would not be held similarly accountable. The lad was irreverent. Titles and royal addresses had long since been forgotten and, in private, the two now behaved as brothers. Juga teased and annoyed him ... and was baited and affectionately cuffed in return. In the absence of brothers of his own, the lad had captured a considerable amount of the Prince's affection. If the fates were not with him in Gorgonathan, Athron hoped that he could shield Juga.

Though now inside of Gorger, they were still nearly a fortnight's journey from Gorgonathan. He could not allow himself to be arrested before he could petition the Council ... and his father.

# CHAPTER 33

Lathaniel was still weak; his legs were sluggish and his steps uncertain. He felt like one of the newly pulled calves in the spring in Lamana, with his wobbles and stumbles. But he was taking each day as it came ...it had been a long time since those words had come to his mind; the last time they'd been said aloud to Chap. It seemed like a lifetime ago.

The skin on his torso was pink and puckered, most of the raw bits were now healed and the scabs were gone. Whatever healing salve the healer had given him was working wonders to keep the new skin supple and pliant. His shoulder was still stiff. It had been bound in a sling, but he had removed that this morning, determined to hasten it to its former strength and mobility.

Through all, the Draconean had never been far away. He didn't coddle but neither did he push. He was just there. And for that, Lathaniel was grateful.

He inhaled deeply. The sea air was cold and bracing. He turned his collar up against the wind but relished the feel of it on his face, and the color it was bringing to his pale cheeks. Gramal had been a busy port, but Lathaniel never thought he would see as many vessels in one place as in Limore. The port was heaving with ships, soldiers, supplies, and bulging at the seams with people of all races and colors. It was the one completely free port on Koorast. Lathaniel watched the comings and goings until exhaustion got the better of him and he was forced to head back to their lodgings once again.

He took a hot cup of tea and nodded off in a chair near the fire, the warm cup untouched but cradled between his hands.

His eyes opened to the keen regard of another. He started with a jerk, spilling the now cool tea on his lap and suspiciously looking at the stranger, whose eyes softened under his stare.

"Please!...I am sorry to have startled you. I have waited many days to see you and could wait no longer. We have met, but I am certain you will not recall, for you were so ill at the time. I am Layne Rev'eara."

Lathaniel's eyes widened as they swept over his visitor. Certainly he was of a size to be a Draconean, for he was nearly as tall as Drake. He appeared well muscled and fit though not quite so broad as Drake. His dark hair was shoulder length, parted in the middle and unkempt, as if he'd just come in out of a great wind. His face was rugged and tanned but lined, and the hazel eyes that held his were tired but sharp in their regard. He wore the clothing of a working man: an unobtrusive leather tunic over a woollen undershirt and leather leggings. His feet and legs were encased in knee-high leather boots. He was without a weapon.

"As you know, I am a Draconean of the north, son of Seuton Rev'eara and a former captain in the Draconean army."

Lathaniel finally spoke. "I understand I owe you my life."

Before Layne could reply, the door opened and Drake entered. Closing it, he drew a chair near to the fire and straddled it, his arms hanging over its back. "So you surface, Draconean. I wondered where you disappeared to."

"I thought it best not to be seen in your company for a time, as I am known in Limore and did not want my presence with you to draw undue attention. You see, many here know that I have been looking for a Draconean. I did not want any to infer from my company with you and our young friend that I had found who I was looking for."

Drake fixed him in a hard stare. "I think you had better tell all."

Layne told of his rise through the ranks in the army and then of the mysterious assignment he had been given by his High Council. He went on to recount the many false starts and leads he had pursued over the years, and then how he came to hear of a strange company heading west.

"I felt the gods had finally smiled upon me, and I set out for the south and west immediately." He went on to describe the leads he had followed and his surreptitious eavesdropping on Gorillian's scouts, whose reports led him to Sitiska and then to the shores of the Loris.

"It was pure happenstance that I was so close when the fire started," he said. "When I heard the fighting, I knew it must be you."

Drake turned to Lathaniel. "He rode in on the blackest mount I have ever seen looking as if he'd ridden out of the black pits of Ethen-jar itself." He smiled slightly, and Layne continued.

"It's been some time since I'd had the pleasure of a battle, for I have kept a low profile these many years." He smiled at Drake. "I should extend my thanks for the pleasure."

"He brought you back here to Limore with great haste, Lathaniel," Drake explained, "and found you a competent and discrete healer. He stayed with you until our arrival but then disappeared."

"I am here now, for I must ask for a return of the favour," Layne Rev'eara said solemnly. "I must ask you to return immediately with me to Dohenheer."

Drake and Lathaniel looked at one another and burst out laughing.

The other Draconean looked quickly from one to the other. "It is not a far-fetched request for, as I have told you, I am pledged to find and return you! There can be no jest in that..."

When he could still his laughter, Drake placed a hand on his countryman's shoulder.

"We find humour only because we have been agonizing over how to get to Dohenheer without the map"

"Map? What map? There are no maps to Dohenheer. As I am aware, none know of its existence."

The silence stretched out until it was almost uncomfortable. Drake had fixed Layne with a hard stare and appeared to be contemplating saying something of importance. Lathaniel was staring at Drake, sure he understood the decision the Draconean was contemplating, and Layne stared from one to the other of them, completely baffled as to what was happening.

Drake broke the silence. Immediately upon hearing him say: "My full name is Drake Sorzin, only surviving son of the Dray Sorzin, the Draconean king of Evendeer ..." Layne Rev'eara first leapt to his feet then fell to his knees, ashen. He was in the presence of Draconean royalty he had been taught were long dead and he was completely at a loss as to how to react.

Drake reached down and drew him to his to feet, then gently pushed him back into his chair. Lathaniel entered the conversation, explaining their search for the Tombs, their discovery of a map to Dohenheer, and their subsequent loss of it during the fight with the Are-Narcs briefly to Layne. He purposely omitted mention of the treasure, believing that to be information only Drake should share.

Layne's expression was grave. "This news that Gorillian holds a map to Dohenheer is most disturbing. I must leave for the north immediately, for my people ... your people ... *our* people must be warned. He could already be on the march, readying for an attack!" He was agitated now.

Drake raised his voice and interrupted, "Captain! I have been fighting Gorillian since before you were able to lift a sword. He will wait, and he will prepare. His mind does not work as you would expect, so while you and I would think to attack when an enemy was least expecting it, he will want to amass his troops, to ensure his enemy knows well he will come, and then intimidate them with his size and strength. You would be surprised at the success such a tactic has had for him across Elënthiá.

"What Lathaniel has not shared is that though the map shows a city in the northern reaches of the Coldain deep in the Ashen Mountains, it does not indicate precisely where it is. To find this, Gorillian will have to decipher runes written in ancient Darrish. This will buy us some time. Then, he will send scouts ahead to ascertain the exact location. Meanwhile, he will amass his troops. Entry of the Draconeans of the North into this war - be it by their choice or by necessity - will have him more than concerned for, I am generally thought to be the last of my race. With no information to the contrary, he will believe Dohenheer to be filled with an army of warriors like me. That may or may not be the case, but if believes the warriors of Dohenheer could turn the tide of this war, then he will not act in haste."

"How did you come to know of his strategies so intimately, your Highness?"

"I am no Highness, Layne. I am Drake to you, just as I was Drake twenty minutes ago. And with regard to Gorillian ... I've had millennia of firsthand observation." Drake turned to Lathaniel, changing the subject. "We will need to mobilize an army of our own to stand in support of the northern Draconeans. We need to get a message to Athron."

"Who is this Athron?" Layne interjected.

"He was the tall, fair-haired man travelling with us. He is the Gor'ean High Prince."

Layne's eyes widened at the news.

"His father is the Fyyther of Gorger and an influential member of the Elënthián Supreme Council. Of any, he would have the power to sway the Council to support a full out Resistance initiative in the north."

Drake paused, his eyes shifting again to Lathaniel. "That is, of course, assuming that Athron gets our message and can speak to him before he is arrested and executed for treason..."

Layne's eyes were filled with questions, but Drake continued on, now addressing him: "In answer to your request for a favour former Captain Layne Rev'eara, my brother from the North...we would be delighted to accept your offer of accompaniment to the lost city of Dohenheer. When do we leave?"

# CHAPTER 34

They were being tracked. Each and every sense was on high alert. Although he hadn't spotted by whom as yet, Athron felt the regard.

"Stay close," he told Juga quietly, his eyes scanning the trees

The tone of his voice was sufficient to alert Juga. "Trouble?" he asked.

"Not yet. But not far away either" was the reply.

The two continued moving through the trees.

"What do you see?" Juga asked quietly as they moved along.

"It's not so much what I can see but what I feel is in the trees watching us," Athron explained. "We will wait. If whoever it is were here to take our lives, we would be dead already. They will show themselves soon, I think."

They'd only continued on a short while when Athron quietly said to Juga, "There, high in the trees off to your left, just to the right of where the sun shines through the leaves. Do you see him?"

While Juga scanned the trees trying his best to look nonchalant, Athron snapped, "Enough of this. Stay here." Then with a great leap he propelled himself up onto a nearby oak branch and easily leapt from limb to limb until he was lost in the greenery of the overstory.

Juga continued to move forward cautiously. Whoever had caused the slight movement in the trees had disappeared before he could get more than a quick glimpse. The minutes ticked by. When Athron had been gone more than ten minutes, Juga began to fret, starting at every sound. He heard a commotion and the rustling of branches and leaves above him. Athron had subdued a very uncooperative Gor'ean soldier and had him pinned against the branches about fifteen feet from the ground off to the left of Juga.. Their struggles set the tree to swaying, and what remained of the fall leaves were floating down like coloured rain.

"Thank the gods, Athron! I thought something had happened to you," Juga said in a quiet voice.

Athron put a free hand to his lips as he continued to subdue his captive. "Quietly, lad. There are others."

Juga reached behind his shoulder to grab his hammer but as he did an arrow buried itself in his forearm. He cried out in pain and sank to his knees. Athron released the soldier and dropped to the forest floor. Before he could reach him, Gor'ean soldiers circled the lad. The soldiers stood between Athron and Juga, holding their ground but not looking pleased about it.

Outraged, Athron looked from face to face and demanded, "Who fired that arrow?"

One of the soldiers smiled thinly. Before any could stop him, Athron grabbed the soldier by the scruff of his neck and slammed him face first into the trunk of a tree. Among the other Gor'eans, not a soldier moved. Athron disarmed the bleeding man and wheeled to the remainder of the soldiers, whipping his bow off his shoulder and notching an arrow. He looked angrily from face to face. "Who else?" he demanded, livid.

He could see the men's gazes locked on someone behind him. He turned in time to see the soldier he'd subdued in the trees drop easily to the ground behind him.

"Athron Mar," he said. "It is my hope that we will not have to harm you. But know this: if you injure another of my men, I will have you killed."

"You *know* that I am the High Prince of Gorger yet you address me in this manner; and worse, you *attack*?" Athron asked, both furious and incredulous.

The soldier raised his chin defiantly. "I am Rowen Sarinn, commander of these men and I carry orders to return you to face the Elënthián Supreme Council and a charge of high treason."

"I am neither deserter nor traitor. I have committed no crime, nor has the Human who accompanies me." As Athron spoke he scanned the line of soldiers between Juga and him, looking for an opening that would allow him to come to the lad's aid.

"Your deliberate disregard of orders from the Fyyther and your exodus with an enemy of the Gor'ean people has marked you as a traitor. It seems we must now add liar to your list of charges," Sarinn sneered, gesturing to one of his men. Juga was dragged to his feet and shoved forward beside Athron.

A soldier stepped forward to take the Anulean hammer from Juga. Juga offered no resistance and released it, watching as the weight of the hammer pulled the soldier to his knees as it fell to the ground. Embarrassed, the soldier stood and bent to retrieve the unassuming tool. Try as he might, he could not lift it. With a pointed, humourless smile and complete disregard for the three foot arrow protruding from his right arm, Juga bent and easily picked up the ancient hammer. Wide-eyed, the soldier stepped away.

Juga drew himself to his full height and glared at Sarinn speaking on his own behalf, "I am the Human Jugarth Framir, originally from the south in Duron. You would be wise to stand down. Those who would question His Royal Highness, the Gor'ean High Prince…" he deliberately used Athron's full title, his gaze swinging across the faces of the Gor'ean soldiers who were looking increasingly uncomfortable, "can do so in less than a fortnight when we arrive at Gorgonathan."

The statement drew an immediate response from the soldiers who, to a one, raised their bows and arrows and aimed at the pair.

Sarinn was outraged. "You would take an *outsider*, a Human, to our sacred city?"

Athron had banked his anger but spat out his response. "Do you think me an idiot? This Human would not accompany me nor even be travelling by my side had he not been thoroughly tested and found to be of courage and character. I would give my life for him in an instant, and would witness your broken corpse burned to ash before I would see him hurt."

He raised his voice, his demeanour now princely as he addressed the Gor'ean soldiers before him. "I bid you fire your arrows now," he taunted, "for it will be only as a corpse that I will be taken forcibly to Gorgonathan!"

None moved.

Athron continued, "While I am aware you are now bound to follow the orders of your commander, know this…my father, Acthelass Mar, your Fyyther ... would demand me brought before him alive!"

He swung his gaze back to Sarinn. "It is not within your power to kill me," he said, his voice powerful and regal. "Are you willing to risk your military career and likely your life on such a blunder as killing a Royal Prince of Gorger." Staring him down, Athron saw the hesitance in Sarinn's eyes and knew he'd called his bluff.

"I thought not," he said dismissively.

Disregarding the soldiers whose arrows though lowered, remained trained on him, he returned his arrow to his quiver and shouldered his bow. He took Juga's arm and steadying his injured arm, snapped the arrow off on either side of his wrist, leaving a jagged spear of wood protruding from either side. He spoke quietly so only Juga could hear. "Lad, this will hurt. Look at me; hold my gaze. I'm going to pull this arrow through and bind your wound. You will not utter a single sound. Do you hear me? Not at a sound."

Athron's gaze held Juga's as he gripped the arrow. At Juga's nod Athron yanked the arrow clear of his arm. Juga inhaled sharply and paled but uttered no cry. The Gor'ean soldiers and their commander watched in silence as Athron took some salve and a strip of cloth from his pack and tightly bound Juga's wound.

With a pointed look at each of the soldiers and at Rowen Sarinn, the two shouldered their packs and weapons and started down the path toward Gorgonathan. The Gor'eans fell in behind them.

"Now what?" Juga whispered quietly.

"There is but one path from here to Gorgonathan, lad. I cannot stop them from following along with us. But by the gods know this. If they harm you again," Athron promised, "I will end the life of each and every one of them."

# CHAPTER 35

Lathaniel had never been one to drink more ale than it took to quench his thirst, but he had to admit he was quite enjoying the pleasant buzz that drinking it in quantity brought to his head. However, the buzz was still not winning the battle against the turbulent thoughts that had driven him into the noisy tavern earlier that afternoon.

He and Drake had been down at the wharf that morning scouting for ships that could take them across the Great Sea. More familiar with their destination and with the intricacies of selecting a reliable ship – and ship's captain – from the hundreds in port, Drake had taken the lead with Lathaniel in his usual role of keen observer. This accomplished, the morning ended with the two of them standing on a rocky rise just above the port. Drake had been silent for a time then had spoken frankly to him.

"I have been thinking about the day we met, Lathaniel. The young, naïve Forsair in the jail cell in Gramal...'Take me with you' you said to me that day. Little did I realize that agreeing, that making the acquaintance of Lathaniel Waythan would change my life forever. I have lived in our great Elënthiá for over two thousand years, lad. There is not much that I have not experienced nor heard, either directly or indirectly. From the moment of your candid introduction, I recognized your name and that you were the heir of Jonas. I knew immediately that by your departure from your small kingdom on Oldo you had forfeited your right to rule. You were an outcast; alone. As am I."

Lathaniel's stomach had knotted as he listened to the Draconean. He turned away from the sights of the harbour and met Drake's gaze as he continued.

"I was going to turn you loose in Zoren. Then in Cap'hannet. Then I thought that I would keep your company through until we solved the riddle of the Tombs and secured both the treasure and the map. Then, I nearly lost you..."

Drake had looked off into the distance for a moment or two before looking back at Lathaniel. "At dawn tomorrow we sail north. I can no longer be so cavalier about your continued companionship; so, Lathaniel Waythan, heir of Jonas and rightful leader of the Forsairean people, I release you. You are no longer apprentice to a Draconean. You are Master Waythan. You are Forsairean royalty. And you are a formidable warrior and a leader. Join forces with the Resistance in Cap'hannet. Find your future and your fortunes on the frontiers of Elënthiá...or go home. It is your fate, and these are your choices. Take time this day to consider them. For my part, I believe you have a greater role to play in both my story and in Elënthiá's future. But what that role is to be is now in your hands.

"We leave at dawn tomorrow. If our paths part, my young Master, then I know they will cross again one day." He had folded Lathaniel into a hard embrace then released him.

Lathaniel had been speechless as he watched the Draconean walk quickly back toward the city. He tossed back the last bit of ale in his glass and signalled for another. He'd been here, staring into the bottom of mug after mug of ale, ever since thinking about his family, Sabine and his friends and mulling over the prospect of returning to Lamana; of what he might find on his return and if a return to life there would be enough now that he had experienced so much of Elënthiá. Yet still, the way forward was cloudy and filled with doubt. *What am I to do…?*

"That's a question I've asked myself a million times, and the answer has yet to be clear. I know just how you feel," a stranger farther along the bar spoke.

Lathaniel was certain he had not spoken aloud but wasn't certain if the cloaked man was speaking to him or someone else, so he ignored him and paid the barmaid when she returned.

"I mean no harm lad," the stranger sighed. "I was simply making conversation."

There was no mistake that he was now addressing Lathaniel. "My eyes have not seen you until just this moment, nor have we spoken. What did you mean when you said you know how I feel?"

"I knew how you felt from the moment I set foot in this room. Sorrow and remorse stains you, lad. And like recognizes like." He paused for a moment to take a long draught of his own ale. He reached up and flipped the hood back from his head and shrugged off his cloak, carelessly draping it across the chair beside him. His light hair was pulled back from a face that was fair skinned and much younger than his voice, but his tired and broken blue eyes held sadness beyond measure and seemed those of one far older than he appeared.

"In my experience there are only three reasons for one to look as you do: family, fortune, or a female. What's your story, lad, and why does it have you looking for solace in a mug of ale?

In the manner of taverns and of ale in quantity, Lathaniel behaved out of character by replying with a half-laugh, "I no longer have a female in my life, and pursuit of a fortune holds no interest for me."

"Ahhh...so it is family."

Lathaniel nodded, taking another sip of his ale. "I am at a crossroads. I am ending one journey and have a choice before I begin another—a choice to continue or to return to my past. But I left: left them, left it all. And I feel that even if I returned, I would find exactly that: nothing left."

The stranger took a gulp from his own mug. "Every lad seeks the thrill of an adventure at one point or another; 'tis the way of things. Those who continue to pursue adventure for the sake of it can find themselves at a point in time where their only companion is loneliness. There are always choices, lad. And sometimes balance is elusive."

"What would you choose, the journey or your family?"

"Sometimes the only choice is the journey. And other times the only choice is family. Sometimes a single choice can answer both. As with most decisions in life, I think the answer is always to follow your heart."

There was silence between them for a time, both lost in their own thoughts. Finally Lathaniel asked,

"What brings *you* sorrow: a female, fortune, or your family?"

"I have wealth untold so need no more. Females are fickle; they warm the night but can be cold of heart. But what I wouldn't give for family." The stranger's last comment was wistful. He remained silent. Lathaniel sat quietly, sensing that his grief was great.

"My sorrow is for the loss of my brother," he spoke again. "Though it has been many, many years now, I still grieve his passing."

"I am sorry for your loss."

"His loss is only a loss until such time as I can bring him back."

Lathaniel turned to fully face him, puzzled. "The dead move on to sit at the feet of Ruahr in the Land beyond. I don't understand. What do you mean 'bring him back'?"

The man did not explain the cryptic comment; rather he stared unseeing across the tavern. "There is a tale told of a stone, the Stone of Humidar. Humidar was the firstborn of Ruahr and his greatest creation until, after a disagreement, Ruahr hurled his son into the depths of the Sea here in the mortal world. It is said that Humidar created the Stone from both the earth and sea as a penance to his Father in hopes that, if he could offer a worthy soul the opportunity for life after death, his father might forgive him. So from the deepest places in the deep, he cut the stone and placed within it an elixir. It is said that if that elixir touches lifeless lips, then the recipient will live once more."

"Surely this is folklore..." When the stranger did not reply, Lathaniel gently said, "Tale or truth, I hope you find a way to make peace with the loss of your brother."

The stranger turned abruptly to look at him. "We have talked of many things, yet I still do not know your name."

"I am Lathaniel, son of Lathart."

"Well, Lathaniel son of Lathart, it has been my pleasure to speak with you. There is something in your manner that brings me great comfort." The stranger seemed to shake off his odd melancholy and rose to don his cloak and hood.

"Perhaps we will meet again," Lathaniel said.

"I think not, for my home is in the far north and visits here to the south are rare. I took some solace from our conversation, lad. The pleasure of our meeting was all mine."

He dropped some coins on the table before them and walked away. At the door, he turned and looked back at Lathaniel once, then left.

Lathaniel ran flat out through the early morning air, dodging merchants, sailors, and street vendors; ducking carts, wagons, and horses; taking shortcuts through alleys and darting down side streets. With every slap of his feet against the cobblestones, he felt his head might split open like an overripe melon and spill his brains upon the street. He ignored the pain in his head, for if he was late, he had no idea what he would do.

His momentum carried him down the hill to the docks almost quicker than his legs could keep up. He skidded to a stop at the bottom of it, turning in a complete circle to orient himself. The wharf looked different this morning, or perhaps it was just the fog in his head. There it was! He spotted the ship and pushed and excused himself through the pressing crowds to the gangway. He spotted Layne on the deck and made for him. Layne's face transformed into a smile at the sight of him.

"We had about given up on you, lad. Drake has nearly paced a trench in the deck, and we're not even out of port." The clap on his back caused unneeded reverberations through his already throbbing skull, but Lathaniel fell in step with the Draconean and boarded the ship.

Drake was in conference with the Captain as they strode up behind him. He finished and turned; his shoulders seemed to relax at the sight of the Forsair, and his face broke into one of his rare smiles. They grasped each other's forearms and moved into a half embrace before walking to the rail.

"We begin again, lad..."

# PART TWO

# CHAPTER 36

Athron stopped so suddenly that Juga ran full tilt into his back.

"My apologies, Athron...I didn't know we were stopping." Juga was stuttering, embarrassed at his inattentiveness.

"We have arrived."

Juga's head snapped up and his eyes darted about him. "Where?"

"Gorgonathan." Athron's eyes lifted as he scanned the trees around him.

Juga did not understand. The forest about them looked as it had looked for the previous fifteen days; full and thick, albeit thinning slightly under the steady advance of the winter. "But every tree looks as every tree has looked during each day of our travel."

"Gorgonathan is as it is for a reason, lad. None can find it who is not meant to."

Athron proceeded off to his left. There, between the trees, vines had intertwined and tangled to fashion a rough arbour, though even if one studied it one would never distinguish it as anything different than other such tangles among the many trees. Juga followed. He'd travelled perhaps a dozen paces of more when a strange unease came over him. He quickly looked over his shoulder then up into the trees. The premonition of great danger was so strong that, with a grimace at the discomfort in his injured arm, he drew his sword from its sheath and his great hammer from its harness. He stepped quickly in front of Athron, forcing him to stop and crowding him against the trunk of a large tree.

"Athron, have a care, for I feel great danger is around us."

Athron's smile was filled with genuine fondness for this Human and his protectiveness. "What you feel is the strength of the protections that are placed around the perimeter of Gorgonathan. Any who approach, save Gor'eans, feel this way - an urge to flee this place. It is a safeguard. Rest easy." He continued forward.

Juga, though unconvinced, reluctantly sheathed his weapons and followed cautiously behind. They arrived at the great Gor'ean city alone. Rowen Sarinn and his soldiers, likely feeling foolish to be trailing along behind them, had disappeared days earlier.

He heard it then. The familiar noises of a great city at first distant but growing louder with each step forward. The path swung round to the right and opened out into the thriving Gor'ean capital city.

Juga stopped in his tracks. Athron was several feet beyond him before he realized the Human was not on his heels. He returned to Juga.

"Forgive me," Juga said faintly. "I think that my injury has turned septic, and I have sprung a great fever for I am hallucinating as happened when we were in the Tombs. Surely what is before my eyes is an illusion; magnificent, but an illusion." His eyes were large and his pupils dilated.

Athron smiled broadly and placed a reassuring arm loosely across Juga's shoulders.

"Welcome to Gorgonathan!"

Gorger was a kingdom of trees. Across the length and breadth of it, trees of every size, height, and species grew thick and bountiful. Such was the magic of the forest that though the kingdom felt the passing of the seasons, certain species of trees within its boundaries remained in perpetual flourish. Within Gorger all trees grew to a girth and a height that far surpassed any in Elënthiá save perhaps those in parts of Nesmeresa, the land of the Elves. Juga had travelled through these forests on their exodus from Gorger and again for the past several weeks. But never, throughout all of these travels, could he have anticipated the sight before his eyes.

The forest was at their backs, and as Juga looked to his left and right, he could see that it ringed the city. The city at ground level looked much the same as he would expect any large city would, though the architecture was most unusual and all buildings were made entirely of wood. However, in front of them was a massive, magnificent tree. The circumference of its base Juga could not even begin to imagine, for it completely dominated the landscape in front of him. As they drew further into the city and closer to the tree, Juga's neck craned backward, as he tried to absorb the sight before him.

The canopy of the tree completely blanketed the sky above them, yet still there was ample daylight. The trunk of the tree was straight and true and seemed to reach to the very heavens themselves. The branches that umbrellaed out from the trunk were of massive girth. It was beyond belief that such a monolith existed. The base of it hosted massive, elaborate, well-fortified gates.

In the air between the tops of the city buildings and the massive whorled leaves of the enormous tree were birds. The cacophony of their songs and chirps could be heard above the city noises, and the sight of the rainbow of colors in their plumage and feathers was spectacular against the emerald backdrop of the leaves above them.

"Gorgonathan is built within and around five such trees," Athron explained. "Each tree is hollowed and houses most of the inhabitants along with certain government and commercial offices that require additional protection and security. The branches above are hollowed and serve as avenues for us to move between the trees.

"How do the trees still thrive?" Juga's neck was tipped straight back and, but for Athron laying a guiding hand on his elbow, he would have veered off into the crowds.

"Unlike other trees who pull their nutrients up through their core, our trees draw nutrients from the ground up through their bark. The bark is porous. It pulls what it requires from the air as well." Athron beamed with pride. "Are they not beautiful?" he asked, indulging in a brief smile. "It has been too long since I have laid eyes on my city."

They'd not moved more than one hundred yards beyond the entry passage and into the city streets before it became obvious that continuing in anonymity was no longer an option. The crowds began to stop and point at them, parting before them as if a great wave was preceding their passage. A contingent of soldiers numbering twenty or more was marching toward them. Leading them was Rowen Sarinn. He marched forward and snapped to halt mere paces in front of them.

Athron spoke first. "You think to meet us at the entrance and escort us forward as if through some great achievement *you* are responsible for our presence here?" His tone was dismissive and filled with disdain. Sarinn's cheeks reddened, but he held his ground. Juga reached for his sword but was stayed as Athron placed a hand over his.

"A wise move, Highness," Sarinn sneered. "For it would be a shame to injure you when we are so close to dragging you before the Fyyther."

"You are very sure of yourself, Commander Sarinn. Sure enough to stand against those loyal to me?"

"I am dispatched as adjunct to the Royal Guard of the King himself. Who would dare to challenge us?"

"*My* Guard..." Athron replied.

At his words men stepped from the crowds on either side of them, throwing off the simple cloaks that had disguised their purpose and unsheathing their swords. They had been shadowing the pair since their first step inside the city walls. Sarinn's guards were subdued before an injury could be dealt.

"The soldiers under your 'adjunct' command may protect my father within the well-guarded perimeter of Gorgonathan, Commander. But my guards are battle-hardened and seasoned soldiers. Their sworn loyalty is to me."

The threat was implied but might well have been trumpeted across Gorger. Commander Rowen Sarinn and his soldiers stepped aside.

High above the city, members of the Elënthián Supreme Council were hurrying to the Chambers having received an urgent summons from the Adjudicator. Word had flown through the city: the High Prince had returned!

In his chambers, Acthelass Mar removed a crumpled parchment from his pocket and reread the message for the thousandth time:

*Highness, my Fyyther, my father:*

*I would ask you to trust me in the face of all evidence to the contrary, to believe in me in spite of all that you may hear, and to have faith that I am loyal to you in my heart and with my life. What I go to do, I do for our great Gorger, for the Resistance, and for the whole of Elënthiá. I will return to you.*

The King crumpled the note again and jammed it back into his pocket, his fist still clenched around it. Thank the gods his son had safely returned! The King would have to be careful these next hours. His actions as the Gor'ean Fyyther had been swift and unquestioned. In the face of the evidence received, he had issued orders for the arrest and return of Athron on the charge of desertion and treason. The Council could find no fault in his actions, for they were swift and deliberate. Behind the scenes he sewed appropriate seeds of doubt across the Council, lobbied for cool heads when Athron was brought before them, and hinted that there could be sound reason behind his son's actions.

Acthelass Mar might not have been the ideal father to his son, but he loved him deeply and the best he was able. He would face the Council now and do what he could to save his son's life without compromising the kingdom of Gorger.

# CHAPTER 37

Athron moved forward through the crowds past the goliath tree they'd seen on entry to the city, and into a larger, bustling cityscape at the center of which stood another massive hardwood. Juga was a step behind and to his right. Another soldier walked slightly behind but close at his elbow to his left. The remainder of Athron's guards fell into formation behind him. As Athron approached the well-guarded gates to this gargantuan, central tree, soldiers posted there snapped to attention. Their party entered without incident.

Once inside it took all of Juga's concentration to keep apace of the soldiers and confine his gaze as best he could to what was in front of him, for what surrounded him defied his imagination. It was a city within a city... within a tree! The entire center of it had been hollowed. An elaborate pulley system moved several platforms up and down between different levels. Spiral stairs wove upwards into the skies above. Gor'eans moved through and about the towering superstructure like busy bees about a hive.

Athron marched forward, and as he approached a junction, the soldier beside him quietly said, "To your left, Highness. We take the third elevated platform to the Supreme Council level."

"Thank you, Darius. It has been many years since I have been back to this city, and in my weariness, my memory fails."

Juga had never thought himself wary of heights, but his head spun as they ascended. When the company finally exited the travelling platform, it was to enter an elaborate lobby. At the far end of the lobby, two sweeping staircases rose on either side to empty out onto a landing in front of massive oak doors. Doors that lead to the Elënthiá Supreme Council Chambers..

A Herald met them at the top of the stairs. Three aides to the Adjudicator were standing against the wall between the sets of doors. Were protocol to be followed, the Herald would greet their party. Their party would wait while he sent an aide to the Adjudicator advising of their wish for an audience. Only when the Adjudicator had given permission did the Herald announce the arrival.

Athron ascended the stairs and while his guard halted at the Chamber's entrance, Athron did not break stride as he approached the Council doors. Rather, he pushed them open and walked directly in, with Juga at his side. The Herald scrambled alongside and hastily announced, "His Royal Highness, the Gor'ean High Prince Athron Mar."

Athron boldly walked up and onto the central platform beside the Adjudicator. The Chambers had fallen completely silent. He paused for a second to scan the balconies, his gaze sweeping around the elaborate room in front of him.

"I believe I have been called to atone for alleged crimes against my country and our Elënthiá," he said in a strong voice offering neither introduction nor apology. "As read, the charges paint me a deserter and a traitor."

A Gor'ean Lord stepped to his feet and called down from his balcony, "You dare enter this Chamber unannounced and uninvited!" It was Cindrick who shouted down from above, but he sat again before Athron could lock upon his voice.

"Dare?" Athron's voice boomed throughout the Chamber, his affront obvious. "Yes, I dare! I dare to return to my country...to my capital city...and to the home of my father and my King! Not only do I dare to enter this Chamber and have audience with this Council, but as the High Prince of this great nation, I demand it!"

High above, though his heart swelled with pride at the regal demeanour of his son and marvelled at his audacity in taking control of the situation facing him, his father remained silent.

"A charge of desertion and treason cuts to the heart of a soldier of Gorger," Athron continued. "It is a charge I would defend!"

Members of the Council began to talk at once, some yelling down calls for his removal, others calling out, "Traitor!" and "Deserter!" Though the Adjudicator was furiously banging his gavel for order, none was to be had.

At that moment a single golden-tipped arrow flew through the air and hit the center of the Adjudicator's podium with a *thwap* that echoed like a thunderclap through the Council chambers. It brought all discussion to a sudden and abrupt halt. Heads swivelled to track its source. There on an upper balcony stood a handmaiden of the Elven Queen, her bow string still quivering and her features set.

"It is time we heard what the Gor'ean Prince would tell us." Queen Allivaris' voice rang clear in the Chambers. When none challenged her, she turned and nodded to the Elven maiden at her side, who took her seat gracefully. The Adjudicator stepped back and took his seat. Athron stepped to the podium to address the Council. Juga remained standing, to Athron's left and a step behind.

"Highnesses, Excellencies, Lords and Ladies of the Elënthián Supreme Council, I bid you greeting." "Your Highness, Fyyther Acthelass Mar, Father...I am ever your servant." With that Athron stepped to the right of the podium, placed his right hand upon his heart, and dropped to one knee, head bowed. It was the appropriate greeting for his King; and for a son. He stood and returned to the podium.

His eyes scanned the balconies until they found the Elven contingent. "Queen Allivaris, my continued thanks for your wisdom and leadership." His eyes met the Queen's and he bowed slightly. She gave a slight nod of acknowledgement.

"I am aware that my sudden departure from Cap'hannet was a direct contravention of orders received from the Fyyther himself. Those orders pulled me from the battlefront and bid me travel immediately to Cap'hannet. There I was to find the Draconean, Drake Sorzin, and personally accompany him here to Gorgonathan. My orders were to 'escort' and 'accompany'... not to arrest the Draconean. While I was not told the reason, nor was it my place to ask, I am privy to information regarding an incident that happened several years ago involving the Draconean and presumed this to be the reason. However, when the Draconean arrived at Cap'hannet, he shared information that I felt was critical to the success of the Resistance effort, to the war against Gorillian and his evil forces, and to the future of Elënthiá."

A ripple of disbelief rolled through the room, but Athron continued before it could swell to an interruption.

"Based upon that belief, I made a decision to travel with the Draconean to investigate the validity of this information. Time was of the essence, and the highly confidential nature of the information was such that I deemed it important to maintain secrecy. With four of my Lieutenants, I departed Cap'hannet with the Draconean and his company heading for the Amarik region. That company included Lathaniel

Waythan, a Forsair; and Jugarth Framir, the Human who stands beside me today.

"When nearing the border of Gorger, we discovered a half-legion of Are-Narcs. In concern that they led a larger incursion into Gorger, I sent my four Lieutenants back to Cap'hannet with a warning. I presume they arrived…"

The Adjudicator answered, "All four of the Lieutenants were killed by Are-Narcs during a battle at Cap'hannet. Your missives were retrieved and distributed as directed,"

Athron's head bowed to his chest for a moment. "May they live on in glory at the feet of the gods…" he said softly. Pale, he lifted his face to the gathered and continued. "Following information held by the Draconean, we uncovered an entrance to an underground chamber in Amarik and there discovered a resource of great value to Elënthiá."

Guffaws of laughter broke out from several of the balconies, and several shouts could be heard, "Let us guess…you found a treasure!" More laughter. "Treasure!" The word went around the room, accompanied by half-hearted laughter.

Athron allowed annoyance to colour his tone. "You have requested information. I have provided it. If you find my explanation to be implausible, then execute me and my companion and be done with it," he replied flatly. "But of course, if you do, then you must know that the knowledge we carry of riches untold dies with us.

This statement brought the room to silence once more.

The Elven Queen spoke once more. "Again, I say let him continue."

When there was no challenge to her statement. Athron gestured to Juga, who brought forth the Prince's worn leather pack. He quickly located the heavily laden leather pouch within it and untied the thong that held it closed. Keeping the pouch itself still inside his leather pack, he withdrew a handful of the precious gems and bent, scattering them across the face of the small platform. The gems snatched at the light beaming down from the magical sky above the chamber and reflected it over and over again until spears of multicoloured beacons were crisscrossing the chamber. Athron then withdrew the entire sack and emptied it until precious stones littered the floor in front of him. The rainbow of light thrown by them was breathtaking. The Elënthián Council was, to a person, on its feet peering over balconies, unable to believe their eyes.

"Where exactly did you get these?" asked one of the Kings of the Realms of Men.

"What you see in front of you represents only one quarter of what we carried out of Amarik and is as a water droplet to an ocean compared to what remains there. We brought only gems, for we were travelling in haste under the constant shadow of Gorillian and did not want to alert him to our discovery."

The Human King persisted, "You have answered where it was found but not what it is...

"It is a tiny portion of the lost treasure of the Draconean race. His Highness, Drake Sorzin, the last living son of the last Draconean King, Dray Sorzin, has bid I make this..." he swept his hand out in gesture to the gems on the platform, "...and what more is required available to the Gor'eans, the Resistance, and the Elënthián Supreme Council to bolster efforts against Lord Gorillian and *to win this war*!" He ended with his voice raised and his fist in the air. Applause thundered within the chamber. The Adjudicator waited until it died and most had resumed their seats before he called the meeting to order.

Before all was silent, a Gor'ean Lord called from above, "You have explained the reason for your desertion but not the reason for disobeying orders from your Fyyther. The treasure is found and delivered. But the Draconean is not. What explanations have you for this?"

"I cannot and will not speak for the Draconean," Athron answered. "He has only said he offered his explanation of the incident already and has nothing further to add on the matter. Though the last of his race, he is still royalty and still an Immortal. Given that he has just gifted Elënthiá with the means to finance and turn the tides of this war, I did not feel it prudent or appropriate to insist upon his return to Gorgonathan at this time. And certainly the use of force to return him here was not an option."

As he finished speaking, Athron's gaze swept the Chambers in search of subtle reactions. He detested politics, but at times participation was a necessary evil. He hoped he had played his hand well.

The Adjudicator banged his gavel then and announced, "I have just received an urgent request calling for an adjournment to this session of the Supreme Council."

Athron was already leaving the Chamber as he spoke, Juga and his guard falling in behind him.

A Council aide awaited him at the platform door with a message. Opening it, Athron scanned the contents and turned to his Guard. "I am bid to join the Fyyther in a reception chamber."

The feeling that he was still, somehow, hallucinating remained with Juga as he stood off to the side in the large lobby below the Council Chambers. Athron had disappeared down a short corridor. Juga and the soldiers of Athron's Royal Guard waited on him. Members of the Elënthián Supreme Council spilled down the two great staircases into the lobby area from the doors above. Royalty from the many races of Humans, Gnomes, Fairies, and others about whom he was uncertain.

His eyes widened at the sight of a being that was half-man, half-horse. The creature approached him boldly, stopping a few feet in front of him. Juga's neck craned backward to look into his face as he rose, for he was nearly eight feet tall.

"I am Wylë, King of the Centaurs." His voice was deep and heavily accented. It seemed to rumble from deep in his chest. The musculature in King Wylë's torso was so developed and pronounced it looked as though it might split. His face was large and more elongated than a Human's, and his eyes were a dull grey. His bare chest was much like a human's but his body became covered with a soft brown fur below the waist where he became as a horse.

Remembering his manners, Juga stepped back a pace and offered a respectful bow. The Centaurean King responded with a toss of his head that swung long brown hair off his forehead and behind the two small horns on his skull. Juga blinked twice.

"Is what the High Prince told us true?" Wylë asked. "Were you among the company that travelled with the Draconean?"

Though naïve to the world of politics and alliances, Juga was astute enough to reply politely yet remained deliberately vague. "The High Prince would not speak falsely."

"I know this well, Human, and I would not imply the contrary. My race has existed since the very inception of Elënthiá. I also know of Draconeans and that only those deemed exceptional are allowed as companions to them. That you were, places you in my highest esteem. If ever you are in need of assistance, I would be honoured to be of service." With that he bent his foreleg and, himself, bowed.

Juga retained the presence of mind to do the same. "My thanks, Your Highness."

King Wylë lifted his head and regally moved on.

The Elven Queen entered the lobby with her entourage. A handmaiden walked immediately to her right, and she was flanked by a large contingent of tall and stately golden-haired Elven Lords. Juga remembered Drake telling him that Humans generally become pliant in the presence of Elven beauty, and he began to understand why as the party approached him. As with King Wylë, he gave a respectful bow in her presence.

Queen Allivaris' voice was light and musical as she spoke: "Rise, Jugarth Framir. It comes to my ears that you are an apprentice of the ancient Draconean. And it appears you are also the companion of the Gor'ean High Prince. How did you come to meet them?"

Again, Juga's reply was indirect. "Through the benevolence of the gods themselves, Highness. That can be the only explanation, for I am a mere Human."

The Queen smiled slightly, recognizing his efforts to avoid answering her directly and appreciating his loyalty in so doing. "Young Jugarth, I do not have the sense that you are 'merely' anything, but I would ask that when next you see your Draconean Master you offer him my greetings. It has been many, many years since I have seen them." The Elven Queen moved on and Juga bowed as she moved away.

Her handmaiden remained. "You speak boldly for one so young." She addressed this to Juga.

"I will shortly begin my seventeenth year. Young in the measure of Elves, I am certain. But by the measure of men, not so young."

"I am Ayleen, handmaiden to her Highness, Queen Allivaris."

Her voice was soft but strong, and her startling blue eyes held his as they spoke. It had been difficult to gauge her height from the balcony above the platform, but Juga saw that she was nearly as tall as he, fit and athletic with light hair falling thickly to the small of her back. This close, her skin seemed almost translucent, and it took all of his discipline to remember his manners and not simply stand and stare at her, slack-jawed.

"It is told that a Forsair was also part of your company. Does he travel here to Gorgonathan with you?"

"May I ask the reason for your interest, Milady?"

"The Forsairs have long been legend among my people. I have held a fascination with the story for many years and wished to meet one, if indeed there is such a being. Is he here with you?"

"No."

Juga offered no more information so she prompted, "Can you tell me where he comes from, if there is truly a kingdom filled with Forsairs?"

He held her gaze for a moment before replying, "I could not say. Both because this is not information he has shared with me and, if he had, it would be for him to speak, not I."

She nodded demurely. "I thank you for your time, Jugarth Framir. Perhaps we might speak again of your travels and the adventures of your company, for I feel there is much you would tell." She moved on to join her Queen's entourage once again.

Athron stopped outside the door and drew a deep, calming breath. The confrontation in the Council Chambers had left his heart racing. The confrontation he was about to have with his father had his stomach in knots. The Grand Hall was reserved for occasions when heads of state needed to meet one with the other in the absence of their entourages. The note directed him to meet with his father in a small reception chamber off of it. Steeling himself for the force of his father's ire, he knocked twice then entered. The Gor'ean Fyyther, Acthelass Mar was conversing with one of the Gor'ean Lords. The conversation ceased when Athron entered, and the tension in the room was obvious.

The Fyyther looked to his Lord. "Leave us."

The door quietly closed behind him. Acthelass Mar stood staring at his only son, his expression hooded. Athron stood at ease with his hands clasped behind his back but his chin high as he met and held his father's gaze.

Acthelass crossed the room to stand before him. Without warning he reached out and grasped his son's shoulders, gathering him into a great embrace. In shock, Athron stood frozen with his arms at his sides, completely taken aback by this reception. He had expected anger, cold distain, even icy silence. But not this. His arms slowly raised and he returned the embrace.

His father cleared his throat several times, composing himself. "Your message…I received your message. I believed in you - never stopped. But you must understand that before the Council my behaviour needed be exemplary. The order for your arrest, the charges, all necessary to demonstrate that I would not exercise favouritism, even for my own son."

He stepped away, once again in full control. "You managed the Council brilliantly today. We have been called into an emergency meeting of the heads of state to determine how to allocate the resources you have brought to best serve the Resistance and the war effort. Even what little treasure you carried with you is significant! We can immediately commission ships, purchase supplies, and pay our soldiers. Many who have swung their support to Gorillian have done so only because he buys their allegiance. Such renewed finances will see a shift in our favour. I will press you for details on what I surmise was a great and dangerous endeavour another time, for the others will arrive any moment now. Remain with me through this meeting. Regarding your return, I will retain my dubious demeanour in the face of the Council...and you must retain your arrogance. Just know that it is theatre for their benefit, for I have never been prouder of you then I am on this day."

There was a knock on the reception chamber door, a summons that the others had arrived. The Gor'ean Fyyther opened the door and entered the Grand Hall, his son on his heels.

# CHAPTER 38

The Pythius was a beautiful ship, nearly one hundred and eighty feet long, her mast reaching one hundred and thirty feet toward the slate clouds they were sailing beneath. She was a frigate for the Resistance, principally tasked with running supplies between Nesmeresan ports and the island of Koorast. She was well gunned, and her crew were both seasoned seaman and accomplished soldiers. Josa Headian, her Captain, ran a tight ship.

Drake and Layne leaned on the hardwood rail and were deep in conversation. The revelations Drake's father had shared with him in the Tombs had left him with many questions. While he had not shared what had happened in the Tombs with his other companions, he felt compelled to have an honest discussion with Layne about what his father had told him. Layne was the only one who could fill the gaps he'd been left with. " ... and while I now know how Dohenheer was built and of the fracture that split the Draconeans into the north and south, I know nothing of what has happened thereafter," Drake explained.

Layne was silent for a time, the two of them staring out across the sea. "What you have shared is as our scholars have taught us. The Dohenheer you will shortly see is not the

Dohenheer that greeted our ancestors those many years ago. The shell of it was there but nothing else. Those first years were focussed on survival. None knew how long the separation with the south would be in effect or if, indeed, we would ever reunite so their priority was to settle. I cannot remember the exact amount of time but as I recall it was several years before an emissary was sent south to Evendeer. You can imagine the shock when the messenger returned with the news. Evendeer had fallen. Our King was dead and there was not a single survivor in the south. They were devastated. Beyond that, the messenger brought news that the entire race of Dwarves had also fallen at Ethen-jar. Exterminated by Gorillian; the same as at Evendeer. The Giants and the Anulé had decamped, unwilling to remain in an Elënthiá so overcome with evil.

"Our ancestors sent emissaries to the Elves in secret asking for their assistance in installing protections around Dohenheer to prevent our discovery. Given the circumstances, the Elven King and Queen vowed to keep secret the fact that more Draconeans existed. The Dwarves knew of Dohenheer, but they were gone. The Giants knew as well, but they'd also left Elënthiá. And so we remained ... hidden and isolated."

Drake was silent as Layne recounted this history. There was so much to understand, to absorb. The two were distracted by Lathaniel who was making his way across the deck.

Lathaniel had finally found his sea legs. His short sojourn on the small craft that brought him from Oldo to Gramal was nothing compared to the vessel they were currently sailing upon. They had been able to see whitecaps before they even left the Limore harbour for open seas. Those first days his stomach had been uncooperative, but now he was enjoying the snap of the sails and the bite of the sea air as he made his way across the oiled pine decks.

It was their fourth morning under sail. The autumn seas were stretching and shrugging in ill humour, pitching and rolling as the ship ploughed through the grey, roiling waves. The crew had fallen into the comfortable rhythm of watches and ship work and paid him little heed as he passed. Drake and Layne leaned against the gunwale on the port side of the ship, talking quietly and staring out across the horizon. Lathaniel joined them.

"The Captain advises that we are a day and a half out from the coastline of Siityth," Drake began without preamble, his discussion with Layne set aside for now. "Gorillian's forces control Siityth and Far'camice and will watch the shorelines carefully. Captain Headian will put us ashore quickly and under cover of darkness then sail back out to sea as soon as possible. Our hope is that we can put in undetected."

Layne used his finger to punctuate destinations as he drew an invisible map in the air in front of them. "We'll put in just east of the port of Jitta. We then head straight north crossing the plains of Thorvana until we reach Crystal Lake. If the gods are with us, we should cover this distance in eight days. From the lake we head north into the Ashen Mountains. Two days to pass the lake and another four days in the mountains before we reach the gates of Dohenheer."

"Would it not have been quicker to sail further north up the coast and port closer to Dohenheer?" Lathaniel asked.

"We could have," Drake answered, "but it was a matter of a reliable ship willing to take us that far north at this time of the year when the seas are at their most unpredictable. And I also have a network of contacts in the Coldain Region that I want to alert en route. Without offering extensive information, I want to spread the word that a military initiative is in the works that may free them from Gorillian's control. This will be welcome news to the Resistance forces in Far'camice,

Siityth, and Illiyish; and quite frankly we will need all the help and information we can get."

"And armies from the south?" Layne inquired. "How will we alert them to our purpose and to the location of Dohenheer?"

"The day we left Limore, I sent two messengers to Cap'hannet by different routes. I have passed information to Athron that he will need to convince the Council to act, and details about where to direct their armies. With the grace of the gods, the messengers will arrive without incident. As for us, once we hit the shore we will need to travel almost continuously for many days so rest well while we are aboard. Lathaniel...are you fit for the journey?"

Lathaniel pulled his bow from his shoulder and notched an arrow. Letting it fly, he buried it in the center of the foremast, startling the seaman standing nearby so badly that he dropped the rigging he was hauling. Lathaniel walked forward and reclaimed his arrow with a warm smile for the seaman, who had not found the incident so humorous.

"Back in fighting form," he replied latently. "Though I am hoping it is awhile before I have to prove it."

Drake nodded in approval. "Go and update Captain Headian on our requirements, Layne. And see to the list of provisions I gave you. I'll want our packs readied by morning in case we need to put ashore ahead of schedule."

Layne moved off to obey, and Lathaniel took his place at the rail where he spent a time in companionable silence with his Draconian mentor.

"Your mind is settled now." It was a statement not a question. Lathaniel had wondered when Drake would initiate this conversation.

"Yes." Lathaniel didn't say anything else, and Drake let the silence stretch out. Lathaniel sighed; it was obvious the

Draconean wouldn't let the matter rest until he elaborated. "'Settled' is as good a word as any. If I return, I return as I left. If my parents have lost their lives at Gramicy's hands, then they are gone and my return will make no difference. Had I stayed, the same outcome awaited them. If they live still and I return, I risk their lives. I have come to understand that returning will change nothing. Nor will fretting about that which may or may not be happening in Lamana in my absence."

He shrugged and continued quietly, "If I remain with you, perhaps I can make a difference in the war against Gorillian. If there is any truth to the rumour that his tentacles are touching uncharted borders and Oldo is at risk, then I can make more of a difference to my people by stopping Gorillian and ending any possibility of an alliance that includes him."

The Draconean listened in silence and said nothing for several moments thereafter. Then he clapped Lathaniel hard on his uninjured shoulder and the two headed below decks to join Layne and the Captain.

"I can't explain it, General. We'd been in skirmishes with them repeatedly for the past two, perhaps three weeks. We'd hunkered down in the Southern Pass protecting all access points to the Clarin Vargor closest to Sethén. They were there…and then they weren't. They simply withdrew back into the Minheras in the night. We tracked them back to the ancient passages and then let them go."

Another General interrupted Athron. "Your Highness, my report is exactly the same. We had been taking heavy losses where our border touches the Marshes - in the area where you and your company spotted them nearly two months ago. We took a particularly bloody assault in the early dawn hours a week back, but by the time the sun had fully risen, there wasn't an Are-Narc to be found. They retreated."

Athron was perplexed. Such reports were not only coming in from Gorger's own borders but trickling in from other hot spots across Koorast. He met Juga's gaze but said nothing. While he had drawn his own conclusions about the reason for the troop withdrawal, he felt it prudent to keep these to himself until more concrete confirmation was received. But for now, there was only one course of action to pursue.

"We must take this information to the Supreme Council. Scouts can be dispatched to ascertain if this is happening further afield or simply on Koorast." He dismissed his senior staff and left immediately, Juga at his heels.

"Gorillian is recalling his troops, isn't he?. He must be amassing them for the assault on the north," Juga whispered urgently when they were alone. "Even if we don't know for certain that there is a city in the Ashen Mountains, *he* must believe there to be."

"We will say nothing. Not until we have heard definitive word from Drake," Athron replied. "But we must report this to the Council. If what we suspect is true, Drake will find a way to get word to us, and he'll be asking for troops. We must use this time to get a sense of troop movement and numbers, for when the time comes, this will be critical information."

The two said nothing further. Athron dispatched an urgent message to the Adjudicator requesting an immediate gathering of the Council.

# CHAPTER 39

Lathaniel's first view of the shores of the Coldain Region was late in the afternoon and filtered through the glass that the Captain loaned him. He was thinking of Juga as he stared through the long glass, of his wish to sail on a ship such as this and see distant realms. Even from this distance, Lathaniel was amazed by the beauty of the coastline. Giant cliffs rose out of the sea; there were stretches where heavy forests spilled over the edge of the cliffs, and where great diagonal slabs of the blackest shale looked like they were sliding into the ocean. As the sun slipped below the horizon, the three companions prepared for a hasty journey ashore.

The Captain used the glass to point out a flat stretch of rocky beach that the three should head for. "You will take one of my oldest skiffs. The oars are good, and it will get you to shore. Once you land, drag it to the north edge of the beach where the rocks begin, and turn it loose. With the coming of the tides, the surf will throw it upon the rocks and it will disintegrate. Any who find it will think those aboard perished or that it broke free of a passing ship. There should be access to the cliff tops near there..." he indicated an area using the glass again, "but use stealth, for the area will be well patrolled.

Once you're beyond the guards atop these cliffs, you should be clear."

Drake thanked the Captain, his hand surreptitiously sliding a pouch of coins into his hands during their handshake. The three checked their packs and supplies one last time, and as soon as the last light surrendered to darkness, they lowered themselves into the ancient skiff and began pulling for shore.

The cove was as Headian had described. They waded along the waterline hauling the small boat behind them, then pushed it out into the gathering surf as directed. Keeping to the shadows at the base of the cliffs, they located a well-trodden path and began to climb, Drake taking point, Lathaniel at his heels, and Layne at the rear.

As they neared the top, Drake gestured for silence. There was that smell again. While it was not so strong as the Cave-Narcs, it was sufficient that Lathaniel's nostrils were quivering. The three could hear the bored discourse between the posted Are-Narc guards, their lax demeanour indicating that they hadn't been seeing a lot of action along that particular stretch of coastline.

One by one, the three made their way quietly through the rocks, using the shadows to disguise their passage. They were soon well beyond the Are-Narcs and quickly moving inland at a long lope.

When dawn broke, they were still moving at a fast clip. As the Plains of Thorvana neared the coast, their geography changed. Scrub brush and low trees grew in thickets and high grasses thrived. Though it was late in the season and most had gone to seed, it still provided cover as they moved inland. They agreed to continue forward until this vegetation could no longer mask their movement, and it was midafternoon before they stopped to rest and take food.

Before them the Plains of Thorvana stretched, mile upon mile as flat as a sheet of tree bark. With no easy way to avoid detection, the three agreed that the lion's share of their travel would have to be done between dusk and daybreak. Drake had taken the first watch but was fast asleep now, and as Lathaniel lay next to him he listened to the easy cadence of his breathing. They were taking two-hour watches, and it was almost time for his. He arose quietly and prepared his pack. Layne's back was to him. He sat on a cluster of rocks several yards away. As Lathaniel approached, he seemed to be humming. So as not to alarm him, Lathaniel cleared his throat then moved to sit beside him. The younger Draconean continued humming for a time. When there was silence, Lathaniel offered to relieve him.

"I'll go in a moment," Layne responded. "I have been enjoying this day. After so many years, I had begun to believe I would never see Dohenheer again and yet, here I am with the Draconean I was sent to find. I am going home and with the Council's blessing, I should shortly return to my army with a commission as General."

Lathaniel was silent as he listened. He imagined how he would feel given the chance to return to Lamana. "Am I permitted to ask of Dohenheer?"

Layne swung his head round to look at the lad. "Given that you journey to my land to stand by my people as they fight Lord Gorillian, I think you have earned that right." Layne turned to stare out over the Plains as if conjuring a vision in his mind of his home. "Dohenheer is built within the Ashen Mountains. Not in them, you understand ... but *with*in them. It is a place more beautiful than you can imagine. Entering Dohenheer is as entering another world, another dimension almost, so grand is it. In my mind I can see it still.

These many years away have not dimmed my memory but have whetted my appetite to see it again.

He spent a brief moment explaining how Dohenheer came to be and the reason some of the Draconeans splintered off and went north. "You can imagine the turmoil we were left in when we discovered Evendeer had been destroyed. Our entire society had been structured around the existence of a royal bloodline. When Evendeer fell, the bloodline of kings ended. We were isolated and afraid for our very existence.

"We re-built our society upon the premise that each and every member of it was vital to the success of the whole. The farmer, the armourer, the baker, the scholar ... all would need to work together for us to survive. So we formed the High Council. It is comprised of four elders. Where lower councils cannot reach agreement over an issue, they act as arbiter ensuring decisions taken are to the benefit of the whole of Dohenheer."

"I thank you for the small favour of information, but know this. Drake Sorzin has not spent a mere twelve years searching for others of his race, but his entire lifetime. Across two millennia it was he who Elënthiá called upon when straits were dire, and each time it has been him standing at the vanguard between Elënthiá and the evil that would corrupt her. Be assured that he returns to your Dohenheer with the full intent of protecting it and what remains of his race with his life. And he will not fail you. But he will not take well to a role as biddable subject reporting to your High Council. And, if your own ascension to the rank of General will be in any way at his expense, know that you and I will have issue."

Then without warning, he gave Layne a great push that sent him sprawling to the ground just as an arrow whipped passed Lathaniel's ear and spent itself in the rocks beyond. Layne was on him in a second, furious.

"You fool!" Lathaniel muttered. "There! In the trees behind us."

The two rolled apart, coming to their feet in a crouch behind some rocks. Layne had his sword drawn, ready. Lathaniel had both of his boot daggers in hand, but cursed his foolishness for his sword and bow were beside Drake, several yards away. Drake was fully awake and armed, assessing their situation. They couldn't remain immobile, for they knew that the Are-Narcs were only quiet because they were preparing an ambush. Drake had the more defensible cover; they needed to get to him.

Lathaniel used his head and eyes to gesture to his weapons on the ground near Drake. Drake nodded his understanding and reached a long arm out from behind the rock to retrieve them. That action garnered a volley of arrows, revealing the location of several of the Narcs. Daggers were loosed, the cries in the underbrush clear indication that they'd found their mark. While the Are-Narcs regrouped, Lathaniel and Layne took off at a dead run, leaping over brush and branches, weaving and darting to impede their attackers, and dove behind the rocks beside Drake who, predictably, was not pleased.

"If this is evidence of a vigilant patrol, you may as well sleep next time!" he hissed angrily.

Layne said nothing. Lathaniel gathered his weapons. He notched an arrow and turned his attention to their attackers. At a sound off to their left, he loosed one and heard a satisfying *thwack* as it found its mark. He followed that arrow with three more in rapid succession, each also on target. Frustrated, the Are-Narcs opted for a full frontal attack and emerged from the underbrush and trees on all sides of them.

Battle hardened as these Are-Narcs were, their eyes widened with surprise as with a loud battle cry, Drake rushed toward them, his four-foot, emerald encrusted sword already sweeping in wide arcs hacking through flesh and bone in its path. He skidded to a halt in a circle of six and began methodically fighting his way through them.

Lathaniel had shouldered his bow and removed his Draconean sword, fully engaging with three Narcs. When his sword locked at the hilt with one, another ran at his back with a battle cry meaning to run him through. A pivot at the last moment had the Narc he'd locked hilts with, run through on his compatriot's sword. While the other Narc was desperately trying to extricate himself, Lathaniel pulled a dagger from his boot and with a whisper-quick motion swept it across his throat. Dagger in one hand and sword in the other, he attacked the third Narc, who fell easily.

He could see Layne engaged in battle several yards away. His sword swung round, clipping a Narc just beneath his ear and effectively lifting its entire head from his body. The head rolled into the underbrush as the body teetered uncertainly before falling. Turning to the remainder of his attackers, Layne grasped the hilt of his sword in two hands, and with some strange flick of his wrists, the single blade became two and he charged the Narcs.

Lathaniel swept the rest of the way around to see a Narc pick up a thick branch and swing it like a club at the back of Drake's head while he was engaged by two other attackers. Remembering their experience in the Minheras, Lathaniel leapt over bodies and caught the Narc with a flying tackle to his midsection. The club went flying, as did the Narc. Their roll in the dirt ended with Lathaniel astride and his dagger buried hilt deep in the Narc's chest. He used both hands to give it a sharp twist before he withdrew it, immediately looking around for other attackers. He caught only the glimpses of Drake and Layne doing the same as dusk settled across the bloody and body-littered clearing.

# CHAPTER 40

It had been nine days since they had arrived at Gorgonathan. Athron spent most of that time completely immersed in meetings with his father and other heads-of-state as messages were arriving daily - at times hourly - from across Koorast and as far afield as Nesmeresa. Where it was appropriate, Juga stood at his side through such conferences; but there were times, like now, when Athron was closeted in the Grand Hall and his presence was not allowed.

Juga sat on an open balcony high in the centrum overlooking the magnificent city. He had a whetstone in hand and was methodically sharpening his daggers and swords, lost in thought. A light cough roused him from his reverie. Ayleen, Queen Allivaris' handmaiden, stood in the arch behind him.

"May I join you?"

Juga quickly stood and gave her a slight bow, shifting farther down the bench he had been sitting upon to make room for her. She sat, and he continued his sharpening, trying very hard to ignore the Elven stimuli that made Humans so vulnerable in their presence.

After a time, she spoke. "I was hoping you would tell me more of the Forsair...of your adventures."

Juga kept sharpening his blades. *Perfect. She wants to talk about Lathaniel!*

"What is it that you wish to know?"

"Where he is from, how you came to meet, where you travelled."

Juga's tone was clipped as he answered her. "I know only that Lathaniel Waythan was exiled from his homeland and that this bothers him sorely. The exact location of it was not information he shared with me, nor were details surrounding his life there or his departure from it. I can tell you that we met in Gramal. He arrived in port on a ship that the Black March impounded. All on it were charged with treason, Lathaniel included. We shared the same jail cell as I, too, was being…ah, detained at the time."

Ayleen's eyes widened, but she said nothing. This Human did not react as did the few others she had contact with. He was not forthcoming with information as she had hoped. And he seemed almost angry.

"I have been apprenticed to the Draconean since I was thirteen years of age," he continued. "He came to rescue me in Gramal, and Lathaniel was brought along."

"Tell me more of the Draconean."

Juga was silent for a time before turning to look directly into Ayleen's eyes.

"Your Queen sent you to question me. You are not here out of your own curiosity or interest. Am I correct?"

Her cheeks pinked slightly and she lowered her eyes. "Yes, my Queen bids me find more about your journey and your companions. But my own interest in you and your company is not feigned."

By the gods, she was beautiful, Juga thought. In her sleeveless simple shift with her golden hair simply styled to fall unadorned down her back, her eyes seemed to catch and reflect the light. He must guard himself carefully, he thought.

Ayleen changed the subject. "Is your Master still in the Grand Hall?"

"I call the Draconean Master, no one else."

"Then why do you serve him? You stand at his side in all but the heads-of-state meetings. He bids you, and you obey. Is that not the behaviour of subordinate to a Master?"

"It is the behaviour of a friend, of a fellow soldier. And he is both."

Ayleen cocked her head slightly as she considered him. "You are young to be a soldier already. Did your parents teach you such things? Did they agree to your apprenticeship to the Draconean?"

"My parents are long dead. I was orphaned and barely surviving as a thief on the streets when I met Drake. He taught me the arts of war and to write and read several languages."

"And the Forsair, did the Draconean teach him this as well?"

"Lathaniel Waythan was of advanced scholarship when I met him. He does naught but question all and everything he sees and hears. His skill as a soldier is beyond mine, beyond that of a Gor'ean. I have only seen him bested by Drake, but then he is only eighteen years of age."

Ayleen's eyes widened at that information. She had assumed the Forsair to be much older.

Looking frankly into her eyes, Juga said, "One day you must reciprocate and tell me how you come to be high among the Gor'ean treetops as handmaiden to a Queen."

Ayleen blushed and smiled gently. "Indeed, a tale for another day. For now I will leave you to your duties and return to mine. Good day Jugarth Framir."

They stood together, their eyes meeting and holding for a fraction longer than necessary. Then she was gone.

Athron's meeting with the Council had been brief and unproductive. So desperate were all in Elënthiá for good news that many of the Council's members had received the information about troop withdrawals as a sign of victory for the Resistance and were reluctant to probe for a deeper meaning. While many others held their comments and guarded their responses, huge contingents within the Council were exchanging self-congratulatory rhetoric about a great victory without stopping to consider that the troop withdrawal might have other serious significance. Between the revelers and the wait-and-see stance of others on the Council, Athron was both frustrated and annoyed.

He was hoping daily for some word from the Draconean and his companions. As yet none had arrived. He'd left the Grand Hall and entered a meeting with his own military leaders. Enroute he dispatched a messenger to find Jugarth Framir and bid him join them. The Human was rarely away from his side these days.

The Gor'ean Fyyther met him at the door to the small room to join in the meeting but deferred leadership of it to him. They gathered round a central table, and Athron rolled out a huge map of Elënthiá. In the bottom left-hand corner was the island of Koorast, and off its shores, the smaller islands of Moldost, Oldo, and Sortaire. Above it was the Coldain Region, the largest land mass and home to most of the Realms of Men within Elënthiá.

East across the Sea was the Vearian Region in the north, and the Zormian Region in the south. The northern Vearian Region was home to the Illisian Elves and the Elleaôerean

Elves, who lived in the north and south of it respectively. Within the Vearian, Elves lived alongside the Unicorns, Fairies, Gnomes, Centaurs, Nymphs, and, before their departure, the Dragons as well.

The Zormian region further south was all but barren. Before the great wars this had been home to several races of Giants, but they had moved beyond the known borders of Elënthiá to avoid following the fate of the Dwarves. The map was common knowledge to those gathered, and all stared down at it as updates were provided.

Captain Caapri addressed them, pointing to his troop placement on the map. "I have two full legions languishing at the end of the Marshlands. We have waited a full week in anticipation of the Are-Narcs' return. We have scouted every possible avenue for ambush throughout the area. Nothing. I tell you, there are none to be found!"

Athron nodded. "Captains in both Sethén and Mai report that the Narc forces have not only retreated but have completely vacated the Forest. A messenger yesterday reported that after a full day of siege on the port at Drataz the ships sailed away in the night. Such are all the reports!"

"My legion languishes in the freezing cold upon the shores of the Pyfra Lake, bored, my Prince! There are simply no Narcs to fight. We wait; we scout; by the gods, we even search! But there are no longer Narcs in the region. Under Gorillian's stranglehold, the flow of supplies from Nesmeresa has all but stopped in recent months. Even if he has withdrawn, if we are to remain there then we require supplies, to survive if not to fight." This, from Revonit Hŭit, a Gor'ean Captain stationed there

Juga quietly entered the room as another Captain piped up. "Aye, my men in the white dunes of Isem Cove are the same. No Narcs left there either. And no supplies!"

Athron raised his voice, bringing the meeting back to order. "Procuring supplies in quantity and payment of Gorger's soldiers is no longer an issue for the Resistance. We now have unlimited financial resources at our fingertips. Rest assured supplies are being carried to your camps, posts, and settlements as I speak. Leave this issue of supplies now and continue with your updates on our troops."

Juga noted that Athron's last bit of news had a marked difference on the tension in the room. Obviously the resources supporting Gor'ean troops had been stretched even farther then he was aware. Athron's team continued to methodically report on all regions across Elënthiá where Gor'eans were deployed.

Glacious Morvic spoke then. He was a veteran of the military, a full Gor'ean General though now retired. In him Athron had an invaluable ally. He had invited Morvic to hear the reports and wanted his take on what it all could mean. "One of two things is happening. Gorillian has come to his senses and decided to renounce evil for his remaining days..." The room burst into laughter, "Or he is regrouping his troops with a specific goal in mind. We all know the former to be false. But if the latter is true, then we must exhaust our every resource to ascertain the location of this massive assault."

# CHAPTER 41

Dusk till dawn six nights in a row. Twelve straight hours of ground-eating lope. The first two nights seemed easy compared to the past four when they'd run through wet snow and sleet, slipping and sliding in places and soaked to the skin. The daylight hours offered little relief, for even if they wanted a fire there was nothing to burn. Instead, they huddled together, sharing warmth, and ate the rations in their packs cold.

Drake had disappeared at two junctures, and neither Lathaniel nor Layne quizzed him on his destination presuming he was rendezvousing with some unknown contacts; though who and where they would be in a place the gods most surely had forgotten, was beyond them.

Loosely the route they were taking followed the Dorvanis River due north. Any settlements in the Plains were established along the River, so they kept well inland of it though occasionally stole a quiet trip to its banks to refill water skins and quietly hook a fish or two.

According to the Draconeans, they would reach Crystal Lake before dawn today. Sunset the previous evening had been glorious; a sign, according to Layne, that the gods were smiling upon them and that their arrival at Crystal Lake the following day would find them under clear and warm skies. Moving through the darkness that night, they could feel the elevations begin to shift and began a constant ascent. When the ground levelled out, they found themselves at the shores of Crystal Lake. As the daybreak approached, it was as if the gods were peeling back the blackness in layers that became successively lighter until the full glory of morning arrived.

The grey skies and low cloud cover had lifted such that Lathaniel could see they were, in fact, quite close to the mountains. Rugged, snow-capped peaks could be clearly seen above the tree line; though distant, this change in geography was a welcome relief after the unrelieved flatness of the Thorvanan Plains.

Crystal Lake was filled with the clearest of mountain waters, and its runoff created the Dorvanis River that flowed south into the Great Sea. The lake itself sat within a great rock shelf. There were no trees on its southern face, and the edge of it fell sharply away to the flat Plains below, allowing any on the lake plateau a clear view in every direction. The northern backdrop to Crystal Lake was the ranges of the Ashen Mountains replete with thick forests, gorges, and craggy cliffs in and amongst sheer rock faces. It was their first defensible position in nearly a week of hard travel.

A sound sleep under the warm sun, fresh fish cooked over a small fire, and the clarity of the air at their increased altitude did much to improve their dispositions, but their good fortunes were not to last long. Layne returned to their camp from a patrol, winded and only slightly ahead of the torches spotted moving quickly their way.

"I could get close enough to get rudimentary information only," he shared with urgency. "They are a company of Are-Narcs: forty-five, maybe fifty accompanied by two Humans, one of which appears to be a guard and the other not a soldier;

more likely a messenger. He carries a large map and stops to frequently check it."

Drake responded, "It would be too much to hope that Gorillian would send a messenger with the original and only map to Dohenheer. But as I see it, we have two choices. One, we attack, slay them all, and get the map. If we do this we take a chance that one escapes and carries the map from our grasp.

"Or we continue on to Dohenheer with a warning of their approach. The down side of that choice is that this is a classic manoeuvre of Gorillian. He will send an advance envoy with a message of peace…'*I have just learned of your existence… perhaps we might meet and know each other better*,' that sort of thing. Whilst there, his envoy and guards surveill the city and its capabilities to report back to him. It gives him the advantage in an attack and often lulls his prey into a sense of complacency that becomes their undoing. Layne, what say you? Be quick with your answer as we are quickly running out of time."

Layne shook his head. "I will never agree to lead them to Dohenheer. We attack."

"Lathaniel…?"

"As ever I am by your side, Drake. What say you?"

"We attack."

The plan was simple. They would move north of the lake into higher country. Layne was thoroughly familiar with the terrain from Crystal Lake through to Dohenheer and suggested a gully not far into the mountains. Lathaniel would take high ground and attack from above with his bow and arrows; the two Draconeans would position themselves in the trees on either side of the gully and ambush the party when they moved to the rocks for protection.

Lathaniel's first arrow was notched and ready. He could just make out Drake and Layne on either side of the gully below. Drake was adamant that they wait until the entire company was in the gully before the first arrow flew; they didn't want to lose any in a retreat.

The Are-Narc commander was no fool. He paused when his company was at the neck of the gully, searching the high walls for any signs of an ambush. He waved his company forward, but they advanced with caution. It wasn't until the last soldier was well into the trap that Lathaniel rose to his full height and drew back the bowstring on his great Gor'ean bow. Arrow after arrow found its mark as the Are-Narcs rapidly fell. When they rushed into the rocks on either side for cover, they were surprised by the two Draconeans. When Lathaniel could no longer fire his bow into the fray for fear of hitting his companions, he quickly descended from his perch. With so many felled by arrows, the three now had the advantage and ruthlessly hacked what remained of the company to pieces.

When it was over, they were winded and not without their own spate of injuries. Layne's cheek was open almost to the bone on the right-hand side, and his thigh was bloody. Drake had taken a slice to his left arm. Lathaniel had only just missed being eviscerated by leaping backward, but not before taking a tidy slice across his abdomen right above the belt of his breeches. Drake moved to the carcass of Gorillian's messenger. He reached in the man's tunic and withdrew the rolled map parchment.

"It's a copy," he reported, "and a poor one at that. It appears he has not deciphered all of the runes as yet because this directs the company through the main pass above Crystal Lake into the Ashen Mountains but gives no further instructions. He was likely hoping they would be picked up by a scout party and could plead their case."

"With no inbound riders, he will not know if his party was received or killed. It may buy us some time." Layne was roughly dressing his wounds as he spoke. That done, he announced he would shortly return with their dinner, as they agreed it best they stop for the night. Drake bandaged his arm, then left to thoroughly scout the vicinity to ensure they hadn't overlooked any Are-Narcs. Lathaniel stayed to make camp. But before he did, he needed to see to his own wound. It was an awkward spot to dress, and he shivered as he shrugged out of his over and undergarments to do so. When he finished, he pulled on a new undergarment and had just donned all of his discarded clothing when he heard a sound. He reached for his sword and dagger, but as quick as he was, it was not before he heard, "Drop them, or die." He slowly set both on the ground beside him and turned to face his captors.

"Identify yourself and do so quickly if you value your life."

There were eleven of them: immense, solid, and fully armed. Lathaniel had grown both in height and girth over the past year, but even at his height and size, they towered over him.

Sensing this to be a turn for the better for his company, he relaxed and calmly replied, "I am Lathaniel Waythan, son of Lathart. I am a Forsair from the south islands and am searching for a lost city of the Draconeans called Dohenheer."

To a one, their features darkened, and they stepped closer to Lathaniel, circling him, their stance intimidating. "If it is a 'lost' city, how came you to know of it?"

"Are you Draconeans?" Lathaniel answered question with question, believing they might as well cut to the heart of the matter.

"You have not answered our question, Forsair. How came you to know of this lost city?"

Beyond them, Lathaniel spotted Drake and Layne moving quietly forward through the rocks. Layne spoke loudly. "Olan! By the gods, Olan? Is it you?"

Lathaniel's dark-haired inquisitor swung around, as did the others in his company, raising their weapons as they did. Everyone seemed frozen.

"Captain? Captain Rev'eara?

Layne walked quickly forward a huge smile breaking across his face. "Indeed, Olan. It is I."

The two embraced, pulled back to look at each other, then embraced again. Layne swung back, his arm still loosely draped over Olan's shoulder.

Drake stood off to the side, an odd look upon his face. Strangely, discovering Layne was a Draconean had not had the impact on him that seeing these eleven did. He took in their size and stature, their armour, the colour of their eyes and hair, the way they held themselves. In them he saw much of himself. His stomach knotted as he stepped forward.

"May I make you known to Drake, a Draconean from the South," Layne introduced. Eleven pairs of eyes gave Drake their keen regard and a nod of greeting. "And Lathaniel Waythan, though I believe you have met him already."

Lathaniel shrugged on his tunic then strapped on his weapons and shouldered his pack. He went to stand by Drake, who remained on the outer rim of the group listening to the excited chatter of the northern Draconeans as they spoke to Layne.

"Your father had given you up for dead! Where have you been these many years? There was no word of you."

"Is my father well?

"Yes! ... and now a member of the High Council."

Layne cut short the chatter then. "We come north in haste, bearing the most serious of news. Dohenheer is now known to Lord Gorillian. His blackness is spreading across the whole of Elënthiá, but now he has turned his sights on Dohenheer and means to attack our city. We came as quick as we could to warn the Council."

The smiles and revelry vanished.

"You can see by the carnage about you that we killed a scout party he was sending north in hopes of finding and securing a peaceful invitation into our city. A ruse while he musters his forces. We must return to Dohenheer immediately, and I must stand before the High Council."

"Aye, Captain." They snapped to acknowledgement in unison.

Olan barked out orders to his men, who dragged Gorillian's dead into a heap and set it aflame, leaving the harsh climate to destroy the remaining evidence of their passage. Opting to continue through the night, the entire company was headed north into the mountains within the hour.

# CHAPTER 42

Juga's footsteps echoed as he approached the doors to the Grand Hall. Yet another meeting to discuss "what-if" was in session, and Athron and the Fyyther were reluctantly a part of it. Used to his presence in the Council wing, the guards snapped to attention at his approach. Juga knocked twice then entered. It was a breach of protocol for him to do so, and as he entered the Hall, discussion stopped mid-sentence and all eyes shifted to him. He searched the room until he found Athron. He locked eyes with the Prince, conveying the urgency of the interruption, then nodded and stepped back out of the room, pacing impatiently up and down in front of the doors until Athron emerged.

Juga motioned him down the hall immediately. When they were in an alcove in the lobby, he reached in his tunic and withdrew two rolled notes.

"These both arrived at Cap'hannet five days ago. Identical, but sent via two different messengers through circuitous routes. I received them not ten minutes ago."

Athron accepted the parchments. "Who is Nizros Ekard? An informant of yours?"

"Look carefully at the name, Athron...and what it spells if read back to front...Drake Sorzin..."

Athron ripped open the message.

*J. my apprentice and good friend,*
*Uncertain of the reception A. would receive, I thought it best to direct this to you. I know I risk much in the sending, but it is a chance I had to take. Our unexpected guest in Amarik is genuine and carries information that replaces what was lost. We head there now and at great speed. All report that G. is pulling in from across E. in preparation for a massive incursion in the north. Those there will not prevail without the assistance of A. and those who stand with him. Depart with many and in haste, for this could turn the war. If you and A. travel in advance, follow the Dorvanis to Crystal Lake then further north along the Zarinn. Send ships in at Cathanlay and up the Callé. Scouts will await.*
*May the great god Ruahr speed your journey and keep you safe.*

"Finally!" Athron exclaimed. He paced back and forth for a moment while he considered his next steps. "My father must know of this; he must assemble the Council."

Athron returned to the Grand Hall to whisper an urgent summons in his father's ear. Acthelass Mar excused himself.

Alone in the Fyyther's chambers, the argument between father and son had grown heated.

"It is not as simple as that, Athron! I cannot simply march in and order the Elënthián Supreme Council about. Gorger is one member of a single voice that is Elënthiá. Yes, our contribution can sometime hold sway over the larger voice, but I cannot order all Elënthián troops to the Coldain Region!"

"This is a chance to turn the tide of the war, Father. Gorillian's strategy has always been to divide and conquer. He isolates individual regions and then relentlessly chips away at their external defences while his envoys unerringly target every weak internal link. He is as a giant panther, patient, but his great black twitching tail contradicts his real intent. This is how he wins! But an open battlefield, Father...an open battlefield with the united forces of Elënthiá would beat him at his own game. Of this I could not be more certain."

"I cannot peddle your certainty, Athron! You must know that those Council Chambers are filled with heads of realms that, for all their rhetoric, are self-serving. And I am no different. While I want a strong and united Elënthiá, at the end of the day I will always do what is right and best for my own country, for Gorger! And they are no different. What we would be asking them to do is to send troops north at the expense of guarding their own borders. What if you are wrong, Athron? What if the Draconean is wrong, and this is all a ruse to draw us north? Were I to do as you ask, Gorillian could simply walk into Gorger, and there would be naught to stop him!"

"All right, Father. If I follow your thinking...if we do nothing but isolate ourselves and protect our own borders, how will that change the current state of affairs? You know as well as I, before Gorillian began to withdraw his troops, we were losing this war! It would only have been a matter of time."

The Gor'ean Fyyther was silent for a time, though the tension in the air remained thick and cloying. The King spoke then, quietly.

"The Council must, of course, know of this note and of its contents. We will call an emergency session and share it with them. It is a matter for discussion and debate, for many of its members will bring an objectivity and wisdom to this issue that will complement our own."

With that, Acthelass Mar stood and left the small meeting room. As the door shut, Athron pounded his fist on the table before him in frustration.

At his father's command, Athron read the message from the Draconean to the Elënthián Supreme Council, who received the news in silence and shock. The implications of it impacted on so many levels, it was no wonder that the initial response to it was silence.

The message confirmed that there was, indeed, a lost city of Draconeans. Though many on the Council had never met Drake Sorzin and most had only just found out he existed, his reputation was such that contemplating an entire city of warriors of his calibre was nearly beyond their ken. If what they had been told were true, and a single Draconean had made such an impact on deflecting the strength of Gorillian and his forces in times past, they were already imagining what an entire city of Draconeans could bring to the battlefield; provided, of course, they sided with the Resistance. And the pull-back of Gorillian's troops...if what the message said were true, then the Council had much to consider.

Surprisingly, once the usual rabble bleated and sputtered their opinions down from on high, cooler heads within the Council prevailed, and deliberations stretched on for hours. The news received was momentous, and the Gor'ean Fyyther had, for the most part, been silent as he listened to Council process the implications of it. He knew well the politics that each must face within their own unique nations and that a decision in this matter would not be quick in coming.

Beside him, his son chafed and fidgeted. Behind him, his Gor'ean Lords were thoroughly engaged in the debate, offering their own perspectives and experience to the exchange. Garnec Cindrick was suspiciously silent. He took a balcony seat as far away from Prince Athron and Jugarth Framir as was possible. He took no pains to disguise his disgust at their presence and the message they'd presented the Council. Acthelass Mar had given him a stern final warning: his obsession with the Draconean had tainted his reason, and he was to keep quiet during the proceedings or risk banishment from them.

Finally a motion was agreed upon and a vote carried. The Council would confer with their domestic counterparts and return to the Chambers in fifteen days with a decision: send all troops north to join the Draconeans in battle with Gorillian, or use Gorillian's pull-back and the new infusion of financial resources to re-bolster troops and supplies on the front-lines around Elënthiá.

Fifteen days…

Juga could barely contain his anger and disgust. Even Athron, the more seasoned at wearing a political face, was obviously frustrated. They were among the first out of the Chambers and down the steps to the lobby where they stood talking of the meeting. Council members lingered in the Lobby using the time to exchange more private personal views on what had just transpired.

Garnec Cindrick belatedly joined the circle where Athron and Juga were talking to several Gor'ean Lords expounding on the importance of quick action and bemoaning the fifteen-day wait.

As soon as he caught the gist of the discussion, he belligerently asserted his opinion. "I disagree! What we do not need is more lying, traitorous Draconeans! The Elënthián Supreme Council is wise and prudent. Mind my words; they will never agree to dedicate our troops in support of a race of blackguards and villains, no matter the source of the request." The last phrase was a deliberate affront to the Prince.

Athron seethed with anger, tired of the elder statesmen's toxic rhetoric especially as it was directed at those whom he held in esteem. "Mind your tongue, old man. It is easy to speak words here in the centrum where you are coddled and protected. It has been years since you have seen battle on the front lines and years since your sight has been clear and impartial enough to hold a valid opinion."

Cindrick reacted instantly to the insult by drawing his sword from its scabbard. The whisper the metal made as it left its sheath was drowned out by the gasp of alarm that could be heard across the room. Athron was unarmed. "You dare to insult me!" he yelled.

Before he could fully draw his weapon, Juga had already stepped boldly in front of the High Prince, and was pulling his Anulean hammer to hand. The crowds leapt back in alarm. Juga felt the sharp bite of Cindrick's sword as it swept across his unprotected upper arm and forearm. Then his ancient hammer was fully to hand, and he used it well to parry Cindrick's thrusts. His stance quickly shifted from defensive to offensive, and he used the long-handled hammer as a battering ram, catching the older man first in the stomach, doubling him over, then under the chin, snapping his head back. Athron, meanwhile, had pulled Juga's sword from its scabbard. Juga stepped aside as the Gor'ean High Prince stood over Garnec Cindrick, the tip of the sword held steadily beneath his chin. Acthelass Mar shouldered his way through the crowds and into the circle.

"You *dare* to threaten my son ... to engage in violence in these chambers?" he bellowed. "Arrest him!"

Cindrick shrugged off the hands that reached down to pull him to his feet. Eyes black with hatred, he stared at

Athron and especially at Juga. Wiping the back of his hand across his bloodied face, he left the lobby with his escort of soldiers.

Juga, cool-headed, turned to the High Prince as he again shouldered his hammer, his eyebrow raised in inquiry. Saying nothing, Athron merely nodded his thanks and handed the Human back his sword. He swung on his heels to depart the lobby with Juga close behind. The crowds parted as they passed, more than a few heads-of-state observing the Human with new respect and regard.

# CHAPTER 43

The Draconean soldiers knew exactly where they were going, thank the gods! Lathaniel concentrated on putting his feet exactly into the imprints left in the thigh high snow in front of him. The night was black as pitch, and his feet were blocks of ice attached to the ends of his legs. He couldn't remember ever being as cold. When the winds shifted just after midnight, they unrolled fur cloaks and collars and bundled into them. All of their faces but for their eyes were shielded from the biting wind, and their hands were buried in fur muffs—for all the good it did.

Dawn was breaking when Olan called a halt. His men dispersed to gather firewood and soon had a blaze roaring. "We crossed a difficult pass through the night," he explained. "It cut our journey by a full two days and allowed us to take your measure." He paused looking from Drake to Lathaniel before smiling.

Lathaniel assumed that his comment was meant to convey that they'd somehow passed some fundamental survival test by keeping up. He really did not care at that point. He was cold, tired, and hungry; and the wound he'd taken the previous afternoon was aching and itchy.

A watch was set, and the remainder of the company gathered round the fire to take some food while Olan drew a rudimentary map in the snow by his feet. "We are here. We will warm ourselves and rest an hour or two. Then we will ascend," he gestured, "up there - almost to the tree line. There is a path down the other side that takes us where we need to go."

Drake wasn't asking, so Lathaniel felt he should. "And that is...?"

"It drops down into a bowl between three mountains. We are at the back side of one of them. On the far side is the ancient city of the northern Draconeans."

Sufficiently appeased, Lathaniel nodded. Drake remained quiet; he and Lathaniel kept to themselves and listened to the northern Draconeans update Layne using names familiar only to them. It was obvious from the tone and manner of the soldiers when they were in his presence that Captain Layne Rev'eara had been held in high regard before he had left the north.

Once rested, they ascended the path as Captain Olan described and carefully made their way down the treacherous, slippery trail on the other side. The "ancient city of the Draconeans of the north" was not what Lathaniel expected.

There was indeed a deep basin nestled at the base of three mountains. Soft wood, coniferous trees grew shoulder to shoulder, sprawling across the valley floor and up all sides of the mountains, their branches heavy and winking in the midday sun with the weight of the previous night's snow. Dilapidated stone ruins were situated in and among the trees at the lowest point of the bowl. One could imagine the streets and dwellings that would have filled the valley at some point, but now it was a tangle of growth and snow. Lathaniel turned to Drake in question, but he said nothing.

The company pressed on through the snow past the skeletons of the snow-covered ruins. The mountain immediately in front of them was one of the three that protected the basin. Lathaniel assumed they were climbing again, but Captain Olan and Layne ignored logical breaks in the vegetation that would ease their ascent and instead lead them straight toward a wide wall of trees.

The closer they drew to it, the more uncomfortable Lathaniel felt. By the time they were almost at the tree line, he had removed his bow from his shoulder and notched an arrow, so wary was he of what was ahead. As they approached, the trees seemed to shimmer; the air held a ripple to it as a water's surface would after one dropped a pebble into its calmness. Lathaniel was feeling nauseous and edgy, as though he needed to depart the basin or forfeit his life. Steadfastly he followed on behind the Draconeans, who did not seem to be suffering from any similar impediment. They marched directly through the shimmer of air before them. What was beyond stopped Lathaniel short.

An enormous entrance was carved into the mountain in front of them. Not a door, but a massive square gate, by Lathaniel's estimation, at least fifty paces across. It was hewn from the rock such that they could walk straight toward it and enter at ground level. The walls to the passage began at ground level and then sloped upward on either side until they met the wall face into which the gate was carved. The sloped sides to the entrance were tree covered and mossy. Snow had drifted heavily in the open passage, and the company had to struggle through hip-deep drifts.

Lathaniel's eyes adjusted to the dimmer light as they passed beneath the arch of the great gate. A passage of similar dimensions yawned into blackness before them. Several steps inside the entrance, Lathaniel was again overcome with apprehension.

Drake said quietly, "It is the work of the Elves – ancient protections in place to deter unwanted guests. I have experienced this elsewhere. It will pass."

Briskly, they pressed forward into the darkness for perhaps one hundred yards. Ahead another great gate faced them. It was twice the size of the entrance from the outside, and beyond it was light.

Lathaniel had stood in awe before the incredible Dwarven halls and galleries within the Minheras, but they seemed diminutive compared to what was before him. One could not refer to it as a hall, for its dimensions defied comprehension.

If the gate they had entered through was one hundred paces wide, then the width of the space before them would be twenty times that. Ahead in the far distance, Lathaniel could see a great stone wall. Within it was another enormous gate on either side of which stood two tall sturdy towers. Two other slightly shorter towers were built into the great wall on either side of these. But this wall was a thirty-minute brisk walk at least. The ceiling stretched several hundred feet above them. Light emanated from hundreds upon hundreds of immense braziers that hung from the ceilings, fuelled by what, Lathaniel could only guess. It was dark; floor, walls, and ceiling all an unrelieved and ominous black. As they walked through the gate and across the massive arena, he could contain his curiosity no longer.

"What is this place?"

It was Olan who answered. "This, lad, is Dinhoriin. Beyond is Dohenheer, the last great bastion of the Draconean race. In the distance you see the first of two outer walls that guard the entrance to our city. Dohenheer was designed as a fortress, to be impenetrable."

"But how could you have possibly hollowed this great space? There are no pillars, no supports."

"There are scholars among our nobility who could better answer your questions, but I can tell you that the our people had aid in the initial excavation from both the Dwarves and the Giants—favours repaid for assistance to them in battle ages ago."

*Giants?* Layne hadn't mentioned Giants ... There was so much of Elënthiá still unknown to Lathaniel. He fell silent, still drinking in all he beheld.

Drake was silent. Having been alone all of his life, his cool demeanour dissuaded most from engaging him in conversation, and his time with the northern Draconeans was no exception. At his request, Layne had not revealed his heritage. All the same, they observed him as an oddity—a countryman, but not, as their terms of reference for their southern brethren came mostly from their elders. As ever, Drake felt an interloper. Across the centuries he would dream of finding and joining what remained of his race, of being welcomed warmly, embraced back into a nation; of belonging. As he walked across the black slate field toward the interior gates of Dohenheer, he had never felt more alone.

A sonorous moan from a horn could be heard from the fortress tower in the distance. One of Olan's soldiers withdrew a smaller horn and responded. As they approached, the great wooden gates swung inward then closed again behind them. They were received by two long lines of soldiers, twenty in each. All were dressed in black tunics thrown back behind shoulders that were covered in eight-lamed black leather pauldrons. A thick shirt of mail hung to their elbows and to the middle of their thighs. Black vambraces protected their forearms and matched the greaves that covered their lower legs.

Their Captain stepped forward to greet Olan, who pointedly stepped to the side leaving the soldier face-to-face with Layne. The Captain's face blanked and then registered surprise as he snapped to attention. Behind him a murmur of surprise rode a wave down the line of soldiers. With precision the two lines stepped back to pivot on their right feet so that they were now facing each other. In unison they then took two great steps backward, forming a corridor through which the company proceeded accompanied by this new Captain. All told, forty soldiers fell in behind the party of ten scouts. It appeared their escort was multiplying.

Before them was yet another, smaller yet strong stone wall at the center of which was an additional fortified gate with the requisite guard towers flanking it. Between the two walls were numerous structures made of wood and stone. Barracks and supply buildings, Olan explained, should there be battle and they have need of them. It was another thousand paces or more to the second gate which, again, swung inward as they approached.

The two fortified outer walls protected a third gate, similar in size to that through which they had entered Dinhoriin, except this entrance had massive doors which at the moment were open. Beyond them, bright summer sunshine was beaming down. Their company moved through the central passage of three. If Dinhoriin was barren and desolate, this place was the complete opposite.

"We will need to meet with the High Council as soon as possible," Drake reminded.

Wondering what their reception might be, Layne nodded and spoke quietly to Captain Olan.

# CHAPTER 44

Deep in Ethen-jar, Gorillian paced circles around his own oversized map table using a long-handled rake to shift his legions around the enlarged parchment. In total he could muster twenty-five legions, perhaps another five if he thinned his troops on the northern borders of Nesmeresa. The majority of his remaining troops were in the frontiers and not easily redeployed. Besides, there were still strongholds elsewhere in Elënthiá that he had taken at great cost, and he was loath to chance losing at this juncture. No…this number would be sufficient.

Koorast had been all but vacated but for his puppets in royal courts of the realms there and his network of spies across the island. The Resistance in Far'camice, Illiyish, and Siityth had been crushed, a happy benefit of their proximity to Ethen-jar. The soldiers who lived had pledged to his service. There would be minimal fallout to removing legion patrols from across the western Coldain and redeploying them for an incursion to the north.

He shifted models representing what ships were not across the sea in the Vearian or Zormian regions around, such that they were evenly positioned along the Coldain coastline, particularly to the south and east. These naval patrols, in conjunction with a loose scout network along the coast, should be sufficient to at least alert him to any danger.

What news he had received indicated that the Resistance was either foolishly celebrating a false victory and buckling under its own self-congratulatory back pats or holding fast to their home borders unable to imagine that he would pull back his forces. Regardless, they were paralyzed, and that worked to his advantage.

The Draconean's map still confounded him. Oblique rune references to magic and to protections had stalled him in his deciphering. He knew Dohenheer's general location in the Ashen Mountains, but he would need to know all before attacking else he be surprised; he didn't manage surprise well.

A quick knock on the chamber door interrupted his thoughts. Karget Gash stood at the threshold awaiting an invitation to enter. At Gorillian's nod, he approached. "A report is in from the messenger and escort we sent north. As of three days ago, they report unimpeded progress. They are following the Dorvanis River closely as you directed. They have not been intercepted as yet."

"The Draconean?"

"No sign of him. Reports from Koorast tell of two entering Gorger, a soldier and a Human, but only the two. No others matching the description of either the Draconean or the Forsair accompany them."

A humourless half-smile crossed Gorillian's lips. "He has divided his company. I am guessing that the Gor'ean and the Human returned to Gorgonathan to try and muster reinforcements. The Prince will have his work cut out for him, for his reception by the Council and his father will be chilly. As for the Draconean, alert all patrols guarding Ethen-jar, and triple the guards along the walls and at all gates. I believe he is coming after his map."

Gash's eyes widened. It took little to shock or intimidate the hulk, but he feared his Master. That Gorillian was sufficiently worried about a single Draconean to fortify his battlements was a curiosity to him. "With respect, my lord, no one would dare approach Ethen-jar or attempt to breach her walls. It would be folly. No ally to the Resistance has been inside the gates for an Age or more.

"Aye, one unfamiliar with this realm would be doomed."

"He has been here?"

Gorillian was looking distractedly down at his map, not giving Gash's dismay any credence. He nodded.

"He is a single Draconean accompanied by a single Forsair, himself not more than a boy. What harm could two bring to us? Is this Draconean a god?

Gorillian chuckled. "No god is he. He would laugh at your comment, as he has long forsaken belief in the gods." He then became serious. "But if ever an Immortal came close to being one, it would be this Draconean."

Gash watched his master in awe while he continued arrogantly, "And if ever there was one to defeat a god himself... it would be me."

# CHAPTER 45

The city of Dohenheer was built as three separate but interconnected pods. To the west were the farmlands, the barns for livestock, the orchards and the dairies. To the east were the markets and the shops for all manner of tradesmen. In the center was Dohenheer city – home to all who lived there, and to the chambers of Dohenheer's High Council.

Lathaniel mused that at heart, he was a simple Forsairean for whom the four seasons came and went, the sun shone, and the moon rose. This was the extent of the magic he knew. What had conjured the sun to shine and a blue sky deep inside the heart of the Ashen Mountains, he could not have imagined...but with the gods as his witness, he felt the welcome warmth of the sun on his face as he lifted it and beheld a cloudless blue sky. They had entered a paradise, he was certain.

The road into the city was cobblestone. Orchards grew on either side of the road as every available space was utilized to sustain the Draconeans. The incongruity of it all was that the distant backdrop on all sides was a cold grey sheer rock face. This was a different version of the huge black arena they had just passed through. It was, indeed, a city of light. Constructed entirely out of white marble, Dohenheer stretched across the horizon in front of them. A large central dome surrounded by six slightly smaller domes dominated its skyline.

At its highest point, the largest dome looked to be well over three hundred feet from the ground.

The base of each of the six other roof domes was encircled with identical tall arches. Below these seven main domes, the city cascaded down in three distinct levels. The top level of the city was a further study in the ornate arches, which multiplied along each side of the city and beyond Lathaniel's vision. A middle level featured more solid walls with less frequent yet still plentiful open arches though these were grouped more to the four corners.

At ground level, the arches were more ornate, their tops narrowing two thirds of the way up and then ballooning slightly, making each opening reminiscent of a keyhole. Where the support columns intersected with the narrowest portion of the arch, they were wrapped in elaborate gold inlay. These lined all sides of the city, and as Lathaniel grew closer he could see that these supported a covered pedestrian thoroughfare of sorts. There were four large entrances in the center of each of the four outer walls. These entrances reached from the ground to the third level.

At each of the four corners of it were tall minarets, which gently flared then narrowed at intervals as they rose into the sky, familiar gold inlay inset at each narrowing. Excepting the gold accents, the entire city was built from the purest white marble. His eyes nearly ached at the brilliance. A quick side glance at Drake's usually impassive face revealed he was as impressed as his apprentice.

As they entered the City itself, Lathaniel became too absorbed in people-watching to detect the finer points of his surroundings. They were being shepherded with haste, Lathaniel presumed, to the Draconean High Council.

The High Council was situated as befitting its name. Its chambers were located on the highest level in the city and beneath its largest dome. Inside the chambers themselves, there was a central dais and below it, a platform. Below that and down a handful of steps there was another larger platform. At the bottom of the room there were elaborate steps that led to double doors.

There was a crescent moon-shaped table situated on the highest dais and behind it four ornate, high-backed chairs upholstered in the finest fabric and cushioned with the softest of goose down. There was not a single seat or table on the platforms below it. Those who came before the High Council, stood.

There were three males and one female Draconean occupying the chairs, and a messenger standing on the first platform before them.

"Speak."

"There is a scout party petitioning immediate audience with the High Council. They are escorted by gate guards. All accompany three new arrivals to the city."

If the Draconean High Council had been bored by the tedium of Council business, that announcement snapped them to attention.

"New arrivals? Explain yourself."

"Visitors not of Dohenheer, your Excellencies."

The four exchanged glances. "Summon them."

The double doors opened and the visitors entered in single file: first Layne – the sight of whom brought gasps from the Council - then Drake followed by Lathaniel. Captain Olan and the Captain of the gate guards brought up the rear. The remainder of the scout party and the escort from the gate stayed outside. With the sound of the doors closing, six new guards filed in from either side of the double doors and stood against the wall, hands clasped behind their backs, staring straight ahead.

No warm greeting nor welcome was offered. Layne and the two Captains had immediately bent to one knee and bowed their heads out of respect for the Council. And, as they had not been given instruction to the contrary, they remained that way. From the dais one of the Council members spoke sharply to Drake and Lathaniel. "One never likes to assume that people of other races are possessed of manners, but before this Council, you bow."

Drake held his gaze and remained on his feet. "And, one would assume that even a race that hosts few guests would be possessed of sufficient manners to welcome them. As to the demand that I bow ... I bow to no one." Drake dropped the haughty demeanor and allowed his annoyance to show. "We have travelled to your city in great haste and at great personal peril to bring you dire news and warning, not to pay homage to your status within Dohenheer."

Faces reddened and eyes rounded at both his breach of protocol and his announcement. Unwilling to concede, the Draconean councillor repeated, "You will bow. Or you will leave."

Drake was tired and angry at their treatment. Also dismayed at the tone and the direction of their meeting, Layne Rev'eara came to his feet.

"By what merit do you demand I bow before you?" Drake demanded. "I have served Elënthiá and my race for longer than any present. I am neither pretentious nor a believer in ceremony ... and I have never hidden behind large gates and strong walls. The blood that courses through my veins runs thick and rich with history and nobility. . .far beyond that of any who sit at your table." Tension vibrated through the room. "My name is Drake Sorzin, son of Dray. I am the last living son of the last King of the Draconeans of the South and heir to the title of King. I bid you speak now if you still feel I must bow before you."

All four were slack-jawed at his announcement. The two captains forgot protocol and came to their feet beside Layne, staring at Drake as well.

Another of the Draconean elders recovered quickly and stood, coming around the edge of the Council table and down the steps to stand in front of Drake. Your Highness, my name is General Fysst and I represent Dohenheer's military on this Council. I knew your father well and often spent time with your family. I bid you welcome to Dohenheer and offer our most sincere apologies to you for your reception." Drake reached out and grasped the elder general's forearm when he would have bowed."

"There is no need for ceremony nor use of titles required in my presence," assured Drake. "I am who I am but it has been millennia since the north recognized the royal bloodline, and I am not here to reclaim it."

The other Councillors had made their way down from the dais. Lilyss Harphh, was slender with dark hair pulled back into a severe knot and securely anchored behind her head. As she introduced herself, she advised that she represented the clergy on the Council. Next was Varis Mauge; portly, balding and shorter than most of the Draconeans they had thus far seen. He squinted through watery eyes up at Drake. "I also knew your father, the King," the scholar said quietly. "We felt his loss keenly." Drake nodded his acknowledgement.

The last of the Councillors was the belligerent voice who had demanded they bow before the Council. His greeting was curt. Drake disguised his surprise when the Draconean introduced himself. "I am Seuton Rev'eara, father to Layne who stands beside you and who remains the greatest warrior Dohenheer has ever produced," he boasted. Drake thought it an inappropriate comment to include in an introduction but said nothing. Rev'eara advised he was the people's representative on Council.

With introductions complete, the general suggested council resume their seats. That done, he spoke on behalf of the Council. "You have said that you have come a great distance and at great peril. Before you share these details, may we ask why you have not made yourself known to us centuries ago?"

"I came to know of Dohenheer only weeks ago. Moments before his death nearly two thousand years ago, my father gave me an encrypted parchment map. It is only through a series of recent circumstances that I was able to decipher it. It led me to the Tombs, which, as you will remember, house the accumulated wealth of our race. There I found a map with instructions to find this place."

"A map!" General Fyyst was agitated. "Our agreement when we left Evendeer was that no such maps would ever be made to this place. If such a map fell into the wrong hands, our security here would be compromised!"

Sensing Drake was close to another outburst, Lathaniel spoke on his behalf.

"I am afraid that what you fear is truth already, sir. Your soldiers say that you know of Lord Gorillian and of the evil he spreads across Elënthiá. We faced an ambush by his Are-Narcs when departing the Tombs, and the map was lost to them. It showed only that this city was located somewhere in the Ashen Mountains. Exact directions to it were riddled in ancient Darrish runes. It was our good fortune that Captain Rev'eara found us when he did and was able to bring us directly to you. We believe that Gorillian has not yet deciphered the whole of these runes but know for a fact that he is amassing his armies for an attack on this place. That is why we've come."

This was devastating news, and all four Council members were visibly shaken by it. Councillor Rev'eara spoke then, addressing Lathaniel disdainfully, "And who are you? What role do you play in this drama?"

"I am Lathaniel Waythan, son of Lathart, a Forsair from the southern islands, General."

"Impossible! Forsairs are myth and legend." The statement and the flick of his wrist was dismissive.

"Then you are truly blessed, old man, for both myth and legend stands before you in the flesh." Drake interjected testily.

"*Iysem-kayda,*" the Councillor muttered beneath his breath.

Drake continued: "At maximum, we estimate that you have two to three months to prepare. We will need to review battle plans and strategies, to establish defensible positions in the valley beyond and within Dinhoriin." The eyes he met as he reviewed the Council were dazed, near to blank. "Have you never once considered that you could not evade evil forever? Have you never prepared for that eventuality?"

"We wouldn't be facing that eventuality if you hadn't lost the only map to our city to the single most evil force in Elënthiá!" This, again, from Rev'eara.

"Be that as it may, Councillor. The fact remains that Gorillian is about to launch a full assault on Dohenheer," Drake snapped.

The general spoke again, "Do we have a sense of the troops he will carry north with him?"

"We estimate thirty thousand," Drake replied. There was a collective gasp across the room. They knew that they could not withstand an onslaught of that magnitude. "The majority of his forces are his own Are-Narcs. These are Cave-Narcs from ancient Oderon that he has bred to Human females for the express purpose of populating his own armies. I believe some of your own scouting parties have had skirmishes with them already. Though not particulary intelligent, they are strong, and formidable opponents, especially in those numbers. The remainder of his force will be soldiers from lands across Elënthiá that have been forced into his service when their lands fell to him."

Lathaniel spoke again. "The coming battle is not without hope. We have dispatched messages to allies within the southern Resistance; strong and loyal allies. They should be rallying their troops and preparing to journey north to join you against Gorillian even as we now meet."

Seuton Rev'eara spoke again, his tone toward Lathaniel continued to be condescending,"Allies? Troops? If you choose to speak to this Council, do so with depth and full disclosure *Iysem-kayda*, for we grow tired of your elliptical comments."

Lathaniel wasn't certain what *Iysem-kayda* meant, but it couldn't have been complimentary. The raspy *ting* of a sword being partially withdrawn from a scabbard was heard then, closely followed by another. Drake had his hand on the hilt of his sword and had lifted though not drawn it. Layne Rev'eara had done the same. The two stood poised as Drake directed his comments to the senior Rev'eara.

"You demand respect, Councillor, but offer none in return. Out of respect for your son, I will not stain this floor with your blood. But guard your tongue well, for I will not see the Forsair bear your insults."

Lathaniel reached across and placed his hand on Drake's wrist, firmly pushing down on it until his sword returned to its scabbard. Unruffled, he resumed his report to the Council as if uninterrupted. "We believe that with the support of the

Gor'ean army and its Elënthián allies we can match or exceed what Gorillian will bring against Dohenheer. But success will depend on preparation."

Drake interrupted, "Three months is not long...but I have done it in less."

"You? We have a newly returned General who can lead us. You speak as if this is your city to protect and defend!" Rev'eara replied.

There was a stretch of silence while Drake let his cold, steely gaze move from one to the other down the Council table. "It is."

With that Drake turned to leave, Lathaniel at his heels. To Layne, he said, "We will need to briefly rest and take food. I will review your troops with you at dawn."

There were sputters of indignance from the Council table behind him. Drake ignored them and left the room. Layne was hard on his heels as he crossed the threshold. He grabbed Drake's arm to stay him, his tone placating. "I know you are not accustomed to the manner north as yet, Drake, but they are our High Council. No matter how you may wish it to be different, their decisions govern Dohenheer. You must remember this and act accordingly."

They were outside the Council Chambers now. The twelve guards from the interior chamber had followed them out where the original ten scouts and twenty gate guards were waiting. All were catching every syllable exchanged.

"*Act?*" Drake responded incredulously. "Think you that it is an act that brought me across the great sea and from one end of our Elënthiá to the other? North or south it matters not. I am a Draconean. This is the last Draconean city and, with the gods as my witness, I will not see it fall to the evil that is Gorillian. As to the rule of the city, with respect, I remind you that they sit in that room because they represent the people, Layne. The people. By your own design, Dohenheer belongs to the people. And the people ... our people are in mortal danger. I will not stand on ceremony. I will not play politics. And I most certainly will not allow Gorillian to take Dohenheer."

The attention of each and every Draconean present was riveted to Drake. His words were a splash of the coolest water against a parched throat. In their hearts, indeed at the most basic of cellular levels, they were warriors bred to fight, to be strong - not to live in seclusion in a manufactured state of perpetual readiness for battles they never had the opportunity to fight.

Captain Layne Rev'eara was at first astonished by Drake's words, then his face broke into a smile, his eyes alight. He snapped to attention and placed his hand over his heart. Following his lead, the assembled soldiers did the same. He leaned forward to Drake spoke: "Word will travel, Drake Sorzin. They will say the sons of Dohenheer have returned and they will follow you." His eyes shifted to include Lathaniel. "They will follow us."

# CHAPTER 46

Drake had requested adjoining rooms, as there was little sense in Lathaniel and him wasting valuable time transiting about the City. Each room was equipped with a bathing chamber. It had been a fortnight since they boarded the Pythius in Limore, and during that time they had lived hard and travelled hard without the luxury of hot meals or baths. The two opted to enjoy the latter before they took food and rest.

Like all else in Dohenheer, their quarters were lavish, marbled and richly draped in fabrics of the most soothing colors. Lathaniel stood before the tall looking glass in his bathing chamber with a towel loosely draped around his waist. He could barely find Lathaniel Waythan in the image that stared back at him. His height had stretched, putting him near to six and a quarter feet in height. His shoulders had broadened, and his waist had narrowed. His long legs were well muscled; and his abdomen, chiselled with well-defined muscles. He was nearly nineteen; this was as it should be. But what took him aback was the evidence of his trials these many months: the spider webs of scars; the pink, puckered burns—all evidence of the soldier he had become. Leaning against the basin, he stared back at his own grey eyes in the mirror. The naïve adolescent was gone. As though a breeze were lifting and flipping back the pages of the past months, scenes flashed through Lathaniel's memory until the wind died and what was before him was his own visage in the glass.

"Soon it will be a year," he said to Drake later as they ate before the hearth. "In many ways, it seems like mere weeks since I left Lamana."

"Are you becoming unsettled again?" Drake put down his utensils and wiped his chin, staring at Lathaniel.

"No. I know now that I am as I am to be; as the gods would have me. But my dreams bring me visions of what could have been were I to have chosen a different path. I look at you, Drake, and I know that I am meant to be your companion in this place and at this time. But, with respect, I also see what I might become. I fear there will be no end to my travels and hardships save death, and it is not how I would want my life to be. Make no mistake; it is not death I fear, only a death without meaning or purpose."

Lathaniel's statement shook him and Drake was speechless for a moment or more. "You have become a formidable soldier, Lathaniel. Save me, your skill as a warrior would see you stand victorious against any in Elënthiá. But it is your mind that sets you apart; your conscience, your sense of honour and duty, your belief in truth and in justice. The circumstances of my life have painted me a warrior and a loner destined to serve, but to stand apart. Your life is new and your experience young. I agree, you are meant to be here now, in Dohenheer. It is destined. But this I also know Lathaniel: you are destined to survive this war, to live. This, I promise you. Your destiny lies beyond a warrior's life, beyond this place. I know your anguish for your people. But what you do now positions you to return one day and free them."

Lathaniel slept without dreams.The Draconean was already gone from his chamber when Lathaniel knocked the next morning. He slept little, and Lathaniel assumed that he was already engaged in understanding Dohenheer. There was much to do and little time.

He made his way to ground level and walked beneath the pillared walkway that bracketed the City. The key-holed arches they'd noticed as they approached the city were mirrored in its interior architecture, the shape repeated itself: white on white for as far as he could see.

Stopping to lean against one of the columns, he looked across emerald green lawns and gardens, fences and enclosures that extended, surreally, in three directions abruptly ending at cold grey granite. He shook his head in continued amazement at the place and let his eyes sweep the crowds. In the distance he spotted Captain Rev'eara in conversation with another Draconean. The High Council had ratified Layne's elevation to the rank of General of the Draconean Army the previous evening. 'General' Rev'eara's delight was obvious.

As Lathaniel approached the two, he had to tilt his head farther back than he usual in order to greet Layne's companion. This one was a behemoth. Nearly seven feet in height, hairless, and with skin of polished oak and eyes as dark as brown currants, the soldier stopped speaking when Lathaniel approached.

"Lathaniel! I thought you would sleep later, lad, else I would have met you within the City walls!" Layne smiled broadly and seemed to forget the soldier beside him.

The mighty soldier stepped forward with a smile. "It is obvious that Dohenheer's newest General's manners are still in his bed, even if he is not. I am Captain Sameer Khan, and the pleasure of our meeting is all mine. You have but arrived here in Dohenheer, and already there is much talk of your skill as a warrior."

Lathaniel did not reply, merely raised a single brow and looked at Layne. The three turned and began to walk as Layne continued. "Drake met with the Draconean captains early this morning, Lathaniel. He has set a training roster for our army. For the next weeks, we will engage in general training in all manner of weapons. Thereafter there will be a series of elimination matches: play-offs, if you like. Warriors from the lowest to the highest rank will compete for points using a variety of weapons. It will allow him to assess ability at all levels, and to target weakness. And it has given the army focus ... and cause for great excitement."

Khan interrupted, "The competitions will identify the finest among us. Your Draconean will enter only when the top five warriors remain."

*His Draconean*? Was he not theirs as well? Lathaniel offered no comment.

"Your silence is perplexing, Forsair." The giant warrior's white straight teeth gleamed in a smile. "If your skills are truly exceptional, then you should train with the other warriors and teach us what you know. *If* your skills are exceptional that is..." The taunt was there, and so was the smile. Lathaniel smiled his agreement. He saw it coming. If he had not anchored his feet and braced, the great clap Captain Khan gave him on the back before he walked away would have sent him flying.

Layne and Lathaniel were left to continue their stroll of the grounds. Talk shifted to Gorillian and the previous day's Council meeting. "I apologize for my father's treatment of you." Layne's voice was quiet and hard. "He has always been a political man. He has obviously used my ascension through the Army, and my absence, to construct his political platform and secure his seat on the High Council." Lathaniel dismissed his concern and the two made their way to the sparring arenas. Captain Khan was already there and walked out to meet them. The Draconean who accompanied him introduced himself as Captain Fabian Dagostin.

"Ahhh...so this is the Forsair," a voice from behind him said.

"Yes, the Forsair," the same voice seemed to say again.

Lathaniel looked first behind and then beside him. Two identical Draconeans smiled mischievously at him, mirror images down to the freckle.

"Pay no heed to those two." Khan smiled.

Captain Dagostin introduced them: "Lathaniel Waythan, may I make you known to Captains Aleksa and Alexi Illic... and no, your eyes do not deceive you. They are brothers."

The two played on their height and circled Lathaniel playfully, purposefully crowding him and looking down at him. "So this is the fearsome Forsair," they joked. "He is so small we must have a care that a blade does not swing and catch him unawares."

They laughed, and Lathaniel laughed with them for it was obvious their jests were well meant. "Have no worries, Draconeans. If a stray blade comes our way, I'll be certain to protect you from it."

That garnered loud laughter all around.

Captain Dagostin spoke then, seriously. "I hear you will join in the elimination. I, for one, give you warning lad for I am a fair swordsman and would not want to cause you harm."

"Nor I you," replied Lathaniel quietly, giving no quarter but softening the reply with a smile.

Dagostin, Khan, and the Illic brothers eyed him curiously.

"We shall have the measure of you soon, Forsair." Dagostin and the other Captains moved on. Layne made his farewells soon after. "I will leave you to your own devices to explore Dohenheer, Forsair, for I have duties to see to."

# CHAPTER 47

It began high with an arc on the left at the top his chest. From there it swept over his shoulder where it split just above the rise of his bicep into three meandering vines that wove around his arm. One blade of the vine ended below his middle knuckle; another finished in a curve above the joint of his thumb, while the third ended just at the underside of his palm.

On his chest above his heart, within the arc of the vine, was a single star with a smaller star to the left above it. With time on his hands and too much on his mind, Juga had contracted a Gor'ean artist to apply the painful body paint to his arm. He'd spent hours pouring over dusty parchments filled top to bottom with designs: Elven, Human, Dwarven and Gor'ean. Athron was correct; the process was not pleasant, but as of the previous day, it was complete.

Today marked the dawn of the fifteenth day. The Elënthián Supreme Council would meet later that morning, and a decision would be taken. Either the Council would send Resistance troops to support the Draconeans of the north, or they would not. There was every indication to believe that they would not. Athron had been called to his father's personal chambers, and Juga escorted him.

"Be prepared to leave immediately after the Council concludes," Athron ordered as they walked rapidly up the steps.

"Have you told the Fyyther of your decision as yet?"

"No. I will this morning." Athron was silent for a few steps. "He is failing. I ask him the cause, and he dismisses my inquiry. Others have also noticed, and typically there are those among the Gor'ean Lords who are circling like vultures."

"I could list them without your help," Juga said with hardness in his voice. "Cindrick would be at the top ... though your father released him and confined him to his personal quarters, many of the other Lords still meet with him there."

Athron grimaced. "He is a fool. But a fool with a following, and there is nothing more dangerous." They slowed as they topped the stairs and entered the corridor to Acthelass Mar's chambers. "Use this time before the Council meeting well. Secure supplies. Weapons and packs at the ready."

Juga nodded, turned on his heel, and walked quickly back the way he'd come.

Athron knocked twice, then entered. His father was sitting alone. The shutters to his balcony were wide open, and the sun bathed the room in warm light. Athron was taken aback at how old his father looked; his invincible, invulnerable Fyyther. Acthelass Mar turned to his son, and his face broke into a warm smile.

"Come sit with me for a time, my son, for I would talk to you before too much more of this day passes."

Athron pulled a hard-backed chair directly in front of his father and sat, leaning forward to rest his elbows on his knees.

Acthelass searched his son's face. "I have not been the best of fathers to you," he began. Athron opened his mouth to interrupt, but the King lifted his hand to stay his protests. "I am an ambitious man, but I am a soldier, a soldier of Gorger and of Elënthiá. The focus of my entire life has been service to both, and I have done so at the expense of my family.

"You are of my blood. I have watched you grow into a strong, proud Gor'ean, courageous and decisive yet fair and compassionate. The measure of a true leader can be found in the devotion of those who follow him; and you, Athron Mar, are extraordinary. You are everything I could ask for in a son and far more than I deserve. My pride and love for you has no bounds."

Their eyes held throughout; both were misted now.

"You are not well, Father," Athron said. "I know this to be true, and yet still you deny me. Can you not tell me what is wrong?"

The Fyyther sighed. "I am an old man, Athron. There is nothing the matter with me that does not happen in the normal course of things. No more questions on this." He changed the subject then. "You know, of course, that the Council will not support a full deployment north." It was a statement, not a question. "I know you think I should have done more, but believe me, I tried to extract every favour owed me to see this done; to no avail."

"Father," Athron leaned further forward, his eyes pleading, "if the Council will not sanction this as a Resistance initiative, deploy our own troops. Deploy the Gor'eans. Though members of the Council, we are still a sovereign nation. It is within your power to do so...with or without the Council's approval."

"No!" Acthelass was already shaking his head. "To do so would be to undermine the authority of the Council, authority I have worked these many years to strengthen and solidify."

"The Council will survive your decision, Father. Elënthiá may not!"

At an impasse, the two were silent for a moment. Then Athron said, "If that is truly their decision - if it is your decision - then I leave immediately for the north. I cannot abide waiting safely inside our borders when I know with certainty that I am needed in the north. I will leave with the Human. We will do what we can to help."

Athron stood and set the chair back in place against the wall. Coming back, he drew to attention, then dropped to his knee in front of his Fyyther, his right fist pounding his heart. It was a gesture of respect and love and an acknowledgement that, in spite of their disagreement, neither would diminish.

When a vote was taken, the motion was declined. Kings of all the Realms of Men still free of Gorillian, along with the Fairies and the Gnomes declined. The Elves supported the motion, but that had drawn some heated comments.

"It is easy to agree to any premise that leaves your troops deployed as they are and sends others in their stead," one Human Kings had called out.

Queen Allivaris took exception to the accusation and replied, incredulous, "Easy to agree? Shake the clouds from your mind and think clearly, man, and you will recall that beyond coping with our own civil war, Elven troops alone hold the southeastern and northwestern borders in the Vearian region. No Resistance troops deploy there. And if you had been following scout reports as they have arrived, you would know that there is no pull back of Gorillian's forces in either of those regions. I think it best you close your mouth, for the emptiness between your ears is becoming obvious."

She was angry and justifiably so. The King sat back, red-faced.

King Wylë pledged the support of his tiny nation without hesitation. The votes of the Centaurs were not sufficient to sway the outcome, but his allegiance was noted.

When the Gor'ean King had raised his hand in support of the motion, a wave of poorly suppressed emotion rolled across the balconies of Lords, some could barely contain their agitation and others, their delight. Beyond voicing his vote, the Gor'ean Fyyther had been noticeably quiet, as was the High Prince.

The Fyyther stood now and moved to the edge of his balcony signalling to the Adjudicator that he wished to speak. His commanding voice rang strong and true.

"The strength and solidarity of this Council are all that stands between a free Elënthiá and the evil that would consume her. As Gor'ean Fyyther I have followed in the steps of my predecessors in supporting the Council's decisions even if, at times, I did not personally agree; or even if decisions taken were not entirely in favour of Gorger. Regarding the matter currently before us, I have witnessed the debate and discussion and feel better informed for having been present when the wisdom of Council members was voiced and shared. However, I find myself unable to accept the results of the vote."

A rumble of surprise rippled across the room, none louder than from the balconies of his own Lords beside and above him. He paused until there was silence.

"As Fyyther, the armies of Gorger are mine to deploy and direct. As Fyyther, while I seek and value input from my own Gor'ean Lords, I am not bound to accede to their wishes in all things. And in this situation I must concur with my son. This is a turning point in the war. With great risk comes great reward, and I believe it time for such risk. I will deploy any and all Gor'ean troops as can reasonably be spared without comprising the safety of Gorger."

The Council erupted in response. The Adjudicator nearly broke his gavel, banging it for order. When the din had faded, Acthelass Mar continued. "As I said, I will redeploy Gorger's own troops to the north...but before I do, I would respectfully ask for the Elënthián Supreme Council's acknowledgement of this decision and a motion of support in this regard."

It was a clever political ploy. In effect the Fyyther was superseding a Council decision, yet at the same time was asking for their approval to do so. It was the perfect way for members who were bound by their own national politics to decline but wished to support the motion to do so.

The Adjudicator asked for a vote. Hand by hand the votes were counted. Though unprepared as a Council to commit all Resistance troops to aggression in the north, the request for support of Gorger carried.

When the gavel hit the block, Athron and Juga were already on their feet.

"Father..." There was much that Athron would say, but nothing that had not already been voiced or that was not evident in his eyes.

"Your Highness," he said, louder. "With your permission I request an immediate meeting with the Generals to cement deployment planning. Thereafter Jugarth Framir and I will leave for the north."

The Fyyther gave his nod of assent.

Athron turned to Juga. "Find Captain Caapri and ensure he waits near the Grand Hall, for I would speak with him before we depart."

The Gor'ean Lords who had supported Acthelass Mar and the Prince stepped forward to voice their support and offer whatever assistance was necessary to prepare. Athron stood by his father's side shaking hands and slapping shoulders, noting that the Lords who had dissented had left the Chambers already. As they made their way out of the Chambers and descended the great stair, the Elven Queen awaited them.

"May Ruahr himself along with all the gods of our great Elënthiá guide and guard you in your mission, Prince Athron." Athron bowed deeply, and the two spoke a moment.

Juga found himself standing next to Ayleen among the entourage that surrounded the two royals. He felt a shy touch as she gently slid her hand into his and squeezed it. "Be safe, Jugarth Framir. There is still much I would ask of you and many adventures left to share." Her eyes faced forward, but her voice was breathless and her face lightly flushed.

Juga never turned to look at her but returned the squeeze, and their hands released. "You may count on my safe return, Milady Ayleen," he said softly, "and on many future adventures we will share."

Captain Caapri and Athron leaned over a map. Athron was giving orders for deployment. "Send immediate missives to all the troops here, here and here," he stabbed at the map. "Have them muster at ports here, and here. Juga and I will leave immediately and put in at Athprai Bay. I want you to sail further up and put in at the Sea of Cathanlay. The seas will be unpredictable at this time of year, and the fleet will need to be mindful of Gorillian's flotilla; but in numbers our ships are sufficiently gunned to dissuade any hasty assault. Once you put in at Cathanlay, follow the Callé river north. We are told that scouts will await to guide you in." He clapped Captain Caapri firmly on the shoulder. "This is a measure of my trust in your leadership and your abilities, Hanna Janheoanus. I will pray the gods speed your journey. Do not fail me."

"Highness, I am honoured by your trust. Be assured I shall not."

Meanwhile Acthelass Mar was having a conversation of his own. "In life one meets many but rarely is blessed with the true friendship you obviously share with my son. That he has also found such friendship with the Draconean and this Forsair, whom I have yet to meet, is unusual. The gods may call me to them before the Prince returns from the north."

Juga paled at this statement but the Gor'ean king continued, "Be that the case, he will need good men, trustworthy men around him. I bid you: guard my son's back well."

"Have you spoken to him?"

"No. Nor will you. I'll have your word on this, Jugarth Framir."

Juga nodded.

Athron had bid him wait in the Fyyther's chambers while he finished meetings with key personnel under his command. When Athron arrived, father and son embraced firmly then held each other's upper arms as they locked gazes. In those few seconds, a million words were said, yet none were voiced. Athron fisted his chest as he bent on one knee; then, arising, he turned on his heel and left without a single word, Juga at his heels.

# CHAPTER 48

Drake Sorzin walked quickly across the open pavilion, his leather soles making little sound on the polished white marble beneath his feet. He could hear many voices as he approached the door to the meeting room. A large table had been shifted to the center of the room. Upon it were maps of Elënthiá, the Coldain Region, and Dohenheer. The Captains of the northern Draconean Army were gathered around the table, heatedly discussing and arguing. The voices quieted as he entered. Lathaniel was there, and the Draconean Army's newest general, Layne Rev'eara. He recognized Dagostin, the two Illics, Khan, Olan, and several of the other twenty-odd Captains that had assembled. He nodded brusquely in greeting, moved to the table, and pulled the map of Dohenheer to the fore.

"I believe I have a possible solution to the defence of Dohenheer," he began. "The city, markets, and farmlands are all protected by the outer walls. These should hold til reinforcements arrive should Gorillian's armies get that close, but if we are to meet him in Dinhoriin in close combat, we will need to develop an advantage, else we will perish."

The murmurs that quietly rippled through the room were unreceptive to his evaluation.

"Hand-to-hand combat will not be our weak point. An Are-Narc has no chance against a single Draconean, nor do ten!" Illic's bravado sparked approval.

"I do not dispute your claim," Drake responded, "for I know well that our individual size and our skills give an advantage. But Gorillian will bring to bear both man and machine against us. We will not survive if we rely on close combat alone."

"That may be so," Layne cut in, "but we do have a cavalry unit. You have told us that Gorillian's force is comprised of men and Are-Narcs only. That being the case, we can ride right over them. No army has ever withstood a charge of a heavily armed cavalry." Again, nods of agreement with General Rev'eara's comments.

"And if they carry spears and pikes?" Drake demanded. "What then? Will we ride ahead regardless and risk the whole of the cavalry? Beyond that, in the confines of Dinhoriin, how will we manoeuvre a cavalry amidst tens of thousands of troops?"

Captain Dagostin took offense. "It is evident that you hold no regard for the suggestions of the General of an army you've presumed leadership of. What say *you* then?"

Lathaniel joined the fray, leaping to Drake's defence. "Mind your tone, Dagostin! You would do well to remember to whom you are speaking."

Aleksi Illic snarled, "It's *Captain* Dagostin to you, *Iysemkayda*!"

Layne interjected, "Dagostin! Illic! That is enough!

Another Captain cried out to Layne in support of Dagostin: "You would side with the southerner over your own soldiers!"

That, in turn, sparked anger in several other Captains who took exception to the insubordination.

Drake pounded hard on the table. "Enough!"

In the jostling around the room, a soldier at the back stumbled, pushing one of the Captains into Aleksa Illic, who in turn fell against General Rev'eara. Alexi Illic gave the clumsy Captain who'd pushed his brother a hard shove into several other soldiers. Fabian Dagostin who had been looking for a reason anyway, waded into the fray toward Lathaniel, who was watching the fracas with interest beside Drake. Without warning, Dagostin threw a punch that knocked Lathaniel back against the wall. Lathaniel shook off the hit and leapt at Dagostin who had turned his head to avoid a stray punch from another soldier. The momentum of Lathaniel's leap took them both across the top of the map table, which crumbled beneath their weight.

Thinking to separate the two, Drake Sorzin moved forward only to be surprised by a blow to the stomach that caught him unawares. One of the young Captains had stepped forward to challenge him saying with great bravado, "If you're a Prince, then I'm an Elf."

Drake straightened and, with a pivot, lashed out with one of his great legs and caught the Captain at midsection with a kick that sent him flying backwards. "Then we best get you to Nesmeresa, lad," he replied.

From there, it degenerated into a full-out brawl. Chairs and fists flew. Noses were bloodied. Eyes were blackened.

The sound of someone clearing their throat and a sense of others entering the room seemed to reach everyone in the fray simultaneously. As if the gods themselves froze the moment in time, all action immediately ceased, fists cocked in mid-air; and heads swivelled toward the entrance.

Councilman Seuton Rev'eara stood at the door with his small contingent of guards.

"If this is how you manage your Captains, Drake Sorzin, then there is little hope for our Army." Shaking his head in disgust, he turned on his heel and left.

Fists were dropped, and combatants stepped away from each other, sheepishly waiting for the reprimand they were certain would follow. Instead, the silence was broken by a deep belly laugh. Drake Sorzin's laughter rumbled from deep in his chest and burst forth across the room. So unusual was it for any, even Layne and Lathaniel, to see him laugh that the room was silent for seconds.

"It would appear we have settled the issue of close contact warfare," he said, smiling from ear to ear and dusting off his clothing. "We should now move on and discuss other strategies."

The Captains relaxed. Smiles were exchanged. Hands were offered to those still on the ground to pull them to their feet. There was nothing like a brawl to clear the air. Dagostin helped Lathaniel prop a makeshift tabletop up with the few chairs that had not been shattered in the fracas. Khan retrieved the maps and rolled them out on the table in front of Drake, who waited until the room was silent, scanning face after face with a steady, serious eye.

"You are strong," he began, "you are bold, and you are capable. Of that, I have no doubt. But while simulated battle within the confines of Dohenheer and the odd surprise attack on Gorillian's scouting parties has refined your technique and your strength, it is not the same as a bloody battlefield."

To a one, their attention was riveted on him.

"I look around this room and do you know what I see? I see the potential for the greatest Army Elënthiá has ever put to a battlefield. But it is only potential. I have much to teach you. And much to learn from you. But, my fellow Draconeans, we have little time. Victorious armies are neither led nor directed by committee. While I will ask for and expect your honest input and your criticisms to plans as they are presented, when the day is done, when my orders are given, they must be obeyed without question and without hesitation. Do I make myself clear?"

During his speech, Layne had turned to stand on Drake's left facing the room. Lathaniel, as always, was at his right. In the silence that followed, Captain looked at Captain; barely perceptible nods were exchanged.

"I said, do I make myself clear?" Drake repeated, raising his voice.

A unanimous "Yes!" was the response. And the strategy session continued, productive and collegial well into the night.

# CHAPTER 49

Training was finished for the day. Dusk was soothing day into evening, and Lathaniel was exploring the markets. His presence within them did not go unnoticed. As he walked through the streets and thoroughfares, he could feel eyes upon him and whispers as vendors and customers alike gathered in doorways.

"*Ayeth-varr*," some said. Lathaniel was becoming familiar with the term, which meant son of light. Where the title came from, no one could say with certainty, but when Drake's name was spoken, the title was as well. Most knew he was a companion to Drake. He also heard "*Iysem-kayda*" whispered, the meaning of which was no longer a mystery to him. It meant "mixed-blood." In truth, Lathaniel took no offense from the moniker. It was as good a description as any.

He was as amazed by Dohenheer as he was by all else he'd seen since he left Lamana, and he was exploring. Busy staring at a display in a storefront, he wasn't watching where he was going and walked into someone. Packages and parcels went flying. He didn't even see who he'd run into, but whomever it was bent at the same time as he to pick them up and they banged heads. Both stood at the same time.

For Lathaniel it was as if everything and everyone in the market around them fell away into a distant blur and there was only this woman and him left. She was tall and slender. Her hair fell in waves over her shoulders nearly to her waist. It was not just one single color of gold but instead, sunshine yellow, finely spun gold, and the purest of whites: a fusion of the palette spectrum that drew and reflected every available ray of the remaining light of the day and reflected it out like a beacon around her. Her eyes were wide with dismay at their encounter, an arresting shade of the same deep blue as the Great Sea on a clear day but shot with white striations. Her skin was translucent and lightly pinked, like the blush that covers a perfect peach.

Standing there beside her there at dusk in the Dohenheer market, Lathaniel felt something shift within him: a visceral pull, a moment of pure clarity that somehow, in her presence, he was finally exactly where he was supposed to be. He had several false starts before he could get syllables assembled to form a word. "I…I, ah…I apologize Milady. Are you hurt?"

Those sapphire eyes held his regard for a second or two before she smiled slightly and answered, "I believe I shall survive."

Lathaniel hurriedly collected her remaining parcels from the ground. "Allow me to carry these for you. Direct me to your destination and I will follow."

That half-smile again. Her shift was a simple white, trimmed in gold threading. She unconsciously smoothed and straightened it as she looked about her, then began slowly walking away. She said over her shoulder, "You may walk with me for a time."

Still partially dumbfounded at the encounter and his reaction to her, Lathaniel stumbled along behind. It took him another moment to summon speech. "Please forgive me for my boldness, Milady. I am not a Draconean, so I am unaware of what is and is not acceptable within your culture. But may I ask your name?"

She tossed a glance over her shoulder. "You assume I am a Draconean."

"You are not? I thought…"

"I am a visitor here, no more. You have said you are not of Dohenheer?"

"No. I, too, am a…visitor. Does Milady have a name?"

"She does, but it is not freely given to handsome strangers met in the Dohenheer markets."

"If I would give you mine and the names of those who would vouch that I am no scoundrel…would you offer your name then?"

She smiled and drew to a halt, turning to lift her packages from Lathaniel's hands.

"Find my name…and you will find me."

Lathaniel stood there blank-faced, uncertain that he had heard correctly and completely bewildered as to what to say next.

The lovely lady leaned in and quietly asked, "But if your efforts are fruitless, how am *I* to find *you*?"

A full smile broke across Lathaniel's face, and his grey eyes sparkled. He began to back away from her, fading into the early evening crowds. "Easily, Milady. Ask for Lathaniel Waythan and you shall find me!" With a jaunty wave, he turned and blended into the crowds.

He didn't see her expression slide into confusion. Nor, a second later, did he hear her call out behind him, "Your name is Waythan? Wait!"

They had been in deliberations with General Rev'eara and his Captains, fine-tuning defence plans and pouring over scout reports when the High Council summons arrived. Annoyed at the interruption, Drake had barked several orders before he and Lathaniel departed. The pace of their lives in Dohenheer was such that they were rarely alone in each other's company. As they made their way from the arenas toward the gleaming white domes, they talked of many things.

"Your studies of Darrish...how are you progressing?"

"Varis Mauge has assigned a scholar to me. It goes well, I guess. Your language is unlike Lamanian - the runes are very different from cursive script. Sometimes the subtle differences in the runes can be of great significance to the meaning."

Drake smiled. "And life among the Captains...there are issues?"

"None. We seemed to have found common ground after the, ah...meeting in your quarters." Lathaniel smiled broadly. "*Accepted* would be too strong a word, but I am tolerated." His smile faded. "Who but Draconeans reside in Dohenheer, Drake?"

Drake's face registered surprise. "None of which I am aware, lad. Why do you ask?"

"A curiosity only. But are you certain there are no other races within this place?"

Drake looked directly at him. "Why are you asking, Lathaniel?"

"No reason." Lathaniel changed the subject. "Have you any idea why we have been summoned?"

Drake shook his head. They were within the City now, just reaching the landing at the top of the grand stair to the uppermost floor. The Council chambers were ahead.

"Speak only when spoken to this time, Lathaniel. While I care not if they are antagonized by your presence, I want to get this over with and back to the troops as soon as possible."

Guards opened the outer doors, and the two were ushered in. Layne was already there, standing at ease off to the side, awaiting their arrival. As before, as soon as the doors closed, the Council guards took up their posts along the walls behind them.

The four sat stiffly in their grand seats behind the polished crescent-shaped table. Dohenheer's High Council had overseen life in their hidden enclave for millennia without challenge and without incident. The sudden appearance of the southern Draconean and the imminent threat of attack on Dohenheer had completely disrupted life as they knew it ... and they were not managing the change well.

"The Forsair was not summoned, Drake Sorzin. Only you," Lilyss Harphh was her usual dour self.

Drake shrugged. "He is my companion. Where I am summoned, he accompanies. What is it that you require of us?"

Harphh opened her mouth to protest, but General Fyyst interrupted. "Please, let us get to the business at hand." He fixed them both with a serious stare. "We have received word from the south."

Drake and Lathaniel tensed expectantly.

"General Rev'eara advises that you are aware that the Elves know that Dohenheer exists. Across time, we have maintained contact with them. At times, a small contingent of Elves remains in residence here at Dohenheer and, as necessary, messengers come and go. A messenger is newly arrived and a representative of the Elven contingent here at Dohenheer joins Council to share the information he carried. We thought it best if you were present for this report."

From the shadows to the right of the upper platform, there was movement. A tall figure in floor-length robes moved to the end of the crescent table near to Seuton Rev'eara. As she moved into the light, Lathaniel's quick intake of air was audible.

"May I make you known to Avion Valia, a representative from our friends in the Elven Realm of Nesmeresa."

Avion inclined her head slightly. As she moved forward, three other Elven maidens moved in to flank her. The General continued: "Her handmaidens Saylia, Aveela and Lairryn accompany her on her journeys to Dohenheer at Queen Allivaris' request." The maidens nodded gracefully then stepped to the rear of the platform.

Drake bowed, acknowledging her presence, unobtrusively nudging Lathaniel who belatedly did the same.

Nerves were an unusual emotion for Avion Valia, for she was never nervous. She kept her arms loosely at her sides and willed her heart to steady as she addressed the gathered. She fixed her gaze on a point on the Chamber walls just slightly above their heads and proceeded to provide a full report on Gorillian's positions within the eastern Coldain near the Nesmeresan borders, and to pass along specifics of the troop roll-backs on Koorast and the establishment of supply lines that were being put in place to support the effort. "Gorillian is amassing all at the western edge of Ethen-dith. By our estimates, you have two months – perhaps less."

While this information supported their own, the finality of her announcement echoed in the Chambers, and for a moment all were silent. Then, ignoring all protocol, Drake spent the next twenty minutes grilling Avion on specifics within her report. She replied calmly and succinctly, clarifying and commenting as appropriate.

When there was silence within the Chambers once again, General Fyyst, "We are left to wonder what is next. What of your Gor'ean, Drake? Will we fight alone in this dark hour?"

"A message has been delivered directly to me," Drake said tightly. "They come. As to what is next...we continue doing what we've been doing since my arrival weeks ago. We prepare."

General Fyyst thanked Avion for her report, and the Elf excused herself, but not before lowering her gaze for a heartbeat to meet Lathaniel's.

As they left the Council, Lathaniel quietly questioned, "I was unaware we had received a message from Athron."

"There is no message."

"It was a ruse then? We do not yet know if they come?"

"They will come. They have to come."

# CHAPTER 50

Juga stomped his feet as hard as he could. And then he jumped up and down. Nothing. He was fascinated.

"It doesn't matter how many times you do that, nor how hard, the water is frozen," Athron said wryly, his arms folded across his chest as he watched the lad. At times it was easy for Athron to forget how young Jugarth Framir really was. And in these last weeks, his youth was never more obvious. *Or perhaps I have become so jaded as to overlook the simple wonders that seem to capture his attention.*

Juga barely slept through the journey by ship. Athron had been worried that the heaving winter seas would take their toll on him given that it was his first voyage, but the lad took to the ship like a fish to the sea. He shimmied up the rigging, threw his muscle into hauling up the halyard, and even convinced the ship's Captain - as ill-humoured a man as had ever set sail - to let him take the helm, peppering him relentlessly about the ship's operation.

He took minimal rest, not wanting to miss a moment of the night sky. He had won over the crew. In spite of the bitter cold, he sat with them through the long night hours pointing out the names of stars and constellations and begging for tales of their adventures.

At the first sight of landfall, he was either glued to the rail with the Captain's glass or beside him with a map, pelting him with questions about where they were and what was ashore. Athron had muttered and grumbled about the bite of the winter cold as they moved further north; from Juga there was not a single complaint. An internal furnace had ignited within him; like the whales and otters they could see from the ship's deck, he had found his element.

Following Drake's instructions, once ashore, they'd travelled due north up the Dorvanis River. When the skies were clear, they could only just make out the Rourgone Mountains off to the far east. At several intervals, Far'camicians or Illyishians had appeared out of the whiteness with food and directions for them and then disappeared again; how and to where, they did not know. The Draconean's network of contacts obviously stretched across Elënthiá.

Now here, at Crystal Lake, Juga was mesmerized by the thought that such a massive body of water could be frozen solid. Juga looked up just then and met the eyes of his mentor, who couldn't help but laugh aloud at the pure delight he saw in them.

"Come, lad. We need to move on."

If the message was correct, it would be only a matter of a few days now before they made contact with the northern Draconeans. With a last look across the unrelieved white of the frozen lake and plateau, to the flat plains beyond, Athron and Juga headed north into evergreens heavy with snow, and into the heart of the Ashen Mountains.

Later, as they hunkered down under a rock face and buried under deep snow, Drake's words came flooding back to Juga: *"You are likely to smell them before you see them."* His nostrils were twitching. There were Are-Narcs close.

They had agreed that if they met an Are-Narc patrol, taking a stand and fighting would be a last resort. They could not afford to be discovered or taken prisoner. Drake's messengers had reported that Gorillian's trackers were crisscrossing the travelled paths in an attempt to ferret out any in the region, and his Are-Narcs were mercenary in their methods of extracting information from those they detained. As careful as they had been in their travels and in covering their tracks, they were now pinned down. The Are-Narc patrol had nearly caught them unawares; too late to outrun them, anyway. Their hastily abandoned camp had been found and the patrol had spread out to methodically search the area. It would only be a matter of time until they were discovered.

The foul smell was stronger now. They could hear the Narc breathing in and out. He was systematically thrusting his sword into the snow banks under the cliff overhang. They had their swords and daggers unsheathed and to hand. When the time came, they would come out fighting. The Are-Narc sword thrust down beside Juga. Then between Athron's legs. The next thrust would hit them for certain.

There was a great commotion then. The Are-Narc stopped his thrusts mid-swing and turned.

"Attack!" was the cry. "We're under attack."

Athron and Juga burst forth, covered in ice and snow and already swinging. Pent up adrenaline blew like a steam release as they hacked the surprised Narc to pieces then bound down from their sanctuary. They had no idea who else was attacking the Narcs, but the ambushers had found two deadly allies.

Their rescuers were clad entirely in white. They appeared as humans—arms, legs and weapons—but were of such a size that the two were left to wonder. The Narc scout party was thirty strong. But, simply put, it was a slaughter. The element of surprise and the ease with which the white soldiers moved through the deep snow, coupled with the deadly aptitude of Athron and Juga, were the Narcs' undoing. As the last Narc fell, Juga pulled back the hood on his cloak to survey the scene. It was macabre: pools, sprays, and splatters of blood stark against the brilliant white of the snow.

There were fifteen of the white giants. They moved toward Athron and his company in an arc. Not certain what to expect, the two kept their weapons in hand and waited warily for what was to come. As the leader approached, he reached up and pulled back a great hood, then removed a tight cap and face covering, unveiling a head of thick black hair and piercing blue eyes. He stepped forward to Athron.

"You would be His Highness, the Gor'ean Prince Athron Mar?"

Athron said nothing, merely held his gaze and nodded.

The soldier bent his head in a nod of deference. "Captain Fabian Dagostin of the northern Draconean Army at your service, Your Highness. We are bid to bring you to Dohenheer."

# CHAPTER 51

The elimination competition was near to complete with the tiers of competitors whittled down throughout the last weeks until five remained. The Illic brothers had faced off against each other with Aleksa winning by a mere point. Aleksa then fell to Sameer Khan the following day. It was left to Lathaniel to battle the giant Captain Khan.

General Rev'eara and the southern Draconean had already fought. There was little sense in Drake participating in the elimination, so obvious and exceptional were his skills. General Rev'eara had challenged him anyway, at the encouragement of his captains. While Layne was a skilled and seasoned soldier and had done the northerners proud in his showing, predictably he had fallen under Drake's superior skills. He would fight the winner of the match between Lathaniel and Captain Khan.

This semi-final bout would be spoken of well into the future. Though all of the northern Draconeans had come to know and respect the Forsair's ability on the battlefield, the bets were heavy that the giant Khan would overcome the much smaller Forsair. The scrimmage ran to nearly an hour. Drake called the points from the sidelines as each was earned.

He also called pointers to each of the combatants as the hours passed, encouraging and teaching them as it progressed.

Lathaniel hurt everywhere. His sword arm felt numb from the barrage of jarring assaults he had received at Khan's great hand. He had learned to use his speed and agility to best the Draconean giant, knowing that in close quarters, the strength of those meaty fists would be his undoing.

Under Drake's tutelage he had learned and refined his skills. With constant training and sparring with the larger, stronger Draconeans, he had sensed a subtle shift within himself; his Elven heritage was becoming increasingly evident in the manner in which he fought. By embracing this, his endurance improved, as did his agility. Both were the downfall of the great Khan who, after a particularly relentless assault by the Forsair, found his sword spun 'round then flipped out of his hand to clatter to the stones below. Dripping with sweat and heaving, he looked down the blade of a sword whose tip tickled his chin, and then into the steady grey eyes of the Forsair.

Khan stepped back and shook himself like a great dog, sweat flying off him like a spring shower. He threw his head back in a laugh and grabbed Lathaniel's other arm, hoisting it high in the air. "By the gods! I would never have believed it! The winner!"

Lathaniel smiled weakly at the acknowledgement and for the first time noted the size of the crowd that had gathered. So intense was his concentration, he had not realized the numbers. With his left hand held high, his eyes swept the crowd and came to an abrupt halt as they met those of the Elven emissary, Avion. Holding her gaze, he accepted congratulations and back slaps from the Captains, gradually working his way over to where she stood. Since the High Council meeting three days prior, he had sought her company during the few moments he found free each day. While protocol demanded that their meetings remain public, that had not impeded the strong attraction between them or their burgeoning friendship.

She gave a slight nod. "You are truly a gifted warrior, Lathaniel Waythan."

"Milady." Lathaniel returned the nod. "Accept my apologies, for I am in no fit state to speak with you."

She smiled. "It is of no matter. I received a message not long ago that an Elven messenger will shortly arrive at Dohenheer, so I shall be with the High Council until early evening. Perhaps we might meet for a walk later on?"

Lathaniel smiled broadly. "Send word when you are free, and I will come if I am able."

The crowd pressed in on them both again, and she was gone.

Late that evening Lathaniel sat alone by the hearth in his chamber. He was fingering the sapphire that he found in the Tombs. It had become a talisman of sorts and he found that holding it, handling it, helped him to focus his thoughts and calm his spirits. He looked up when Drake entered the room.

"It is late, Forsair. Why do you not sleep?"

"Too many thoughts, Drake. Somewhere beyond these great caverns, the largest Gorillian army ever to take to a battlefield is amassing, its sole focus on destroying this place. Sitting here by the hearth, it is hard to conceive of the danger that is approaching."

He hesitated, watching Drake shrug off his weapons and place them near the fire, before continuing, "And my thoughts are with Athron and Juga. We have had no word as yet. They should have arrived by now." He turned back to the fire, continuing to shift the sapphire between his palms.

"What have you there?"

Lathaniel looked down, only then realizing what he held and that, for all his good intentions, he had never shown the stone to Drake nor offered it to him. He cleared his throat and spoke apologetically.

"It is a sapphire. Here." He handed it to Drake, who took and turned it in his own hands. "I found it when we were in the Tombs. In truth, I picked it up just as Juga discovered the map and slid it in my pack to show you. I've meant to, truly..."

Drake was shaking his head. "It is a beautiful gem, to be sure." He handed it back to Lathaniel, who tried to refuse it.

"Go ahead, lad. It is yours to keep. It is but a stone to me, a beautiful stone but nothing more. If having it brings you comfort, then it is yours."

Lathaniel took it and nodded his head in thanks.

Drake sank into the chair beside him and released a weary sigh. The two were silent for a time. Then Lathaniel said, "Did I ever tell you of my last night in Limore?"

Drake shook his head. He let his head rest against the back of the chair, his eyes closing.

Lathaniel told him, then, of the stranger in the tavern and of their unusual conversation. "...and then he said, *'If the elixir touches lifeless lips, then the recipient will live once more.'* Do you suppose there are such stones in this world, Drake? That the Stone of Humidar truly exists?"

Drake was quiet for a moment. "I have heard this story and of the Stone. The tale is told that the gods placed four such stones in Elënthiá, individually of great power. Perhaps the stranger in Limore told you his own version of this myth. As to the truth of any version of these tales, I could not say."

They sat in companionable silence for a while longer. Then Drake opened his eyes and looked at the young Forsair. "You recall that we left the haven under Horon unexpectedly?"

Lathaniel nodded.

"While Draconeans join all of Elënthiá in worshipping Ruahr as the almighty, our principle deities are Dyváriiare, the god of darkness, and his wife Suvillwa, beloved goddess of light. Suvillwa has come to me in dreams twice in my lifetime. Once immediately after Evendeer was destroyed, and again…in Horon. She spoke to me of many things. It was she who told me of the starting point for my father's map was in Sitiska. It was she who confirmed that, were I to find the Tombs, I would also find a map that would lead me here. I find it interesting that this tavern stranger would say to you that *'sometimes the only choice is the journey'*…and that you have chosen as you have. For, Suvillwa also told me that my fate rests in your hands."

Lathaniel was dumbfounded. Drake smiled warmly at him. "In ways you could never understand, lad, her words are daily proven true."

# CHAPTER 52

Anticipating battle at any moment, a pall had settled over Dohenheer. All knew that the days were counting down and what lay ahead would define the future of their race; either they would emerge victorious and live, or they would go the way of their southern brethren and be lost forever.

The Ayeth-varr was their saviour, they believed. No one from peasant to merchant had escaped his influence, for the southern Prince had met with representatives from all sectors of Dohenheer. All would play a role in the defence of it, he told them. Supply lines, replenishment of weapons, triage for the wounded, burials for the dead, dried food provisions, even the simple tasks of filling and delivery of water skins to the front lines had been discussed. The High Council was another matter, but the Draconean people had embraced their Ayeth-varr.

Drake continued to plan and prepare Dinhoriin and to drill the soldiers on formations and strategies within it. The elimination competition had given him the opportunity to gauge areas of weakness, and he drilled the army mercilessly to improve these. They were nearly ready, or as near to ready as he could make them.

Tensions ran high, and for that reason he gave pause to all training to allow audience to the last of the elimination rounds: the Forsair, Lathaniel Waythan, would fight their beloved General Layne Rev'eara.

Layne and Lathaniel faced off at the center of the arena. After a brief nod to one another, Drake reminded the two that no blood could be drawn below the waist. The winner would be declared when blood was drawn on the torso only. They would need restraint, as the intent was not to wound fatally, which heightened the challenge. Drake called the match begun.

Layne wasted no time in taking the offense. He plunged toward Lathaniel, stabbing, swinging, and thrusting. Lathaniel allowed himself to be driven back, taking the opportunity to map the Draconean general's attacks, seeking weakness. The attack halted with the two locked at the hilt. They gave a mutual push to separate, and then attacked again.

Layne had watched the Forsair enough to know that his agility gave him the advantage, so he pressed him relentlessly, giving him little space to move. Seeing an opening, Lathaniel slid in low, feet first under Layne's sword, and swept his feet from beneath him. The crowd went wild. Layne rolled quickly to his feet again, but this time it was Lathaniel who attacked relentlessly. The advantage shifted back and forth between the two for nearly thirty minutes. Both were soaked with sweat and single-minded in their focus. Crowd noises had long since slid into the background.

Lathaniel's Elven heritage was proving more difficult than Layne had anticipated; the Draconean was tiring, and he knew Lathaniel knew it. He pressed forward with a series of thrusts and in a wild sweep caught Lathaniel across the front of his shins. Feeling the bite and the blood, Lathaniel dropped his guard, believing the match to be lost, for the rules had been broken. In the second that his guard dropped, General Rev'eara nicked his shoulder and, again, the crowd went wild.

Drake was approaching them. Lathaniel could tell by his face that he'd seen the shin slice and was about to call the foul. Lathaniel met his eyes and gave a frantic but barely noticeable shake of his head. He walked to the Draconean General and grabbed his left hand, thrusting it high in the air to signify the General's victory.

General Rev'eara was overcome by his countryman and hoisted to their shoulders as the victor. Drake made his way to Lathaniel who pulled him into an embrace and said quietly in his ear, "The Draconeans need their Ayeth-varr *and* their General to be invincible. Leave it, for it is best this way." Lathaniel was drawn back into the crowds then, congratulated on his excellent showing.

It seemed to Lathaniel that he'd only just closed his eyes when he was shaken awake by Drake. "Get up, lad. There are scouts approaching the outer gate." He was brusque and impatient.

Lathaniel wasted no time in donning boots, tunic, and weapons and following him. As they rounded the lowest stair and headed out the south gate of the City, General Rev'eara fell into step beside them, having also received word. They assumed this scout party would bring news of Gorillian's troops...and that it wouldn't be good.

Their long strides quickly consumed the ground between their quarters in the City and the first gate. They'd just passed through it and were part way to the second gate when they heard the sonorous moan of the watch tower horn reciprocated by a smaller scout horn. The outer gates slowly swung open.

Two separated from the scout troop, pulling off their hoods and hats.

*Athron and Juga!*

The reunion of the five was warm and heartfelt. Captain Dagostin and his scouts stood off to the side watching in wonder. Not so long ago, apart from infrequent visits from the Elves, the northern Draconeans had lived in complete isolation from the rest of Elënthiá. Now, mere weeks later, they witnessed Human, Forsair, Gor'ean, and Draconeans—of both the north and south—exchange the warm and heartfelt embraces of old friends.

General Rev'eara excused himself to hear Dagostin's report and to welcome back his troops while Drake and Lathaniel led their companions through the second gate and central passage toward the city.

Lathaniel and Juga sat to one side of Drake's chambers. Juga was sitting at the table jamming food furiously into his mouth as if he'd never eat another meal. He hardly paused for a breath, nor did he take any notice that his mouth was filled with food as he updated Lathaniel on their adventures since departing Limore. Lathaniel had straddled a hard chair and sat with his arms draped over its back, rapt at all the news. Being the storyteller, Juga's murmurs from the corner were occasionally punctuated with loud guffaws as the two broke into laughter.

Drake and Athron spoke of more serious issues. Athron brought the Draconean up to speed on the events in the Supreme Council and made his own reports on the deployment of Gor'ean troops to the north. If all went according to plan - and there were no guarantees given the season and the seas - the flotilla of troops should have come ashore in the Coldain at the base of the Hills of Asgoth by now and should be enroute to Dohenheer. Fourteen and a half thousand, perhaps fifteen, Athron reported. The Draconean army numbered just under eight thousand. Combined, they would still be outnumbered, but if the Gor'eans arrived in time, victory could still be theirs.

The two spoke of battle strategies and preparations through the remainder of the night. Drake updated the High Prince on what he might expect when he was brought before the High Council the next morning, and they were in solid agreement on how best to manage the politics of the meeting.

Athron was the first royalty that the Draconean High Council had ever hosted, and it was evident that they were anxious that they comported themselves as was fit. As it unfolded, Athron's innate graciousness and amiability won the day, and soon the formalities were set aside and more serious topics were broached. Juga attended, as did Lathaniel, Layne, and Avion.

Athron largely repeated the summary he had given Drake the previous night. Before they could progress further, there came a frantic knocking on the Council chamber doors. The chamber guards opened the door to admit Alexi Illic.

"General, they approach."

"May the gods save us," Lilyss Harphh intoned quietly.

"I'm certain I speak for the Council when I reiterate our belief that we should ride out to greet this Gorillian and ask he spare Dohenheer. We are outnumbered! If we engage, it will be our certain death!" This plea was delivered by an ashen Seuton Rev'eara.

"After all of our meetings, our briefings and our discussions I cannot believe you could make such a suggestion!" General Rev'eara was aghast and embarrassed at his father's cowardice. "This discussion is ended. We have a war to win." He turned on his heel and left. At the news, Drake followed on his heels.

Athron replied to councillor Rev'eara's comment and to the Council generally, "Gorillian will spare no one, Councillor. What he will do is recognize the value of Dohenheer for what it is. He will butcher every last Draconean and take this city proudly as his own. There is no halfway measure in this battle." Athron then bowed politely to the Council and took his leave followed closely by Juga.

Lathaniel stepped to the side to speak with Avion.

"There is still time for you to leave Dohenheer, Avion," Lathaniel said urgently. "This is not your war! Remaining here in Dohenheer will see you in grave danger."

Her blue eyes snapped with anger. "Do you truly think I could leave? Beyond the years that I have spent seconded to this place, these past weeks have become precious to me, Lathaniel Waythan. Though we've not spoken of this, I see but one road ahead of me, and it is a road I hope we will walk down together. My duty requires I be circumspect in this place, but when you win this battle..." She held her hand up when Lathaniel would have interrupted. "And you will. When you win this battle, if you agree, I will petition my Queen for permission to consider you."

That statement stopped Lathaniel in his tracks. He could not deny he was losing his heart to the Elven maiden. Lamana, his obligations there, Sabine, Drake, Athron, and Juga...all of these things rushed through his thoughts. He took her hand in his. "Let us take each day as each day comes, Avion. Let us see what the close of this battle brings; then we will determine a way forward together," He could see Drake leaving and with a last look at Avion, he followed him out.

Dohenheer mobilized for war. Weeks of meetings, preparing, and planning were paying off. The northern Draconeans were overcoming paralyzing fear with the best possible medicine: action. There was no panic, no mayhem. Beginning with General Rev'eara and his Captains, the army, down through to each and every farmer, merchant and tradesman ... all set themselves to the duties that had been described and assigned to them.

Drake had taken over a barracks between the outer and inner walls and was running his command from there. The map of Dohenheer was spread on a central table. Captains Dagostin and Khan were reporting to Drake.

"Troop estimates?"

"As best we can tell there are twenty-eight, maybe thirty thousand."

"Location?"

"It is as you predicted, Ayeth-varr. They have split here." Dagostin pointed the map. "They enter the outer valley of the old ruins through these two passes. The majority of them will be in the bellies of the passes by midmorning."

"Are our soldiers in place?"

"Yes. Two here and two here. On the agreed signal, they will sound the battle horns."

"Will it be sufficient?"

"The day is clear and mild, and the sun is bright. The snow on the upper slopes is heavy and unstable. We should be able to trigger avalanches from above. At the very least, the chorus of battle horns ought to give them pause."

"And the archers?"

Athron answered this. "Lathaniel and the Captains Illic have taken our best archers and are situated in hides built into the trees of the valley walls here and here. Once Gorillian's troops reach the ruins, it will be an ambush."

General Rev'eara interrupted, "But our window with the archers may be limited, Drake. Winds have started lifting snow off the southern faces in the high peaks. We'll have weather by late afternoon."

"Send a messenger and let Lathaniel know they are to take no chances," Drake ordered. "If the weather shifts, they are to immediately move through the protections and back into Dinhoriin."

He surveyed the gathered. "Gorillian has obviously deciphered the runes and knows exactly where he is headed. He will also be aware that our location gives us strategic advantage. He will be expecting ambush in the passes and within the valley, so we will have no element of surprise there. He will push forward on the strength of pure numbers alone. Remember, he cares not for the lives of his Are-Narcs. He all but manufactures them within Ethen-jar, so he will have no hesitation in accepting losses as he presses in on us. We will exact what damage we can in the valley and delay their entry into the passage to Dinhoriin for as long possible. If the gods are with us, it will give us the time we need for the Gor'eans to arrive.

"General, finalize the defences just inside the Dinhoriin gate. Leave only sufficient gaps through which our troops can retreat. Have the men ready."

Drake dismissed them all. And it began.

Lathaniel was glad to be out of doors. He was exactly where he preferred to be, his great Gor'ean grey bow in hand with several quivers filled with arrows strapped across his back. He, Aleksa, and Alexi had situated themselves in three corners of an imaginary triangle, and from their respective perches the valley floor was covered. They each commanded one hundred of Dohenheer's best archers. Hides had been built in the sturdiest trees around the rim of the valley bowl, and care had been taken to clear sufficient branches to allow for line of sight to the valley floor but not to compromise their positions. The sky was a clear and frigid blue, and the sun was achingly bright. The winds through the valley were light. If the gods were with them, the weather would hold.

The sound of Draconean battle horns startled him from his thoughts. One, two, three, and...there it was, four. By the gods they were loud! The echo of them reverberated off of the mountain walls for a full moment after they were sounded. Then the mountains themselves seem to shrug and shudder. A deep rumbling could be heard in the distance. The intensity seemed to increase until they could feel even the trees they perched in shiver at the menace. It was done. If the avalanches worked as planned, there would be some troop losses and what remained would be impeded by the volume of snow.

It was now early afternoon. The Draconeans were well attired against the snow, sitting or leaning in their shelters. Suddenly it was if the mountains themselves exhaled, sending an icy wind down the valley. On the breath of that exhale, Lathaniel smelled Are-Narcs. He straightened immediately and gave signal to his men and across the valley to the Illics. They were here.

The Narc's dull black armour threw the white snow around them into sharp relief. They carried tall shields of pounded leather and wood. The vanguard carried the shields in front of them. The last soldier at the end of each row carried the shield to his side. All troops within the center carried the shields above their heads. Gorillian had anticipated their archers.

Lathaniel gave the signal to fire, taking careful aim below and between the shields. All they needed was a break in the formation to gain a foothold. The Draconean archers were marksmen. Arrows flew. Some imbedded in the leather bound shields, but more and more found the creases between the shields and vulnerabilities below them. As soon as a soldier dropped, the archers took advantage of the exposed troops to pick others off with deadly accuracy.

Within the ruins, the Narcs had little room to manoeuvre. The space on the valley floor was limited and soon the bodies became an impediment. They pressed forward relentlessly.

Unfortunately, the gods were not with the archers. That earlier icy breath of wind was a caution of weather that would follow. By late afternoon, the skies were dark and overcast; and large, wet flakes of snow began to fall. Lathaniel gave the agreed signal, and by turns the archers abandoned their hides and moved through the protections back into the safety of Dinhoriin. The great entrance was sealed behind them. When the sun rose the following day and the weather cleared, Gorillian held the outer valley.

# CHAPTER 53

The tension was thick and the mood sombre within the barracks. The months of anticipation were now at an end. Death was quite literally at the gate. Estimates put his day one losses at three, maybe four thousand. Gorillian had sent his troops through the passes by battalion and so had only lost less than two thousand in each to the avalanches. Archers had sent nearly three thousand arrows into the valley. Estimating a third hit their targets put the count of dead or injured at a thousand or more. The odds were still overwhelmingly in Gorillian's favour, but the day's end was not without gain.

It was day two in the battle for Dohenheer, and Drake had ordered the entire Army gathered. They marched out through the inner gate across the keep and out into the great blackness of Dinhoriin.

The Draconean army was a vision of black on black. The massive warriors wore full breastplates of reinforced black leather. At the center of their chests was a silver crest in the shape of a shield, in the center of which was a six-pointed black star. Outside of the shield insignia and to the top right of it was a second smaller star of silver. Thick buckles and leather straps held the breast and back plates together. The greaves and vambraces were of similar design with the two-starred motif common to every piece.

The cadence of their march echoed off the black slate walls until the last battalion stopped and marched once in place. Then the silence was absolute. Thousands of civilians lined the ramparts of the great outer wall to see the spectacle and to hear the words of the great Ayeth-varr. The braziers overhead were fully fired and sent an eerie cast of shadows upon the great black battlefield.

The Army had divided in two: four thousand on one half of Dinhorinn; the rest on the other side. A great avenue was left open down the middle of it. Drake Sorzin, Prince of the southern Draconeans and Ayeth-varr to his northern brethren, rode onto Dinhoriin on a great black stallion. It pranced and rose on its hind legs to paw at the air in protest and excitement at the spectacle in front of it. Lathaniel had never seen Drake Sorzin astride a horse, and the picture he painted in those early morning hours would forever be burned into his memory.

Drake's voice seemed to come from deep within him, thunderous syllables that echoed off the bedrock and filled the corners of Dinhoriin.

"Sons of Dyváriiare and Suvillwa, grandsons of the almighty Ruahr himself... The lost city of the Draconeans is lost no longer. The whole of Elënthiá now knows we exist, knows of our great bastion, Dohenheer. What Elënthiá has found is a great nation as befitting our ancestors and our heritage. A nation of warriors. Proud. Strong. Capable. This day, Dohenheer - indeed our existence as a race - is in great peril. Beyond Dinhoriin's gates, evil gathers. But beyond the valley walls, help approaches. Mighty Gor'eans twenty thousand strong march to our aid. But until they arrive we fight, Draconeans! We fight!"

So deafening was the noise from the Draconean army and the civilians lining the outer wall that it felt as if the walls of stone might split from the force of the reverberations. Drake's stallion reared and pawed. His rider expertly ran him up and back along the front lines of the troops, his massive, ancient sword held high above his head. After a final pass down to the last of the troops, he rode back through the gate of the outer wall and dismounted, handing the stallion off to a nearby soldier.

The General was on the field with his troops, some of whom were now moving off Dinhoriin to take up positions on the outer and inner walls. Others were assuming defensive assignments well down Dinhoriin close to the exterior entrance, which was sealed closed and had been reinforced for strength. Drake was giving his final orders to Lathaniel, Juga, and Athron when they heard the first assault on the outer gate.

Use of the cavalry in an engagement of this magnitude within Dinhoriin would not have been practical. But mounts were available to facilitate ease of movement of Drake and senior officers up and down the battlefield. The four of them mounted and moved down to the front line of battle.

Dinhoriin was more than a mile wide and double that in distance from the entrance to the gates of the outer wall. Anticipating the breach of the outer entrance, great spikes of wood had been tied together and intertwined to form a deadly fence over which the Narcs would have to climb in order to move up the great battlefield. About two hundred and fifty feet back from this, wooden barricades had been fashioned in an arc facing the entrance. Small steel barrels were situated behind these and lit with fires. The barricades were simple and could easily collapse if strategic supports were removed. Archers were positioned three deep. They had been drilled to move in to the barricade in intervals to fire tar-tipped arrows. At five-hundred-yard gaps, the deadly spiked fences and archer barricades were repeated through to the midpoint of Dinhoriin.

The pounding was relentless, and the tension among the Draconeans waiting inside the gate was palpable. They could see the great door buckle and groan as it slowly succumbed to the battering. The first crack in the thick wood gate echoed through Dinhoriin like a thunderclap. On and on, they rammed the door until the last of the supports surrendered. One side of the great gate fell from its moorings; the other splintered, and Are-Narcs rushed forward with bloodthirsty battle cries.

"Fire!" Drake and Lathaniel rode their mounts back and forth behind the front line of archers. Are-Narcs surged forward through the breach, the first impaling themselves upon the spikes unable to fight the momentum behind them. Burning arrows were loosed into the thick of the fray, and screaming filled the air. The close quarters made it impossible for the attackers to avoid the crush of bodies lit afire as they frenetically staggered about while they were burned alive. The stench of burning flesh stung every nostril, and the volume of screams was deafening. Yet still they pressed forward, climbing over bodies and moving steadily toward the first wooden barricades.

Hours passed. Gorillian's troops had nearly reached but had not yet breached the first barricade when a horn sounded from deep in the tunnel outside of Dinhoriin. Gorillian was pulling back his troops. A great cry of victory swept the Draconean lines.

"He has breached the outer gate and has now had a glimpse of Dinhoriin - enough to know what he is up against." Drake was talking to Layne and the Captains. Athron, Lathaniel, and Juga were also present. "His losses were heavy today, and the tunnel access is blocked by bodies that he will have to clear before his next assault. Abandon the first barricade and reposition behind the second," he ordered. "Double check all fences and reinforce if and where possible. Athron, we may have need of the oil channels before tomorrow passes. Is all in readiness?"

Athron nodded and provided an update. They girded themselves for the strength of Gorillian's next assault.

They did not wait long. The respite lasted only hours. Gorillian immediately deployed shielded troops down the ramp, their only purpose to drag their dead out of Dinhoriin and up the tunnel. There was no honour in the removal; it was driven by pure practicality, as Gorillian wanted a clear entry for his next attack.

When the last of the bodies were dragged away, hooves could be heard coming through the tunnel. Gorillian himself entered Dinhoriin. His great grey gelding reared, danced, and spun in several circles before settling. He was alone.

He urged the grey forward a hundred yards or more, then waited. It was a parley he was after, and in his arrogance he held his mount steady, as though daring the Draconean to ride out to him.

Drake wasted no time. Seuton Rev'eara had positioned himself on the outer wall and came at a run, determined to join him. He was ignored. Drake rode out on the black stallion accompanied by Layne, Athron, Lathaniel, and Juga.

Spikes were pulled back and barricades parted. Gorillian rode forward. Every archer's bow was drawn and aimed. Fully armed and armoured Draconean soldiers parted to create an avenue for his passage. The two parties met a third of the way up the battlefield. They stayed astride their mounts. For all but

Drake, this was their first view of the evil others in Elënthiá had long been fighting.

Gorillian's smile was tight and his eyes empty and cold. "Draconean…my old friend. It has been several hundred years."

Drake interrupted him. "We have not gathered to exchange pleasantries. Withdraw. Immediately. Or die here."

"Straight to business as always, I see." Gorillian's eyes swept the warriors behind Drake. "You are keeping better company these days. The Gor'ean High Prince…hmmm, what happened? Did the Fyyther cast you aside for your association with this cur? I do not blame him."

Athron was silent, his face expressionless, but his eyes held Gorillian's and were fearless.

"And who is this boy who rides with you? Is this the Human I have heard about? What a disappointment."

Juga's face flushed with anger, but he took his cue from Athron and held his silence.

"So that leaves you as the Forsair." Gorillian addressed Lathaniel directly and eyed him with great curiosity. "I did not believe the reports when I heard them. I see now that I was wrong."

Drake drew the attention back to himself. "Withdraw from this place immediately. You have no hope of success, Gorillian."

"Yield the City and I shall spare its inhabitants and all who pledge service to me."

Drake laughed. And then laughed some more. Though Gorillian kept his face carefully blank, Drake's laughter angered him.

"Turn on your horse and ride away, for this is the one and only glimpse you will have of the great Dohenheer. If it falls, it will only do so after each and every Draconean has first fallen."

"Ah...so this is how it is to end, Draconean."

"Aye...with your death."

The madness surged through the warlord then. "No! I will not die today. I will emerge triumphant finally knowing that each and every Draconean will be wiped from the face of Elënthiá, a disease that our world will be well rid of. I ask one last time. Submit to me now. Or die."

All the laughter was gone from Drake's voice and face. "It is you who will die, and at my hand. It has been battle you have craved these millennia, Gorillian...and it is battle that you shall have! Let us see how you fare against Draconeans who are not ambushed and slaughtered as they sleep. Let us see how you fare against this Draconean army! Turn and ride away from this arena like the coward you are, and allow us to get on with the business of wiping the carrion you call an army off the face of this world. Be gone!"

Gorillian wheeled his horse in a circle. And then another. His face was near purple with rage and madness. The blood fever within him longed to leap from his mount and fight the Draconean right to the death that instant, but some whisper of reason kept his wits about him sufficient that he rode away and up the ramp at great speed.

There were no horns bleating to mark the beginning of the third assault. As Gorillian rode up it, Are-Narcs overflowed out of the tunnel and into Dinhoriin, thirty across and at a dead run. As before, the archers loosed hell with their arrows, and again, the Are-Narcs fell; but this time the onslaught was rapid and intense. Some carried hastily crafted ladders they thrust against the ten-foot spiked fences. As many fell as pressed forward, and within an hour the first spike wall was breached, and Drake gave the order for the archers to fall back. As they ran through prearranged breaks in the next fence and barricade, the spaces were closed, and soldiers rolled and anchored the next spiked fence in place.

The third line was breached and by midday so was the fourth. Behind the fourth barricade, battalions of soldiers awaited. Behind them one final spiked fence remained. When the archers were recalled and the barricades fell, fresh Draconean troops rushed forward to engage the Are-Narcs. Drake, Athron, Lathaniel, Juga, and General Rev'eara led the charges followed by the Draconean Captains and their battalions.

Hammer in one hand and sword in the other, Juga ran forward then stopped suddenly, sweeping the great hammer around. Screams accompanied the sickening crunch of bones. Any who did not fall by his hammer, were hacked through as he advanced again, swinging and slicing.

Drake was again wielding his great sword like a scythe as he waded forward. Limbs and body parts rocketed off into other soldiers as he unleashed hell on the attacking Are-Narcs. Centuries of pent-up fury, worry, longing, and hate had congealed into a hard knot at his core. Now in this final face-to-face battle with Gorillian's troops and, gods willing, Gorillian himself, the knot of emotion began to loosen and fall away.

Athron and Lathaniel, like their comrades, had waded into the thick of the battle. Beside and among them, the Draconean soldiers, themselves honed to giant killing machines, comported themselves admirably in their first real engagement in more than two thousand years. But the crush of Are-Narcs still pouring in through the Dinhoriin Gate was endless. And though the toll they took on Gorillian's forces was substantial, the Draconeans were forced back.

Drake saw the moment the tides shifted.

"Back!" he cried. "Sound the horn! Athron! Lathaniel!" His head swung back and forth until he located them. "The oil!"

At the sound of a battle horn, the Draconeans turned and ran, Are-Narcs hard on their tails.

As part of battle preparations, Drake had had teams mine the floor of Dinhoriin. Into it were hewn six shallow trenches, twelve inches wide, six inches apart, and six inches deep. Lathaniel and Athron leapt astride mounts and rode full out for huge wooden drums strapped to the side walls of the great enclosure. With a swipe of their swords, spigots were released, and tar-like oil flowed rapidly down into the trenches from each side. At a signal from Drake, archers on the walls ignited the trenches, and a wall of fire arrowed across the width of Dinhoriin, effectively blocking further advance of the Are-Narc troops.

A second identical set of trenches had been hacked out of the floor fifty yards further back. Lathaniel and Athron released the oil into these as well, but the archers, too caught up in the passion of battle, did not wait for a second signal and fired on these as well, igniting a second firewall.

Most of the Draconeans had already pulled back and were behind the second firewall. The few who were caught between, fought the trapped Narcs valiantly. Drake worked his way down the space between the two firewalls, ruthlessly cutting down what enemy remained. Ahead of him, he could see Alexi Illic doing the same.

With the call to pull back, Juga and Athron and their assigned Captains had taken command of the outer wall, positioning archers and preparing fortifications to drop in place when the outer gate was closed. General Rev'eara was on the battlefield just outside of the outer gates, marshalling and directing troops into their next positions. Captains Khan and Dagostin remained on the field with their respective battalions, as did Aleksa Illic. Lathaniel was with them.

Drake and Alexi were not more than twenty yards apart when it happened. As if it were nothing more than a morning mist, Gorillian walked forward through the nine-foot wall of flames with a bloodcurdling scream. Alexi reacted immediately before Drake could stop him.

"Alexi! No! Stop!" As Drake leapt forward, it was as if he were trying to run through a thick cloying fog. His limbs could not move quick enough yet the action before his eyes seemed to accelerate. Alexi Illic, Captain in the Draconean Army, charged the immortal warlord. Gorillian strode forward purposefully, his eyes locked on Drake. Alexi stepped into his path, ignoring Drake's shouts, and engaged the warlord.

It was over before Drake could intervene. Gorillian allowed only a precious few parries with Aleksi before, seeing Drake approaching, he grew impatient. His met Aleksi's sword with one, strong thrust and spun his wrist, pulling the young soldier off balance and leaving his right side open and vulnerable. Gorillian abruptly released Aleksi's sword and arced his own weapon downwards into the torso of the Draconean, killing him instantly. Beyond the second wall of flames, the agonized screams of his brother rent the smoke-filled air. His fellow captains held him back, else he would have charged the wall of fire.

When he saw Aleksi fall, Drake stopped and waited for Gorillian. Aleksi Illic's death was just one more reason the warlord needed killing. He was the assassin of Drake's race and the cold-blooded murderer of his brothers and his father. Drake felt a curious calm wash over him. The only thought he could form was *finally.*

Madness filled Gorillian's eyes. Blood oath forgotten, there was a maniacal light in them. His demons had overrun all vestiges of sanity, and what faced Drake was pure evil. The swords of the two titans clashed once, and their hilts immediately locked. Each gave a great shove, thrusting apart and began to circle each other.

Drake heard three long, deep blasts from a horn. Then three more. He smiled at Gorillian. "You are finished. The Gor'eans arrive."

A great cheer could be heard from the outer walls as the Draconeans saw the first of the Gor'ean troops surge in through the distant gate. The Are-Narcs, separated from their leader and trapped between the approaching forces and the fire, lost all focus and were falling rapidly.

In seconds, Lathaniel took it all in. The Gor'eans had arrived, but Drake was embattled to the death with Gorillian. Between the twin walls of fire before him was the closest he would ever have to father, brother, and mentor embodied in a single being. Surely if he combined his skills with the Draconean's, Gorillian would be defeated. With neither fear nor further thought, he sprinted for the wall of flames and leapt through them, skidding to a halt several feet from the embattled two.

The intensity of their engagement was both terrible and incredible to behold. Titans both, the clash of their swords was ear-splitting as, with great grunts, sheer strength was pitted against sheer strength. Arrows were still pelting across the wall of fire from Narcs, who desperately held to the thought that their lives could somehow be saved if their leader lived.

Lathaniel was already moving forward when he saw the first arrow hit Drake in the thigh of his right leg. As Drake raised his sword, a second arrow caught him beneath his left arm. He fell to his knees.

A thin smile crept across Gorillian's face as he drew his sword back to deliver the killing blow.

Lathaniel screamed wordlessly as he skidded in under Gorillian's sword to counter the killing blow. As he did he felt the strength of it reverberate up his arm and into his shoulder. The power of it shook him. He was on his feet, engaging Gorillian sufficiently to draw him several feet away from Drake. Lathaniel countered, spun, swung, and held his own against the enraged titan for several minutes; but the warlord was the better swordsman, and Lathaniel knew he couldn't hold him for long.

A parry and spin pulled both swords to the side and brought the two shoulder to shoulder. Gorillian gave a great heave that lifted Lathaniel off of his feet and flung him to the ground. As he did, his long, filthy nails caught the Forsair across the face and sliced his skin like knives.

Lathaniel sprawled on the ground, his vision lost for seconds as blood poured down his face and into his eyes. Gorillian left him, walking back toward the Draconean who was still on his knees, incapacitated by the arrows.

As Gorillian approached, he swung his great sword back to take Drake's head just as Lathaniel let loose with one of his Gor'ean daggers. The dagger struck just below Gorillian's right shoulder blade, his sword arm, causing him to drop his shoulder and hesitate. At that moment, Drake surged up with his sword and, with a mighty thrust and ran the warlord through.

Gorillian was face-to-face with his nemesis in those last moments, his expression frozen in disbelief and incredulity. With his last strength, Drake gave his sword a twist and yanked it further up, eviscerating Gorillian, who fell off to the side, skewered upon the Draconean's sword.

Lathaniel struggled to his feet and ran to Drake, sliding to his knees to catch him as he let go of his sword and slid sideways to the ground. Each second seemed to stretch to infinity. Lathaniel was vaguely aware of screaming, "Noooo!" as he gathered the great warrior's head into his lap.

The arrow Drake had taken beneath his arm had punctured his lung. Frothy pink blood was bubbling at the corners of his mouth.

"Drake! Drake, can you hear me?"

Lathaniel had dropped his weapons. He frantically ran his hands over Drake's torso and around his great head as if, somehow, his touch could brush away the cobwebs of death.

"Drake! Stay with me. I will get you help. Stay with me."

"I'm here, lad ... still here with you. Is he dead?" Drake whispered. His eyes were open now and locked on Lathaniel's, but there was a fog starting at the corners of them that Lathaniel refused to acknowledge. Lathaniel nodded. He looked up then and screamed again for help.

Drake gripped Lathaniel's hand and pulled him close. "Leave it, Lathaniel. I am done. Gorillian is dead...my father, my brothers, my people avenged."

Tears were flowing freely down Lathaniel's cheeks now, his words mixed with great sobs.

"No! Please, you can't leave me, Drake ... you can't. What will I do without you?"

Drake's response was no more than a croak; a whisper. "You will go on, lad. You will fight for that which you love. Your wisdom and honour will serve you well. I have taught you all that I can in this world and I shall await you in the next. You must let me go..."

The great soldier coughed then, releasing a stream of blood and mucous. The fog of death continued to creep across his eyes, and one by one the lights in those brighter emerald flecks dimmed and were extinguished. Drake slowly closed his eyes.

This was a loss so huge, so irrevocable, that Lathaniel's mind balked at its measure.

"But I was supposed to save you," he whispered.

His beloved Draconean's mouth lifted in the faintest of smiles. "Don't you realize, lad ... you already have."

"No!" Lathaniel cried again, shaking him. "No! You listen to me, Drake Sorzin. I will bring you back! If it takes every day of my life and the last breath from my body, I promise you...I will find a way to bring you back!" Amidst the dying flames, the stench of death, and the shouts of victory from Draconeans and Gor'eans alike, Lathaniel held the fallen warrior. There was the slightest exhale of air; then Lathaniel took the full weight of the warrior as his body went limp. The Draconean was dead.

# KEY CHARACTERS & PRONUNCIATION GUIDE

|  |  |
|---|---|
| Elënthiá (Eh-len-thee-ah) | The world in which *The Draconean* takes place |
| Coldain | A region in northwest of Elënthiá |
| Vearian (V-air-ee-an) | A region in northeast of Elënthiá |
| Zormian | A region in southeast of Elënthiá |
| Koorast | The largest island in the southwest corner of Elënthiá; surrounded by the smaller islands of Oldo, Moldost, and Sortaire |
| Lamana | An enclave on the island of Oldo; home to the Forsairs |
| Forsairs | A race of half Elven/ half Humans |
| Lathaniel Waythan | By blood, the rightful heir to the Forsairean throne |
| Lathart | Lathaniel's father |
| Sayra | Lathaniel's mother |
| Jonas Waythan | The original Human royal ancestor of the Forsairs |

| | |
|---|---|
| Ethena Waythan | The original Elven maiden who gave her love to Jonas |
| Bracher Gramicy (Braah-cher Gram-i-see) | The current, corrupt leader of Lamana |
| Chap Garous (Gar-oss) | Lamana's butcher; a friend of Lathaniel |
| Sabine | Lathaniel's childhood friend, confidante and love |
| Jameth Panemon | Lamana's blacksmith; a friend of Lathaniel |
| Darryn Eariish (Ear-ish) | Friend of Lathaniel |
| Gorger | Realm of the Gor'eans |
| Gor'eans | A race of men influenced by Elves, inhabitants of the Realm of Gorger |
| Gorgonathan (Gor-gone-a-th-an) | Capital of Gorger and home to the Elënthián Supreme Council |
| Cap'hannet | A hidden Gor'ean military stronghold – headquarters to Elënthiá's Resistance |
| Acthelass Mar (Ack-the-lass) | King of the Gor'eans |
| Athron Mar | High Prince of Gorger; a General in the Resistance and son of Acthelass |
| Fyyther (F-eye-ther) | The Gor'ean word for 'King' |
| Garnec Cindrik | Former General in the Gor'ean army, now a Lord on the Elënthián Supreme Council |
| Hanna Janheoanus Caapri (Jan-ee-oh-an-us) | A Gor'ean; a Captain in the Resistance |

| | |
|---|---|
| Gorillian | Immortal warlord threatening freedom in Elënthiá |
| Cave-Narcs | Underground creatures living under the Minhera mountains |
| Are-Narcs | The fighting force of Gorillian's army |
| Pouris Gaul | Human Captain in Gorillian's army |
| Karget Gash | Human General in Gorillian's army |
| Evendeer (Ev-an-deer) | Home of the Draconeans destroyed by Gorillian |
| Draconeans | A race of Immortals in Elënthiá |
| Darrish | The language of the Draconeans |
| Drake Sorzin | A Draconean – the last of his kind in Elënthiá |
| Dray Sorzin | The Last Draconean King – father of Drake |
| Iysem-Kayda (Eye-sem-kay-dah) | The Darrish word meaning 'mixed blood' – a derogatory term |
| Ayeth-Varr (Ay-eth-var) | The Darrish word meaning 'son of light' |
| Jugarth Framir | A Human; Drake Sorzin's apprentice |
| Allivaris | Queen of the Elves |
| Naris | King of the Elves |
| Ayleen (Eh-leen) | Queen Allivaris' hand maiden |
| Avion Valia (Ah-vee-on Vay-lah) | Elven ambassador to Dohenheer |
| Wylë (While) | King of the Centaurs |
| Anulé (Ann-oo-lay) | A race of Giants that lived in the mountains of Oderon; they left when evil became prevalent in Elënthiá |

| | |
|---|---|
| Dohenheer (Doh-hen-ear) | A city in the Ashen Mountains in north-western Elënthiá |
| Layne Rev'eara (Rev-ee-air-ah) | Captain in the Dohenheer army sent south in search of a single, surviving Draconean |
| Seuton Rev'eara (Soo-t-on) | Layne's father and the People's representative on Dohenheer's High Council |
| Lilyss Harphh (Lill-iss Har-ff) | Represents the Clergy on Dohenheer's High Council |
| Varis Mauge (Var-iss M-oh-gg) | Represents the Scholars on Dohenheer's High Council |
| General Fysst (F-eye-st) | Represents the Army on Dohenheer's High Council |
| Sameer Khan | Captain in Dohenheer's army |
| Fabian Dagostin | Captain in Dohenheer's army |
| Aleksa Illic | Captain in Dohenheer's army |
| Alexi Illic | Captain in Dohenheer's army |
| Ruahr (Ru-ah-r) | The principal god worshipped by all in Elënthiá |
| Erenthoris (Eh-ren-thor-iss) | The Elënthián God of the Sea |
| Surias (Sur-ee-ass) | The Elënthián Goddess of the Sky |
| Allimar | The Elënthián God of the Earth |
| Nesmeresa | The Elven Goddess of Nature; the name of the Realm of the Elves |
| Suvillwa (Soo-vill-wah) | The Draconean Goddess of Light |
| Dyvariiare (D-eye-vair-ee-ah-r) | The Draconean God of Darkness |

# A MESSAGE FROM JAKE AND LUKE ...

Thanks for reading *The Draconean.* We hope you enjoyed meeting and following our characters throughout this story. Look for them as the story continues in the second volume of our trilogy: *The Draconean – An Immortal's Gift* coming soon.

Our website is at www.draconean.com. Be sure and let us know what you thought of the novel.

# ABOUT THE AUTHORS

Jake and Luke Reaume are 17-year-old identical twins. Though they started life in rural Canada, they have lived most of their lives in the Middle East and have travelled the world extensively.

LaVergne, TN USA
16 April 2010

179554LV00005B/77/P